spider blue

also by Carla Damron

KEEPING SILENT
A Caleb Knowles Mystery

spider blue

a caleb knowles mystery

CARLA DAMRON

BellaRosaBooks

SPIDER BLUE
ISBN 0-9747685-6-1

First Printing: January 2005

Library of Congress Control Number: 2004195072

Printed in the United States of America on acid-free paper.

Book design by Bella Rosa Books

BellaRosaBooks and logo are trademarks of Bella Rosa Books
vii

This book is dedicated to the memory of Olivia Williams, a mighty advocate for people with mental illness. Your work lives on, friend.

acknowledgements

I want to thank the following friends for their advice, editing, and words of encouragement: Bert Goolsby, Judy Hubbard, Karen Murphy, Susan Craft, John Bolin, Ann Furr, Paula Benson, Sam Morton, Jeff Koob, Pat Willer and Ed Owens.

I'd also like to thank my family for giving me love and an endless supply of material: Katie Damron, Ed Damron and Vidisha Mallik, Pam and Hank Knight, Faye and Ernest Hussey, Sam and Mary Ann Combs, and Essie Mae Clark.

Also, a thank you to Lt. Joseph Pellicci and the Richland County Sheriff's Department, Susan Gray and Linda Barnes for helping out a mystery writer who had some strange requests involving tricycles and crime scene tape.

I'm especially grateful to my loving husband, Jim Hussey, who accepts that writing must come before vacuuming. I couldn't do this without you.

chapter one

Caleb Knowles pulled his beat-up suitcase out of the truck and stared at the front of the cottage. It was close to midnight and his home was lit up like a Wal-Mart Superstore. Hadn't his girlfriend just given him that little talk about wasting electricity, asking if he knew lights could be turned off as well as on? He smiled. Payback time, Shannon McPherson.

The front door opened before Caleb reached it, Shannon standing there with purse in hand. "I tried to call you."

Caleb glanced down at his cell, wincing when he realized he hadn't turned it on after the flight. "Sorry."

"How was the social work conference?" Shannon had a strange look on her face, her thin lips taut, a little crease appearing between her brows.

"Riveting. My butt's still asleep." He wondered why they were having this conversation on the front steps. "Is something wrong?"

"I have to go over to Maggie's." Maggie Wells was Shannon's best friend. The beautiful, often tragic, Maggie Wells. Shannon fumbled in her purse for keys, trying hard not to look at him, something she did when she was upset.

"Honey?" Caleb reached over and squeezed her arm.

Blue eyes met his, misting. "Maggie's neighbor died. Maggie found her. She was murdered."

"Murdered?" That word felt strange in his mouth.

"Frances Callahan, the one with the kids. She was stabbed. Maggie's trying to take care of the children." Shannon blinked at him, her eyes pleading. "She needs us, Caleb."

He slung the suitcase inside and followed her out to her car.

Three miles separated them from Brenton, Maggie's neighborhood, but Shannon did the drive in five minutes, ignoring red lights and disregarding Caleb's terrified grip on the dashboard. She took the right turn onto Sims Avenue and only slowed when she spotted the six police cars lining the street in front of Maggie's house, sealing off the drive. She parked a block away, climbed out of the car and jogged up to Maggie's door.

Caleb eased his car door shut. A huddle of police officers and forensic technicians standing beside a crime scene van turned to stare at him. He wished he'd had the chance to brush his teeth or comb his hair after his flight, and he still longed for the hot shower he'd been denied, but maybe charm and grace would make up for bad grooming with the cops. Or not.

The talking ceased as he drew near. One of the officers scowled at Caleb as if he were just another one of the nosy neighbors he had apparently had to deal with all night. "Something I can do for you, sir?" he asked, stressing the "sir."

"We're friends of Ms. Wells," he answered over the buzz and crackles of police radios.

"Who?" He glared harder at Caleb.

"Never mind." Caleb got the too-familiar feeling that he was stepping into something he shouldn't. "Who's in charge here?"

The officer pointed with his clipboard. "She is."

A cluster of more police personnel had gathered under a street light and Caleb spotted Detective Claudia Briscoe giving orders as she scribbled into a small notebook. Caleb took a step in her direction, but the officer placed a hand just in front of his chest. "You stay right here. We don't need anyone else in the scene right now. I'll let her know you're here, Mister . . . ?"

"Knowles. I'm a therapist. I've worked with the police department some."

"Wait here Mr. Knowles," the officer ordered, looking decidedly unimpressed. Yep, definitely stepping into it.

He looked beyond Claudia, to a section of the Callahan's yard enclosed in crime scene tape. More yellow tape made a web around a rust colored spot on the sidewalk and a toppled Red Rider tricycle beside it. The whole scene seemed surreal.

"Caleb? What are you doing here?" Claudia came over to him, taking his hand. Despite the chill, her grip was warm and moist. "This is a mess, I'll tell you."

"Shannon's best friend called. She lives there." He pointed at the small cottage with yellow siding.

"Right, the lady who took the kids. It's a good thing she was here."

"What happened?"

Her coal black glare berated him. "A woman's been killed. Sorry if that sounds blunt, but really, that's all I can tell you."

He gave her a sad smile. They had a long, interesting history together, beginning in the early nineties when she came to him for counseling. Five years later, Caleb had been recruited as a part-time police consultant and Claudia had been promoted to Detective. Their careers, and lives, had been curiously intertwined ever since. "I'm here to help with the kids. Do you know anything I can tell them?"

"They just lost their mother. What do you tell them after that?" Long, crimson nails scratched her mahogany chin. "She was stabbed, right here in front of her house. All the neighbors are panicked, telling me over and over how this is Brenton, not the projects, and this kind of thing doesn't happen here. A nurse bleeds to death beside her kid's tricycle. People want answers faster than I can give them."

"Where's the father?"

"Down at the station giving a statement."

Caleb stared at the dark pool where the life had leaked out of Frances Callahan. It looked brutal, like she'd lost a huge amount of blood. "You thinking this is domestic?"

"We're questioning Mr. Callahan because he was here when it happened, but I'm not ruling out anything at this point. We'd question Gandhi, too, if he'd been on the premises." She glanced over at Maggie's house. "You better go see to those children. They got a rough road ahead of them."

As he started to walk away, Claudia called after him, "Hey Caleb?"

"Yeah?"

She came in closer, almost whispering. "Listen, if the kids say anything, and I mean anything, that you think might help us catch a break here . . ." She let her words trail off.

Caleb acknowledged that he understood. "I'll let you know."

Caleb made his way up the walk and opened Maggie's front door, finding a somber gathering in her living room. "I was talking to Claudia," he whispered, taking a seat beside Shannon. He glanced up at Maggie. A small child had affixed herself to her, its tiny arms clinging to her neck, its tiny face buried in Maggie's long, dark hair. The girl looked to be about four years old, with paper white skin and long, spindly limbs.

"How are you holding up, Maggie?" Caleb asked.

Maggie's dark, frightened eyes swept past him to Shannon, to the child, to the window that looked out on strobing police lights. The child sobbed a little and tightened her grip.

Shannon reached for her. "Come here, sweetie. Let's go find your brother."

The girl pulled back, scrunching her petite shoulders up. She started to cry.

Maggie touched her chin. "Emma, you remember Miss Shannon, don't you? You've met her before."

The child nodded.

"Why don't you take her in my room?" Maggie said to Shannon. "Seth is in there. Maybe she can lie down with him and sleep for a bit."

Shannon slipped her hands under the girl's arms to lift her. Immediately, the child clutched Shannon's neck with fierce desperation, holding on as if her life depended on it.

"Can I get you anything?" Caleb asked Maggie.

"No," she answered. "Thanks for coming." She reached up to wipe the tears filling her eyes.

Caleb noticed a box of tissues on the coffee table and handed her one. "You've had one hell of an evening."

"How does something like this happen? I just talked to Fran this afternoon. Everything was so normal. And now—" Her voice faltered. "I just don't understand it."

"You knew her pretty well?"

"She was my neighbor, for Chrissake. And my friend." Maggie narrowed her eyes at Caleb, like he had moved far away and was hard to see. "I haven't been sleeping well lately so I piled into bed early with the TV on. I don't know when I finally got to sleep. But I woke up when I heard this screaming. I thought it was the TV, like a horror film or something, but I heard the screaming again—so loud, I thought it was an injured animal. I went to the window." She paused for a long moment, then continued. "It was dark outside, except right under the street light, where the light was almost pink. I saw two people, shadows really, one leaning back against the other. I couldn't tell who they were. I grabbed the phone and dialed 911. When I looked out again I only saw one person, lying there on the sidewalk." Her eyes darted back and forth like she could still see it.

"Fran?"

"I couldn't tell at first. I saw a little movement, like maybe a hand reaching up, grabbing at the air. I went outside but when I got to her I didn't know what to do. How to help. She reached up for me and said 'Maggie, I can't breathe.' But her voice was gurgly and I could barely hear her. I got on my knees to get closer—that's when I saw what had happened. What they'd done to her."

Maggie's eyes fell to the floor. "There was blood everywhere. I took her hand and told her to be still, to breathe, but she couldn't seem to get her breath. Each time she tried, I heard that same gurgling, gaspy noise. I'll never forget that sound." She shuddered, her hands shaking in the folds of her arms.

"What happened then?"

"Then Paul was there. I don't know where he came from. He was panting and sweaty, and he laid down beside her, holding onto her, telling her she would be all right. Dear God . . . Paul!" A tremor made its way through her, vibrating her hands, her breath, her lips.

"That's Fran's husband?"

She nodded. "How can he survive this? And the kids? They're just babies—"

Caleb tried to fathom it himself. If his daughter lost her mother . . . if he lost Shannon . . . It was unthinkable.

A door creaked open and Shannon appeared. Behind her, a blond-haired boy, about six, held the hand of his younger sister. They looked like Hansel and Gretel, lost and frightened in the forest.

"Caleb, I'd like you to meet Seth." Caleb heard the forced bounce in Shannon's voice. "And I think you've already met his sister, Emma."

Caleb went over to them and crouched down so they were eye to eye. "How you guys doing?"

The boy pulled his sister close. "Where's our dad?"

"He's talking to some people right now. But I know he wants to be here with you." He looked at the girl's face, her eyes wide blue beacons scanning the unfamiliar giants in the room.

Caleb hated feeling impotent. What could he say? *Sorry your mom got murdered. How about a cookie?*

"We called our grandma," Seth said, taking charge. "She said she'd come get us. I want Dad to know where we are." His skin was fair, like his sister, and his lips were drawn in tight. His eyes were pools of haunted gray.

"I'll make sure he knows, Seth," Maggie said.

A gentle rap at the front door made them all jump. Caleb opened it and showed Claudia Briscoe in.

"Ms. Wells? Could you come here for a moment?"

"Why?" Maggie eyed Caleb, looking terrified.

"I'll come along, if it's okay," he said.

Claudia shot him an irritated look but assented. She led them out of the house, around the back, and through the welded-wire fence that enclosed Maggie's back yard. In the far left corner of the property, three officers stooped down to study something on the ground.

"Now, I need both of you to follow in my footsteps exactly. We've found a piece of evidence and we need to wait till daylight to see if there are any foot impressions around it," Claudia said.

"Excuse us, gentlemen." She motioned them out of the way, dropping to her knees and pointing to a bed of dense ivy. An officer aimed a flashlight at a glimmer of silver metal nested in the dark green leaves. Maggie and Caleb knelt down for a closer look.

"That look familiar to you?" Claudia asked.

"No." She pointed to the blade. "There's blood on it."

Claudia used her pencil to force back a thick ivy vine and nudged the object onto its side. It was a knife, about nine inches long with a treacherous scalloped blade coated with a thick rusty brown substance. Blood. "Bag this," Claudia instructed one of the uniforms. "And take a couple of these leaves so we can match the blood."

Caleb looked over at Maggie, who was shivering in the cold, moist air. "It could have been me," she whispered. "The murderer was here, in my yard. He could have killed me."

"Go back inside, Maggie. I'll be right there," Caleb said.

"Follow the same path out as you did coming in," Claudia called after her.

After she left them, he turned to Claudia. "That the murder weapon? It looks like a regular kitchen knife."

"Actually, it's an expensive one. High carbon stainless chef's knife, probably eighty bucks or so at one of those fancy kitchen stores." She looked back at the house. "Kids okay?"

"No. They need to see their dad soon. I sure hope he didn't do this. They don't need to lose both parents."

She peered up in his face. "If this is your subtle way of trying to pry information out of me, forget it. I don't know who did this and if I did, I wouldn't tell you. So let's move on to some other subject."

He shook his head. He didn't want to know more. He just wanted to spare those kids another loss if he could.

They heard voices and what sounded like a wail coming from the front of the house. Caleb and Claudia ran to the commotion and found a middle-aged woman leaning against an older man. She was crying, sobs heaving from the depths of her. The man's feeble arms tried to hold her up as he stared at the chaos around him. The front door opened and the children ran out to the woman, who scooped them up and held them close.

Shannon found Caleb and whispered, "Fran's parents. They're taking the kids."

He watched the small family huddled together, bracing themselves against waves of grief. Maggie walked over to them and talked for a moment, then led the children to the grandparents' car.

"Maggie's coming home with us," Shannon whispered.

"Makes sense to me. No way I want her staying here. Have her pack a couple of days' worth of clothes."

Shannon gave him a grateful hug. "I'll go help her get her things."

chapter two

The next morning, Caleb blinked away the fog of sleep and spotted Shannon's nightgown where she'd left it on the dresser. His eyes trailed up to the window. There was already a heaviness to the day. Dark clouds hung low, leafless trees fingering up into a pewter sky. The bleak South Carolina winter would soon pass, Caleb reminded himself. It could evaporate in a day; winds would stir, soft rains would come, and color would pour back into the gardens. He just had to get through the next few weeks.

He untangled himself from the sheets and made his way to the mirror, which was its usual unfriendly self. Some time during the night, an invisible squirrel had nested in his auburn curls, leaving an unflattering, chaotic mess. Shadows under his light brown eyes testified to his lack of sleep. He growled and plodded to the shower.

After shaving, Caleb threw on a robe and tiptoed down the stairs, wincing as the steps' creaks and groans threatened to wake their houseguest. In the kitchen, he found a half pot of coffee waiting for him. That blessed nectar, caffeine.

He dropped into a chair to peruse the newspaper spread out before him. Under the headline story about the Tindall Mill was the sketchy article about last night, "Pediatric Nurse Found Dead." There was a photograph of the Callahan's narrow brick home, with a tiny tricycle overturned on the walkway in front. Emma's tricycle, he remembered, with pink streamers on the handlebars, a few feet from where Emma's mother had been found.

Caleb heard a clatter of keys against the back door. Shannon dragged in, looking thoroughly exhausted. Most of her dark curls were contained in a barrette, but a few escaped to dangle over her face. She wore Caleb's blue work shirt over a white cotton T-shirt that was only half-tucked in her faded jeans. She kissed Caleb and made her way to the coffee pot.

Caleb held out a chair for her. "Where ya been? Get any sleep?"

"Not much. Maggie and I stayed up talking. She was too scared to lie down."

"Where is she?" He made his way to the refrigerator. After a quick inventory, he retrieved a carton of eggs and a couple of bagels that would do for their breakfast.

"I took her to get her car so she could head over to check on the children. She should be back soon." Shannon let out a sigh. "Maggie's had a rough year. I sure hope this doesn't push her over the edge."

Caleb quelled the urge to point out that every year had been a rough one for Shannon's crisis-ridden friend. Comments like that always got him in trouble. He broke a couple of eggs into the skillet and asked, "She still seeing that guy with the big teeth? Barry What's-His-Name?"

"No. He moved out three weeks ago," Shannon said, her stare daring him to say something smart.

"They were together a long time, weren't they? I mean, long for Maggie." He slid bagel halves into the toaster oven.

"About two years, off and on. More off than on," she conceded. "I was relieved when he finally left this last time. And I hope he's gone for good. The break-up was pretty bad."

Caleb kept an eye on the skillet while setting the table and freshening their coffee. He slid a spatula under Shannon's eggs and plopped them on her plate. "All of Maggie's break-ups are bad. She gets depressed, then you get depressed, and I walk around feeling guilty for even having Y-chromosomes."

Shannon piled half an egg on her fork, blew on it, and popped it in her mouth. "Breaking up with Barry was about the bravest thing she'd ever done. She was doing terrific until this happened. Right now, I don't know."

As Caleb buttered his bagel, he pondered the dynamics of men and women. His thoughts flashed to last night, to Fran Callahan's death. Had her husband killed her? Had there been a jealous rage where tempers escaped the bounds of self-control?

He'd been a therapist for fifteen years and often believed he'd seen it all. He'd seen sick, unbounded relationships where violence and turmoil were a way of life. He'd seen cold, distant families where nobody gave a thought to the pain of another. But rarely had anything moved him like last night—like the face of Emma Callahan.

Shannon reached over and squeezed his hand, drawing him back from the dark thoughts. He lifted her fingers to his lips and kissed them.

The ringing phone seemed too loud and Caleb snatched up the receiver. "Caleb? Did I wake you?" Dr. Matthew Rhyker, Caleb's boss, sounded hurried.

"No. What's up?" Caleb looked up at the clock. Not even 7:30 yet.

"We've got a mess. You know that EAP contract we have with Tindall Manufacturing?"

"Sure. I see about a half-dozen of their employees." The Employee Assistance Program was a special contract between the factory and the counseling center where Caleb, Matthew, and Grey Lazarus worked. It gave the factory employees the benefit of free, short-term counseling and an occasional workshop on job stress. In exchange, the factory paid the counseling center a flat annual rate—a comfortable deal for everybody.

"All hell broke loose there yesterday. One of the workers

reported for the first shift, worked a few hours, then pulled out a handgun and opened fire. One of the mill workers was killed, two others injured."

"Jesus." Caleb glanced at the newspaper article he hadn't read.

"It's a bizarre case. No precipitants that anyone's aware of. They arrested the guy. His name's Murphy Lumford. Know him?"

"No," Caleb said, relieved the murderer wasn't one of his clients. "Who was killed?"

"A floor supervisor, Buck Swygert. Sally Weston was a machine operator. I think Beard did electrical work. We don't have charts on any of them."

"They hurt bad?"

"Beard is. Abdominal. A lot of bleeding before the EMT's got there. Weston took a bullet in the collar bone. Swygert was hit in the face. Dead instantly."

The death talk was getting to him. It was too much, especially after last night. He shook his head slowly at Shannon, who moved in closer. "What do you need me to do?" Caleb asked.

"Come in as quick as you can. Grey and I are going out to the mill and we'll debrief the folks there. I suspect we'll be pretty swamped all week. The other workers may be traumatized, too. May mean a long few days. I want them scheduled immediately, so maybe at forty minute intervals, until we get them all in. That all right with you?" Matthew's voice sounded strangely mechanical, as if he was on automatic pilot. A logical approach, given the situation.

"Sure. Anything else you need from me?"

"No. We'll get back to the center as soon as we can. You mind the shop till then."

Caleb wished him luck and hung up, relieved that Matthew and Grey Lazarus, the center's part-time psychiatrist, would handle the first slew of victims. After last night, Caleb didn't need to look at any more devastated people.

Pouring himself a third cup of coffee, he filled Shannon in on his call. "Remember when Westville was a calm little town?" he added. "Ten years ago, a fender-bender on Main Street made the front page. Now, we have two murders, two brutal murders, in one day." He paused, the gravity of his words slowly sinking in. He thought of his young daughter sleeping across town in his ex-wife's home. "I don't want this kind of world for Julia."

"What's Westville going to be like when she's a teenager?" Shannon grew quiet as she stared out the window at the wintry day.

"You okay, honey?"

"I can't stop thinking of those kids. And that man killed yesterday at the factory. I wonder who he left behind?"

Caleb's eyes met hers for a long, uncomfortable moment. Finally, he said, "I'd better get to work."

March is South Carolina's bipolar month. Even its first few days had been a weather roller coaster: highs close to seventy, lows that could freeze bone marrow. Caleb looked out his kitchen window at webs of white frost on the grass. This day was destined to be a frigid one. He grabbed his Polartec parka from the closet, put on gloves, and carried a steaming cup of coffee out to the truck. At 7:50 A.M., extra caffeine was definitely in order.

Twenty minutes later, Caleb sat in his office at the counseling center sipping cup number four of black, industrial strength coffee and scowling at his appointment book. As promised, Matthew had booked him with back-to-back clients from Tindall Mill. His first intake was due any minute. Damn, he hated having to be coherent before nine.

"Good Morning." Janice Birchstead's voice sang out over the phone. In his six years with the clinic, he'd never seen their secretary in a bad mood.

"Morning yourself," he growled back.

"Claudia Briscoe's on line two."

He punched the lit extension. "You catch Fran Callahan's murderer yet?"

"Not that it's any of your business, but no," Claudia sniped back. "Unfortunately, I'm calling about another murder. You heard about the incident at Tindall?"

"Yeah. Bet you're just loving your job."

"I'm still in yesterday's clothes," she groaned. "Anyway, we got the killer, Murphy Lumford, in custody. He tried to kill himself last night. We put a suicide watch on him, but we need you to give him a look."

"How on earth could he try something like that?" Caleb knew jail protocol meant Lumford would be stripped of his belt, laces, and other worldly possessions.

"Tried to hang himself. Almost succeeded, too. That's why we're bringing him to you."

"Claudia. Matthew's out at the plant trying to put the pieces of that crew back together. We've got a dozen of your guy's co-workers scheduled here. I don't think they need to bump into the man that shot at them." Caleb didn't want to evaluate Murphy Lumford. He wanted no part of a faked insanity plea, or guilt-driven squawks about suicide. From what he knew, Lumford had coldly, sadistically gunned down three innocent people.

"We'll bring him in through the back, like always. You're the jail consultant, so you get to do a screening. I told the secretary he'd be there at ten."

"Today?" He glared down at his cramped schedule. "You're kidding, right?"

"Thanks for your help," she interrupted. "I'll call for a report."

Two hours later, a couple of police officers flanked Murphy Lumford as they escorted him into Caleb's office. Lumford wore the traditional orange jail jumpsuit as he shuffled in, hindered by shackles that rattled on his arms and legs. He was a short man, maybe five-foot-six, with thin, oily hair graying at the temples. Silver wire Coke-bottle-glasses perched on a small nose and what Caleb could see of his face looked calm and personable. He looked like he should be a professor or an accountant, not a gun-wielding assassin.

"Take those off," Caleb said, pointing at the chains.

A large officer in a buzz cut stepped forward. "Can't. It's against the rules."

"No it isn't. You can check with your boss. Our contract says we have to provide assessments on your inmates, but you remove handcuffs and leg irons, at the counselor's discretion. Mr. Lumford looks pretty calm right now. You'll be sitting right outside my office, so there shouldn't be any trouble, right?"

Buzz-cut locked his thumbs in his creaking gun belt and fanned out fingers the size of sausages.

Caleb reached for the receiver and waved it at him. "Call Detective Briscoe."

The man fished keys out of a crowded pocket and handed them to his partner. "Here, Saunders. It's okay, he probably won't bite or nothin'. You take the irons off while I talk at this doctor here for a moment."

Caleb followed him into the hall. Glancing up at the policeman's name badge, he said, "Okay, Officer Wright. What's the situation?"

"You got yourself a case in there." He punctuated this profound insight with an arch of thick black brows.

"Tell me about the suicide attempt."

"What's to tell? He tried to hang himself."

"Mind telling me how that could happen? Weren't his belt and shoe laces removed?"

"Yep. But not the sheets. He worked himself up some contraption, I tell you. He turned the bed over on its side. He rolled up the sheet real tight, twisted it around his head, and hooked it around the top of the bed frame. It would have worked, too. That much pressure against the carotid artery . . ." he paused, squinting an eye. "The sheets must have gotten loose. We found him on the floor, his face as red as a balloon. We don't know how long he'd been there. It's a wonder he wasn't dead."

"Did he say anything?"

"Nothin' much, except he denied it. Said he hadn't meant to kill himself or anything like that. Now, I'm in there untangling a knotted-up sheet from around his head and he looks me in the eye and says he didn't try to hurt himself. I guess a ghost came in and tried to hang him. Or maybe it was his 'other personality.'" Officer Wright chuckled at his own joke, but Caleb made no effort to smile. He returned to the office, held the door until the other officer departed, then closed it.

Murphy Lumford never looked up. Caleb extended a hand, startling him. Reluctantly, his patient took it. "I'm Caleb Knowles," Caleb said, feeling the bones, close to the skin, in Lumford's hand.

"Thanks Mr. Knowles. For this." Lumford held up his freed wrists. A wide, raw band of flesh marked where the handcuffs had been.

"No problem. I know it's hard for anyone to get comfortable, chained up like that." He pointed to a chair and his new client took a seat. Though Lumford kept his head bowed, Caleb caught a better glimpse of his face. He was startled by a strange scar, the bright red color of recently healed flesh, that encircled his eye socket, merging with his wiry gray brows. Caleb couldn't imagine what might cause a scar like that.

"I'm sorry, Mr. Knowles," Lumford said.

"For what?"

"For them bringing me here, taking up your time. I saw all those people in your waiting room. You don't need to waste your time on me."

"How about I decide if it's wasted time?"

"I don't really have anything to say to you, except that I'm not crazy. I didn't try to kill myself. I don't need to be here."

He said it matter-of-factly, with no hint of defensiveness.

"The police say you tried to hang yourself."

"They're wrong. Yes, I tied the sheet to the bed frame, but not to hang myself."

"Why then?"

"I'd rather not go into it." Meek, apologetic eyes peered at Caleb from behind the thick lenses.

"Okay . . ." Caleb grabbed a pen and pad from his desk. "So we have an hour to kill here, Murphy. Why don't you tell me about yourself?"

"What do you want to know?"

"Have you been to a counselor before?"

"No. Well, not for me. My ex-wife went to a therapist back in Charleston. I went with her a few times."

"For marital therapy?"

"No. She had a drug problem."

"Did she get into recovery?"

"For a while. I took Joyce to Narcotics Anonymous meetings and I went to Alanon, myself. We moved a couple of times, you know, to get her away from the people she used with. The longest she stayed straight was eight months."

"Where is Joyce now?"

A shadow crept across his face. "She died."

"I'm sorry. How did it happen?"

"It's been five years. We divorced in '96, because of the drugs, and I got custody of our boy. She never could quit using after that. She started prostituting herself, got arrested two or three times on a strip near the naval base." His eyes fell down to his lap. "They found her body in an empty field. She'd been shot in the head. She had fresh needle marks from using. The police said a drug dealer probably killed her."

Caleb nodded ruefully. He knew, far too well, a dozen stories like Joyce's. He'd been the counselor for cocaine-addicted clients, plenty of whom never made it to sobriety. He'd also been the son, watching in disgust as alcohol chipped away at his father, fracturing the family in its wake.

"You mentioned getting custody of your son. Where is he now?"

"Kevin? He stays with my mom. He's fourteen now."

"Has he seen you since you've been in jail?"

Lumford lowered his head again. "I don't want him there. I don't want him anywhere near that kind of place. I called my mother and she promised to keep him away. I'm gonna hold her to it."

"How's your mom taking all this?"

Murphy Lumford gave his thumbnail a thorough inspection. "They didn't bring me in here to talk about my mother or my family."

"No."

"They brought me here to see if I'm crazy."

"You look pretty sane to me."

"You mean for a murderer, huh?" Lumford's sarcasm was surprising.

"Okay. You brought it up. Tell me about yesterday."

"What's to tell? You've heard it all. Or read it in the papers. I went to work. I had my gun with me. I worked part of my shift. Then I pulled out the gun and shot three people. Buck Swygert, Mike Beard, and Sally Weston. Then the police came and arrested me." He relayed this so mechanically that Caleb half-expected him to add, "and I had tuna fish for lunch." The placid face held neither guilt nor remorse. The entangled fingers of his hands—the same hands that fired three bullets into a crowd of innocent mill workers—were relaxed, casual. Did those fingers remember the feel of the gun? Could they recall the heat of the steel, the jolt of each shot?

"It sounds like you remember it all quite well," Caleb said tightly.

"Most everything. Look, I didn't hear voices in my head telling me to shoot people. I wasn't possessed by Satan and I don't have a second personality that made me do it. So there's really nothing you can do for me." Lumford lifted his hand to his head. His forefinger pressed into a spot above the left ear and moved in a tight, circular pattern. He closed his eyes halfway.

"Okay. You've explained that you weren't mentally ill and you remember shooting those people. Can you tell me why you did it?"

"No." He squeezed his eyes shut.

Caleb studied him, perplexed. The amiable face now looked contorted in pain. Was it guilt? Was he reliving what he'd done on some dark mental screen? Caleb leaned closer, asking, "Are you feeling okay?"

"Headache. I didn't get any coffee this morning. I'm addicted to caffeine, I guess."

"I can relate to that. You take your coffee black?"

His nod was more of a flinch than a head movement. Caleb punched Janice's extension to put in the order and a minute later, she rapped at the door.

Caleb opened it, flashed a quick grin at the officers, and took two steaming cups from Janice. "Matthew busy?"

"He went on rounds. Dr. Lazarus is on his way," she whispered.

"Buzz me when he gets here." Careful with the hot coffee, he maneuvered back to the office and closed the door with his foot. His client looked even stranger now. Both hands were positioned on the sides of his head, along the same latitude as his brows, and his closed eye lids flickered like a strobe light. He opened his mouth slightly, breathing in a slow, even rhythm. A flush like a crimson butterfly spread across his nose and cheeks.

"Murphy? Can you hear me?" Caleb asked.

Lumford's nod was barely perceptible. His eyes blinked open as he reached a shaky hand for the coffee.

"You don't look so good," Caleb commented. "Do you have blood pressure problems?"

"No. The coffee will help."

"Do you take anything else for the headache?"

"No. I don't like medicine. I guess after Joyce—" Slowly, he sipped at the steaming cup.

"Dr. Lazarus will be here shortly. He'll take a look at you."

"I thought all I had to do was see you."

"I'm just the social worker," Caleb said. "We have to be thorough."

"I don't like doctors," Lumford whispered, holding the cup close to his lips.

"Me neither. But Grey's a decent guy. It should be painless." He noticed the flush had left Murphy's face and his eyes were more focused. "You feeling better?"

"A little."

"Can you stand a few more questions?"

"I guess."

"I asked you to tell me why you killed those people. You said you couldn't."

"I said I won't. It's really none of your business. All you need to know is that I wasn't crazy."

"Okay. But you have explained it all to your lawyer, haven't you?"

He took a noisy slurp from the coffee and set the cup down. He laced his fingers together, chest level. "I refused counsel."

Caleb's eyes widened. "I thought you told me you weren't suicidal."

The corners of Murphy's mouth eased back into a tense smile. "Point taken. But again, that doesn't relate to my coming here, does it?"

Janice buzzed his extension and told him of Grey's arrival. Caleb left Officer Wright with Lumford and beat Grey to his office.

"Man, am I glad to see you," he exclaimed.

Grey peered skeptically at him over his bifocals while fumbling with his door keys. "Why?"

"I need you to take a look at a new client, Murphy

Lumford. You know, our famous town murderer? Supposedly tried to kill himself, but he doesn't look suicidal to me. One odd fellow, though. No evidence of thought disorder. Oriented, cordial. Remembers the crime, recounts it with no emotion, like he's reading a grocery list."

Grey returned the tangle of keys to the pocket of his lab coat. "That's not uncommon with violent criminals. It's an internal defense, of sorts. Janice said he tried to hang himself."

"That's weird, too. He twisted up a sheet, tied it to the bed frame, and wrapped it around his head. But he denied trying to kill himself."

Grey studied him for a moment. "It could be scarfing."

"What's that?"

He motioned Caleb into the office and closed the door. "Hypoxyphilia, a form of autoeroticism. You wrap something around your throat, like a cord or scarf, to cut off circulation. You masturbate, then release the cord just as you ejaculate. It's suppose to produce an incredible sexual high."

"Jesus," Caleb uttered, not really wanting to know how Grey knew things like that.

"It's actually a quick way to see Jesus. It's caused a number of accidental deaths."

Caleb grimaced. "I can't see that fitting Lumford. But he's not your typical client, so I don't know. Had a killer headache in the session with me. His face turned bright red, he kept rubbing his head. Said it was from not having caffeine."

Grey lowered himself into his desk chair and ran his hand through wiry gray hair that probably hadn't seen a comb that morning. He wore a faded plaid shirt, navy pants, and antique loafers that showed way too much of Grey's thread-bare white socks. Grey's salary had to be six figures but he dressed like a street person. "It could be a brain tumor. Lesions on particular areas of the brain can make folks behave bizarrely. Might explain the shooting. Then again, he could have faked the whole thing. Any drug seeking behavior?"

"He says he doesn't want medication." Caleb opened the door then turned back towards his colleague. "I leave him for you to fix, then. You ready for him now?"

"I suppose. We've got them lined up out the door, you know. It's going to be a long day."

Caleb brought in Murphy Lumford as the policemen moved their chairs outside Grey's door. "Dr. Lazarus has some questions for you. Try to be as straight with him as you can so he can help you, okay?"

He nodded, muttering meek thanks as Caleb closed the door.

chapter three

Janice intercepted Caleb on his way back to his office. "You have two clients waiting. The intake's a referral from Tindall named Meredith Spencer. The other client is Helen Fleck," she said with a hint of humor.

"Uh–oh." For the past three years, Helen Fleck had a standing ten o'clock Wednesday appointment, which she kept about half the time. It being 11:15, on Monday, meant Helen probably wasn't doing too well. "Okay Janice, here's the drill. You give Ms. Spencer the intake forms, and a Depression Inventory, too. That ought to keep her busy while I see what's up with our Helen."

Janice nodded and a moment later returned with his client. Helen Fleck sauntered in, peculiarly graceful, and stood in the middle of his office. She wore a full olive green skirt and beige sweater that needed washing. Her long hair was collected in a silk scarf that framed a wrinkled, weathered face. Her wide, aimless brown eyes searched the room as if she was unsure what to do next. A bad sign.

Caleb pointed at the chair that she'd occupied for three years, reminding her to sit. She twirled dramatically, breezed over to the seat, and glided down.

"What brings you by, Helen?"

"Why, I came to see *you*, of course." Her voice had a familiar sing-song quality as she tilted her head coyly at him.

Despite the deterioration in almost every other area of her life, Helen's social graces were intact. There was comfort in that, Caleb supposed. Helen's illness chipped away at her short-term memory, concentration, and articulation skills, but the lady had her charm. "It's always nice to see you. But our usual appointment's on Wednesday. Can you tell me what today is?"

Her lips parted, then closed. The brown eyes darted about, confused.

"It's okay," he smiled. "Today's Monday. You could probably tell that from just looking at my tired old face. Now, can you tell me what month we're in?"

She stroked her cheek with a partially polished fingernail. "It's not the same as last time."

"Right. Last time you were here, it was February. What about now?"

She squinched her eyes shut, then said, "Now's a good time."

He shook his head, his concern mounting. She'd been unable to follow a simple train of thought. She looked worse, too. Blotches of bright pink rouge floated like clouds above her angular cheekbones. The lipstick had missed its target, covering most of her upper lip. Her arms looked bony, the flesh on her hand surprisingly pale. He wondered if she was remembering to eat.

"Did you have breakfast this morning?"

"Yes. It was lovely. I had eggs, toast, juice. Have to have that vitamin C!"

"And last night? What did you have?"

Her index finger tapped her lip as she thought. "Last night, I had a lovely evening!"

Caleb reached for his notepad and jotted down, *short-term memory impairment.*

He asked, "I mean what did you eat last night? What food did you have?"

She smiled with enthusiasm. "That's certainly food for

thought."

If she was forgetting to eat, then she might also forget to take her medication, he realized.

She leaned towards him, draping her arms over the folds of her skirt. "Are you single, Caleb?"

"Are you flirting with me, Helen?"

She grinned and actually batted eyelashes at him. "Still some fire left in the old girl, huh?" The "old girl" was only sixty-two, living the daily tragedy that was her illness. Ten years ago, she'd been a restaurant manager of a five-star establishment up in Boston. Ten years ago she had a husband, a family, a nice home.

There was no clear explanation for Helen's fate. She developed a severe drinking problem, that poison damaging her brain. A quick downward spiral found her homeless, lost, and starving. No one knew how she ended up in an abandoned warehouse in Charleston, South Carolina, but when the police found her rummaging through garbage and arguing with herself, they plopped her in the State Hospital. A dutiful social worker managed to locate her family but they recoiled in embarrassment at what she had become. Now she lived alone, struggling to survive as Alzheimer's disease devoured the remains of her mind. She had no contact with her family except the middle son, who was married and living in Virginia.

"So what am I going to do with you, Helen?"

"Dinner, a little dancing . . ." her voice lilted youthfully.

"Now, cut it out. We have to get serious here. I'm worried about you living by yourself. You look like skin and bones. You need to be somewhere safe, where someone can take care of you. Make sure you eat right, take your medicine, and maybe even pamper you a little. Have you talked to your son lately?"

"Jeffrey? I worry so much about him. He's so busy at the bank, they make him work such long hours." She paused, a shadow of sadness passing across her face. Then suddenly, she jerked back and added, "I saw his little league game last week! I was so proud of him. He's small for his age, but he tries hard. I watched him catch a fly ball, Caleb." She probably did. Twenty years or so ago.

"Mind if I give Jeffrey a call? I have a few ideas I'd like to discuss with him." He knew Jeffrey sent the checks to pay for her medication and therapy from the small trust her ex-husband had set up to supplement her disability payment. Maybe there would be enough to cover a placement in a retirement home or other type of sheltered housing. If not, Caleb would have to get more creative.

"Yes, yes. Of course you can call Jeffrey. He gets home from school at three."

"So. I'll talk to him today. You come back and see me on Wednesday, at our usual time." He wrote the appointment down on a card and gave it to her, then jotted a reminder on a sticky note to call her son. "I want you to bring me your medicine bottles, okay?"

She nodded, grinning coyly at him. It was a long shot. She might remember the appointment, but it was unlikely that she'd bring the pills with her. If she didn't, he could drive her home and check out the medicine then. The tougher job was going to be getting her placed somewhere safe and comfortable.

He walked her to Janice, who said she'd be happy to call and remind Helen of the appointment. Helen complimented Janice on her hair bows, "That lovely blue, the color of the ocean . . ." then whirled around and glided out the door.

Janice grinned up at Caleb.

"He wants to see you. Before your next appointment." She twitched her thumb towards Matthew's office. Caleb grumbled and looked at his watch, then complied with the summons.

Matthew nodded into the phone and motioned Caleb into the office. Caleb took his usual seat, stretched out his legs and glanced around Matthew's office.

It was hard for Caleb to believe Matthew could keep things so organized, given the general chaos of their work. The huge mahogany desk glistened under the banker's lamp, only a phone and small notepad disrupted its pristine surface. The Oriental rug felt like marshmallows under his feet. A massive bookcase held hundreds of books and journals arranged by topic. Paneled walls displayed dozens of diplomas, licenses, and special certificates that attested to his specialties in cognitive-behavioral psychiatry, addictions, and family therapy.

Matthew hung up the phone. "Sorry for booking you so heavily. There was no avoiding it."

Caleb shrugged. "I suppose you're entitled, since you do sign my paycheck. Meager as it is."

Matthew grinned, but his eyes looked hurried. His finger traced the thin, perfectly shaped silver mustache under his pointed nose. "Well, I'm about to make your day even worse. I need a favor from you."

"Okay."

"I got a call from a friend of mine last night. He'd had a devastating tragedy. His wife was murdered."

"Is your friend Paul Callahan?"

Matthew nodded, his hand reaching in his suit jacket to retrieve his pipe. "I suppose you saw it in the papers. Really tragic, isn't it?"

"I'm afraid I have more of a first hand connection." Caleb went on to explain the visit to the murder site. "It was horrible, Matthew. You can't imagine what it's like for those kids."

Matthew's intense green eyes squinted over the pipe as he lit it. "I've met them. Beautiful children."

"So what's the favor?"

"Maybe you can't help me out, after all. Paul's concerned about the girl. She hasn't slept or eaten. She barely responds to him at all. She's not even crying, which really has him worried. He's bringing her in tomorrow, but I'm way too close to the situation. I was hoping you'd take a look at her."

Images from that night paraded through Caleb's mind: the bloody spot on the street where Fran Callahan died, the encrusted knife in Maggie's yard. The tiny child wrapped around Maggie's neck, the desperation in that child's gaze. "I don't really have a connection to the family. I was there as a favor to Maggie. The girl would probably remember me, and that might actually help. Of course, it might scare her. She may associate me with the events of that night. Tough call."

"Grey's due at the hospital all day tomorrow. I'm too close to the family to be objective. I suppose if you're comfortable, we could give you a shot at her."

Caleb shrugged, unsure how to squeeze Emma Callahan into an already impossible schedule. He stood, stretching his long legs, arching his back. "Guess I better get hopping."

"Your intake appointment. You get a look at her yet?"

"No. Why?"

Matthew grinned under twirls of blue smoke. "I may not owe you any favors after all."

You didn't have to be Stephen Hawking to pick up on what Matthew was grinning about. Meredith Spencer was gorgeous. Drop dead gorgeous. The kind of gorgeous that might have a less self-assured man knocking at the knees.

"Uh–uh–have a seat." Caleb suddenly realized that she was already sitting and tried to hide his embarrassment by turning away. As his chair swiveled around, his leg bumped the desk and jolted his mug, spilling a pool of coffee on his appointment book. He snatched a tissue from its box to blot up the hot liquid. Smooth, he thought. Really smooth.

"Thanks for seeing me, Dr. Knowles."

"Call me Caleb. We try not to be formal around here."

"Okay, Caleb," she said, flashing a dazzling white smile. Light brown hair framed her face and fell in soft curls off her shoulders. Big, thickly lashed green eyes didn't hesitate to make direct contact.

Caleb found his own eyes pulling down, focusing on the Intake Form in his hand. It said she was married, no children, no history of prior treatment. She was one year short of a college degree. Both parents were living. She'd worked for Tindall Mill for two years. The form didn't mention her Jodie Foster cheekbones or her liquid eyes that reminded him of Shania Twain.

He could have turned the sheet over and spent another five minutes avoiding eye contact, but maybe it was time to switch attention from his hormones to his job. He looked up at her and she smiled.

"You're here about the shooting?" he blurted out, immediately regretting it. He hadn't established any sort of relationship with her before delving into what was probably the most traumatic event of her life. It was the kind of blunder he made back during his internship. In three short minutes with this woman, fifteen years of clinical experience flew out the window.

It didn't seem to phase her. "Yes. I was there. I was standing right beside Sally when she got shot."

He was surprised by how calmly she said this. In fact, he was surprised by everything about her. He'd worked with plenty of employees from Tindall, who tended to be big-haired women with protruding middles and smiles that lacked dental attention. But Meredith didn't fit the mold. She was petite, maybe five foot three, with a lean dancer's physique. She didn't have the stained, rough hands of a mill worker; hers were manicured, with long, apricot-colored nails. She wore a pale blue dress, belted at the narrow waist.

"What do you do at Tindall?" he asked.

"I work in human resources. I rarely go on the floor. But Sally Weston had just passed her three-month anniversary, so I was working up a benefits package for her. I needed to verify the level of coverage and I went down to talk to her. I had just found her when—" She looked down and studied her manicure.

"I imagine that was upsetting," he coached.

"It was horrible. I knew Murphy Lumford, you see. I had met with him just a few weeks ago. He was a nice man. I thought his sense of humor was sort of sweet, almost boyish. I liked him."

Caleb thought about other mass murderers he'd read about. The media always interviewed an acquaintance or neighbor who said, "Such a nice man, never bothered anybody. Always seemed kind of quiet . . ." But then, Ms. Spencer's assessment of Lumford wasn't too different from his own.

"It was so hot on the floor," she went on. "They run air conditioning almost year round, but when the looms are going, you just can't cool the place down. Even in the winter. I remember I was perspiring as soon as I opened the door. I was walking over to Sally to ask her something. Then I notice Murphy Lumford standing off the line, in the middle of the floor. He doesn't say anything, just stands there, perfectly still, for several minutes. I remember thinking that was odd. Buck Swygert, the floor supervisor, notices him too. We're both staring at him when I see him move. He reaches in the pocket of his work pants and pulls out this gun. He points it and shoots. I think he got Buck Swygert first. Then he slowly turns, firing the gun—" She held her hand out, forefinger extended. "He shot Sally, then turned some more, and shot Mike Beard. He kept turning, until he'd gone full circle. Then he carefully set the gun down at his feet, bowed his head, and waited." She drew her finger in, making a fist, then dropped her hand in her lap.

"What did you do?" Caleb whispered.

"I just stood there for a moment, sort of in shock. Then I went over to Sally and tried to help. She bled all over the place. Somebody brought a towel and kept pressure on her arm until the ambulance came."

"How long did that take?"

"I couldn't tell you. I know our security got there first, and they put handcuffs on Murphy. Then I think the police got there, then the EMT's. It seemed like it took hours, but it was probably more like twenty minutes."

He studied her for a moment, glad that his therapeutic eye was now working harder than his hormones. "How has the incident affected you, Meredith?"

She took in a deep breath. "I was scared to death. After it was all over, and the police left, and the ambulances left, we all just sort of stood there, looking at each other. Frozen. Like we didn't know what to do next."

"You still feel that way?"

She leaned back in the chair and fingered the neckline of her dress. She turned her head slightly, her eyes watching him from the corners. "Maybe. I get these waves of fear, you know? Like I start shaking and feel real cold. I called my husband. He's pretty worried about me. He's the one who insisted that I come today."

"Tell me a little about him."

"What do you want to know?" She stiffened in her chair and her tone changed, a hint of defensiveness leaking in.

"Whatever you're comfortable sharing. Like what does he do, how long have you been married, that sort of stuff."

Her eyes fluttered and she looked up, as if sorting through a mental Rolodex trying to decide what to pull out. "Alec and I have been married four years. My first marriage, his second. He's British, and I fell in love with his accent first. Then him. No kids yet, but who knows? He works as a professor at the university."

"Oh? What does he teach?"

She grinned. "Psychology."

Caleb started flipping through his own mental Rolodex but the name "Alec Spencer" wasn't familiar. "Does he have a practice in town?"

"No. He's more into research, really. Anyway, we met when I was in school. We got married. I decided to postpone the degree. I've enjoyed office work and hoped to climb through the ranks at Tindall."

"You're speaking in the past tense."

She shrugged. "I'm not feeling so terrific about my job at the moment. Which, I would think, is understandable."

"When are you planning to go back to work?"

"When I leave here."

"Did you think of asking for some time off?"

"I did think about that. But really, I'm not sure it's good to avoid going in. The longer I wait, the harder it will be. You know, like falling off a horse. It's best to get back on right away."

"Unless the horse injures you. Sounds to me like you did suffer a wound from this." Caleb's gaze was soft but probing.

Hers evaded him. "I was upset, that's all. It seems like that's perfectly normal."

"Absolutely. Listen, I've had traumatic events that messed with my head some. I had sleep problems, I didn't want to eat. I had to give myself time to heal. That may be what you need."

She inspected her nails again. "Alec would agree with you. I thought he was being overprotective."

"I think you should do what feels right to you. If it means you take a few days off, I think you should give yourself permission to do it." Caleb sensed tension between them, like this simple issue had blown up into a power struggle. He wondered if he'd stumbled on a theme in their marriage. Like a lot of other couples, maybe Alec and Meredith regularly vied for control. But whatever triggered it, she looked like she needed for him to back off.

"When I get a new client, it's helpful to get background information. Is it okay if I ask you some questions?"

She narrowed her lashes at him. "What kind of questions?"

"Mainly information about your history. Your childhood, family, that sort of stuff." He smiled and hoped it looked reassuring. He couldn't figure out why she responded so defensively; every effort to connect with her failed. Of course, his initial glandular reaction had given them an awkward beginning.

"Okay," she said, relenting. "What do you want to know?"

"Where were you born?"

"Japan, if you can believe it. My father was Air Force. I lived there until I was two. Then we came back to the states."

"Any brothers or sisters?"

"Yes. Two sisters. I'm in the middle. Alec says that makes me a peace-maker, because middle children are great compromisers."

"How far apart were you?" Caleb asked.

"My oldest sister, Sandra, is thirty, I'm next, twenty-seven. Teresa was the baby, she would have been twenty-four."

"Would have been? What happened to Teresa?"

She sighed, and he couldn't tell if it was exasperation or sadness. "She died when she was ten. Somebody ran over her with their car." Her voice had softened, but there was little emotion there.

"Were you close to her?"

"Yes." She leaned forward, her eyes zeroing in on his. "I don't think I know you well enough to go into how that affected me. I don't mean to sound negative, but could we just change the subject?"

He nodded, confused by this latest roadblock. "Okay. You said your father was in the Air Force. Did you move around a lot?"

"Sure. Every two years or so. Dad finally got transferred to Sumter when I was fourteen, then wound up retiring there. I came to Westville to go to school, met Alec, et cetera, et cetera." She was smiling now, as if recounting these details were more comfortable for her. He decided to keep things light for a bit.

"Did your mom work?"

"Off and on, after we started school. Mostly secretarial stuff. Dad's retired now, but dabbles in insurance. They're still happily married."

"That's impressive. So they've probably been together,

what? Thirty years or so?"

"Thirty-two years. My sister Sandra is single. She says she won't get married until she finds someone as terrific as Dad." The tone was more relaxed, almost buoyant now. Maybe she was ready for a more serious line of questions.

"Sounds like you're close to your parents."

"Yes. We talk every day."

"So you probably told them what happened. What did they say?"

"I'm not telling them, if I can help it. It would just upset them. They think Westville's a big, violent place and this would just get them more worried." She gestured with both hands, like an adolescent would do. Her expression was open and animated, a complete switch from her reserved posture twenty minutes earlier.

Suddenly, she angled her hand to look at her watch. His wall clock said it was 9:50, which meant she'd been there less than a half hour. "Well, I think I'd better go," she said breathily.

Caleb nodded. An hour had been scheduled for her, but apparently she wouldn't be using all of it. Since it was her first session, he decided to let her take the lead. "Okay. But before you go, I would like to know how I can help you. Would you like to reschedule? Maybe later in the week?"

She strummed her thumb along the tips of her manicure. "I'm not sure. I don't feel like I'm the basket case Alec thinks I am. But then, I don't know if I'll have some lasting effects from the shooting. Could I call if I feel I need to come in?"

"Sure. I'll give you my card. One other thing. For counseling to be effective, it's important that the client feel comfortable with her therapist. If, for any reason, you think you could work more effectively with someone else, just let me know. I'd be happy to refer you."

She shot up in her chair. "Are you saying you don't want to work with me?"

He blinked, surprised that she interpreted his comment as

rejection. "Absolutely not. I'd be delighted to work with you. But sometimes clients have a preference related to the therapist's style. Or, sometimes they want a therapist of the same gender. I want you to get what you need, Meredith. You've been through a lot. I want therapy to help you get over what happened."

"Well then, I'll give that some thought." Her tone was flippant. She took the card from him and studied it. "Caleb Knowles, M.S.W. That means you have a Masters in Social Work, right? But not a Ph.D. I didn't realize." She held the card by its edge like it was a used tissue, then opened a large leather purse to drop it in. She stood, straightened her dress, tossed her hair behind her shoulders, and approached the door.

When Caleb rose to show her out, he was struck again by her diminutive size. He reached to shake her hand. "It was nice to meet you, Meredith."

As she left, Caleb dropped back in his chair and mulled over the session. The end had been like a courtesy job interview for a position he wasn't qualified for. Nothing about Meredith Spencer had been easy.

He was jotting down a few sketchy notes about the session when Janice buzzed him. Your brother's here and I'm sending him on back. Your next appointment isn't due for another twenty minutes or so."

Sam sauntered in, looking fresh. He was over six feet tall and with his pronounced carpenter's muscles, he easily filled a room. He wore a brown wool sweater that complemented his blond hair. His hands were wedged in the pockets of freshly pressed khakis. His running shoes looked bright white and ready for action. Sam strolled over to the window and opened the shade so that the sunshine spilled in, the light feeling curiously therapeutic.

Caleb waited until his brother sat down facing him, then signed, "Make yourself at home."

Caleb's older brother had been deaf since an accident at

age sixteen. Although Sam spoke clearly and read lips well, the best method of communication was a combination of signed and spoken words.

"You look like hell," Sam said aloud, eyeing him intently.

"I'm always a beauty after three hours of sleep," he signed. "We had a bit of an adventure last night." He told Sam about Maggie, about the murder, and about the two devastated children.

Sam's eyes, the only window to his world, read Caleb's words and every meaning beneath them. "Anything I can do?"

"No. Let's change the subject before I get too depressed to work with the two hundred depressed people I'll probably have to see today. What brings you by?"

"I need a favor."

"What?" Caleb signed, striking his right index finger across his left palm.

"I need to borrow your ears tomorrow."

"Well, okay. But I'll be wanting them back."

Sam scratched at his thick hair and groaned at the joke. "I just tried to meet with a real estate agent. I never needed an interpreter so bad."

"Why did you meet with a real estate agent?" Caleb signed, brushing fingertips across his forehead, then extending his thumb and little finger.

Sam took a deep breath, like he was about to say something difficult. "I'm thinking about selling the house."

"What?" Caleb glared at his brother. "You spent a year restoring that place. You promised I'd never have to move you again."

Sam's eyes dimmed a little. "After Anne's death . . . I thought about leaving, but I couldn't stand another change, you know? Not so soon. At first, when I walked around in the studio, all I could remember was her body. It was weird, but I think that sort of helped me accept her death."

Caleb nodded, remembering, and not wanting to. Claudia

had called him right after the murder happened and he'd been the one to identify Anne's bludgeoned body for the police. He remembered Sam, covered in his fiancée's blood, staring out at the turmoil around him. A few days later, the police arrested Sam and charged him with Anne's murder. As Caleb worked feverishly to prove Sam's innocence, he learned of Anne's pregnancy and other dark secrets—secrets that nearly drove Sam to self-destruct before the real murderer was uncovered. It had been a close call for Sam. For both of them.

"It's different now, though," Sam went on. "Now, I remember the nicer things. When we bought a new bedspread because Anne thought my old one was too masculine. When we cooked supper together and then ate slowly because we had so much to talk about. I think about late mornings in bed together, or just times when we poked around, each doing our own thing, but somehow together. Connected. I feel her presence there, you know? Does that make me batty?"

Caleb signed, "Well, if you want my professional opinion, I'm afraid I'll have to bill you for it."

"Put it on my tab. God knows, yours is pushing five digits, little brother."

Caleb brushed fingertips on his forehead then extended his thumb and pinky, signing, "So why leave now?"

"I need more space. I outgrew my workshop years ago. I thought about building in the back, but I really don't have much yard and I'd have to take out those great oak trees. My agent thinks I should rent a separate workshop and studio. She said it would help out on my taxes. Which means I'd only be using the mill house for living space, and it's way too big for that. So maybe I should sell the place, then separate my work from home. Don't you think it's smart to shake things up a bit, to try new things?"

"I guess," Caleb said. "It would be like a self-imposed boundary. The day is done, you go home. And home is a separate place from work. That's not exactly an unusual way to live, you know."

"Well, it would be unusual for me. I get a bit immersed in my work, as you like to point out. The idea of taking free time—what would I do?" Sam looked puzzled by his own question.

"Here's a novel idea. Why don't you get out and date?"

Sam studied the window for a while. His eyes looked a little uncomfortable with this reference to his social life. "I don't think I'm ready."

Caleb reached over and tapped his brother's hand so he'd look up. "It's been over a year, Sam. And I'm not talking about any big commitment thing, I'm talking about having fun. Getting to know some new people. If you meet someone special, that's just icing on the cake. You can't keep living like a hermit forever."

Sam waved him off and returned to his study of the window. After a long moment, he said, "It's not easy dating, you know. I remember you put us all through hell before Shannon. And I don't even know where to start. There aren't too many single deaf women in Westville, and hearing women? They're pretty tricky."

Caleb almost commented that trickiness was an inherent quality of the double-X gender, deaf or not. But he knew Sam's issue touched on something more sensitive.

Sam functioned extraordinarily well in the hearing world, but the accident twenty years ago had affected more than his hearing. He had been the stellar Knowles child, the handsome athlete, the straight-A student. The motorcycle accident landed him head-first in a silent, lonely world. He had to leave his school, his friends, and his home to commute to a special school that trained him in signing, lip-reading, and "community adjustment." When Sam returned to the family, he was a very different young man. He spent afternoon hours closed up in his room, avoiding all the family, but especially their father.

Samuel Knowles, Sr. didn't help matters. He made no effort to conceal his disappointment in Sam, using the

accident as another reason to drink, another reason to curse
the fates. Another reason to hit his children. And it was
Caleb's loyal older brother who absorbed most of those
blows.

Fourteen-year-old Caleb didn't understand why his brother
had become the silent stranger in the next room. So Caleb
enrolled in sign language classes at a local church, talking the
teacher into private tutoring until he knew enough to help
Sam with his school work. And gradually, Sam had adjusted
to his new life. But being a "late-deafened" person meant he
didn't quite fit in either world. While he was fluent in
American Sign Language, or ASL, his "native tongue" was
spoken English, with its grammatical structure. And he got
along so well in the hearing world that people tended to
forget he was deaf. Little things, like not facing him directly
when addressing him, meant he couldn't understand what was
being said, which was a source of constant frustration and
confusion for him. And it really pissed off his protective
younger brother.

Caleb gave him a scowl.

"What?" Sam asked.

"I do remember dating. You're right, I wouldn't wish that
on anybody. But you need to get out. Shall I ask around about
available women?"

"Not if you want to stay my brother. So, back to why I
stopped by here. I've got the realtor coming over tomorrow.
She speaks a mile a minute, and I suspect she may talk out of
both sides of her mouth. Can you help?"

He nodded, waving his fist in signed assent. Of course he
would. Sam so rarely asked for his help. "So you're really
serious about selling the mill house. It's hard to imagine you
anywhere else."

"Seven o'clock."

"Okay. If you feed me."

"Janice said I only had you for a few minutes because
she's got eight zillion clients lined up for you to see. Have I

told you lately that I don't want your job?"

"I'm not too wild about it, myself, just now."

chapter four

Three hours and three long sessions later, Caleb stopped by Janice's desk, picked up a stack of messages, and sifted through them. He leaned over Janice to peruse the weekly master appointment schedule, which had never held so many names. Caleb's column had back-to-back sessions scheduled, Matthew had filled up two lunch breaks, and Grey Lazarus had even scrawled in some extra hours.

"Jesus, Janice. What are you doing to us?"

She grinned sympathetically. "You know I'll help how ever I can."

"Can you clone me?"

She rolled her eyes over her bifocals, giving him that look she probably saved for disobedient grandchildren.

"See you in the morning." Caleb gave her a wink and made his way to his truck. The air was cool enough that he zipped his jacket. Dusk was sneaking down on the city and promised a colder night. He realized this was the first time he'd been outside since eight that morning, which wasn't good. Taking some semblance of a break in the middle of the day was one way he stayed sane in the pressure cooker business of mental health. He'd have to do better tomorrow.

Traffic had died down. The rest of Westville's working class were already home with their ties off and jeans on, settling down at their dinner tables. The town housed many government offices and the mass exodus always hit at five o'clock on the dot. Those government employees knew the real meaning of 'quittin' time."

He eased around Maggie's Honda and parked in the tiny space beside Shannon's behemoth car. Stiff from the endless day of sitting, he hauled himself out of the truck and trudged up the walk.

In the kitchen, he found Maggie and Shannon sitting behind half-empty bottles of Heineken. Two empties rested on the counter. Caleb made his way behind Shannon, laid his hands on her shoulders, and kissed the top of her head. She grinned up at him, the slight scent of beer breathing out of her.

"What's for dinner?" he asked.

"I was about to ask you that," she said, taking a swig of her beer.

"What? Two beautiful women in my kitchen and no dinner's been cooked?" He feigned astonishment.

"And when do you return to your home planet?" Shannon leaned her head against the bottle in her hand.

Caleb took a seat beside them, pondering his empty stomach and the empty oven. The unwritten rule was, first person home started dinner. Shannon's turn usually meant Chinese carry-out or pizza delivery.

"Actually, we have been discussing food," Shannon said. "It would be nice if we had some. But Maggie and I pooled our resources and concluded we could maybe manage grilled cheese sandwiches without burning the house down. Then we had beer and decided even that would be too hard."

"So Maggie, you saying you don't cook either?"

Maggie shook her head as she scratched at the label on her bottle. A tidy pile of green and silver flecks lay in front of her on the table.

"Oh Maggie, tell him about the survey," Shannon said with a laugh.

"Please don't make me." A smile had eased on her face,

the first he'd seen since the murder. And her color was better, he thought. Her brown eyes looked less haunted and had some sparkle back. Her ample black hair hung loose about her face in a style that flattered her. Maggie was an attractive woman, Caleb had often noticed, with the kind of intelligent beauty men easily appreciated. Unfortunately, she had the not-so-uncommon habit of selecting the unhealthy, damaging ones to be romantic partners.

"Well, I'll tell him then." Shannon leaned forward and set her beer down. "About a month ago, Maggie gets this phone call from a guy doing a survey. What was it? The chamber of commerce?" Her friend shrugged, so Shannon went on, "Anyway, this guy's taking a poll, you know, about restaurants in Westville. Well, Maggie considers herself somewhat of an expert in the area, so she agrees." She paused for another sip of beer. "The guy asks 'Ms. Wells, how many times would you say that you've eaten out in the past month?' And Maggie replies, 'Sixty.'"

"No kidding?" Caleb grinned.

Maggie peeled the final strip of label.

"Then he asks, 'How many times have you eaten Chinese?' She says, 'Fifteen.' 'Mexican?' She says, 'Ten.' 'Fast food?' 'About twenty-five!'"

"Now that's pathetic," Caleb said.

"Isn't it though? That's my life all right," Maggie said.

"You live your life exactly like you want to and you know it." Shannon punctuated her statement with a wave of the beer bottle. "If you wanted to cook, you'd learn how. Like Caleb. He could learn how to change the oil in that neglected truck of his if he wanted to. But instead, he leaves that to me. You just need to find a man who cooks and hold on to him."

"That's what Shannon did," Caleb said. He stretched his arm around her and opened the refrigerator, grabbing one of the few remaining beers for himself. "Should we call for pizza?"

"Excellent plan." Shannon grabbed the phone and dialed

the number from memory. Maggie stared down at her pile of beer label shavings.

"How are you doing?" Caleb asked. "Feeling any better?"

She nodded. "A little. I guess the shock's wearing off now. I talked to Paul and he said you were going to see Emma tomorrow. I know you can't talk about it, confidentiality and all. But I do appreciate your helping them."

He smiled, wishing she'd change the subject. Rules of confidentiality meant he couldn't acknowledge any contact with Paul or the Callahan family—not to Maggie, or even to Shannon. It was something he had firm ethics about.

"I talked to the police again. That Detective Briscoe that you know?" Maggie said. "She wants to see me tomorrow. I can't imagine what else I can tell them."

Caleb took a swallow from his Heineken. "I'm real familiar with how Claudia works. She knows you were in shock last night and that veils your awareness of things, particularly details. Once you've had time, your memories will probably look clearer to you. So she may ask some of the same questions she did before, hoping you remember more."

Maggie raked her hands through both sides of her hair, lifting it away from her face. It was a nervous gesture he'd seen her do many times. "I can't help but wish it was all over, you know? That they'd arrest whoever did this, and let me and Paul and the children get on with our lives."

"And whatever you tell Claudia might just help that happen."

Shannon finished her call and was about to take a seat again when the phone rang. As soon as she answered it, Caleb read on her face that it was someone she didn't care for. "For you, Maggie. It's Barry."

Their friend looked like she'd just been hit in the stomach.

"I'll tell him you're out. Or I'll tell him to go fuck himself, if you'll let me. Your call." Shannon made no effort to hide her disgust.

"I'll take it in the other room." A knowing glare passed

between the two women as Maggie moved to the den. Shannon gave her a moment, then hung up.

"Damn him," she muttered.

"Does Barry like, have a job?" It always seemed like Barry had way too much idle time on his hands.

"Supposedly, he helps his father selling some kind of insurance." She wrinkled her nose as if she smelled something rotten.

"This seems stronger than your usual dislike of her ex-boyfriends. Of course, I never liked him. Too intense. Too tanned. And all those perfect teeth, lined up like piano keys . . ." His voice trailed off. Shannon didn't look like she was paying him the least bit of attention, her turquoise eyes staring at the telephone like she was trying to see the conversation taking place.

Caleb drank more of his beer and pondered getting Shannon engaged in the conversation he realized he was having with himself, but she looked furious.

"If he tries anything, Caleb, I swear I'll—"

"What do you think he's going to try?" he said evenly.

"To get her back. To move back in, to be all protective and concerned and sucker his way back into her life. She's so vulnerable right now."

"Seems like it's her choice to make. It's her life, isn't it?"

She glowered at him. "You have no idea how bad he is for her."

"Tell me then." He resented the anger she was inflicting on him, and wondered if this was one of those situations where he represented the entire male sex, evil as it was. He hated it when their talks regressed to that level.

She sat back at the table. "I can't really go into it. Suffice it to say that Barry Waters needs to crawl back into the pit he came from and stay the hell out of Maggie's life."

Caleb gave her a neutral nod. Given the mood she was in, Caleb resolved, there was no way he'd argue with her. She could have told him that the pope himself was a child molester and he'd have sat there nodding, not wanting to make an issue of the pontiff's personal habits. He was beginning to wonder if the specter of PMS had crept into his happy home.

But that was okay, moodiness in Shannon was a pretty rare event. And Caleb's marriage to Mariel, especially the last two years, had been like boot camp preparing him for female hormonal wars. He went to the refrigerator, grabbed her another beer, and waited for the pizza.

It came twenty minutes later and Shannon convinced Maggie to tear herself away from the phone. They ate quietly, the silence tense with unspoken opinions. When Maggie finished her beer, she turned to Shannon. "I need to run by my house and get a few things," she said. "That is, if you can stand putting up with me."

"I want you here till it's safe for you to be home. Maybe Caleb could help you get your stuff."

Caleb remembered the SEC game he'd hoped to catch on TV and started to say something, but he caught the look in Shannon's eye. "Good idea," he said with as much conviction as he could muster. He finished his last bit of pizza and followed Maggie out to her car.

Caleb pushed the passenger seat back as far as he could as Maggie eased her Civic onto Saluda Street. A light, chilling rain drummed the hood of the car and spattered the windshield. She turned on public radio where strains of sultry saxophone jazz almost matched the rhythm of the rain. As Caleb listened, fatigue settled in, his bones wanting to melt into the car seat. He needed to get to bed early if he was to survive the rest of the week.

He glanced over at his companion. Maggie's hand tapped her steering wheel in no particular beat with the music. Suddenly, she reached for the radio and turned it off. A few seconds later, she switched it on again and punched the button to a rock station. Sting hadn't made it through one verse before Maggie pulled against the curb in front of her house, just a few yards away from where Fran had been murdered.

They sat there for a long moment, staring ahead at the now clean spot on the sidewalk. There were no blood stains, no police tape, no signs at all of what had happened. But suddenly, the air became very cold. Caleb glanced over at Maggie. "You okay?"

She was trembling. Her hand covered her lips, as though holding back words that couldn't be spoken. "It's almost like I can see it all over again."

"Are you up to going inside?"

"Inside's the easy part." She opened the car door, tightened her jacket around her, and trotted up to the house.

The steps to the dark porch squeaked as they climbed them. Maggie fumbled through a dozen keys until she found the right one, which she slid into the lock. She turned it left, then turned it back, then pulled the key out and stared down at it. "That's funny. I think the door was unlocked."

"You forget to lock it?" he asked, motioning her aside as he eased the door open.

"No, not after last night." She touched his arm. "This is scaring me."

Caleb squeezed her hand, whispering, "Wait out here."

When he stepped into her living room and looked around, he found everything as it had been the night before. He switched on the light, crossed through the room and inched open the door to the tiny den. A thin shaft of light spilled in, showing him the TV and stereo were in place. Everything else looked okay, too, except for the roll-top desk in the corner.

Every desk drawer gaped open, papers and notebooks spilling out like someone had ransacked it, looking for something. Had the police come back here? Or maybe there had been an intruder. Warily, Caleb eased over to the other door leading to the kitchen.

It was then that he heard the noise. A creaking sound, like

an old door. At first he thought Maggie had come in, except the noise seemed to come from the back of the house. He froze against the wall, breathless, listening. Silence. He waited another moment and heard nothing. He was probably just hallucinating, he decided, and maybe Matthew could work him in tomorrow, see if he needed medication. He started down the hall.

"What the fuck?" A voice boomed. It was a deep, throaty voice with a Spanish accent, coming from the bedroom.

Caleb froze again, terror clinching like a fist inside him. He needed to get to a phone and call the police. But first, he definitely needed to get out of there. He looked down the length of the hall that seemed to have expanded by about fifty feet. He could bolt, throw open the front door, grab Maggie and—*Maggie*. As if summoned by his thought she appeared, making her way through the living room. He tried to motion to her, to signal for her to run, but she was looking in the other direction.

"Try the closet," the voice said. Mumbled words followed, something about a "spider." Caleb flattened himself against the hallway wall, craning his neck to see if Maggie had heard the intruders. She was gone. He prayed that she had made it back outside.

There must be two intruders at least. What did they want? He pinched an eye shut, hoping to make out their shapes through the crack between the door frame and the door. He could make out an outline of one figure, large and quick, darting about the room, which looked like it had been overturned. The mattress teetered off the bed, clothes lay scattered on the floor, bureau drawers sat upended against a wall.

Caleb sucked in air, unsure what to do. He heard another noise, this time coming from the kitchen. Maggie. He held his breath.

"What was that? Go check." The Spanish accent said. A huge man swung open the bedroom door and immediately, a flashlight beam swept Caleb. He tried to run, but it was too late.

"Who the fuck are you?" the man boomed, slamming Caleb into the wall. The man's breath, hot on Caleb's face, smelled as rancid as cat litter.

"A neighbor. I was just—"

The man pressed his forearm into Caleb's chest, crushing the breath out of him. Instinctively, Caleb thrust his knee up, hoping for contact with the man's crotch, but hitting a muscled thigh instead. The man lifted his other hand, which held the long, industrial size flashlight, and shoved it hard into Caleb's ribs.

A red hot, disorienting pain shot through him. Caleb gasped, grabbing for the man's hand and digging his nails in, but it didn't phase his assailant. The man pressed his mouth into Caleb's ear and whispered, "Don't look at me, fucker. Only way you'll stay alive."

Caleb tried to speak, but no words came. He tried to move, but his body wouldn't obey. His lungs hungered for air. Out of the corner of his eye, he saw a head. Huge, bald, pale. It attached to a neck as wide as the head. Then came shoulders that bulged out like basketballs. He dared not look any more.

"What should I do with him?" the man asked his colleague.

"Put him out," the Spanish accent said from behind him. Caleb felt himself being lifted, then hanging as limp as a rag. The pressure in his chest was like boiling lead. He couldn't seem to get his arms moving to fight back. He thought about Maggie and hoped to God she was safe and maybe even getting help for them, like the police or . . . A massive fist poised in front of him, moved, coming closer. A milky fog spilled in, taking him away.

"Caleb? Caleb!" The voice called to him from somewhere very far away. It annoyed him, and he wanted it to leave him alone. "Caleb!" it screamed again. All right, all right. He tried to move towards it, through the tangled slinky in his mind. But as he got closer to the voice, a searing, needle-sharp pain exploded in his ribs.

"Caleb," the voice cried now. He worked against the weights on his eyelids and pried them open.

Maggie peered down, looking frantic. "Can you hear me?"

"Yeah," he whispered.

"You scared the shit out of me. Can you move?"

He took a quick inventory. His arms moved sluggishly and his eyes and ears seemed to be in working order. Neurons were firing away in his brain, particularly the ones that registered pain. He laid a hand on his raging chest.

"I called for help. They should be here soon," she said.

All at once, he remembered why he was on the floor. "Where are they?" he asked, panic tightening his inflamed lungs.

Maggie laid a soothing hand on his head. "They're gone. I was in the kitchen when I heard them. The next thing I knew, one slammed you into the wall. I hid behind the kitchen door until they ran out the front door. They jumped in an old car and drove off."

"Good riddance." Caleb pressed his palms into the floor and lifted his torso. That bit of exertion sent waves of electricity up and down his neural system and he let out a staggered groan. With help from Maggie, he slid over to the wall and leaned against it. "Shit," he muttered.

Sirens howled in the distance, coming closer and getting louder and louder. Soon, police officers and EMTs streamed in, the officers asking questions as the EMTs got to work measuring his heart rate and blood pressure. After more probing of his head and ribcage, they offered an ambulance ride, which Caleb declined. Maggie promised to drive him to the emergency room as soon as the police were done with him.

Claudia arrived next. She surveyed Caleb up and down, shaking her head. "They called me from the precinct. Since the address was so close to the murder site, I thought I'd better come take a look. And who do I find here but you? You sure got a knack for getting into trouble."

"I just do it for attention."

"Well, this could have gotten you attention from the coroner. Are you okay?" She sounded genuinely concerned.

"I think so. But you got more criminals to catch."

"So I hear." She pulled out a notepad and went to work. She glanced around, her sharp eyes taking in the scene, her quick hands jotting down notes. She questioned Caleb about the men, wanting physical descriptions and other details about his encounter with them. He wished he remembered more than he did, but the fog that had filled his brain seemed to be distorting his memory. He told her one had a Spanish accent and the other was made out of four hundred pounds of granite, but Claudia ignored his humor and kept on writing. After finishing with Caleb, she approached Maggie and motioned her into the kitchen.

"Maggie? I'm looking for Maggie Wells," a man's voice called out. Barry Waters tried to push past an officer who blocked him at the door. "Where is Maggie? Is she—"

Caleb waved off the officer and motioned Barry over. "Maggie's fine. She's with a detective."

"Thank God." Barry let out a relieved sigh. "I was driving by and saw the police cars and Maggie's Honda. It scared the piss out of me." He looked it. His lips quivered under the dark bush of mustache as his wary close-set eyes peered at the officers around him.

"Driving by? How did you happen to be 'driving by'?" Caleb squinted up at Barry, who seemed to ignore the question, and noticed a large coffee stain on Barry's sweater. He'd never seen a coffee stain or even a speck of dust on Barry's clothes before. Poor Barry must be having a tough night, too, he thought.

The officer approached Barry again and asked, "Who are you?"

"Barry Waters. Ms. Wells' boyfriend. What the hell happened here? Who's in charge?" Barry's anxiety quickly evolved into his usual take-charge manner. He glared down at the young officer who scurried off to fetch his boss.

"I thought you and Maggie broke up," Caleb muttered.

"We're working things out," Barry said with confidence that Caleb hoped wasn't warranted. "We always do. By the way, why are you sitting on the floor?"

"I think I'll try a chair now." Caleb heaved himself up with a little help from Barry, then limped into the living room and collapsed on the sofa.

"You don't look so good," Barry said, ever the perceptive one. But his eyes shifted beyond Caleb, to the doorway where Maggie appeared. As soon as she saw him, Maggie's face lit up. She ran to him and fell into his arms, her face burrowing into his chest. They muttered quiet words to each other the way reunited lovers do.

"That's Barry Waters, Maggie's used-to-be ex-boyfriend," Caleb whispered to Claudia. "Shannon says he's a toad."

Claudia turned hard, detective eyes on Barry, who replied with the usual ingratiating grin. "You better get Caleb to the hospital to get checked out," she said to Maggie. "We'll finish up here."

Maggie pulled herself away from Barry's grasp. "Let's go, Caleb. Shannon will kill me if I don't get you tended to."

"I'll ride along," Barry volunteered.

Claudia stepped up to him. "I'd rather you stay for a moment, Mr. Waters. I have a few questions for you."

He smiled, revealing a half-moon of perfect teeth that didn't seem to impress Claudia. "I'll be glad to answer anything." He kissed Maggie on the forehead. "I'll catch up with you in a bit, honey."

Bryant Wheeler, M.D., was covering the emergency room at Westville Memorial, which was a lucky break because the waiting room was full of coughing, wheezing people, probably struck by the flu. Bryant spotted Caleb as he came in and hurried him into an examining room. "What happened to you?"

Caleb grinned up at his friend and poker buddy but Bryant didn't grin back. He wrapped a blood pressure cuff around Caleb's arm, and used a stethoscope chilled to well below freezing to listen to Caleb's ailing chest. Caleb gave him a Reader's Digest condensed version of what had happened. "Did you lose consciousness?"

"Just for a minute. Most of my faculties seem to be working."

Bryant reached in the pocket of his lab coat for a flashlight. He aimed it in Caleb's pupils as his hands groped the back of his head. "Ow!"

"Nice bump there. Looks like you'll have an attractive bruise on that chin, too. I'm more worried about the ribs, though. The X-rays will show if any are fractured." Bryant spoke slower now, the triage doctor converting to the concerned friend.

"Can I go home now?"

"No. You get X-rayed first."

Caleb glanced at his watch. Ten o'clock. Shannon was sure to be worrying by now. "Can we make it quick? I need to get home."

Bryant pursed his lips. "Well, I'm glad you could squeeze us into your busy schedule. I just bumped you ahead of about eight patients, Caleb. You need to let me do my job here."

Caleb looked appropriately chastised and let himself be worked through the loops of medical red tape. An hour later, Bryant wrapped his chest to stabilize the broken rib, which hurt like a mother, and handed him samples of medication with instructions to rest and avoid exertion. Caleb thanked him and went to the nurse's station to check out.

"Code Management, Bay Three!" a technician yelled as he ran out of an examining room, cradling his blood-soaked arm. Screams and clanging noises resounded behind him. As his colleagues at the desk looked up in alarm, a quick nurse grabbed the phone and paged security.

Bryant Wheeler nearly leapt over the counter to get to the examining area. Through the opened curtain of the cubicle, Caleb spotted a Hispanic teen wearing a leather jacket and red bandanna.

The teen stood poised, his arms outstretched, his hands positioned like claws. His eyes, huge and electric, darted around the room. With what looked like super-human strength, he jerked away from two large attendants trying to subdue him, all the while wailing out in an incoherent tangle of Spanish and English. Before Bryant could grab his arm, the man hurled a technician to the floor. A nurse who tried to help was shoved into a gurney. Then he turned to Bryant, his fingers poised and aiming for his throat. "Wait here," Caleb cautioned Maggie as he pushed his way into the examining area.

Two security guards stormed in, shoving Caleb aside. They pried the patient's fingers from around Bryant's neck, but somehow the kid got a second wind and pulled away from them. He lunged for Bryant once more. Bryant slid back, looking petrified. Before Caleb could reach him, the larger of the guards came from behind and reached around the guy's neck, snaring him in a headlock. The teen panted, eyes bugging out, as the men slammed him face down on the gurney. A few seconds later, they had the kid's hands and legs gripped in restraints.

"You okay?" Caleb asked his friend.

"Getting too old for this." Bryant helped a nurse prepare and administer an injection as the patient strained hard to bite Bryant's hand. "This guy's on something nasty, I hope not the same stuff as the guy last week." He gave more orders to the nurse and instructed the security guards to plan on a long night.

Bryant walked Caleb out. "New drug on the streets. Heroin—which is making a big come-back, by the way—they cut it with scopolamine, the stuff they use in motion sickness pills. It makes for a great high until you go berserk like our friend in there. Last week's victim was only seventeen years old. He died of cardiac arrest, after a two day spell of rabid psychosis." Bryant used a paper towel to wipe sweat from where his forehead grew into his baldhead. "Just what our town needs, huh?"

"No kidding." Caleb noticed two other young men in bandanas at the nurse's station, pointing at the closed door behind them. "I think I'll hit the road," he said.

Bryant looked over at the men. "Wish I could join you."

chapter five

Despite the drugs from Bryant Wheeler, Caleb slept fitfully that evening. Just after midnight, he heard Maggie answer a gentle rap at the front door and heard Shannon tiptoeing out of the bedroom. Sometime after, he heard her return and lean over, checking on him. He heard the phone ring, much later. Each small movement and every inhaled breath fanned the flames that wouldn't die in his chest.

Too soon, the alarm pierced through the last dregs of sleep. He swatted blindly at it, his third swing making contact and silencing the annoying buzz. He crawled out of bed and limped over to the bureau mirror. The bruise on his chin wasn't as bad as he thought. No one would even notice it unless he turned his head into the light. Gingerly, he removed the wrap to check out his ribs. Not bad. The injury glowed crimson red like a sunset, with traces of pale blue radiating out. A soft hammer banged away against his chest, but it was nothing a few aspirin wouldn't take care of. He took a gentle shower, re-wrapped his chest, and dressed in chinos and a loose fitting sweater.

In the kitchen, Shannon greeted him with a gentle peck on the lips and a coffee cup. Cleo, their seventy pound sheepdog, greeted him with a cold nose to his abdomen. "Good morning to both of you."

"How ya feeling?" Shannon lifted his sweater to check out

the ribs.

"Sore, but okay. You look rough."

She nodded and drew her lips in tight. "Long night. Are you going in to work?"

"I have to. We're swamped."

"They could survive without you, you know."

He thought he caught a chill in her eyes, but knew better than to ask. "No they couldn't. The center would probably collapse on itself without me. I am Atlas, bracing all of Westville's mentally ill on my strong, worthy shoulders." He flexed his muscles like he was Governor Schwartzenegger, immediately regretting it when his ribs flared again.

She didn't seem to find him funny. "Please, be careful. Don't overdo it."

He downed the rest of his coffee and walked out the door.

"Thanks for seeing us, Dr. Knowles," Paul Callahan said. He looked older than Caleb remembered from his brief introduction to the man several months ago, but then, Callahan had probably aged twenty years in the two days since his wife's murder. Sandy blond hair fell in thinning wisps across his forehead. His red-rimmed blue eyes met Caleb's head-on, but there was nothing genuine in his smile. He wasn't as tall as Caleb, maybe close to six feet, with a lean build like a long distance runner.

"Call me Caleb. I'm not a doctor, anyway. I'm a clinical social worker." After yesterday's session with Meredith Spencer, he decided to be perfectly clear on that point.

"I know that you're a good friend of Maggie's," Paul said. "I think we met before, didn't we?"

Caleb nodded and motioned him into the chair beside his desk. "I'm very sorry about what brings you here."

Paul's bottom lip started vibrating and he pulled it in, stabilizing it with his teeth. Caleb looked down to give the man a moment to regain control.

"Sorry," Paul said finally. "I've got Emma in the waiting

room, with her grandmother. She's not doing well."

"That's understandable. She's about four, right?"

"She'll be five in April."

"I don't know if you're aware that I met Emma that night."

"Maggie told me. She said you stayed with the kids while I was being questioned by the police." His eyes brimmed and he looked away, embarrassed. It was hard for Caleb to imagine that this grief-stricken man could have committed murder.

Paul cleared his throat before continuing, "I don't think Emma remembers you, though. It's hard to know what she's taking in, what she understands of all this. She isn't talking. She isn't sleeping much. Or eating. She hasn't even cried." He paused again, glancing up at the closed office door. "When your kid's sick, you know what to do. You give 'em Tylenol, feed 'em soup, rock them until they fall asleep. But this—I have no idea how to help her."

"I have a daughter Emma's age. Pre-schoolers are still a bit primitive. They have powerful, raw feelings. But they also have an impressive capacity to heal. You've surely seen that before. Your kid gets sick and looks nearly comatose, and the next day, she's in the back yard running around like nothing happened."

"So you think this is just a temporary thing? She'll be okay?"

Caleb studied the desperate father, imagining himself in his place. "I can't say for sure. Let me have a session with her. Then I'll want to get a good developmental and family history on her. We'll see after that."

Paul nodded, looking like he would cling to any thread of hope he could. Caleb smiled sympathetically and said, "How about I go meet your daughter now?"

The play room was the most beautiful spot in the restored brick home that now served as the Westville Counseling Center. The second story room had originally been a traditional southern sleeping porch. A long wall of windows looked out on a magnolia that had probably been planted before the Civil War. Sunlight filtered through its huge branches to splash against buttery yellow walls. One end of the room had shelves lined with Lincoln Logs, Tinker Toys, and other building gadgetry. Another wall held several large doll houses and about a dozen dolls of various sizes and races, some with genitalia, some without.

In the far end of the play room, shelves and tables made up the Game Section. Foam darts, a bean bag toss, a train set, and a small Nerf basketball hoop were spaced around so that loose race cars and Tonka trucks could maneuver between them.

The center of the room had been more devoted to the creative arts. Play Dough, finger paints, crayons, molding clay, and poster sheets lined shelves that surrounded a child-size work table. There was even a miniature covered sand box that Caleb used with smaller children who had less developed motor skills.

This was Caleb's favorite place to work. He and Matthew had designed it and afterward had a special consultant, Caleb's daughter Julia, test out their final product. Thankfully, it had passed the three-year-old's scrutiny.

Caleb escorted Emma into the playroom, instructing Paul to wait outside. "Your Dad's gonna be right out there, okay?" He gestured toward the chair in the hall where Paul took a seat. Emma watched them both, saying nothing.

Caleb closed the door and eased into one of the small chairs by the work table, the movement irritating his throbbing chest. He hoped his discomfort didn't show on his face. As stiff as a statue, Emma stood in the middle of the room.

She was a pretty child, in some ways like his Julia. Her long blond hair fell like silk ribbons down her shoulders. She wore a white sweater over a green dress with frills at the hem and sleeves. Caleb almost smiled. To get a dress like that on

Julia would require bribery. And he couldn't even imagine his child in the black patent leather shoes Emma wore, or the tights that matched the pale green bow in her hair. She was thinner than Julia, pale and long-limbed, with wide four-year-old eyes absorbing everything around her.

"Okay. Here's how we work here," he said to the girl. "This is your place for the next hour. You can play with anything you choose, and I mean anything. We've got a nifty train set, some dolls, some play dough. You just take your pick. The only rule is that you and I clean up our mess when we're done. Deal?"

She bowed her head and studied Caleb's feet, which probably looked huge to her, jutting out from under the pre-schooler's table.

Caleb tore off a sheet of drawing paper from a pad on the table and picked up a crayon. "Me, I like to draw. So I'll just sit over here with my crayons, unless you have another idea." He grinned at her, hoping his smile could convince her that this would be a safe place. But for Emma, it must have seemed the whole world was veiled in a new black terror. Nowhere would feel safe.

He kept his head down but rolled his eyes up to look at her. He wondered what she had looked like two days ago, before the shadows overtook her world.

He glanced over at the doll house. He'd love to get her over there, to have her play out her fears and grief with the family of dolls. But it was way too soon. It was better to start with the crayons, which might feel safe, non-threatening.

"I have another chair over here, Emma. Why don't you come over and sit down?"

She looked up at him. A hand rose to her face and the thumb inserted itself in her mouth. Good, he thought. Take comfort there, Emma, if you can.

Comfort, he thought. Maybe she needed something tactile, something to hold. He reached over, lifted a plastic crate, and laid it on the floor before her. "Emma? Could you do me a favor? These stuffed animals have been shoved in this crate for a long time. Could you help me get them out? I think they need some air."

Her eyes focused on the crate, on a bear's head that peeked out. "Yeah. Take Mr. Teddy bear there. I don't think he's had someone to play with for weeks. Would you mind letting him out?"

She moved very slowly, but gradually eased over to the crate and peered down. Caleb leaned back and returned to his crayon doodles, watching her out of the corners of his eyes.

He read confusion on her face. *It should be such an easy thing*, he thought, reaching in to grab that bear. But she couldn't. She looked lost, like she was buried somewhere deep inside herself. She gazed at the bear, her cheeks rhythmically throbbing as her mouth sucked on her thumb.

A few long moments passed and Caleb realized she needed prompting. He laid down his crayon and held up his drawing to the sunlight. It was his usual, a scrawled sketch of Cleo, his sheepdog. "So what do you think?"

She didn't look up. She kept her eyes on the crate and the animals confined inside it. Her chin quivered up and down as she worked on the thumb.

Come on, Emma, reach for that bear. Hold it close, let it give you some relief from the horror you must be living. Caleb closed his eyes, wishing he could telepathically heal this child who now seemed too much like his own daughter.

He set the drawing down and scrambled onto the floor, feeling an immediate scream from his ribs. Her gaze moved from the crate to him. He forced a grin and lifted the teddy bear, which he handed to her. "Here, Emma. Hold him for a moment."

In slow motion, she raised her free hand and took it, clutching it by an ear and gazing at the bear's face. Her eyes widened and her brows lifted a little. Caleb repositioned himself so that he could look at it, too.

"Well, I think he feels better all ready. That face is about to smile, don't you think?"

She tilted her head to the side, studying the bear. This slight movement and the subtle change in her expression were positive signs. She sucked the thumb with less vigor.

"I think he likes you, Emma," Caleb said.

Her eyes softened as she pulled the bear against her tiny chest, braced it with an elbow, and slid her left arm around its middle. Her head eased down so that her chin buried itself in the soft tufts of fur.

Caleb leaned back in front of her. "I'll bet that feels good to the bear. I think that bear needed to be hugged."

Emma squeezed it tighter as her body started to sway. She rocked to the right, then to the left, then back to the right, moving in a gentle rhythm, her face pressing in the bear's fur. Caleb watched her carefully, looking for surfacing fear or grief, but her tiny face revealed nothing.

"Can you feel how much the bear likes that, Emma?"

Her nod was almost imperceptible.

"Then you just keep on holding it. Let it know that it isn't alone. Somebody really cares for it."

Caleb fought an impulse to scoop up Emma and hold her as tightly as she clung to that animal. He wished he could rock her and tell her the world was safe, maybe take away the horror of that night. But it was too soon. She didn't know him and she couldn't trust him. Not yet. And for now, her only contact with the world was that stuffed bear, which had an important job to do.

After a few moments, Caleb touched Emma's hand with his finger. She looked at him, startled, but didn't recoil. He stroked her hand with the finger, in rhythm with her rocking. Her eyes stayed on him, but didn't let him inside.

There was a policy at the Westville Counseling Center that Caleb was about to gladly break. No toy was allowed to leave the premises. Children often attached themselves to trucks or dolls or puppets, and would ask to take them home. Since these toys were a part of the therapeutic process, they needed to remain in the therapy space.

But Emma needed the bear. She'd experienced quite enough loss already. To tear it from her arms would be unthinkable. Stuffed bears were inexpensive and easy to buy, anyway. Comfort was not.

He tapped her hand again, then sat back on his haunches. "Emma, how about you take that bear and keep it a few days? I think we'll go see your dad now, and talk to him about when you can come back and visit me again. Okay?"

She gave him a slight nod and when he reached out his hand, her fingers took hold of his index finger. He smiled down at her and escorted her out the door.

Paul Callahan looked up as they approached from the playroom. Emma walked to him and leaned against his knees. As he slid his arms around her, she stiffened again, and Paul looked beseechingly at Caleb.

"We're still getting to know each other. I think it would help if you could bring her back soon."

"I'll bring her tomorrow, if you want."

"Friday would be better. That work for you?"

Paul nodded.

Caleb stooped down to speak to his young client. "So you bring the bear back in two days, okay?" He held up two fingers and counted them for her. "Then you and I will go back in the play room and see what else we can find in there."

Paul took her hand and started to leave, but hesitated at the stairs. "You mentioned something about getting information about her history."

"Yes. I'd like to meet with you privately about that. We're a little swamped today. Could you stop by in the morning? It shouldn't take more than a half hour or so."

"Okay. I have to be at the funeral home by ten-thirty." He swallowed and looked down at his child. "Could I come before?"

"That'll be fine. Thanks, Paul."

* * *

After seeing seven more clients without even a break for lunch, Caleb drifted into Matthew's office. He found his boss reading notes into a Dictaphone with surprising articulation, given the pipe wedged in his teeth. Matthew switched off the machine. "I've been expecting you."

"You have? Were we supposed to meet?" Caleb asked.

"No. But you've had about a dozen clients today so I wanted to make sure I gave you plenty of time to chastise me about it. Twenty minutes do it?"

"Doesn't even scratch the surface." Caleb dropped in a chair, immediately feeling a sharp twinge in his chest.

"How'd you get that bruise on your chin?" Matthew asked, moving in for a closer look.

"No, Shannon isn't abusing me," he said evasively. "But you are. I'd go on strike if you weren't working harder than me. You even have Grey doing overtime."

Matthew rubbed his eyes. "That shooting at Tindall has been a real nightmare. The people who where there are traumatized, the people that should have been there but called in sick, or were in another building, or were out on vacation time—they're traumatized, too, and feeling guilty. I saw one lady who had been standing right beside Buck Swygert, the man who was killed. She had just walked away to check a machine when Buck was shot. She says she found the Lord that day."

"Then how come she needs you?"

"The Lord's not happy with her little cocaine problem. I sent her to the detox unit. Grey's admitting her now." Matthew shook his head. "So how about filling me in on Paul's kid."

Immediately, a mental picture of Emma cradling the bear filled Caleb's mind. "She needs intensive work. Probably three times a week, which is impossible because we're so swamped, but I don't think we have a choice."

"Of course not. Do what you have to. Is she talking?" Matthew asked.

"No. She's shut down. I have no idea what she's processing."

"Give her time. The whole family's just beginning to deal with what happened."

"You never told me how you know Paul."

Matthew turned his head and exhaled a stream of sweet-smelling smoke. "Is that important?"

Caleb scrutinized his boss, surprised by that response. "I guess not.

"We're old friends, let's leave it at that. I'm worried about him, about the whole family. Fran's death is such a horrible waste."

Caleb wondered if Matthew would say more but he didn't. He glanced down at his watch. Close to 7:00 P.M. "Is it okay if I head on out? I'll be in early tomorrow."

"How kind of you to ask. It makes me feel like I actually have some control over your behavior. Illusions can be wonderful things."

Caleb stopped by his office, spotting the sticky note reminding him to call Helen Fleck's son. He dialed the Virginia number and got an answering machine, a lilting Southern voice encouraging him to leave a message and have a nice day. He left the message, hoping he'd get a return call the next morning.

chapter six

As Caleb turned onto Lake Drive, he heard the moaning horn echoing down the train tracks. He eased up to the railroad crossing and waited as the seemingly endless train snaked its way north. He turned off the truck, the way he often did on his way to visit Sam. There seemed to be no real pattern to the train's travel, no way to predict it. Except if Caleb was running late, he could pretty much count on a two-hundred-car coal freighter.

Sam's combination house and studio bordered on the track, just a block from this crossing. Trains howled by a half dozen times a day and would have driven Caleb or anyone else to madness, but with Sam, it literally fell on deaf ears. He could feel the vibration of the train, enough to know it was coming and when it had passed, but the noise never affected his concentration or disturbed his sleep. He'd bought the property for next to nothing and had done a beautiful restoration to the mill home, claiming to be the perfect resident for that particular corner of Westville. And now, Sam would be moving. It was hard to imagine his brother living anywhere else.

At last, Caleb spotted the final car. "Hallelujah," he muttered, cranking up the truck.

When he arrived at Sam's, he spotted Tessa Solapé's Volvo in the driveway. He let himself inside and found Sam's agent in the office that adjoined the studio. She was punching numbers into Sam's computer with Sam watching behind her. He motioned that he needed five more minutes with Tessa and shut the door, muttering something about privacy.

Caleb shrugged at the closed door and decided he'd use the time to peruse Sam's latest work. He made his way through the studio where a new sculpture caught his eye, a pale swirl of wood, glimmering in the cone of light from the track system above.

Caleb had seen it before, in a rawer state, and had been impressed. But now, it was magnificent. The music stand stood about four feet tall, with a round base and supple neck that gently sloped upward. About eighteen inches from the top, the neck widened into a detailed square composed of curved strips, a tapestry of wood. Mahogany, cypress, cherry, tiger oak, burled maple, and a few rarer woods Sam had ordered from Africa were intertwined in a basket-weave fashion. A strip of maple protruded from the base of the "fabric," a lip to hold the musical scores. The piece was playful, complex and quite beautiful. Caleb ran his fingers along the upper edge, absorbing the contours, feeling the subtle changes in sensation as he touched each texture of wood.

"What do you think?" His brother startled him.

"It'll do. Once you slap some paint on it." Caleb signed "paint" by brushing two fingers of his right hand down the palm of his left.

Sam moved closer to study him and asked, "How'd you get that bruise on your chin?"

"Tell you later," Caleb signed, gesturing towards Tessa. He didn't want to go into the previous night's events, if he could avoid it. Caleb pointed back at the music stand. "This is a great piece."

Sam's worried gaze shifted from Caleb's injury to the sculpture. "Staining it was a nightmare. The African wood takes the stain in a peculiar way. Two days ago, I wanted to trash the thing."

"Glad you didn't." Caleb pointed to a paper tag attached at the bottom. "*Music to My Ears*. What does it mean?"

"I try to remember music. Sometimes I get an image of Mom putting a classical album on the stereo, a symphony or something. I remember how all the notes from the different instruments seemed like threads. Some fat, some coarse, some thin and very delicate. That make any sense?"

"So the notes are woven together into this fabric. Perfect. It's the best thing you've ever done."

Sam waved him off. "You always say that."

"This time, he's right," Tessa said, cradling a stack of papers that smelled like they had just come off the printer. She wore a purple tunic with sleeves like batwings. A chunky pendant of a bird's claw holding a blue stone dangled over her chest and it looked like she'd tried to paint her eyelids the exact same shade. Today's jewelry assortment included a hoop on her eyebrow, four sets of earrings, and a yellow stone on the side of her nose, which made Caleb wonder what the heck she did when she had a cold.

Tessa owned the Solapé Gallery and had recently appointed herself as manager of Sam's artistic career. Despite Tessa's rather unconventional appearance, she had developed quite a reputation for promoting new talent. She also knew more about the business of fine arts than just about anyone in Westville. Flashing a dimpled smile at Caleb, Tessa said, "It is his best piece. And I think I've already sold it."

"No kidding?" Caleb asked.

"The Cultural Council in Columbia hired a hot-shot conductor for the philharmonic. They want to buy this as a gift to welcome him on board. Since he'd already heard of Samuel P. Knowles, renowned sculptor, they figure it's a great way to suck up to the new guy. Who are we to argue?" She positioned herself so Sam could easily read her lips, clearly practiced in communicating with her prodigy.

Caleb winked at Tessa. "You got a good price, I hope."

"Your brother would shoot me if I quoted money to you. But put it this way, it's enough for all three of us to take a long Caribbean vacation, then maybe buy one of the islands."

"I'll start packing," Caleb grinned.

Sam stepped between them and opened the front door. "Leaving so soon, Tessa?"

"Okay, okay. I get the hint." She kissed him artist-style, on each cheek, then waved goodbye to Caleb.

"So when does the real estate person get here?" Caleb asked as she left.

Sam checked his watch. "Should be any time now. You in a hurry?"

"Not in the least. Shannon and Maggie went out so you have me as long as you need me. So how much is Tessa making for you? Ready to claim me as a dependent?"

Sam ignored him by turning away and walking to the apartment behind the studio. Caleb followed him, freezing in his tracks as they entered the living room. Apparently, Sam had done a spit-and-polish cleaning for his anticipated visitor. The oak plank floor gleamed beneath the arched wood floor lamp, one of Sam's early works. The kidney-shaped coffee table, topped with etched glass, held only a vase of eucalyptus sprigs instead of the usual assortment of magazines, sketchpads, and gallery flyers. The forest green sofa and matching chairs had been fluffed and tidied, with pillows scattered around.

"Who lives here?" Caleb signed, hands shaped like guns passing over his torso.

"My alter-ego. Everything look okay?"

"Everything looks great. You know, this realtor is someone that *you* hire. You don't need to worry about what she thinks. You just have to decide if she's the right person to sell your house."

He nodded, but looked nervous. His eyes widened when they caught the flash of light from the door signal. "Guess that's her."

Caleb followed him to the front door and together they greeted the visitor. She introduced herself as Vanessa Montague. She wore a business suit with a skirt that showed well-toned legs. Her puffy, pale blond hair resembled spun like cotton candy. He put her age at about fifty, but it was hard to be sure. Her brown eyes were so huge they gave a look of constant surprise and Caleb couldn't decide if she was a victim of a thyroid condition or bad cosmetic surgery. She waved her hand and led them to the back of the house like a museum tour guide.

They gathered around Sam's kitchen table and Vanessa opened her briefcase. She pulled out a stack of papers and dropped them in front of Sam. "What I've done here is a fair market value analysis of your home in comparison with other property that has sold in Westville over the past six months," she said with machine gun rapidity, tapping figures on the papers with a lethal-looking crimson fingernail. "It's actually a difficult analysis, because, as you know, this property is unique. Which can be an advantage and a disadvantage."

Sam looked at the papers, then at her, then at Caleb, dismayed.

Caleb raised his hand to stop her. "Vanessa," he signed, speaking slowly. "Sam is deaf. Whenever you speak, you must slow down and face him. He cannot listen to you and read at the same time. So start again and I'll sign for him, then we'll look at the papers."

Her face flushed. "I'm . . . sorry."

"Vanessa," Sam said, and she looked up at him. "In addition to being deaf, I'm illiterate in the area of real estate. Tessa referred me to you because she believes you are the best person to help me find my way. Caleb here," Sam laid a hand on his brother's shoulder, "is even more mathematically impaired than I am. So go *real* slow, because I may have to explain things to *him* for you."

She grinned and the smile did wonders for her, crinkling her eyes, softening her face. For the next two hours, they plodded through facts and figures and about a dozen documents. A contract was signed that said Vanessa Montague would represent Samuel Knowles in the sale of his property. The home would be viewed only by appointment, and Sam would have plenty of notice so that he could make himself scarce.

Vanessa loaded the documents into her briefcase and stood to leave. At the front door, she faced Sam and said carefully: "I know a few realtors in Atlanta. If you want a referral, let me know."

Sam looked awkwardly at Caleb. "My plans are uncertain right now, Vanessa."

As Sam closed the door, Caleb watched him, an uneasy feeling spreading in his gut. He signed, "Atlanta? What was she talking about?"

"She didn't know what she was talking about," Sam said dismissively.

Caleb moved in front of him, that bad feeling spreading all the way to his toes now. "Tell me what's going on."

Sam leaned back against the door jam, avoiding Caleb's glare. "Tessa's been marketing me up in Atlanta. There's a gallery that's shown my work twice before, and it did okay. Tessa thinks I should move there because I'll be more accessible to galleries and there's a mint to be made in commissions. The artistic community there would be good for me. Atlanta also has a very active deaf culture, which is, of course, attractive."

"Damn. You're serious." The news swirled around in Caleb's head, unsteadying him.

"I don't know if I am or not. There are things about moving that appeal to me. But Westville's been my home forever, and I don't know if I'm ready to leave it. I didn't plan on talking to you about this until I had a better handle on what to do."

"You didn't think you should talk it over with me?" Caleb's flush of anger surprised him.

"I didn't think you'd be objective."

"Objectivity isn't my strong suit when it comes to family." Caleb did his best to look unflustered, knowing Sam saw right through him.

"I really don't know that I am leaving. So let's not deal with it unless it does happen, okay?"

"Okay. If that's how you want to play it." Caleb fished his keys out of his pocket. "I guess I'll head on home."

Sam stepped in front of him. "Hey, this isn't an easy decision. Give me a few days to sort it all out. Then we'll talk."

Caleb nodded. He wished he could say "It's all right Sam. I'll support you whatever you decide." But those words just weren't there. It was definitely a good time to leave. "I'll wait to hear from you, then," he muttered.

"You never told me what happened to your chin."

"Shaving accident," Caleb signed, and hurried out the door.

Lights were off in the cottage; Shannon and Maggie must have already turned in. He parked the truck in its usual spot and let himself in the back door. In the kitchen, he opened the refrigerator, more out of habit than hunger. Nothing appealed to him. He could down a beer, to take the edge off, but thought better of it. The Knowles family had an ugly tradition spawned by that kind of thinking.

Switching off the light, he tiptoed up the stairs. The door to his bedroom was closed so he slipped off his sneakers, jeans and T-shirt before opening the door. He laid his clothes on his bureau as he eased into the room.

Shannon was in her usual spot, in the center of the mattress, sleeping soundly. He lifted the spread and slid his body in beside her, careful not to jostle the bed. Instantly, she shifted and turned, curving into him, her head leaning on his chest, her arm slipping across his waist. These were familiar, primal moves, their bodies unconsciously seeking each other, even in sleep. Caleb exhaled, grateful for her touch. He'd been feeling so damn lonely.

He leaned over and gently kissed her on the lips. Her hand unwound itself from his middle and reached up, grabbing his neck, pulling him down to her. Their lips found each other again, tongues hungrily probing. He could feel her hands seeking him as their bodies stirred, awakened, aroused.

He rolled on top of her as she pushed up, kissing him again. Her gentle fingers found him, caressed him, guided him inside her. Their cadence began at a swifter rhythm than was their custom, quickly swelling to a frantic, driven pace, fed by private fevers and by their desperate need for each other.

Shannon's body, strong as steel, moved him, moved with him. They stared into each other, breathless, suspended beyond time for those incredible seconds. And when they finished, they collapsed on each other, drenched and panting.

They lay wordlessly together for a long time, Shannon nestled in the familiar crook of his arm. "God, I needed that," she said finally.

He kissed the top of her head.

"Did I hurt you?" she asked. "Your chest, I mean."

"No," he lied. Someone had rudely left an anvil on his chest. What had Bryant said about exertion?

"I was pretty hard on you this morning. Am I forgiven?" She looked up at him. She was so beautiful.

"I think so. This reconciliation ritual is one of my favorites. Everything okay with Maggie?"

"No. But let's not talk about her now." She snuggled into him tighter. "Everything okay with Sam?"

He lifted a curl of her hair and caressed it. "No. But let's not talk about him, either." He rolled over and laid his face in the soft white cradle of her neck.

chapter seven

Caleb was the first one up, so he threw on a robe and trotted downstairs to get the coffee going. When he heard no movement from the sleeping women, he hit the shower. He knew he needed to be quick because the cottage's antique plumbing system gave, at its best, about twenty minutes of hot water. Twenty divided by three . . . Well, he never claimed to be a mathematician. At least, that would be his alibi.

The scalding torrents bounced off his auburn hair and cascaded down the length of his spent body. The bruises on his chest had softened to a dull purple and a fire burned underneath them, a souvenir from the acrobatics with Shannon. No question, it was worth it.

He closed his eyes and held his face to the water, his mind drifting back to the talk with Sam. He should be glad his brother had this opportunity. Sam was so gifted and Caleb wanted him to have all the success he deserved.

But Atlanta. Almost four hours away, not ten minutes. No more impromptu poker games or free babysitting or gourmet suppers. And then, there was Atlanta's size. A big, sprawling monster of a city with clogged traffic arteries and a rush hour that lasted all day. How could Sam live in a place where every street had the same name? Peachtree East. Peachtree Drive. Peachtree Parkway. Wasn't there any other fruit around when the city planners scrawled their maps?

Sam had been born in Westville and raised in Westville. He knew how to maneuver around. Caleb sometimes worried about him on his bike, but Sam knew what streets to avoid because of dangerous hills or blind curves. Atlanta, with its fevered arteries congested with too many cars and Sam on his bike. A car horn blaring an unheard warning . . .

Caleb raised his face again so that the water pounded out that image. Don't go there, he told himself. Don't go there.

He turned off the water, grabbed a towel and rubbed himself dry before tiptoeing into the bedroom to dress. On his way downstairs, he heard clattering noises in the kitchen and found their houseguest pouring coffee. "Morning, Maggie. You sleep okay?"

"Yeah, thanks." Her red, puffed out eyes contradicted her.

He poured himself a cup and took a gulp of the scalding hot, blessed caffeine. "I saved you about three minutes of hot water. You might want to try and beat Shannon."

"I'm in no hurry. I told the principal I wouldn't make it into school until after lunch. I have to be at the police station by ten."

Shannon appeared like a ghost in the doorway, hair tousled, eyes at half mast.

"You need coffee." Caleb filled a mug for her.

She mumbled something, sipped, and mumbled some more.

"You had two and a half beers last night!" Maggie berated her. "And now you stumble in here, looking like death. What a light-weight." She found an aspirin bottle on the window sill over the sink and handed it to her.

"Would juice help?" Caleb queried, suspecting the problem was more likely dehydration from their late night activity.

"I doubt it." She turned to Maggie and said, "I almost hate to ask. That was Barry who called again, wasn't it?"

"Yeah. He's pretty upset about Fran. And about the break-in."

"I suppose he is. So he comes to you for comfort. That feels dangerous to me."

Maggie chewed at her bottom lip and eyed both of them. "You're being a bit protective. I don't need you to be my mother."

Ouch. Expecting fireworks, Caleb backed away from the breakfast table.

"And I don't want that job. But I hope you remember what it was like with him. It's easy to remember the good times and overlook the pain. That man was toxic for you."

Maggie stood. "I do remember. But I think I have an advantage over you. I don't work in a field where I see the underbelly of humankind all the time. I still believe that people can change." With that, she set her cup on the counter and headed upstairs.

Shannon winced at Caleb. "Well, I certainly handled that well, don't you think?"

"You were a bit intense. What's so awful about this guy? I mean, compared to her others."

"Let's see. He's a liar. He hit Maggie once. He has a drug problem. That about cover it?"

Caleb flinched. "I'd say so."

"And she has huge blinders on about him. He comes to her full of apologies and promises to change. Tells her he can't live without her. She checks him into detox, and he stays clean maybe a month."

"What does he use?" Caleb asked.

"Alcohol. Cocaine. God knows what else. He was trying something new last time she took him back, but I don't know what."

"Maggie into drugs?"

"No. Her father was an alcoholic, and her brother's been into marijuana. Maggie has a healthy fear of those influences."

"Sounds like she confines her addiction to men."

Shannon muttered noises of exasperation and buried her head in her hands. "I know I have to be more patient with her. I'm just worried she's gonna make a disastrous mistake with Barry.

"She hates to be alone, you know? Especially at night. That's why she grabs onto men. Men that use her, but stay with her. As long as someone's there, breathing, beside her, she feels safe. Until they screw her over."

Caleb set down his coffee cup and walked over behind Shannon. Tenderly, he touched her tense shoulders and started a gentle massage. "You are a loyal and loving friend. But you can't fix everything. Maggie's gonna do what she wants. And lucky for her, you'll be there to put the pieces back together."

Thirty minutes later, Caleb stood on the front porch of the Westville Counseling Center. The sky was an ominous gray, threatening to burst open with a cold, drenching rain. Good. Maybe the rain would drive away some of their business.

Caleb twisted the knob on the massive oak door but it didn't give. He retrieved his keys and unlocked it, pushed it open, and hit the light switch. He checked his watch, 8:15. Matthew was usually in long before now. Of course, he'd probably seen clients until late last evening and may have indulged himself by sleeping in until 6:00 A.M. Then would come the five-mile jog, then a disgusting wheat germ/oat bran/tofu concoction for breakfast. He'd only get half way through the *Wall Street Journal*, Caleb reflected, before coming to work. Matthew's lifestyle was as foreign to Caleb as the president's Mid East policy.

Caleb wandered from room to room in the giant house, turning on lights and adjusting thermostats. The heating and electrical system had been updated last fall, and Matthew installed storm windows during the summer. But the tall ceilings and wide-planked floors held a chill, particularly after cold, damp evenings.

He stepped into the break room and got the coffee going before unlocking the door to the reception area. Janice's phone had been transferred to the answering service so he dialed the familiar code and retrieved a dozen messages, most of which were for Matthew. He filled out pink message forms and stacked them in Matthew's mail box.

He barely got the door to his own office unlocked in time to catch the ringing phone. "Westville Counseling Center," he said, panting.

"I'm looking for Caleb Knowles." The voice had an English accent.

"You got him."

"I'm Alec Spencer. I'm calling about my wife, Meredith."

"What can I do for you, Mr. Spencer?" It was always awkward when a client's family member called. Usually they phoned out of concern for the client, but rules of confidentiality limited what the therapist could say. Family members could also be valuable resources, if the therapist used a little finesse.

"Doctor Spencer," the voice corrected him. So much for finesse. "I wanted to make another appointment for Meredith. She didn't sleep last night, but was reticent about contacting you. She agreed to allow me. Might you see her today?"

"I'd need to check my schedule. Is Meredith there now?"

"She's in the bath. I suggested it to relax her."

"Can I have your number? I'll call back as soon as I can get to my book." It was a ruse, his appointment book was right in front of him on the desk. But his session with Meredith had taken such curious turns, he knew he'd better deal with her directly if there was any hope of a therapeutic connection. The monotone British "Doctor" gave him the number and hung up. Caleb waited fifteen minutes, then dialed back.

Meredith Spencer's voice sounded weak and tentative. Yes, she could use another appointment and yes, she wanted Caleb to be her therapist. He scheduled her for the next day at eleven. As he hung up, he reflected that if he kept up at this pace, he'd be averaging about a dozen clients a day. Too many. Way too many.

He made his way back downstairs into the break room and interrupted the brewing coffee to pour himself a cup. He was about to return to his office, to the mounds of paper work that he'd rather avoid for another decade or so, when he heard the front door creak open. Grey Lazarus rumbled insincere morning greetings as he shuffled in and went straight to the coffee pot.

Grey wore a beige rain hat that dripped water onto the carpet. His tweed sports jacket didn't conceal enough of his crinkled shirt. His khakis looked like they'd done too much time in the dryer, about four inches of frayed white socks peeking out under the cuffs. Grey moved quickly and gracelessly, grabbing a mug, pouring coffee, stirring in three spoons of sugar, then tossing down the spoon.

"You're early," Caleb commented.

"Got a mother of a day ahead of me," he muttered over the cup.

"Matthew booked you up, too, huh?"

"Matthew's checking on a patient in detox. And I have to go do hospital rounds. How's your day looking?"

"Like a disaster."

Grey downed the rest of his coffee and dropped his mug in the sink. "I'd better get to the hospital. I hate to go out in this mess. I should be back by ten-thirty, so mind the shop."

Caleb grinned. "I'm in charge? Me? A lowly social worker?" He watched Grey trudge off and pondered his new power. Usually when left like this, he made policy changes like redistributing caseloads according to zodiac signs or instituting a mandatory two o'clock nap break. Maybe this time he'd change the center's dress code, forbidding Grey's pathetic white socks.

Janice stepped into the break room and smiled at him. Her wispy blond hair was gathered in a scarf the same flamingo pink as her skirt, belt, and shoes. As she heated herb tea in the microwave, she said, "Your appointment's here."

"Which one? I seem to have thirty or so scheduled."

"It's not that bad, is it? I'll help however I can." She handed him the thin, incomplete record for his client. "Emma Callahan" had been typed on the tab. "Her father's here. Shall I bring him up?"

Caleb nodded, refilled his mug, and took the file to his office.

Paul Callahan looked bad. His face had an ashen pallor and appeared deflated, as if the skin barely clung to bone. His slate eyes seemed to be set deeper than before, if that were possible, and his gaze roamed the room like an escaped bird. Both hands clutched a large photo album. He sat down, gripping the book in his lap as if it was a lifeline. "I hope this isn't too early for you. I have a lot to do today."

Caleb remembered that Paul had mentioned a visit to the funeral home. That morning's newspaper had said Frances' funeral would be tomorrow morning. "This is fine. I'll only need a half hour or so."

Paul's attention drifted down to the book in his hands. "You said you wanted to get some history on Emma. I thought this photo album would help."

"I bet it will. Thanks." Caleb's hands rummaged through the mound of papers on his desk to retrieve a notepad and pen. "Before we get going, tell me how she's doing."

"She finally got to sleep last night. That's the first time since—well, you know. She curled up with the bear you gave her, put her thumb in her mouth, and went out like a light. Slept straight through until morning."

"I'm glad to hear it."

"She hasn't eaten but a few bites of food. And she isn't talking. But at least she got some rest." He looked imploringly at Caleb, as if wanting reassurance that this meant his daughter would recover.

"So tell me what you can about Emma. Start at the beginning, before she was born."

He drummed his fingers along the cover of the scrapbook. "Seth was almost two and we decided to try to have another kid. When Fran got pregnant again, we both hoped for a girl. Of course, more than anything, we wanted a healthy child. But if we had a choice, we wanted a girl. A balance for Seth."

"You said she was planned. Did it take long to conceive?"

He shook his head. "We're Catholic, so we never really practiced birth control, except the rhythm method, which miraculously worked for us. We stopped monitoring Fran's cycle, and within three months, Emma was on her way."

"How was the pregnancy?"

"Easy. Fran took good care of herself, so she was very healthy. She had a little morning sickness, but that's about it."

"How about her delivery?" Caleb asked.

"Both babies were delivered by C-section because Fran had a tilted pelvis. But there weren't any complications. Emma was an amazingly beautiful baby, everyone said so. Fran stayed home the first three months, then returned to work."

"Did she breast feed?"

"Yes, for both kids. Emma was the happiest baby you ever saw. She smiled all the time, nothing ever seemed to bother her. And Seth adored his baby sister. Would you believe that her first word was 'Seth'? Not Mama, not Daddy, but 'Seh', for her big brother. He got a real kick out of that." That memory prompted a phantom smile. Paul opened the album and sifted through a few pages until he found what he wanted, a picture of the family. Fran holding a cherubic, grinning infant, the pre-school boy with a huge smile, all teeth. They looked happy. Loving. Normal.

"How old was Emma when she talked? And walked?"

"Around eleven months for talking. Walking came soon after. She potty-trained quickly, too. Around fourteen months."

Caleb recorded these details on his pad. So far, everything looked fairly normal, except the toilet-training may have been a few months premature. "When she was a toddler, did she have a transitional object? By that, I mean a favorite blanket or stuffed animal, something she wouldn't go to bed without?"

"Oh yeah. Her stuffed puppy. She calls it 'Muffin'. Fran gave it to her when she was about a year old, right before Fran had to go away on a business trip. Emma wouldn't go any where without it. Once we accidentally left it at a hotel up in Charlotte and didn't realize it until we got home. Emma was inconsolable. At ten that night, I drove all the way back up there to bring the thing home to her." Caleb smiled, remembering a similar experience with Julia's favorite Tonka truck. "Does Emma still have Muffin?"

"It's in her room, but she won't touch it." Paul rubbed his face with both hands. "Every night after prayers, Fran put Muffin in the bed beside Emma and said 'Take care of my Emma while she sleeps and remind her how much Mommy loves—'" His voice broke. "Dear God, I hadn't realized. You gave her that stuffed bear yesterday. At least that's something she can hold. Something that doesn't remind her that her mother's dead."

Uncomfortably, Caleb watched the grief pour out of Paul's eyes. After a moment, he asked, "Can you tell me more about Emma's family life? Before Sunday, I mean."

Paul reached for a tissue from the box on Caleb's desk and wiped his face. "Uh. Okay. We had our ups and downs, but Emma's always been a happy kid."

"Tell me more about the ups and downs."

Paul turned his head to the window. Rain streaked the rippled glass and pounded against the window frame. The dreariness of the day seemed quite fitting. "I guess I should level with you. Fran and I had problems. I mean, we weren't heading for a divorce or anything. We'd never do that to the kids. But the last year or so has been . . . difficult."

"Kids usually pick up on problems with their parents. They may not understand it, but they can tell when something's wrong," Caleb said carefully.

"I know. Emma and her mother were very close. Whenever Fran was upset, Emma could tell. She'd crawl up in her lap and wrap her arms around Fran's neck. Fran wanted to protect Emma from our problems. We both did." Paul reached for another tissue.

"What was going on between you and Fran?"

He sighed, his eyes filling with regret. "It was me, mostly. I loved Fran deeply, but I didn't feel that I should be married to her. It felt dishonest. It's hard to explain. I really don't understand it myself."

Caleb nodded. He'd heard the tale a thousand times. He'd even lived it himself: the slow death of a marriage. The disease strikes. The relationship struggles, fights to hold on, but gradually succumbs. Some couples try marital life supports like therapy, or changing homes, or having a baby, or a myriad of other diversions to delay what's inevitable. Not that Caleb was the least bit skeptical about the institution of marriage. "Is there anything else I should know about Emma?"

"Not really. I just want her back, you know?"

It seemed a simple request, and Caleb understood the desperation on Paul's face. "Like I said before, kids can be remarkably resilient. But this has been a horrible trauma. Give us time to work with her, okay?"

"Her mother's funeral is tomorrow." Paul's face contorted again at the mention of burying his wife. His lips parted as though he meant to speak again, but no words came.

Caleb took a tissue from the box on his desk and handed it to him. "I was thinking, Paul, that it might be a good idea for you to see our psychiatrist yourself. You're feeling the grief in a healthy way, if there is one, but maybe you need to talk to someone. What do you think?"

"Matthew mentioned another doctor here. Can't remember

his name."

"Grey Lazarus."

He nodded. "But I don't think I need it. What I really need is for the police to catch the son of a bitch who killed my wife. Nothing else is going to help me." A knot of muscles throbbed on his jaw, as if working hard to contain a great reservoir of rage.

"I can understand—"

"How could you?" Paul blurted out. Abruptly, he rose and crossed to the window. He gazed out at the swollen dark clouds hanging over the day. "They keep questioning me. Over and over. And harassing Fran's parents. They think the answers are hidden somewhere in the family." He reached for the cord dangling over the mini-blind and wrapped it around his knuckles. "This town used to be a safe place. I used to love it here. I mean, I knew the rest of the world was crazy as hell. But here, I thought I could keep my family safe. I thought Westville was a little sanctuary, like nothing could touch us, you know?"

"But not any more?"

"No. Hell no. I'm moving out of here as soon as the police catch Fran's killer."

"You said the police keep questioning you. Do they know about the problems with you and Fran?"

He kept his back to Caleb as his shoulders rose and fell. "Some of it. Fran was someone who treasured her privacy. I can't tell you how important it was to her. It would violate her memory to drag out the details of our married life, particularly since they have no relevance to her murder. But the police questioned Maggie this morning, so they probably know everything now."

"Maggie? What does she have to do with it?" The mention of her name made something churn in Caleb's gut.

"She's been a good friend to both of us. She and I have spent some time together, comparing sob stories, I guess. She's a terrific listener, and it's great hearing a woman's perspective. And I think I've helped her, too. She has such low self-esteem when it comes to men.

"I was at Maggie's the evening Fran was killed. Another neighbor told the police I left her house around eleven, so now they think Maggie and I were embroiled in a sordid love affair, which is absolutely unbelievable. And every second they waste probing my life is another second they could spend finding Fran's killer. It seems every second counts, doesn't it?" He turned to face Caleb, his eyes wide and challenging.

Caleb didn't respond. He drew his lips in tight, hoping to conceal his own fury. He thought about Maggie, his houseguest, Shannon's best friend, who had omitted this tiny detail that she had been implicated in the murder. He looked at the man across from him, Emma's dad, who may have murdered his wife. Caleb realized his decision to be Emma's therapist was absurd, given his personal connections to the case. After a tense moment he said, "Look, Paul. Let me step out of my therapist's role for a second. I work as a police consultant and I know how they work. Having the police turn over every leaf of life is difficult, painful, and at times, humiliating. But it is the only way to get at the truth.

"You aren't doing yourself any favors by being secretive. The police will see right through it, they probably already have, and it will just make them probe harder. My advice is, level with them. If that feels too risky, then hire yourself a lawyer to guide you through the process. Do you understand what I'm saying?"

Paul sat down hard in his chair and leaned forward, his gaze scrutinizing. "I didn't kill Fran. I need you to believe me, for Emma's sake. If you have questions about that, I'll answer them, and I'll answer straight.

"But first, I want you to talk with Matthew Rhyker. He knows all about me. Tell him I give permission for him to tell you anything you need to know. If you need me to sign a release, I'll do it. But you talk to him. Promise me that."

Caleb sat back, winded by his own frustration. Sure, he'd talk to Matthew. In fact, he'd like to ring Matthew's neck for getting him into this mess.

Paul checked his watch then shot out of the chair. "I'm real late. Look, I'll make sure Emma gets here tomorrow, but, because of the funeral, it probably won't be me bringing her. I'll call after, if you don't mind."

Caleb didn't bother seeing him out. He reached for the phone and dialed the number to the hospital, asking for Dr. Matthew Rhyker. When Matthew came to the phone, he answered with a weary hello. "Sorry to bother you boss, but I have a question."

"What?"

"I just saw Paul Callahan. He told me the police have been questioning him pretty extensively about his marital problems, which probably means he's a suspect. I hate to think he did it, especially because of the kids. He says I should talk to you, and he gives you permission, and I quote, to tell me everything. So out with it."

A heavy silence resounded on the other end.

"Matthew? You there?"

"Yes. You're sure Paul meant to tell you everything?"

This time Caleb fell silent, stunned that Matthew would question his word. "Jesus, Matthew. You have to ask that? I shouldn't even have to make this call. You should have already told me anything relevant before I took Emma on. I'm feeling set-up."

"Calm down, Caleb." His tone was somber now. "I didn't mean to doubt your word. It's very complicated. I will talk to you more about it, but not now. Not over the phone."

"Okay." But it really wasn't okay.

"I'll get back to you later. We both have clients waiting, you know."

chapter eight

After three more morning sessions, Caleb grabbed a quick, fast-food lunch that scarcely placated his empty stomach. The afternoon wore on. His one o'clock appointment, Mary Beth Plowder, decided to cut down on her medicine. She'd had to double the anti-anxiety medication after 9/11. The replayed media footage of the towers collapsing had escalated her panic attacks to the point where Caleb almost went to her house and confiscated her TV. But enough time had passed and she felt better now, she said, so she cut her dosage in half—should she have waited and discussed that with the doctor? Caleb pointed out how that might have prevented the rebound of anxiety symptoms, but praised her decision to use less medication.

Gus Seawell, his two o'clock client, had missed three shots of Haldol, the one fragile barrier between him and long-term institutionalization. When the voices in his head told him that the world was about to end, he came to warn his therapist. Caleb was thankful the voices got Gus to the center where Grey gave him the much-needed injection.

After finishing with his last client at 5:30, Caleb dialed the number for Jeffrey Fleck, Helen Fleck's son, who hadn't returned Caleb's earlier call. Someone finally picked up on the seventh ring.

"Hello." The voice was feminine, with the unique Virginia

accent.

"This is Caleb Knowles from South Carolina. Is Jeffrey Fleck in please?"

"No. I'm his wife, Gloria. Jeffrey's out of town. Is something wrong with his mother?" Mother came out mothah, with the refreshing lilt in her voice.

"No emergency, but I am concerned. When will Jeffrey be in?"

"Not until Friday. He mailed her check before he left. Is she out of money again?" she asked, with a hint of irritation.

"No, it's nothing like that."

"Jeffrey's very busy," she said. When Caleb didn't respond, she added, "You know, she left the family when Jeffrey was just a boy. I think it's asking a lot to expect Jeffrey to drop everything just because Helen's having problems." Now the charming southern voice oozed annoyance.

Caleb was feeling right annoyed himself, but strained to keep his voice even. "I just need to ask Jeffrey a few questions. Could you have him call me?"

Curtly, she said she would and hung up. Caleb wrote himself a note to call again on Friday, having little faith that Gloria Fleck would relay his message to her husband. He hoped Jeffrey would be more receptive.

He dropped his stack of charts on Janice's desk and was about to head out when he noticed a light on in Grey's office. He stuck his head in and asked, "You finishing up?"

Grey looked rough. His tie sported lunch stains and hung off-center down his chest. Pink message slips peeked out from every pocket of his wrinkled lab coat. He sat at the desk, Dictaphone in hand, mounds of records surrounding him. "I think I'll be here till midnight. Why did I take this job?"

"Out of a great sense of civic duty. Or masochism, take your pick. I never got to ask you about your session with Murphy Lumford. What did you think?"

Grey scratched his head with the end of a ballpoint. "One

strange Homo Sapien, that one. Hard to believe he shot those people. He looks like he'd have trouble killing a spider. You were right, he's not suicidal, not when I saw him, at least. He refused meds. He's seen a neurologist so I sent for records. I told the police to keep a close eye on him, call us in if there's another problem. They'll bring him in on Friday for follow-up. I told Janice to put it on your book."

"Thanks," Caleb groaned, wondering how to fit Murphy in with all the others.

Grey removed his bifocals and cleaned the lenses with his tie. "You know, I've done probably three hundred prison consults in my life. I've seen anti-socials that would make your hair stand on end. But this guy, Lumford, doesn't fit the mold. He admits to this gruesome, cold-blooded crime, but you look at the quiet little guy, all twisted up with what looked like a mother of a migraine, and you just don't see it."

"I know what you mean," Caleb said. "It makes me wonder if he's really psychotic, but covers it up well."

"Could be. That's why you're seeing him."

Caleb looked at the mounds of paper around Grey and was beginning to feel guilty for leaving. But he had an important date with cute little redhead, and nothing would keep him away from her. He waved at Grey and said he'd see him in the morning.

Wild red hair flying behind her, Julia Knowles burst out of the front door of what used to be Caleb's home. "Daddy!" she screamed, jumping in Caleb's arms. Caleb squeezed her and kissed her neck and wondered how a kid could grow so fast. She was at least an inch taller and five pounds heavier than last week. She had on overalls and a sweatshirt with grass and mud stains on the cuffs. His ex-wife would be horrified.

"Hey monkey-face! How's my girl?"

She squirmed down, grabbed his hand, and dragged him to the truck. "Let's go, Daddy."

He let himself be led and slid into the seat after her. He

watched her buckle up, then asked, "Do you want to get something to eat?"

"When we get home." He loved it that she called his new house "home," too. He loved everything about this kid. "Is Shannon there?" she asked him.

"I hope so. And her friend Maggie is staying with us. You remember her?"

"Are we having a party?"

"No, honey. It's just gonna be us." He turned on the radio and pushed the button to Julia's favorite station. She was soon humming and swinging her legs to Dwight Yoakam as Caleb pointed the truck towards home.

Cleo was in the yard and ran over to them before they could open the truck's doors. Julia clambered out and threw her arms around as much of Cleo as she could. Caleb's eyes followed the reunited best friends to the back yard where games of tag and fetch began. Julia was such a happy, free kid. He hoped she never changed. He hoped she never experienced the world where Emma Callahan now lived.

"I'll be back out in a second, honey. You stay with Cleo," Caleb called from the back porch. He opened the door to find Maggie alone in the kitchen.

Shannon had left a moment ago, she reported, to run errands. She had said to eat without her. Maggie had already put the leftover pizza in the oven and Caleb asked if she could be trusted with the oven on and all, so Maggie swatted him with a towel. She seemed to be feeling better.

He made his way up the stairs and into the bedroom to change into his favorite ten year old sweats, making sure the latest holes didn't expose anything significant. He checked the elastic bandage around his chest, noticing that the swelling had gone down, the color now an attractive dark purple. As long as he didn't make sudden moves, or sharp turns to the side, the pain was manageable.

When he wandered back into the kitchen, he grabbed two beers from the fridge and handed one to Maggie. Out the window, Julia was braiding the hair on the top of Cleo's head. "Want to join me on the patio?" he asked Maggie.

"Sure." She unscrewed the top from her bottle and followed him outside.

As they sat at the wooden picnic table, Julia and Cleo scrambled over to greet them. Maggie complimented Julia on her hair styling talent and promised to watch as she jumped into backyard swing. "She's such an energetic kid."

He nodded. "Her goal is to make the swing go so high that it goes all the way over the top and back around. Shannon says it can't be done, that the laws of physics won't allow it. Of course, I think my daughter can do absolutely anything she puts her mind to."

She laughed. "I can't wait until she's a teenager."

"As soon as she pubes, I'm putting her in an all-girl Catholic school. Some secluded area, like say, Antarctica." He took a sip of beer, the foam cold against his teeth. He turned back to Maggie. "So how did it go with the police today?"

"Terrible. They found out Paul had been over to my house. You know, before Fran was killed. I hadn't mentioned it before because it didn't seem important. But our neighbor, Mrs. Pritchard, saw him leave. She's our neighborhood Aunt Bea, always in everybody's business. After Detective Briscoe questioned her, she spent two hours or so with me. The same questions, over and over. Now they want me to take a polygraph, like I'm a suspect or something. It's so damn ridiculous."

"So why was Paul at your place?" he asked, not liking how his personal life was colliding head-on with his professional one.

Her finger fidgeted with the rim of her bottle. "He stopped by. We've become pretty good friends over the past year. He and Fran were having problems—I guess most married people do. So he came over now and again and we'd talk. He helped me understand my problems with Barry. I owe him a lot." Maggie's gaze locked on Caleb.

"I know what you're thinking," she said, her tone cool. "Look, Paul and I were friends, but nothing more. And I loved Fran, Caleb. She was a good friend. She knew Paul and I were close, but she wasn't threatened by it. You have women friends. Do you sleep with all of them?"

He shook his head, embarrassed by the thought of it. He looked over at Julia to make sure she hadn't overheard. "Of course not. I—"

She slapped her hand on the table, palm up. "You see? That's why I didn't mention it to the police before. People are so sick. They see trash everywhere, even in the most innocent situations."

He shrugged, wishing he felt more relief. Her fire made him want to believe her. But he wasn't so sure what to believe about Paul Callahan.

The next morning, Caleb took Julia to kindergarten. He loved the way she held his hand as he walked her inside, the way she showed him her latest drawings and the rocking horse that was her personal favorite. He barely had a chance to kiss her goodbye before she scampered off with two other pre-schoolers. Such an amazing kid, he thought for the thousandth time. If only she could stay just like this forever.

He was the last to arrive at the clinic. He parked beside Grey's BMW and braced himself for the onslaught. The waiting room was full and Janice had a stack of messages waiting for him. "You have Meredith Spencer at nine, and Emma Callahan at ten. I've been trying to call Helen Fleck because from what I can tell in the record, she's run out of medicine. But she doesn't answer."

"Her son hasn't returned any of my calls," Caleb answered. "Keep trying to reach Helen. Let me know if you do."

"Matthew and Grey are already in session," she said hurriedly, as two phone lines rang. She grabbed her message pad and started punching buttons.

"Good morning," Caleb muttered to no one in particular and limped back to his office.

Meredith Spencer arrived on time for her appointment. She wore a tight, beige skirt that left a lot of leg uncovered. A green silk sweater flattered her eyes. She had on more make-up than he remembered from their last encounter, making her lashes look thick as brooms.

"I wasn't sure I should come back," she began.

"I'm glad you did. I know we had an awkward beginning."

"My husband, Alec, thinks it's important I see you. He's very worried about me."

"Why is that?" Caleb asked.

"It's his way, I suppose. I . . . haven't been back to work yet."

He nodded and took a long sip of the coffee. He wanted to probe but needed to pace it. "Are you nervous about work?"

Her lips parted slightly and her tongue reached out to wet them. "It's stupid, I know. I tried to go to work yesterday. I got in my car and drove up to the highway. But suddenly, I couldn't do it. I started shaking so bad I had to pull off the road. My chest started hurting, and I couldn't seem to catch my breath. I called Alec on my cell and he talked to me until I calmed down. He said it was probably a panic attack. He wanted me to mention it to you."

"I think he's probably right. Have you ever had one before?" Caleb asked.

"Not that I can remember. What was I panicking about? There was nothing, but I was so scared I couldn't breathe."

"What did you do?"

"Alec wanted to come and get me but I wouldn't let him. I felt like such a fool, interrupting his work like that. I managed to get home and I went straight back to bed. And finally got some good sleep."

"Have you been having nightmares?"

Her eyes widened and a strange, coy smile crept across her

face. "Yes, how did you know?"

"It's typical when someone has experienced a trauma. Can you tell me about yours?"

"I only remember one, and it was strange. I was at the mill, talking to Murphy. He had the gun in his hand. Blood dripped off his wrist. But he was talking to me about his insurance program, saying he wanted to change over to an HMO. I knew he shot those people, but we just chatted on and on about the virtues of managed care, like nothing was wrong." She blinked her eyes as if trying to focus them. "Then the next thing in the dream was a woman lying in a bed, with blood all around her."

"Was she familiar to you?" Caleb asked.

"No. Yes. Sort of. In my dream I knew her, and I cried out when I saw her, very upset. But I can't remember now who she was. I remember knowing she was older. Though she didn't look older, she looked my age. And I remember the blood on the bed and cuts on her wrists." She looked down at her own thin arms.

"What did you do?"

She arched her head back and looked at his ceiling. "What did I do? Nothing. I couldn't move. I stood there, staring at the woman, screaming. That's when Alec woke me up."

Caleb studied her strange expression, deciding he needed to be careful. "Do you want to work on that dream?"

"Work? What do you mean?"

"Well, sometimes our unconscious sends up messages in the form of dreams. The problem is, these messages are in an abstract, symbolic language and you are the only one who can translate them. I could teach you how, if you want."

She stroked her eyebrow with a long fingernail. Its iridescent tint flickered in the light. "I suppose we could try."

He reached in his drawer, retrieved a pad and pen, and handed them to her. "We can start here, but you'll need to finish it at home. It takes a little while until you get the hang of it. Now, the first thing you do is write down the entire dream, in as much detail as possible. It doesn't matter if it doesn't make sense, or if it seems like a series of disjointed images. Most dreams are. The next thing you do is take each image, one at a time, and let yourself free-associate. For example, the gun. What do you think of when you envision that gun in the man's hand?"

She did as he instructed, writing "gun" on the top of the page. "I think of violence . . . fear . . . movies I've seen. I think of Alec's gun in the closet. The fight we had when he brought it home. I think of last Saturday, and those people falling to the floor around me, moving in slow motion, like a sick ballet. I remember how small Murphy's gun seemed, yet it caused so much destruction."

"Well, you seem to be taking to this like fish to water." He grinned. "Now, you write down all those thoughts, and keep on writing, till the well runs dry. Then you move on to the next image, which might be the HMO. You may wind up with pages and pages, and that's okay. When you've finished with each image, you go back. You look at each association and figure out which ones stand out to you, which ones feel the most relevant. You highlight those. For example, you review the images you wrote down for "gun." Maybe Alec's gun stands out in your mind and the conflict about it."

"This isn't a Freudian thing, is it?" she asked suspiciously.

He laughed out loud. "No, no. Sorry. Maybe that was a bad example."

She grinned back at him. "I'd hate to tell Alec we spent the session talking about his big gun."

Caleb was both surprised and relieved by her effort at humor. "I suppose he might misinterpret that," he laughed.

"Okay. I think I have the hang of it. I'll give it a try."

"Besides the nightmares, how are you doing?"

"I got a call from my boss this morning. She said everybody there keeps talking about Murphy, wondering how he could do such a thing."

"How well did you know him?" Caleb probed.

"Not very well. I did his benefits package. Like in the dream." Tension returned to her face in creases around the lips and eyes. "I didn't have a clue he'd do something like this."

"Of course you didn't."

"We don't have a space on our job application where it asks 'Do you ever think of bringing a gun and shooting the people you work with?' If we did, we might get some strange answers."

"I imagine so." Caleb nodded. She'd given him a lead, but he wasn't sure how much to pursue it. Gently, he asked, "Do you find yourself feeling responsible, like you should have anticipated what happened?"

She narrowed her eyes at him like he'd accused her of something, but Caleb kept his expression soft and accepting.

"I wonder if I could have done something. Before that day. Or even a moment or two before he pulled out the gun. Maybe I should have paid more attention to him, asked him if something was wrong. Maybe if he'd had someone to talk to . . ." her voice trailed off.

"You're giving yourself a lot of power, don't you think? I mean, everyone said he looked like a normal guy. It looked like a normal day. I don't think he gave off any cues, do you?"

She smacked her full, perfectly lined lips like she was about to speak, but said nothing. She crossed her legs and bobbed the top foot up and down so that her shoe dangled from her toes. A curiously seductive gesture.

Caleb forced his gaze to move from her legs to the taut lines of her face. "Did you know any of the victims?"

"Yes. I had only just met Sally Weston, because she had recently started with us. I knew Buck Swygert, but not well. I helped him with his insurance forms after he got out of the Bruce Hill Center. I guess he had a drinking problem or something."

"How long ago was that?"

"He went in a couple of times. I don't know that it helped much. He always looked pretty rough to me." She wrapped her arms across her chest as if chilled. Tears squeezed out of the corners of her eyes.

"Something's upsetting you."

She nodded. "I–I just had an image of him, from the other day. He was shot in the face, you know. I remember all the blood and that huge hole where his eye had been." She shuddered.

The image made Caleb's chest tighten and sent a wave of pain around his bruised torso. He sucked in a deep, slow breath. "Is that the first time you've seen someone dead?"

"No," she whispered, looking away. A heavy silence fell between them. Finally, she said, "I saw my sister, right after the car hit her. Theresa and I were riding bikes. We lived in the country on a quiet road, and we were on our way to a friend's house. I had passed her, and heard a horn blaring, and squealing tires, and I turned around and saw the car swerve and drive off. Theresa had been thrown thirty feet. Her body was twisted and so still. I ran to her and screamed her name, but she didn't hear me. She never woke up." She reached for a tissue and wiped her face. "I haven't talked about that in years. It was so long ago. A lifetime, really."

The vividness of her description struck Caleb. "They ever catch the driver?"

"No, they didn't." Carefully, she dabbed at the mascara streaks under her eyes. "I must look a mess."

"You look fine."

"I hate for people to see me cry."

"It means you're human. Just like the rest of us, I'm afraid." He watched her for a moment. "Theresa's death must have devastated your family."

"Like I said, we don't talk about it." She glanced down at her watch. "I really have to go."

Caleb glanced at his clock. Just like last time, she'd been there less than a half hour. "Are you sure? We have more time if you want to use it."

She flashed a nervous smile. "I saw all those people in your waiting room. They probably need you more than me."

"But this is your time, Meredith. You don't need to be concerned about anyone else."

She stood, straightening her skirt and gathering her purse under her arm. "Thanks for seeing me."

"Okay. Can we reschedule?"

She nodded and they agreed on a time for the following week. She accepted his appointment card, carefully placing it in her wallet.

He took that as a good sign.

chapter nine

Wrapping her tiny hand around two of Caleb's fingers, Emma Callahan allowed herself to be led into the playroom. Her other arm squeezed the neck of the bear Caleb had given her last session. She wore coveralls and a pink sweater that matched the tiny pink bows peeking over the sides of her pink sneakers. Caleb smiled, thinking how he struggled to get his own daughter in matching socks.

Emma wouldn't look at him. Her spiritless eyes stared straight ahead, as if expecting something terrible to leap out at her at any second. But when Caleb coaxed her into the playroom, she moved directly to the center of the room and looked around, an improvement from last time.

"You remember the rules, Emma? You can play with anything you want in here."

She glanced up at him with her wide, blank eyes. He grinned down at her, reinforcing her attempt at eye contact. Celebrate every little improvement, he reminded himself, because there was still a long road ahead.

Emma moved in slow motion. One small step, then another, until she stood over the large blue crate that contained a tangle of stuffed animals. Caleb positioned himself on the floor between the crate and the doll house. "Do you see something you want to play with?"

She nodded, pointing in the crate.

"Good. Why don't you pick out what you want."

She reached inside, carefully selecting a stuffed panda, a kitten, and a Yoda doll. After arranging them in a circle, she pulled herself up on her knees and studied the animals surrounding her. Her face puckered as if something just wasn't right. She surveyed the room until she spotted the tan-colored bear she'd abandoned on the floor. She crawled over to it, maneuvering between Yoda and the kitten, to bring the bear into the center of the circle. She pulled it into her lap, her thin arms cradling it close.

Caleb wondered about the arrangement of creatures encircling her. Did they represent a wall, protecting her? Was there special meaning to the number? Three animals . . . the three other members of her family?

Emma closed her eyes and began a gentle sway from side to side. She moved in a languid rhythm, her hair waving like wheat stirred by a soft breeze, the bear's face jostling against her stomach.

Caleb watched her for a few minutes, but soon sensed her slipping away. "You've taken such good care of that bear, Emma. See how happy it is?"

She looked at him, then down at the bear.

"He sure likes to be rocked, doesn't he?" he added.

She nodded.

Caleb slid behind the circle of animals. He reached over and touched the panda's head. "Does this guy know your bear?"

"Girl. It's a girl bear," she said unexpectedly.

"Oh, right," Caleb said playfully. "Does she have a name?"

Emma nodded. "Mama."

Good, he thought. *Play it out.* "Mama huh? She looks like a mama bear."

Emma reached for her, sliding the panda in front of her and laying the smaller bear across the panda's legs. They toppled over, the smaller bear tumbling a few feet away.

Emma dropped her hands helplessly in her lap.

Caleb gave her a moment, then decided to help. He repositioned the panda so that it was braced against his foot. Then he lifted the smaller bear and said to it, "You miss your mama, don't you? Well, here she is!" He laid the bear in the panda's lap while Emma watched. "How does he look now? I can't see his face."

She bent over and peered into the bear's eyes. "He likes it."

"Great. I like our bears to be happy."

As Emma studied the two bears, something stirred behind her eyes. Slowly, she reached over, touching the mother bear's nose and her mouth, tracing a line down her chin. She dropped her hand to the child bear, stroking its cheek. Then, in a sudden gesture, she swatted it out of its mother's lap and onto the floor. Emma leaned way over to the side so that she was nose to nose with the fallen child bear.

Captivated, Caleb watched his young client play out this ritual with the bears. Emma had made an unconscious connection with the child bear, her bear. As she played out her own separation from her mother, he needed to read her cues to learn what Emma understood about her mother's death.

Emma picked up the smaller bear and stared at its face before returning it to the panda's lap. "Bad bear, bad bear," she said in a stern voice.

"Is the mama bear scolding the little bear?" Caleb asked, perplexed.

She ignored him. She touched the smaller bear's head and swooped it off the lap again, this time with enough force to send it hurling across the room. Quickly, she crawled to it and returned it to its mother's lap. "Bad bear!"

Caleb sat up, locking his arms around his knees to free up more space for her. This bear-hurling ritual might just expand to other parts of the room.

Again, Emma knocked the smaller bear away from the

panda. It landed in a heap several yards away. She waited a moment before collecting it again. This time, her scolding was even more forceful. She wagged a punitive finger in the bear's face and plopped it in the mother bear's lap. She didn't drop a beat before knocking it away again, retrieving it, berating it, then returning it to its mother.

Troubled, Caleb studied his client. Though there was fire in her eyes, it was way too soon for her grief to enter the anger phase. And the anger was directed towards the child bear. *Was it self-hate? No. Self-blame.*

Of course. At age four, Emma probably held to the belief that the whole world revolved around her, which meant her mother's death must have been in her control. Emma believed her mother died because she was bad. "Bad bear," she had said.

Caleb blinked, absorbing the realization. He fought a strong urge to take Emma in his arms, to assure her that this was not her fault, that she was a wonderful child who did not deserve this tragedy. As the impulse passed, he turned to Emma, who knelt in front of the abandoned smaller bear. Caleb slid over to her. "That bear sure looks sad," he prompted.

She glanced at him and turned back to the bear. The rage had evaporated, but she looked sullen and confused.

Caleb turned the bear over so that it faced her. "You know what? I don't think this is a bad bear. I think it's a very good bear." He eased the bear towards her and she reached for it, lifting it to her chest.

"That's very nice Emma. He really needs that. He's a very good bear, but he misses his mama."

She buried her face in the nape of the bear's neck. Softly, Caleb ran his hand up and down her delicate back, feeling her rigid tension there. "Hold on to him, Emma. He needs to feel you close." A quiet sob heaved out of her. Caleb continued to stroke her back, hoping she'd reach for him. But she couldn't seem to let go of the bear.

"Emma? Why don't you sit here?" He guided her down beside him and rested a hand on the back of her neck. "That's right. Yeah, hold on to that bear. And maybe I'll hold on to you for a moment." She leaned against him and he gave her a gentle squeeze. Gradually, some of the tension melted away.

And she started to cry. She sobbed mournfully, her tears pouring into the bear's fur. Caleb leaned into her ear and whispered that she was all right, that it would all get better soon. After a long moment, the tears stopped flowing and the thumb made its way into her mouth. Curving against Caleb, Emma soon fell into a heavy slumber.

When he realized it was time to finish the session, he touched her shoulder to wake her. Sleepy, unfocussed eyes looked up at him. He grinned back at her.

Emma stiffened, drew back from Caleb, and said loudly, "Water. I want water."

Caleb removed his hand from her back. "You're thirsty?"

"Water!" she yelled.

Caleb stood and approached the small sink. He took a Styrofoam cup from a cabinet and filled it, then handed it to Emma. "Here you go."

She stared into the cup for a second, a confused look on her face. Without taking a drink, she handed the cup back to him. Caleb shrugged, dumped out the water, and reached for the smaller bear. "Here's your friend. I want you to keep him and bring him back on Tuesday. That's in four days." He held up four fingers and counted them. "Do you think you can remember?"

She nodded. She lifted the bear under her arm and followed him out of the playroom.

"You taking lunch today?" Shannon's voice sounded hurried over the phone.

He glanced at his watch, which read 12:30. He perused the schedule of appointments and noticed that Janice had squeezed out an hour, bless her soul. "Sure. Want to meet somewhere?"

"Pasta Fresca? They're fast. And close."

"I'll be there in ten minutes. If you beat me there, order for me."

Relentless traffic made Caleb late. He parked by Shannon's car in the parking lot's one remaining spot. Inside, Caleb scanned the chattery lunch crowd until he saw Shannon in a corner booth of the restaurant. Hammered silver earrings bobbed through her thick brown curls. She wore a hint of makeup that gave a blush to her cheeks, a splash of pink to her lips. The eyes needed nothing, the pale blue sweater perfectly reflecting their crystal clarity. He leaned over to kiss her before taking the seat opposite her.

"I ordered for you. I couldn't decide if I wanted ravioli or lasagna, so you get the ravioli and I get to taste it. I thought we'd split a salad."

He grinned. As usual, the stresses of her life had not affected her appetite. "So how's your day going, dear?"

"It sucks," she said, plopping a lemon wedge into her water. "And yours?"

"The same. Eight zillion clients, most in crisis. It's a good thing I took my Geritol."

"How are you feeling?"

"A little sore. It's okay if I don't breathe though."

She fidgeted with her water glass and looked tense. "I thought we should talk, maybe catch up a bit."

"Sounds good to me." He could tell something was swirling around in her mind.

"The other night, you said things didn't go well at Sam's. What's wrong?"

He sipped at his water and wished she hadn't brought it up. He'd done a fine job of suppressing the issue, and in fact, the whole conversation with his brother. But here she was, churning it all up again. "It's nothing bad, really. Sam may be moving to Atlanta. Tessa Solapé knows several galleries there who want to take him on. She thinks the artistic stimulation would be good for him. He says the deaf culture is alive and thriving, so he'll find himself a niche."

"Atlanta. That's so big. And so far away."

"Only four hours or so." It was no big deal, really. Four hours was nothing. There would be weekend visits every few months or so. And Sam would make so much money, he could fly home whenever he wanted. Caleb felt eyes boring holes through him and looked at Shannon, suddenly very uncomfortable.

"You're having a hard time with this," she probed.

He reached for his glass. His throat constricted making it hard for the water to go down.

She took his hand. "It might be a good opportunity for him."

"I know. And he deserves it."

"You're worried something will happen to him. You're so used to being his ears, maybe he'd need you and it's too far for you to get to him."

The knot of tension worked its way up his throat and he swallowed it. After all, that was his family heritage. "I don't want to go into it now, okay?"

She nodded, her eyes sad. The food came and she divvied up the salad. He stared at his portion with little interest. "So what about you? Everything okay?" he asked, feeling more than a little bit wary.

"Maybe it can wait."

"Look, as crazy as our lives have been, this may be our only time alone."

She poked at the lasagna and he leaned back, waiting.

"It's about Maggie," she said finally.

"I figured."

"She's my Sam, I guess. I'm scared she's going to do something stupid. We had a marathon session last night."

"About Barry?"

"I need to let up on her about him. She's going to make her own decisions, it's not like I have any control over her. She called me a while ago and said she felt uncomfortable staying with us because I was being so hard on her. I promised to lay off because I really want her with us until the killer is found. She's seeing Barry this afternoon, and I hope she doesn't decide to move in with him."

"From what you've said, that would be self-destructive." Caleb wondered where all this was leading.

"Not according to her. I told her she deserved better, that she'd find someone who would be as good for her as you are for me. You know what she said? She said she didn't want what I have. She likes you, but she's not sure you're good for me."

Caleb dropped his fork. "Why did she say that?"

Shannon leaned her head against her hand. "I love you, Caleb. You know that. And I love Julia. I don't think I could love her more if I had given birth to her."

"I hear a but coming—"

"Maggie says I'm in suspended animation. We've been together two years now, but we aren't married. She says people like you never want to get married again. She says I know that but I stay anyway, like I don't really think I deserve any better. But that's not it. Sometimes I feel okay like this, and I think we could go on forever. But sometimes I don't feel so secure." She paused, staring down at her food like it held all the answers.

He looked down at his and wished it did. "I didn't realize."

She looked up again. "She asked me what if we don't make it? I've given up my home, and two years, and I love that kid so much and if we split, I'd have no rights to her." The words rushed out of her so fast, like they'd been trying to find their way out for months.

She went on, "It seems we're stuck, you know? We're not moving forward. Maggie calls it 'suspended animation,' but maybe it's stagnation. You don't want to hear it, but I need to be honest. I'm scared, Caleb."

He watched her spill it all out. He had no idea, really, that she felt that way. He should have known. She'd been so tense lately, he should have read her better.

Shannon's eyes reached out to him. "Say something. Anything."

"I don't know what to say," he answered. Even though she wanted more from him, there was nothing else to give.

She studied her partially-eaten food. "This was a bad idea."

"No, I want to know how you feel."

"It's better when the road goes both ways, isn't it?" she said with uncharacteristic bitterness.

And suddenly, it was like time travel occurred right there at the table, taking Caleb back two and a half years. He could see Mariel, his ex-wife, sitting across from him, wearing that same expression of hurt and frustration as she listed the hundred ways he had disappointed her. He pushed his plate away. The very idea of food made something roll in his stomach.

"So you're not going to say anything?"

"I . . . I can't really describe how I'm feeling. This is sort of coming out of the blue," he said, though it really wasn't true. They rarely talked about marriage because he never let the subject come up. The idea of it scared him to death. Mariel's disapproving face hung around the fringes of his thoughts.

Shannon looked at the others around them enjoying their lunch. "Well, we've been here before, haven't we?"

"Look, we need more time for this. Maybe tonight."

"Not with Maggie there."

"Then we'll walk down to the park. We'll talk all night if we have to." He heard a hint of desperation in his own voice.

"It's going to be cold tonight." Her eyes told him that she'd left the table, left the restaurant, left him. He should have seen it before. "I have to go," she said suddenly. She stood, eyes evading, and walked briskly towards the door.

Caleb stared down at his meal, which offered nothing for

the emptiness growing inside. Dark clouds swam around in his head, familiar death clouds. They had come when his mother died. And through the slow, painful death of his marriage.

He dropped a limp twenty on the table and made his way out the door.

The afternoon wore on and automatic pilot handily kicked in. Caleb dialed Helen Fleck's number a few times, but there was no answer. He screened two new clients, met with one of Matthew's regulars and returned a dozen calls. He finished a few clinical notes. He wrote a report for a managed care company.

He was numb.

When his desk phone rang he hoped it wasn't a client. He was out of fuel.

"Caleb?" Matthew said over the phone. "I'm at the hospital. Bryant Wheeler mentioned that you'd been mugged a few nights ago. Asked how you were recuperating. Why didn't you tell me?"

"It's no big deal. And I knew I couldn't miss work."

"Any shortness of breath? Fever?"

"I'm feeling okay," he mumbled, aware it was a half-truth. "What's up?"

"I'm about to head home, but Janice has a couple of files I need to work on. Would you mind bringing them by the house? And maybe stay for a drink?" Matthew asked.

"Okay. I'll be there in a bit."

Matthew lived in Reynolds Park, Westville's most prestigious old neighborhood. Large brick and stone homes, shaded by towering oak and pecan trees, lay surrounded by lush gardens and expanses of lawn perfect enough to be Astroturf. Matthew's two-story Tudor-style home had four bedrooms, a library, and a greenhouse. There was a garage that could park a small jet and a tool shed the size of a miniature barn. It was way more than one man needed, unless that man was Matthew Rhyker.

Matthew was a collector of everything: antique furniture, modern art, rare coins, and first edition books. His library, so vast it had a card system, contained everything from the latest Barbara Kingsolver to the complete works of William Blake. His CD collection, including jazz, classical, and folk, was the envy of everyone who beheld it, especially Caleb Knowles. Devices Caleb couldn't identify, much less use, lined Matthew's kitchen counters and his wine rack contained the finest reds Caleb had ever tasted.

"Thanks for these," Matthew said, taking the records and ushering him inside. Caleb followed him into the library and sat on the plump leather sofa that made sighing noises underneath him. Matthew poured two glasses of wine, handing one to Caleb.

Caleb sipped at the cabernet, which tasted dry and expensive. He was more of a Molson man himself.

Matthew twirled the stem of his glass, looking distracted. "I guess you're wondering why I asked you over."

"You wanted the files."

"Yes, the files." He studied the wine as if it was suddenly fascinating. "But there's something else. Something difficult for me to discuss with you. I suppose I should have told you this several years ago. But honestly, if I had a choice, you and I might never have this conversation. That's the honest truth."

"It sounds serious."

Matthew didn't answer, but regarded him over the wine glass. "I have a friend coming to town tomorrow. You've met him before. Ben Aldridge."

"Yeah, I remember Ben. I met him at your birthday dinner last year." Caleb recalled a tall, muscular guy with a ready smile and stories about travel in New Zealand and China. "Isn't he some kind of computer whiz?"

"Yes. He works for Microtech. He's been in Australia for a year. He'll be living with me," Matthew said into his glass.

"God knows, you have the space."

"Yes, I suppose I do. But my point is Ben will be living

here. With me."

Caleb blinked, knowing where this was going and wanting so badly not to go there. He'd always suspected, but found the "Don't ask, don't tell" strategy from the military worked just fine for him. Until now. "Okay, Ben's living with you."

"Exactly."

"So you're saying . . ."

"I'm gay."

"You're gay," Caleb repeated, the word tumbling out of his mouth.

Matthew retrieved the wine bottle from the bar and topped off Caleb's glass. Caleb took a long swallow that burned a little on its way down.

"You'd figured it out, hadn't you?"

"I suspected. Thought it wasn't really my business."

"Thank you for that. I prefer to keep my private life private. Westville is a conservative town and the professional community isn't much more liberal, I'm sad to say. I can't bear to be the subject of gossip, you know me well enough to know that."

"Yeah, I guess I do." He looked around at the expensive paintings on the walls, the antique roll-top desk in the corner. The stained-glass sunrise hanging over the window. "Why are you telling me now?"

"I had to. But not to make you uncomfortable." Matthew studied him, appraising.

Caleb sipped at the wine. "Well, Jeez, Matthew. You're gay. It's not a big deal, really." He hoped he sounded convincing.

"So. You have any questions?"

"Questions? I can think of about a hundred. Have you and Ben been together a long time?"

"Four years. But as you know, he's been overseas a great deal, which has been hard. He took a long vacation and came back the first year. And last fall, I met him in England for a week."

Caleb tried to imagine it. Did Matthew feel about Ben what he felt for Shannon? How did it work? His mind conjured up images that immediately made him squirm. As much as Caleb wanted to be accepting, to be politically correct, the idea of two men. Together. He glanced nervously at his boss.

Matthew's stare was poking at him, probably reading Caleb's discomfort. "I've always liked you and respected you, Caleb. But I've never lusted after you."

Caleb laughed. "I don't know if I should be relieved or insulted. So does all this have something to do with Paul Callahan?"

"He's one reason I came out to you. I met Paul through a mutual friend, who's also gay. Paul's become a part of our small, very discreet, social circle. Paul is coming to terms with his own sexuality, but it's caused him great guilt and confusion.

"Paul met Fran in high school, dated her throughout college, married her right after graduation. Then came the kids, the home, the distractions of young family life. Paul is a devout Catholic, so church became a center point of their lives." Matthew paused, wiping tiny beads of claret from his silver mustache.

"Paul found himself feeling dissatisfied with his life. He described it as being hungry, but not knowing what he needed to sate him. He got to know a few of us and it helped him realize what was missing from his plate. His Catholicism conflicted with his emerging sexual identity, which made him feel very guilty and even a little depressed.

"Paul loves his children. And he also loved Fran. He didn't believe in divorce. He felt—and still feels, I think—that he betrayed his family."

As Caleb absorbed the story, his mind's eye filled with a freeze-frame image of Emma. He supposed that it was a betrayal of sorts. Paul's homosexuality would have threatened the security of Emma's home life. And, for a four-year-old, home was the entire universe.

"Is Paul seriously involved with anyone?"

Matthew hesitated before answering. "I . . . I don't think so. Paul's confused and needs time and space to work it all out."

"You said Paul didn't believe in divorce. That's not an issue now, is it?" Caleb said more wryly than he meant to, and noticed Matthew pulling back in response.

The phone rang and Matthew left the library to answer it.

Caleb finished his wine and stood, the movement stretching his torso and aggravating his ribs. He limped over to the marble fireplace to look in the mirror tilted over the mantle. He wasn't wild about the reflection. Fatigue and stress had pulled the color from his face. Gingerly, he ran his hand over the bandages on his chest, wincing when his fingers found the tender spot.

He was a mess. His life was a mess. Shannon was probably going to leave him. His brother was moving away. His job was about to suck the life right out of him. And how would this revelation change things with Matthew? He hoped it wouldn't. Caleb might have an embarrassing trace of homophobia in him, but Matthew was his friend.

Matthew shut the French doors behind him. "That was Grey. He's just leaving the hospital and wanted us to appreciate how hard he's working." He walked slowly back to the sofa and lifted his glass by its stem. Idly tilting it from one side to the other, he watched the swirling purple liquid. "You brought up the fact that Paul didn't have to worry about a divorce now. But believe me, that brings him no relief. He is devastated by Fran's death, especially since the last few months were so hard for her. She knew what Paul was dealing with and knew it was way out of her control. She, too, was a devout Catholic."

"I suppose they both felt trapped."

"That's a good word for it. But they loved their kids and, in spite of all that, they loved each other. They'd have worked something out."

Caleb couldn't imagine how they would. The rigidity of Catholicism wouldn't allow for Paul to express his sexuality; it would be a mortal sin. Divorce would also be a violation of church doctrine. The church would expect them to live a lie, Caleb supposed. "I guess you don't think Paul killed Fran."

"I know he didn't." He stared into the empty fireplace for a moment. "Besides," he went on, "You don't need to play detective here. That's for the police to do."

"Yeah, well, I need to know if Emma's going to spend the next ten years visiting Dad in prison."

"How's she doing?" Matthew asked.

"She's starting to play it all out now. Pretty tough to watch."

Matthew nodded. "I knew you'd be the right therapist for her. Sorry if it hits too close to home."

"I'll survive. She's a great kid. Be nice to see her smile one day." He stood, resting his drained wine glass on the table. "So about this secret, I won't tell anyone."

"Thanks. With this police investigation, I think Paul's situation will have to come out. But I'd like my name kept out of everything. It's okay to talk around Shannon and your brother, but others . . ."

"You mean Sam knows?"

Matthew grinned. "And apparently, he's pretty good at keeping secrets."

chapter ten

Caleb's house was dark, except for a lone porch light flickering, a pale beacon in the cold. Shannon's car was gone, which was just as well. He wasn't ready for round two with her. He opened the back door and switched on the stark fluorescent kitchen light. A plate of meatloaf, covered with plastic, lay on the table. An attached note read: *Salad in the fridge. Maggie's out with Barry. I'll be home later. S.*

He stared at the note, wondering if there was subliminal text between the lines. Missing was the usual smart-ass comment: *I made pork chops. The number to Poison Control is by the phone,* or *Here's my casserole. Consume at your own risk.*

He slid the plate in the microwave and decided to forego the salad. He wasn't hungry, even though he'd barely touched his lunch. The news he'd digested all day left his stomach unsettled.

After eating as much of the meatloaf as he could handle, he dumped the rest in Cleo's bowl and watched her lunge for it, slurping it up with a noisy vigor. She licked the last trace of sauce from her dish and rolled her eyes up at him adoringly.

"Nope. That's all there is." Caleb stroked the long fur that fell over her clueless eyes and wished that his own life could be so simple. Food, water, plenty of naps. Remembering where she left her favorite tennis ball. Keeping an eye on their neighbor's sneaky cat. Maintaining a squirrel-free yard. Yep, life wasn't exactly a tightrope of stress for Cleo.

She followed him into the den and plopped down by the sofa. As Caleb stretched his long, tired legs the full length of the couch, his damaged ribs made their presence known. A dull, throbbing ache began at the point of impact and radiated around his left side. Not bad enough for painkillers, but annoying just the same.

He reached for the remote control and began the sacred male ritual of channel surfing. The Bobcats were taking a beating against the Pacers, so he surfed on. He skimmed over a few driveling situation comedies, passed through shopping channel hell, and paused at the cable news station. A special on the recent disease outbreak in Rwanda wouldn't help his mood in the least.

He pressed the button to his favorite channel, the Aquarium Station. For twelve hours a day, a TV camera filmed a live, fresh-water aquarium to the accompaniment of jazz music from a local radio station. Caleb watched as two angel fish played tag to Branford Marsalis, remembering the time Shannon had left fish food on top of the TV, with a post-it note, *I fed them this morning.*

Shannon. God, this house would feel empty if she left him. Empty and cold. Caleb touched the sore area of his chest, aware of a deeper hurt growing there.

He'd pretty well burrowed down in a self-pitying reverie when the phone rang. He winced as he reached for it. "Hello?"

"Caleb. I left about a dozen messages for you. Don't you ever check your answering machine?" Detective Claudia Briscoe sounded only mildly annoyed.

"I was going to check it next week, weather permitting. What's up?"

"I wanted to meet with you. How about I buy you breakfast tomorrow morning?"

"I'm flattered. And suspicious. You must want something."

"Of course I do. Eight o'clock okay? The Bread and Bagel?"

"Make it a quarter till. I have to be in the office early."

"Okay. I'll meet you there."

He hung up the phone and resumed his channel surfing. He ventured back to the Bobcats game in time to see the Pacers tie the score with a tricky lay-up. A few minutes into the Pacers revenge, Caleb was sleeping soundly.

He awakened an hour later when he heard the front door creak open. His confused, bleary eyes tried to focus on the two bodies that came in, lit only by the video flicker from the TV.

"Caleb?" Maggie said, groping for a wall switch. "You must have been asleep."

"Yeah. What time is it?"

"Eleven. Shannon here?"

Caleb looked up the hall where the stairs were. Surely Shannon wouldn't have come in and gone to bed without waking him. "Good question. You see her car?"

Barry Waters walked over and peered down at him with wide, kinetic eyes. "Not there. God, I love that car. 1969 baby blue Impala. Mint condition. Worth a fortune, I bet! If she ever wanted to sell it, I'd scarf it up." Waters' words exploded out of his mouth like a geyser. He was probably buzzing off his latest substance of choice, whatever it was.

Maggie sauntered to an armchair, all smiles and perkiness, like a shampoo commercial. "We had a great time tonight. We went downtown, to the River Walk area. I haven't been down that way in over a year! We ate at Fellini's, then went to "Just Desserts" for cheesecake, and sat outside people watching. Everyone looks so young, Caleb. It has to be that. I refuse to believe that I'm getting old." She was Maggie at her best, all lit up from inside. The Maggie from two days ago— the frightened, haunted Maggie—was gone. And Caleb knew what had caused the transformation. He looked over at Barry.

"So, how you feeling there?" Barry asked, with no concern in his voice. "You recover from the other night? That was one hell of a scare, I'll tell you. I suppose they could have killed you."

"Thanks for the cheery thought."

Barry grinned at him as if he'd made a joke. A mop of thick black curls framed a face too tanned for the season. Thick black brows shaded his dark eyes, giving him a look of mystery that women seemed to love. At least Maggie did. She was positively filled up with him.

Caleb pulled himself up and plopped his feet on top of Cleo. The sheepdog rolled over, demanding a stomach rub. "Maggie, did you hear anything else about the break-in?"

"Not a thing," she answered. "Detective Briscoe said they didn't find any usable fingerprints. She said it wasn't your typical robbery because it looked like they were looking for something specific. She asked me if I knew what. I told her I don't exactly make enough to own stocks or bonds or anything else of real value. I don't even have much jewelry, except a small cameo collection. The burglars went through my jewelry box, like everything else, but didn't take anything." Maggie fell back in the chair and kicked off her shoes. Long, lean legs appeared out of the folds of her skirt, awakening primal male drives in Caleb. He found his eyes scanning her pale, delicate ankles and her taut, muscled calves. Embarrassed, he looked away.

But Barry didn't, he noticed. Barry's thirsty eyes drank up those legs, his lips moving as if he could taste them.

"Anyway," Maggie continued, "Whoever broke into my house had something to do with Fran's murder. It only makes sense, doesn't it? Two serious crimes, so close together? It couldn't be coincidence."

"No, probably not coincidence," Barry said with an air of authority. "People read the papers. Sometimes criminals read the funeral announcements so they can break into the home of the bereaved family while they're at services. Pretty disgusting, but true. As much media attention as this has gotten, someone probably figured out the Callahan house would be unoccupied. Your car was gone so they checked out your house, too."

Maggie's chestnut eyes widened, as if fascinated by Barry's theory. "You think that could be it, Caleb?"

"I suppose it's plausible. I'm meeting Claudia in the morning. I'll ask her what she thinks." He caught an unhappy glare from Barry, probably because Maggie had asked for Caleb's opinion. He stood and carefully stepped over Cleo. "I think I'll put my weary bones to bed. Maggie, would you mind letting Cleo out before you come up?"

"No problem. Good night."

Caleb trudged up the stairs, undressed, and slipped on a T-shirt. He piled into his side of the bed and picked up a social work journal that was sure to put him to sleep. He'd finished half an article when he heard Shannon climbing the stairs.

She inched open the door, not expecting him to be awake. When she noticed that he wasn't asleep, she hesitated. She mumbled an awkward greeting, dropping her keys on the bureau.

"Are Maggie and Barry down there?" he asked, wanting to break the silence.

"Yes."

"You know what I like about Barry?"

"I can't imagine," she said coolly.

"His teeth. You can't grow teeth like that. You have to pay for them. Some orthodontist put a kid through college thanks to Barry's bicuspids."

"Sam has teeth like that. He grew them on his own."

"Sam who?" Caleb asked.

"Sam your brother. You know, big, deaf guy? Looks sort of like Adonis?"

"Oh yeah. Him."

Shannon pulled off her sweater and bra. She grabbed the

flannel gown that was hanging from a hook on the bathroom door. "I was just over there."

"At Sam's? How'd that happen?"

"I don't know. I ran a couple of errands, then I was just sort of driving around. Thinking."

He didn't want to ask, but had to. "About us?"

"About me, mostly. I found myself driving up Lake Drive, came to Sam's house, and saw his lights on. So I stopped in."

Caleb dog-eared the page and tossed the journal on his night stand, not liking the direction this conversation was taking. "Sam okay?"

"He's a little mad at you. For not staying in touch, especially with all that's going on. He hates to be excluded."

"Me, too."

"Relax. We talked about things other than you."

"Like what?"

"Like Atlanta. Sam still doesn't know what to do. About Maggie. Sam says I have to be patient and supportive, even if that means watching her fall flat on her face. He says it's what he does with you."

"Sam's a funny guy."

"Sam's a perceptive guy. I didn't say a thing about lunch. And I know you haven't talked to him. But he says, sort of out of the blue, that I need to remember how you are your own worst enemy. He said you never feel like you deserve to be happy."

Caleb closed his eyes. Maybe Sam moving to Atlanta wasn't such a bad idea. He hated being the subject of talk between them. He didn't like being exposed. These two people that knew him so well, sharing their lights to see the darker places inside him. He opened his eyes to find Shannon studying him. She offered a weak smile and crawled into their bed, sideways, facing him. "I did realize one thing," she said.

"What's that?"

"We have so much going on right now, we need to postpone dealing with our problems. I mean, until Maggie's safe and moves back out, until Sam's situation is more settled. How does that sound to you?"

He looked deep into her ice blue eyes and felt a deep sadness. Yes, he was glad for a reprieve, even if it just postponed the inevitable. "Whatever you want, Shannon, is fine with me."

"Okay, so we work at surviving the next few weeks, then we talk this out."

"Agreed." He wanted to grab her, to scream out how much he loved her, how much he needed her. He wanted to make love the feverish way they sometimes did, to feel himself deep inside her.

She reached over and pecked him on the lips. "Good night, then."

"Good night."

On Friday morning, Caleb maneuvered his mismatched, tri-colored '92 Toyota pick-up truck into the last remaining spot in the parking lot of the Bread and Bagel Café. He was glad to be adding class to the collection of Lincoln Navigators, BMWs, and Saabs perched under leafless trees that were planted more for decoration than shade. Passing Claudia's CRV, he opened the heavy glass door to the restaurant.

Claudia had claimed a window table. She sipped coffee while perusing the *Westville Chronicle*. Her black hair was pulled back and gold disks the size of quarters hung on each earlobe. In the dark suit and charm bracelet, she looked more like a high school principal than a cop. She reached to take his hand, her smile warm enough to make Caleb even more suspicious about their meeting. "I haven't ordered yet," she said.

"Sorry I'm late. I didn't reserve shower time last night, so I had to wait on the women. What's up?" He spotted a waitress in snug black skirt and spandex sweater and waved her over, ordering coffee and a bagel, Claudia opted for a full breakfast of an omelet, grits, and a biscuit.

"I have something for you." She reached into a briefcase beside her chair and pulled out a folder with a familiar document inside. "You aren't going to like this. It's a release of information form signed by a new client of yours."

"Damn." The sheet was the standard "HIPPAA" consent form used by Westville Counseling Center, this one signed by Murphy Lumford.

"As you know, this is about the hottest case we've had in years. This form authorizes you to give me any information about Lumford that I need." She was smiling now, full crimson lips just shy of gloating.

Caleb scowled down at the signature on the form. "What can I tell you that you don't already know? He confessed to the shootings. You've got about a dozen eyewitnesses. You have the murder weapon. What do you need from me?"

Her gaze wavered. She lifted the coffee cup to her mouth, blowing before sipping. A red half moon appeared on the rim of the cup. "You're right, we do have a solid case against Lumford, but there's one missing piece. Motive. The solicitor's office is worried he'll plead insanity. Me, I don't know if maybe he is insane. You've seen him. Give me your professional opinion. Is he crazy or what?"

He squinted at her, unsure what he should do. She was right, the consent authorized him to tell her whatever she wanted. But sometimes clinical ethics overrode sheets of paper. "Come on, Claudia. All the solicitor has to do is have Lumford admitted to the forensics ward at the state hospital. Dozens of eager psych residents would swarm around him like sharks. You'd end up with a battery of personality tests, psych profiles, and forty-page clinical assessments. And you'd have your so-called expert witnesses chomping at the bit to have their day in court. I'm a lowly community social worker. You don't need me."

She wagged a finger at him. "Ah, but I do. Powell Mercer, the new assistant solicitor, has been assigned to this case. You know him?"

"Nah. I saw his picture in the paper. Looks sort of like Richard Nixon, only without the boyish charm."

She rolled her eyes. "He's tough. And very political. Mercer loves it that this case has so much media attention. He's playing up Murphy Lumford as a cold-blooded assassin. His words, not mine. Mercer wants this to be a death penalty case, which means he needs to kill any chance for an incompetency or insanity plea. He has no plans for any psych testing or anything else that could potentially distract from his case."

The waitress reappeared, oozing sultriness. "Cheese omelet," she said, in a breathy, knowing way, and set the plate in front of Claudia. "A bagel, cream cheese on the side." She smiled at Caleb, tilting her head so that her blond hair cascaded down over her cheek and into her cleavage. Not a bad way to encourage tips.

Claudia seemed oblivious to the sultry waitress, who drifted away from their table. Claudia continued, "Lumford's playing right into Mercer's hand. He's doing nothing to defend himself, he's declined counsel. Eventually, a judge will order court appointed counsel, but he needs a lawyer right now. Someone who'll make sure he gets the testing and psychiatric care he needs. I mention this to Lumford, he says, 'No way.' I think he wants the death penalty. Which seems pretty insane to me."

"Well, well, well." Caleb popped a quarter of the bagel in his mouth as he scrutinized his breakfast companion. "Let me see if I have this right. You're worried that Murphy Lumford is really wacko and won't get a fair defense. And all this time, I thought it was the police's job to make sure the *prosecution* had a good case. Why are you switching sides here?"

It looked like his question made her uncomfortable. She lifted the cloth napkin from her lap and wiped the edges of her mouth with great care, mulling. "I guess I just want to be sure Lumford has a fair go of it. And honestly, not having a motive is a huge hole in our case. Anyway, I've spent hours in interrogation with him and he's a strange little guy. He readily admits to the shooting, but shows no remorse, which is why Mercer sees him as an assassin. To me, that just doesn't fit. He doesn't have that anti-social glint in his eye. He doesn't play the manipulative games we always see, where the bad guy cries buckets, faking remorse, playing for sympathy. Lumford's always polite, always candid, and says without flinching that he shot those people. But he never says why."

Caleb nodded. Her assessment matched his, and Claudia looked just as confused as he was. "So what does your boss say about all this?"

"Captain Bentille is giving me a free hand. He knows that if we find motive we strengthen our case."

Caleb raised skeptical brows at her. After Sam's ordeal last year, Caleb didn't exactly trust Captain Frank Bentille. "So what exactly do you want from me?"

She reached over and tapped the consent form. "This says you got to tell me everything you know about Lumford. Out with it."

It still didn't feel right. Lumford was self-destructive. He may have signed the consent form without caring about the consequences. "Tell you what. I've got Murphy Lumford scheduled this afternoon. I want to hear from his mouth exactly what he wants me to disclose. Then we'll talk."

"You do understand that I'm trying to help."

"Yes. You seem to want to save Lumford from himself. And I'll give you what I have, if he tells me he understands and agrees." He glanced down at his watch. He was ten minutes away from the center, and his first appointment was probably already waiting. "I gotta go, Claudia."

She leaned forward and laid her hand on his, stopping him. It was an uncharacteristic gesture. When he looked in her eyes, they seemed to be pleading with him. "Call me, Caleb. As soon as you finish your session with him."

"Okay."

She released his hand to reach for the bill and he let her take it. He stood, thanked her for breakfast, and promised to be in touch before leaving work that day.

chapter eleven

Trish Havenaugh, Caleb's nine o'clock appointment, told him all about her miserable evening with her miserable husband and his miserable parents. Apparently, the medicine she took to control her depression had no effect on her depressing home life. Trish was thinking of leaving her husband, she told Caleb for the seven hundredth time, and going back to school. Maybe she'd get a degree in counseling, maybe find a job helping people. She could do it, he reminded her once again, if she set her mind on it. Caleb hoped the tedium didn't show on his face. He needed to confront her again about the rut she'd dug for herself, but he didn't have the energy today. When their session ended, she thanked him and walked out, back to the life that was slowly suffocating her.

Janice intercepted him in the hall to tell him that his intake appointment had canceled and hand him Helen Fleck's chart.

"Mind reader," he said.

"It's not like her to forget to show at all. I mean, she may come an hour late, or two days early, but she always comes. I hope she's okay."

"Me, too. We ever hear from her son?"

"Maybe he didn't get the message."

"Or he didn't care enough to call," Caleb said bitterly.

Janice looked down at Helen's chart. "It's a shame. She's a fine person. Always smiling, always a kind word. It's not her fault she has this awful illness."

Caleb smiled into her soft, pillowy face, grateful for Janice's empathy, grateful someone else in the world cared what happened to Helen Fleck. "I'll call when I find her."

It had been two years since he last visited Helen's apartment. Back then, she belonged to a discussion group at the library, volunteered at an adult day care center, and wrote movie reviews for a senior citizen's newsletter. It was hard to think of all the changes in Helen, now that the Alzheimers infiltrated every aspect of her life.

Caleb drove down Legare Street into the Briarwood area, Helen's neighborhood. Clusters of small homes and duplexes lined poorly-kept narrow streets. Steady pedestrian traffic streamed down the rutted sidewalks, particularly the ones close to the small liquor store. Behind that popular establishment were the projects—housing for the poor, in the form of claustrophobic shoe-box apartments—lined up in endless rows like freight cars. A seven-foot chain-link fence, topped with three rows of barbed wire, enclosed the projects. Caleb wasn't sure if it kept the bad element out or in.

He turned down the street behind the projects, took a left onto Helen's street and parked in front of her duplex. The porch light was on, and envelopes bulged out of her mailbox. He stepped out of the truck, immediately noticing street activity close to Helen's house. A cluster of older men passed around a bottle poorly concealed in a crumpled paper sack. A half block down from them, two gangly adolescents cursed, posturing nose-to-nose, poking each other into a fight.

Beyond the boys, a dilapidated, abandoned home hid behind a curtain of kudzu vines. The windows with broken out panes looked like eyeless sockets. The front porch sagged, steps in front missed crucial pieces of wood. The weed-choked yard, covered with broken bottles and garbage, was probably home to rats and other vermin. This shack had all the makings of a crack house. And it was directly across from Helen.

He rang Helen's doorbell. He thought he heard stirring inside, but the door didn't open. He rang the bell again, and once more heard a muffled noise. "Helen? It's me, Caleb. Open up!" he yelled into the door. This brought a flurry of sounds. A chain lock rattled, bolts clicked, and finally, the door creaked open.

"Caleb. How lovely to see you," she said softly. He could barely see her in the muted light.

"Hey, lady. I was getting worried about you. Can I come in for a minute?" He thought he caught a flicker of smile, a glimpse of yellow, neglected teeth. The door opened wider allowing him to step inside.

Helen's living room had a musty smell, like the air itself was antique. A radio somewhere played an old Dean Martin song. Dark drapes over the windows sealed out any trace of sunlight, and a lone table lamp did meager battle against cave-like darkness. He squinted at the walls until he located a light switch and flipped it on.

"Helen!" He rushed to her, sickened by what he found. Helen had been beaten. One side of her face was a puffy mass of teal and red. Specks of dried blood encrusted her lip and chin. Her left arm cradled her right elbow, which looked swollen and painful. "What happened to you?"

"Caleb! How nice of you to stop by. Won't you stay for tea?" Her enthusiastic smile contrasted with the tears glistening in her eyes.

"Come over here and tell me what happened." He guided her over to the old sofa and supported her injured arm as she took a seat.

She whispered, "Did we lock the door after you came in?"

"I think so, but I'll double check." He stepped around the cluttered coffee table and tugged on the door knob, the lock seemed sound. He slid the chain lock into its slot for added security. "All locked up," he said, returning to the sofa. "Now, tell me what happened to you."

"What day is it?"

He blinked at her, reminding himself that the illness and recent events made her even more confused. "It's March seventh."

"So three days ago was the fourth, when my check from Jeffrey comes. I always know to be home then, and the mailman rings my bell so I can sign for it." She paused a moment, then continued, "I keep a calendar on my refrigerator so I won't forget. And he reminds me, too, if he sees me. He'll say 'remember tomorrow, Mrs. Fleck,' to help me." She smiled then, warmed by thoughts of her friendly postman.

"So did something happen with your check?" Caleb coaxed.

"The door bell rang, and I asked, 'Who is it?', and Mr. Lawson said he had my check, so I opened it. I signed for it and wished him a good day, and he said he thought it might rain later. We need rain, you know. My pansies aren't doing well at all."

"So the postman handed you the check and—"

"And he left. I thought he did, anyway. But a second later the bell rang again. So I knew it had to be him. I opened it and two men—" Her hand found its way to her mouth, stopping the words.

"It's okay now, Helen. You're okay. Tell me what happened with the two men."

"They shoved me and came in the house. I told them to leave, but they laughed. One of them asked, 'Where is it?'" She lowered her voice, imitating him. "And I said 'What?' So he replied, 'your check, bitch.' He hit me across the face and I fell to the floor. I landed on my elbow, here." She showed him the dark, swollen spot on her elbow.

"What did the men look like?" he asked, remembering the two teenagers arguing on the sidewalk.

"One was black. The other was white. He had a brown hat on and a leather jacket. He was older than the other. He was the one that knocked me down. The black kid had light skin, like coffee with cream in it. He went over to my table and found my check from Jeffrey. They took it and ran out."

Did you call the police?"

Tears streamed down her face and over her quivering lips. "They said if I did, they'd come back and kill me."

"They said that to frighten you. You're safe now, I promise." He winced, imagining how, over the past two days, she'd cowered in her home, watching from a window, too afraid to call for help.

"Are you sure you locked the front door?" she asked again.

"Positive."

"I promised Jeffrey I'd be careful."

"Does he know about the robbery? Have you talked with him?"

"He's been very busy lately, with his final exams coming up." The Jeffrey of her world was the loving, dutiful college son, not the business executive too tied up in his own life to check on a disabled mother.

"Does he know you were hurt?"

"I wouldn't want him to worry."

Caleb leaned over for a closer look at her arm. "I want to take you to get that X-rayed."

"I can't leave! Who'll watch my house?"

"We won't be gone long. Jeffrey would want you to see a doctor, wouldn't he?"

She looked in his eyes, a mixture of fear and relief spreading on her bruised face. Caleb helped her up and gently led her to the door. He used her keys to lock the deadbolt and gave the knob a jostle and push to reassure her it was secure. She froze on the porch, her gaze darting up and down the street as though looking for would-be assailants. Thankfully, the men who had been loitering on the sidewalk had disappeared. If they watched her leave, they might decide to break into the house while she was gone. Of course, that was infinitely preferable to breaking in while she was there.

Caleb helped her into the truck and drove to Westville

Memorial Hospital. Carefully, he eased her out of the passenger seat and guided her through the heavy glass doors leading to the emergency room. At the reception desk, he asked, "Is Bryant Wheeler here?"

"Yes. He's with a patient." The young man behind the glass window clicked away at a computer without looking up.

Caleb rapped on the glass. "I have a client here that needs to be seen. Could Bryant take a look at her?" He hoped using Bryant's first name would speed up the process.

It didn't. The young man handed him a stack of forms and pointed at the crowded waiting area. "Bring them back when you're done."

Caleb carried the forms to Helen and they plodded through them. She did better than he expected. She had copies of her Social Security card and Medicare documents, and managed to remember her date of birth and phone number. She did fine until the form asked her age and she replied "thirty-one." She went on to say she lived in Brooklyn, New York, with her husband and three young sons. After finishing the forms on his own, Caleb returned them to the annoying young man whose eyes never left the computer screen. It looked like they'd be waiting a while, so Caleb clicked on his cell phone and dialed the office.

"Did you find Helen?" Janice asked.

"Yeah. She's been mugged. I brought her to the hospital to get checked out. I could be a while. How are my appointments looking?"

"Your eleven o'clock is here, but she said if you didn't make it back, she'd reschedule."

"Put her down for next week and offer my heartfelt apologies. Is Matthew available?"

"I'll check." She clicked the phone on hold and Caleb groaned when the Muzak came on. Stairway to Heaven, done on organ. Hell would probably have music like that.

"Caleb? How's Helen?" Matthew asked.

"She may have a broken wrist. And she's very confused. I

doubt she's been taking the Cognex."

"She was robbed?"

"Yep. That neighborhood's gone all to hell. No way she should be staying there. Too dangerous."

"Maybe we can find a group home for her, but that will take time. Is there any family around?"

"Family's not interested. All she has is us," Caleb said dismally. "She can't go back to that apartment. The neighborhood will eat her alive."

"Okay, okay," Matthew said, and Caleb could almost see the gears turning in Matthew's mind. "Tell you what. I'll see if we can get her admitted. We need to get a neurological work-up on her, anyway, to see how far the illness has progressed. They should keep her a few days, which gives you time to work out a placement. How does that sound?"

"Thanks. I owe you one." As he hung up, he noticed Dr. Bryant Wheeler staring at him over wire-rimmed bifocals. Bryant had a chart in his hand and a harried look on his face. "How's it going, Doc?"

"You having problems with the ribs?" Bryant reached over and lifted Caleb's shirt, checking him out.

Caleb swatted him away. "No, I'm fine. But I'm here with a client." He pointed over at Helen, who was thoroughly engrossed in a Disney cartoon on a wall TV.

Bryant took a hurried glance at his watch. "What can you tell me about her?"

Caleb filled him in, letting him know about the beating and Matthew's plans to admit her for testing. Bryant promised he'd look after her and told Caleb there was no need for him to stick around. As Caleb escorted Helen to the examining area, she clung to his arm like a frightened child. He helped her on the table and said, "Dr. Wheeler will take good care of you. Then Dr. Rhyker's coming to visit you."

"Won't that be lovely!"

"He may want to keep you here for a few days. Just to make sure you're okay."

She shook her head with vehemence. "I have to go home. Who will look after my things? The children will be home from school soon and . . ." her voice trailed off.

Caleb laid a gentle hand on her shoulder. "Your children are being taken care of. Maybe Jeffrey can come down and look after your place. If not, I'll go back and get your valuables. I'll bring them to you here or put them in the safe we have at the office."

She stared up in his face, fear conflicting with her desperate need to trust him. Smiling as reassuringly as he could, he said, "You have to let us look after you, lady."

The tension melted from her face. "If I was only a few years younger, I'd make you take me out dancing."

Caleb grinned at Bryant, "Watch out for her. She's a notorious flirt."

"I'll be on my guard," Bryant said.

chapter twelve

Caleb stared down at his appointment book. The list of clients coming in that Monday was twice as long as usual. And Caleb was bone tired. It had been a strange weekend. Shannon spent most of it with Maggie, probably avoiding him. He only had one day with Julia because a roller-rink birthday party claimed her Saturday—the kid was a terror on the rink. So it was Caleb and Cleo most of the time, and even she looked bored with him. He'd almost been glad when Monday arrived, but that thought vanished when he realized what he'd be facing.

His desk phone buzzed. Time for his first client.

Murphy Lumford dragged his chains into Caleb's office and dropped into a chair so the police officer could remove the hardware. He looked pale and troubled. The red scar encircling his right eye had a brighter tint as if something had aggravated it. Caleb eyed the two officers. "You can wait outside. I'll yell if I need you."

As they left, Murphy massaged the chafed area where the cuffs had been.

"How are you feeling?" Caleb began.

"Got a bit of a headache."

"They seem to trouble you a lot. Dr. Lazarus has asked for your neurologist's records."

"I doubt they'll say much. He called them 'cluster

headaches' and gave me pills that didn't hardly touch it. Anyway, I told you how I feel about drugs. Every once in a while I'll get one that'll put me in the emergency room. They usually give me an injection that helps, but it leaves me feeling sort of mealy-headed."

"That's quite a scar around your eye there. How'd you get it?"

Murphy lifted his hand, his fingers following the puckered rim of the scar almost exactly. He didn't answer.

"Was it a fight?"

"With myself, maybe." Murphy's eyes squeezed shut as the hand pressed into the scar.

"What do you mean?"

Murphy shrugged.

"Murphy, open your eyes and look at me." Caleb's tone was firm. Lumford complied, regarding him blearily, like someone deprived of sleep. "Tell me what happened to your eye."

"I don't think so. It doesn't have anything to do with me being here. Let's talk about something else." He said it matter-of-factly, with no hint of hostility.

"What do you want to talk about?"

Murphy turned toward the window to stare out at the chilly day. "We could talk about my son. I need to talk to someone about him."

"Kevin, right?"

Murphy nodded. "This has been harder on him than I realized. He stays with my mother and they let her visit me yesterday. She said Kev's been giving her a time."

"How old is he?"

"Fourteen. Going on thirty. Kevin's always been a challenging kid, with a mind of his own, even when he was little. But he's bright, and talented, too. He draws things. I think he could be an artist someday, if he gets his act together."

"Are you pretty close to Kevin?"

"Yes. He doesn't live with me, but I still spend a lot of time with him. I didn't grow up with a father around, so I make sure Kev knows I'm here for him.

"He's had a rough couple of years. His grades dropped and he cut a few classes. Then he started hanging around with this kid, Leon Spears, and things got worse. I don't like this kid. He seems like trouble to me. I think he may even be in one of those gangs the papers talk about, but Kevin says no. Anyway, since he hooked up with this Spears kid, he's been getting in fights, missing school, staying out all night. But then, he's a teenager, so what do you expect?" Murphy looked up at Caleb, as if wanting reassurance.

"Did he get in trouble with the law?"

"A couple of times, but nothing too serious. He and Leon were caught setting fire to a mailbox last fall."

"Is Kevin into drugs?"

Murphy Lumford closed his eyes again. As his hand slid up to massage the scar, veins throbbed under the translucent flesh at his jaw.

Caleb leaned in, closing the distance between them. "You okay?"

"Damn headache again. Give me a second," Lumford whispered.

"Take all the time you need." He could tell his client was in serious pain. His lips parted, inhaling and expelling air in a controlled, rhythmic way. Caleb wondered if Murphy was easing the pain by regulating his breathing, a common relaxation technique. He noticed the flicker of Lumford's eyelids as his face turned chalky white. His hand pushed into his brow bone, fingers aligning with the bright red rim of the scar.

"Can I get you something?" Caleb asked.

"Water," he muttered.

Caleb stepped out of the office, explaining to the officers he'd be right back. He grabbed a cup from the break room and filled it at the water cooler. He was careful not to spill it as he opened the door, but the cup hit the floor when he spotted his client.

Murphy knelt on the floor, Islam-style, with his face pressed into the rug. His head moved side to side, like he was burrowing his flesh into the carpet.

"Murphy? You alright?"

Lumford jerked back, staring at Caleb through slitted eyes. "Damn headache."

Caleb stared for a moment, unsure if he should approach. He glanced back at the closed door, wondering if he should call in one of the officers, but his client didn't look threatening. He moved closer and helped him into a chair. "What were you doing on the floor?"

Again, Murphy's fingers sought out the scar, now bright red and inflamed by carpet burn. His eyes were closed tight.

"Murphy? You okay?"

"Getting there," he whispered. After a moment, he pried his eyes open and squinted into the light. "That was a bad one."

"Why were you on the floor?" Caleb repeated.

"Now you *will* think I'm nuts. I had to put pressure here." He rubbed a finger around the edge of the scar. "Sometimes the texture of carpet helps. If I rub my eyebrow against the rug, it brings a little relief. Weird, huh?"

"So that's how you got the scar," Caleb said, intrigued. "How does it help?"

"The docs say it's got something to do with vascular swelling. Pressure against this one spot kind of relieves it a little. Sometimes it makes the blood flow better up in my brain."

"What about the suicide attempt, when you had the sheet wrapped around your head?"

"I tied it around my eyes and twisted it tight. It didn't help much, though. Then the guard came in and all hell broke loose. No way I could tell them the truth. They really would think I was loony."

"How often do you have them?"

"They come in spells. I'll get two or three a day, for maybe a month, then none for a week or two. Lately, it's every few hours."

"But you don't take anything for it?"

"Not usually. I don't want to get hooked on any drugs."

"You mean like Joyce did." Caleb watched him, hoping he'd pushed a wedge into his defenses. But his client ignored him. Caleb waited a moment, then said, "Are you up to answering more questions? We were talking about Kevin. I asked you if he was using anything."

"Yes. We found out last summer he'd tried cocaine and marijuana. Given his mom's problems, well, let's just say I blew a gasket. I hate to think of him taking after her."

"So what did you do about it?"

"I took him to N.A. and Alateen. We put him on a strict curfew, and watched him real close. He seemed to get better. But now Mom says he's back with the same kids. I can't help but think he's using again."

"You know your wife's history puts Kevin at risk."

He nodded. "I should be there. I need to be there to help him."

"What would you do for him if you were there?"

"I'd keep him out of trouble. Like a father's suppose to do." His voice broke and he turned away, embarrassed.

"He's very important to you."

"He's all I have." Murphy shook his head. "Anyway, he's young. He could turn around, you know. He could turn out okay."

"Yes."

"But I'm not sure he will. And I won't be around to help out."

"Because you're in jail now. Because of the shooting."

"I didn't mean to hurt Kevin." This was the first trace of guilt Murphy Lumford had expressed. While Lumford had freely acknowledged his responsibility for the shooting, he had never before voiced any remorse.

"We don't live in a vacuum," Caleb answered. "What we do affects those around us. Your shooting those people affected many others, including your son." Caleb was careful to keep his tone neutral.

Murphy Lumford arched his head back, staring at the ceiling. "I can't expect you to understand."

"I'd sure like to. You're a bit of a mystery to me, Murphy. You come across as a decent guy, a devoted father. But you are also a man who shot three innocent people."

"Three innocent people," Lumford repeated at the ceiling.

"I have to admit, I'm perplexed. I don't know how to help you if I don't get a clue as to what's going on in your head."

"I don't want you in my head." His tone was cool.

Frustrated, Caleb swiveled his chair back and let silence hang between them. After a moment, his client looked over at him, his face softening a little. "I know you're just trying to do your job," Murphy said. "But I can't tell you anything."

"Then at least talk to a lawyer. Dealing with charges as serious as yours without legal representation is suicidal."

"No, not suicidal. My strategy is simple. I want this resolved as quickly as possible. I want my name out of the papers so Kevin and my mother can go on with their lives."

"Without you?"

"That seems obvious."

"And look how well your strategy's working. Your kid's a truant who's into drugs and God knows what else. And believe me, you'll make headlines for a long, long time. The solicitor will see to it."

Murphy cocked his head, a limp strand of greasy black hair falling over his face. "You just don't get it."

"I'm wondering if you do. You know how much your kid needs you. Yet you won't help yourself, so that you can be around for Kevin."

Murphy studied Caleb for a moment. "Are you a father?"

"Yes, I am."

"Then you know. Sometimes you have to make sacrifices."

"Sacrifices like what? Like self-destructing?"

Murphy Lumford stood up and crossed to the window that looked out on the bleak day. The sudden movement startled Caleb and made him slide his chair back a few feet. He never let himself forget this client was a murderer.

"I'm not going to hurt you," Murphy said, a sardonic flicker in his eye.

"Glad to hear it."

After a moment, Murphy added, "That police detective— Briscoe. She had me sign a release so she could talk to you. I want you to answer whatever she asks."

Caleb nodded. "I will. Because she wants you to get a fair trial, Murphy."

"Is this my last visit here?"

"Do you want it to be?"

"I think it helps."

"Okay. We'll work it out for you to come back next week. And I will talk to Claudia. She's a cop, but a fair cop."

"Thanks," Lumford said. "I appreciate you trying to help, even knowing what I did. And I want to ask you for a favor."

It surprised him. "What?"

"I want you to see my boy. I want you to be Kevin's counselor."

Caleb didn't answer at first. He was thinking of all the new clients filling his appointment book.

"I pray to God it's not too late for him. Maybe you can get through."

"Okay, I'll give it a try."

Caleb watched as the officers closed the manacles around Murphy Lumford's hands, Murphy wincing as shackles pinched flesh.

"Sorry," the younger officer said.

"It's okay. I'm getting used to it."

chapter thirteen

"Well, well, well." From his desk, Caleb squinted up at Claudia Briscoe. "The detective makes a house call."

"More like an office visit. Got a sec?" She didn't wait for a response before dropping in a chair and unzipping her portfolio. "So. Tell me everything I need to know about Murphy Lumford."

Caleb reached over, picked up a pencil, and drummed it against his desk. He soon had a nifty jazz rhythm going, but his visitor didn't seem to appreciate it. "I'll tell you about Lumford after you answer my question," he said over the syncopated beat.

"Which is?"

"Which is why are you so interested in him? I mean, I know what you said before—pursuit of justice, blah, blah, blah—but it runs deeper than that. What's up?"

She pursed her lips at him, looking quite annoyed, which happened pretty often when Caleb was around. He drummed the pencil with more vigor and decided he sounded just like Buddy Rich.

She reached out, snatching the instrument from his hand. "I think we covered this at breakfast. Breakfast I paid for."

"And it was a good breakfast, too. But I know a half-truth when I hear it." He could see stubborn resolve on her face, but he could be just as stubborn. He needed to be clear on

Claudia's motives before he discussed Lumford in any detail.

The tip of her tongue came out to moisten her lips. "Sometimes, I wish you didn't know me so well. It's awkward."

"Awkward how?"

"You were my therapist before. It was a long time ago, a lifetime ago, really. But damn, you have a good memory." There was a forced levity in her voice.

Caleb remembered his first meeting with Claudia. She'd completed the university with a degree in Criminal Justice and joined the ranks of Westville's finest. She was a bright, competent, but insecure black woman tiptoeing into the land of the "Bubbas." She was the police department's answer to affirmative action and she knew it, which didn't lessen her anxiety.

It didn't take long for her to work through her fears. Progressive relaxation took care of her anxiety symptoms. Claudia's drive and tenacity helped her work through the rest. When her superiors and colleagues realized how capable she was, the race and gender issues disappeared and she became Officer Briscoe, part of the team. Three years later, she was promoted to detective. Caleb wouldn't be surprised if she made captain one day.

"I hope you don't think I've taken advantage of our previous relationship. I would never mean to—" Caleb looked at her, looked deep into her eyes, seeing a vulnerability there he hadn't seen in years.

"I know that. And you haven't. I have always trusted your ethics." She slowly rubbed the palm of her hand against the arm of the chair. "I'm use to being tough, impenetrable. I have to be or this job would eat me alive. But you see right through it."

"Maybe I do see beyond that thick skin of yours, but I like what I see. You are a terrific lady. I wish others got a chance to see you like I do." Caleb stretched back in his chair, lacing his fingers behind his head. "So. What is it you aren't telling me about Lumford? And I'm asking that as a friend. Not as your ex-therapist. Not as police consultant."

"I guess you are, damn you. A friend I mean." She looked around the familiar office. "You remember me talking about my father?"

"Sure. He lived up north somewhere. He died a couple of years ago, right?"

She nodded. "We weren't close. My mother and grandmother raised me. He dropped into my life now and then, but never for more than a few months at a time."

It was all coming back to Caleb. Claudia's father was a rogue who had more than a few brushes with the law. He supported himself gambling and running scams, never settling in one place for very long. When he ran out of money, he'd charm his way back into her mother's life, stay long enough for young Claudia to get attached, then take off again, no warning, no goodbyes. He taught his daughter to be tough, to guard her heart. He taught her to be a survivor. "How did your father die?"

"He died of self-neglect. He drank too much, smoked too much, lived way too close to the edge. They diagnosed him with throat cancer, kept on smoking. Then he got stomach cancer, kept on drinking. He had no insurance, no savings, no way to care for himself. He died alone in a nasty little hotel outside of Fayetteville." She eulogized her father with no struggle, no emotion leaking out.

"I'm sorry."

"Like I said, we weren't close. But it was a stupid way to die. And a lonely one."

"Not many of us get to choose how we go," Caleb said reflectively.

"Yeah, well Pop did. He could have lived another ten years if he just changed a few habits and tried to take care of himself. But he wouldn't. It's like he looked death straight in the eye and toasted it with his Jack Daniels. He committed suicide in a slow, gruesome way."

"You think he wanted to die?"

"I know he did. Mama never gave up on him, even though he'd long ago given up on himself. Mama begged him to come stay with her so she could take care of him. He wouldn't come. He said life had done enough to him and he was ready to go."

"Your mother loved him?"

"To the bitter end. She misses him, even now."

"And you?" he probed.

"Me? I grieved, but mostly I was pissed at him for being so pigheaded. Then I moved on. I vowed I'd never end up like him." She stared at Caleb as though worried she'd revealed too much.

"I don't think you need to worry. You've pretty well got your life together."

"I'm named for him, you know. He was Claude Lafitte Briscoe. He was born in Louisiana. His people were Bayou people."

"Claudia suits you, but that doesn't mean you take after him."

"And I don't intend to. But this Murphy Lumford. He bothers me. And I figured it must be related to Pop. You taught me that, you know. When something nags at you and you can't figure out why, then you just figure out what it reminds you of. 'Unresolved issues,' you called them. I think Lumford wants the death penalty so the state can carry out his suicide."

Caleb nodded. "I see the similarity. Because your father wouldn't help himself."

"I don't want Lumford to use the system to carry it out. Not the system I work for. If Lumford gets a fair trial with a good defense, and then gets sentenced to death, then so be it. But thinking that Lumford can manipulate us to carry out his death sentence makes me nauseated. Do you see my point?"

"It doesn't set too well with me either."

She opened her hand, gesturing towards him. "So what can

you tell me about Lumford?"

"Not much, I'm afraid. He's a real puzzle. He isn't psychotic, at least, not that I've seen. He has some depression, but who wouldn't, given his situation? He suffers from migraine headaches that appear to be debilitating. He's divorced. His ex-wife was a drug addict. He has a teenage son who's in trouble. Lumford wants me to start counseling with the kid."

"What's his name?"

"Kevin. Age fourteen. He lives with Lumford's mother."

"I'll check with juvenile, see if they have a record on him."

"They probably do, he's been arrested before. Lumford's worried about the kid. He comes across as a normal, frustrated father, yet he's gotten himself locked up for this heinous crime. He's a tangle of contradictions."

"Has he told you why he shot those people?"

"No. He refuses to discuss it. Says it isn't pertinent." Caleb swiveled his chair back and forth as he reflected on his client.

"You have any theories? I know you love playing detective."

"Not really. I don't think it was random though. Somehow, I think Lumford planned out what he did, and I wouldn't be surprised if he knew exactly who he wanted to hit. I know it sounds strange, given the way he fired those shots."

Claudia pointed her finger like it was a pistol. "He held out the gun, fired. Turned, fired again. Turned once more, fired again. When he completed the circle, he laid down his gun."

"But he didn't just splay bullets around everywhere, did he? It's like he knew who he was aiming for. Lumford strikes me as a careful, methodical person. That's why I think he knew exactly what he was doing."

She clicked her nails against the chair, looking pensive. "It's an interesting theory. We haven't established if the three victims were connected. They all worked the same shift, but in different areas. Buck Swygert was a floor manager. Mike

Beard, an electrician. His specialty was troubleshooting whenever there was a problem, so he worked all over the plant. Sally Weston was new, she did production work."

"Are Beard and Weston saying much?"

"Beard's been pretty sedated. He had a nasty wound, but he's stable. Weston says she'd only met Lumford once." Claudia shook her head. "It wouldn't hurt to dig a little deeper. Talk to Swygert's family and associates. Run a background check on all of the victims, see what comes up. Question more of the workers from that shift." She opened the portfolio and started jotting down notes on a paper with the heading: "To Do List." Caleb had one of those once, but lost it.

"Your boss gonna be okay with you opening this can of worms?" Caleb asked.

She smiled. "Captain Bentille is no fan of Powell Mercer, so he wants me to make the best case I can. I told him I was talking to you."

Caleb raised his brows at that. "Well, give him my love."

She stood, straightened her skirt, and zipped up the portfolio.

"Before you rush off, any news on the Callahan murder? Do you know who assaulted me yet?" Caleb asked.

The end of her ballpoint found its way up to her mouth and dangled there like a cigarette needing a light. "We're making headway. I can't give you specifics, of course." She hesitated, then added, "Ms. Wells's boyfriend, that Barry Waters. How well do you know him?"

"Well enough to want to steer clear. Shannon thinks he's dangerous. I usually trust her opinion."

"She could be right. Off the record—and I mean that, Caleb—Waters has been under investigation by narcotics. I wouldn't spend too much time in his company."

"Thanks for the warning."

She opened the door. "You get any brilliant insights about Lumford, let me know."

"You, too, Claudia."

At six that evening, Caleb locked the door to the office behind him and stood out on the back porch, marveling at the brilliant sunset sky. The sun hung on ribbons of gold, coral, and crimson. A lace of clouds muted the colors just at the horizon. Soon, the sun would plop down, putting itself to bed, and night would bring another chill. But at that moment, the breathtaking dusk was the perfect apology for what had been a cold, leaden day.

As the color faded, Caleb got into his truck and cranked it awake. He eased onto Harwood Street, passing the small Presbyterian church. The crisp white lines of its steeple etched on the cardboard gray of the twilight sky. He'd always appreciated the church for its simplicity. It looked like a small village church where everyone knew each other. A Walton family church. Not that Caleb had ever attended there, or anywhere else in recent years. He'd given up organized religion before puberty and doubted he'd ever find his way back.

He turned onto Sumter Street, where the Calvary Free Will Baptist Church had its empire. It was the biggest church in Westville; a billboard overhead attested to it. It occupied two city blocks with its new gymnasium, new church school building, and new sanctuary that could hold a thousand people. Matthew called the Calvary Baptist complex "Six Flags over Westville."

Every Sunday, Calvary's service aired on live TV. Impassioned gospel singers with gravity-defying hair sang into microphones and wiped tears of Christian joy from their eyes. It was more entertaining than the Grand Ole Opry, although Caleb preferred the twenty-four hour aquarium station.

Caleb headed right on Main Street and found a parking spot in the crowded visitor's lot at Westville Memorial Hospital. He needed to check on Helen Fleck. Since he'd had no success reaching her son, she would be all alone yet again. Where were all those good Christians when you needed them?

"Hey, lady. You awake?" Caleb slipped through the door to Helen's hospital room. Helen lay propped up in bed. A cast enclosed her right arm which rested on a triangular piece of foam. Her dim brown eyes stared at a game show on a suspended TV. Caleb pulled a chair close to her bed and squeezed her good hand. "What ya watching?"

She looked down at his hand, which was as big as a bear's paw compared to hers. "Hello there," she said to it.

"Hello yourself. How are you feeling?"

"I'm just dandy." A weak smile inched across her face. "Are you here to take me home?"

Caleb leaned closer so that their faces were at the same level. "No. You have to spend the night so that Dr. Rhyker and Dr. Wheeler can run a few tests on you, remember? I've been trying to call your son, Jeffrey, so that he could come and check on you. But I can't seem to reach him."

"Well now, boys will be boys." She arched her penciled-in eyebrows at Caleb knowingly. "He's been so busy. Soccer season takes up a great deal of his time."

Caleb squeezed her hand again. "You and I have talked about how this illness messes with you. It confuses your thinking and your memory. Jeffrey isn't playing soccer now. That was twenty years ago. Jeffrey works at a bank. He's married now, and lives in Virginia. Do you remember that?"

"How silly you are!" She clicked her tongue, berating him. "Jeffrey tells me he'll be a doctor when he grows up. Now Mitchell might be a banker. That child loves to count things. Alford is my dreamer . . . he'll be a poet or an artist, I think." She closed her eyes like she was imagining her boys all grown up.

"Helen," Caleb said firmly. "Alford is a lawyer. Mitchell teaches at a private school in New Jersey. Jeffrey lives in Richmond with his family. I've been trying to get him down here to help you."

His tone startled her and she pulled her hand away. "I want to go home."

"No. You have to spend the night here." Frustration and fatigue from this endless day was leaking out and he immediately regretted it.

Helen's eyes moistened and she turned away. "I'm sorry. Don't be mad at me," she whispered, choking on her words.

"Ah, Helen." He sighed deeply, hating himself for the pain in her expression. "It's okay. Now look at me."

Like an obedient child, she did as instructed. He rewarded her with a soft smile. "Remember me now? I'm Caleb, your counselor."

"Caleb! How lovely to see you. Can I get you some tea?"

"No, Helen. I don't need a thing."

The door swung open and Bryant Wheeler stuck his head in. "Hey, Caleb. Can I see you?"

Caleb told Helen he'd be right back and followed Bryant out the door. "She's more confused than I've ever seen her," Caleb said.

"Her neurologist says she's sundowning. Often patients with dementia experience a worsening of the confusion and disorientation at this particular time of day. We don't really know why. Some say it's the change in the light brought on by sunset. Some claim it's neural fatigue."

"I've heard of sundowning but I've never actually seen it." Caleb looked at Helen's door. This disease was cruel. "How bad's the arm?"

"It's a simple fracture. But the neurologist agreed with you and Matthew, she needs a work up. She's been off the Cognex for four or five days, which accounts for some of her decompensation. We put her back on it, so she may be a bit more lucid tomorrow." Bryant pulled off his wire-rimmed glasses and rubbed his eyes with the back of his hand.

"Long shift?"

"Interminable! We're down a staff physician in the ER, so

I'm pulling double shifts. I tell you, I'm too old for this."

"Whatever happened to that kid in the ER? The one who tried to bite you."

"He had a couple of seizures. I wouldn't be surprised if he had permanent brain damage, but we won't know for sure because he walked out of here against medical advice. Emergency medicine ain't what it used to be."

"You love it and you know it. You get off on the adrenalin rush. You'd go completely bonkers if you had a quiet little family practice in the 'burbs."

"Yeah, yeah. But I could do a specialty. Maybe get into plastics. Three days a week, I'd do tummy tucks and breast enlargements. The rest of the time, I'm on the golf course . . ." He pantomimed a golf swing that sent an invisible ball way down the corridor.

"I've been thinking of getting my nose done. So I'll look even more like Brad Pitt," Caleb said.

"Then again, maybe I should try proctology."

"I don't think I could play cards with you any more."

Bryant's beeper squawked and he squinted down at it. "Better get going. I'll keep you posted on Ms. Fleck." He walked briskly away, his open lab coat flapping behind him.

When Caleb returned to Helen's room, she had dozed off with her head tilted to the side and her glasses dangling off the end of her nose. Caleb watched her for a moment, wondering how her sons could abandon her. Of course, there had been the drinking years. There must have been many disappointments and broken promises.

Caleb thought about his own father, Samuel Knowles, Sr. His alcoholism had darkened Caleb's childhood, the addiction running the gamut. He could be the gregarious drunk, full of bluster and jokes or the belligerent drunk, full of rage and venom. The vicious battles that erupted left mental and physical scars on the Knowles children. Then would come the thick-tongued apologies, the promises to quit drinking. And, perhaps the most damaging of all, their mother's heart-wrenching pleas that if the boys just behaved maybe their father wouldn't need to suck down his bourbon.

Caleb couldn't leave home soon enough. After his parents finally divorced, he rarely visited his father. Those scars never quite healed. Maybe that was how it was for Jeffrey, and for Helen's other sons.

He reached over and tapped her good arm. "Helen? Wake up, lady."

She opened groggy eyes and smiled up at him.

"Is there anything you want from your home?" he asked her. "Anything you need me to put somewhere safe?"

Her eyelids drooped down, as if fighting the pull towards sleep. "My papers," she murmured. "I keep them in my bureau in the bedroom. An' my mother's opal. It's in a pink sock. In my stocking drawer. Get them for me, Caleb. Don't let those men have my things." She pointed down at the cabinet by her hospital bed. Caleb opened it and retrieved her purse. Weakly, Helen fumbled with the clasp until it snapped open. She handed Caleb her house keys. "The boys will be home from school soon. See that they get a snack."

Dusk had come and gone. Lingering clouds webbed across a three-quarter moon; city lights blinked on across the horizon, turning the sky a pinkish gray. Caleb zipped his jacket as he headed out to his truck.

He knew it was too late to be heading into the projects, but he'd promised Helen. And her unoccupied house, at night, would be an easy invitation to a thief. He needed to move her things into the office safe before it was too late.

As he turned on Legare Street, he was struck by a strange, unsettling awareness—the projects had a very different feel from before. Too few streetlights pierced the darkness. No cars moved on the silent roads. On the sidewalk, Caleb could barely make out the shapes of young men coming out to reclaim the streets.

He parked as close as he could to Helen's place, climbed

out, and surveyed the surroundings. The winos from the afternoon had disappeared, but he spotted movement in the abandoned house across the street. He squinted, trying to adjust to the darkness, and caught a flash of red as a figure passed by the broken out window. A second later, two young men in matching red jackets ambled up the sidewalk. Each jacket had an insignia on the back, a long knife dripping with blood. The men took no notice of Caleb as they headed into the abandoned house.

Caleb jogged up the walk and unlocked Helen's door, hoping to get in and out of there as quickly as possible. Despite the chill, temperatures on her street were on the rise.

He hit the lights and headed straight for Helen's bedroom. She had heavy, dark furniture, straight from the 1930s, that was in sore need of refinishing. The scarred headboard of her single bed was concealed by the dozen brightly covered pillows that topped a flowered comforter. Lace doilies that reminded Caleb of his old Aunt Martha's living room covered every available surface in the room, including a small chipped table lamp.

Caleb pulled out drawers in Helen's bureau, finding a stack of papers gathered in a satin ribbon. He thumbed through insurance documents and bank information, along with a few handwritten letters that Helen probably treasured. He tucked the papers under his arm.

Adrenalin had him moving fast. He opened more drawers until he found her socks. He groped the toes of several cotton crews, located the opal pin, and slipped it in his pocket. He collected four framed photos of Helen's children and grandchildren, bundling them up in a nightgown. He jerked the closet door open and grabbed a terry robe, house shoes, and a blue dress. It felt strange, handling her things like that. It felt invasive.

He checked around the room one more time to see if he'd missed anything important. On the night stand, he spotted a worn leather Bible and added it to the pile. He made his way over to the window before heading out. The moon sent out a little more light and he spotted a rusted out junker parked at the end of the block. In the abandoned house, two men in red jackets came out to the porch. One pointed to the street.

Coming up the sidewalk were three other men, two black, one white. They wore matching black jackets, bomber-style, with immense shoulders and a strange, swirling gold insignia on a patch on the left side. They moved slowly, swaggering abreast each other, as if their approach had been choreographed. They stopped in front of the house.

The two men on the porch didn't speak, but the three newcomers had a lot to say. Something about the "fucking money" and the "fucking deal for the fucking stuff." Voices grew louder, hands gestured threateningly. The situation was about to explode.

Two other men came out of the house to join their colleagues on the porch. The red jackets out numbered the black jackets by one and the yelling reached siren level. Caleb glanced over the living room until he found the telephone and dialed 911. He gave the dispatcher Helen's address and hung up.

They were all screaming now, gesturing home-boy style with the backs of their hands. Soon weapons would come out of those jackets. There would be a bloodbath. How long would it take the police?

But then the police didn't rush to answer calls in this neighborhood, he thought. Gang warfare often turned deadly, and the gang members had no respect for badges.

Like a driver passing a car crash, Caleb couldn't tear his eyes away from the altercation. They were just kids, really. No more than sixteen, seventeen years old. They probably grew up hungry and poor. They were taken in by "the streets," which had its own culture, its own pecking order. And the streets turned them into soldiers. Soon—too soon— these soldiers would be dead.

If he could just distract them until the police arrived. The social worker in Caleb reared its ugly head. He sucked in a deep breath and reminded himself that what he was about to do only proved he needed professional help. He opened the front door.

He ambled out onto the porch. Out of the corner of his eye, he watched heads turning toward him. He'd been seen, just like he wanted. "Hey! Hey there! How ya'll doing?" He yelled out in his thickest southern drawl. "I'm new here. Come to see my Mama. My name's Bud. What's yours?" He waved boisterously at them and plastered a wide moronic grin on his face. "Sure is gettin' cold tonight, I tell you what!"

The three adolescents on the sidewalk mumbled and poked at each other, confused by the idiot white man.

"My mama didn't tell me it would get this cold, no sirree!" Caleb shook his head in amazement over the brisk 50-degree weather. His eyes stayed fixed on the cluster of jacketed men.

"We don't fuckin' care!" One of the men yelled from the porch.

"Now, watch your language," Caleb said. "The Lord don't like nobody with a filthy mouth! Have you found the Lord? Have you accepted Jesus as your Lord and Savior?" He waved the Bible at them, then drew it to his chest and clapped his hands together prayerfully.

"Shut the fuck up!" the man bellowed.

His larger colleague laid a pacifying hand on his shoulder and said, "He's mental. Be cool."

"*I'm* cool, I tell you what!" Caleb yelled. He unbuttoned Helen's flamingo pink robe and slipped it on, then twirled in a circle for his admirers across the street.

"He don't shut up, I'll do it for him." The shorter man reached in his pocket and pulled out something. Caleb knew it was probably a gun, probably aimed at him. There were five men over there. With guns. And one of him.

The idiot white man armed with a nightgown and a Bible.

"Why don't you go inside to your Mama?" One of the red

jackets asked. It sounded like an appeal, with the subtext, *Do it for your own good*. Caleb decided it was a sound idea.

"Well, okay. I was just being friendly and all. I reckon it's close to supper time and . . ."

Three squad cars careened onto the street, two from the south, one from the north. The cruisers jumped the curb in front of the dilapidated house and focused spot lights on the dispersing gang members.

"It's the fuckin' cops!" One of the red jackets yelled as spotlights swept over them. Caleb crouched down behind the porch rail and waited.

The three red jackets took off south, jumping a fence and disappearing into the night. The men on the porch ran inside where more yelling erupted. The officers shouted warnings, drew guns, and converged on the house. A few minutes later, they returned to the yard without any prisoners. Caleb heard the creak of leather as guns reentered holsters. One of the officers announced into the police radio that the suspects had dispersed, but a variety of illegal drugs had been confiscated from the abandoned house.

From the darkness, Caleb called out, "Officers, I'm Caleb Knowles. I called you."

A flashlight beam shot towards him and he waved into the cone of light. "You'd better walk over here, Mr. Knowles."

Caleb eased forward onto the steps. One arm clutched Helen's belongings, he held the other in the air as he approached an officer who looked vaguely familiar. "I'm a social worker. I was visiting a client's home and noticed some suspicious activity over here. So I called you."

"Hold it right there." The policeman came up close with his light, a black officer approached from his left. Caleb froze in his tracks, aware that in Helen's bathrobe, he was one suspicious looking fellow.

"Knowles." The man shone the light in his eyes. "You Detective Briscoe's friend?"

Caleb nodded, recognizing the buzz-cut man. "Hey,

Officer Wright. Any idea who those kids were?"

"Those 'kids' were gang members. We got two local gangs tangling with each other for the past month. They're competing for the drug trade around here. We've had a couple of shootings already. You probably just prevented another."

"Postponed it, more likely," the young black officer said, shaking his head in disgust. "They'll meet up again. And we'll get called to collect the bodies."

Caleb looked at him, surprised to hear so much cynicism from someone his age. "So you don't think our Governor's Hugs not Drugs campaign is working?"

The officer let out a howl at that. Officer Wright shone his flashlight at the robe Caleb had on and asked, "Care to explain your get-up?"

"I think you police people call this a diversion. It's the only thing I could think of to keep them from killing each other."

"Well you sure found a creative way of doing that." He took out a notepad and asked Caleb a series of standard questions. He explained to Caleb that the young men in red jackets belonged to the Blades, an up-and-coming gang around the projects. The black jackets were from the City Lords, an older, more established gang, with a monopoly on Westville's drug trade. "Of course, you being a social worker and all, you probably think these kids just need a little love and understandin'."

"I think they need to stop being hoodlums so maybe they'll live to see twenty."

chapter fourteen

It was close to nine P.M. when Caleb finished locking Helen's belongings in the office safe. He was famished, tired, and cranky. Westville used to be a quiet little town, he reflected. If someone vandalized an abandoned building, that was an *event*. Now there were drugs and gangs and murders. Now children had guns.

He didn't want this climate for his daughter. He pictured her across town in his ex-wife's home, probably arguing about bedtime and pleading for more stories to be read. He wanted her to have a hometown where the streets were safe and her innocence protected until maybe age thirty-five or so. But then his mind flashed to Emma Callahan, whose innocence had been snatched away at the ripe old age of four. So damn unfair, he thought.

Instead of turning toward home, he found himself headed to Sam's, to a visit he had been avoiding. When he pulled in Sam's drive, the van was missing, which probably meant Sam had run out for supplies or take-out supper. Caleb could afford to wait a while, he had nowhere else to be. He parked the truck and climbed the back steps. He knew were Sam's house key was hidden, but elected to wait outside. The frosty air felt good.

He sat at the top of the porch steps and looked up at the night sky. It was so quiet here, except for the faint whisper of a chilling breeze. Sometimes, when it was silent like this, Caleb thought about how Sam's world was like this all the time. There was never music in the air for him. Never laughter. Never the welcomed sound of a familiar voice.

The van parked in its usual spot and Sam climbed out. He had on ancient jeans, covered in sawdust, holes exposing both knees, and a tattered flannel shirt he'd had since college. He ambled up the walk and stopped in front of Caleb, peering down. "You look familiar. Red hair. Weird eyes, like a product of alien cross-breeding. Too skinny." Sam pondered. "I used to have a brother, looked like you. I wonder whatever happened to him."

Caleb looked up to grimace at him. Sam's face didn't look amused.

"So," Sam said.

Caleb wiped a hand over his face and said, "I was sort of in the neighborhood."

Sam reached over and tapped his hand. "You're already out of practice. Either move your hand from in front of your face or sign it."

"Damn," Caleb berated himself. "I mean, sorry." He circled a closed fist over his heart.

"Come inside where I can see you better."

Caleb followed him through the back door and watched as he turned on the track lighting. That done, Sam turned and looked at him. "You don't look so good. How are the ribs?"

"Sore." He signed a fist with the thumb extended, which he pressed and twisted against his chin. "Wanna see?" He didn't wait for Sam to answer. He lifted his sweater and pointed to the purple bruise radiating out from the ace bandage. It was something they'd done since kindergarten, comparing scars and cuts and scraped knees.

Sam looked grim. "Shannon told me what happened. Lucky you weren't killed. Have the police caught them yet?"

"No."

"Do they think it has something to do with Fran's

murder?"

Caleb lowered the sweater and signed, "They're looking into that. But Claudia isn't saying a whole lot."

Sam brought him a soda. "You should have told me what happened the other night."

Caleb didn't answer, remembering how he hadn't told Sam the truth because he'd been pissed off that night and was acting all of about twelve years old. He wondered if he should mention what he'd just been through in the projects, but couldn't imagine signing the scene of him wearing Helen's bathrobe.

So the brothers sat across from each other, a loud silence hanging between them. Caleb started to sign something, but couldn't think of what to tell his hands to say. Instead, he rubbed them together, then laid them on his knees. Sam sipped and waited. After a moment, Caleb set down the drink and signed, "I know about Matthew. About his being gay. You knew already, though."

Sam leaned forward, serious eyes fixed on Caleb's face and hands. "Yes."

"You know about his friend?"

"Ben? I met him when I did that work at Matthew's a few years ago. Ben helped me out. That massive banister I made, and the mantle—Ben helped with the sanding and the installation. He's a real decent guy. He always treated me, I don't know. Normal, I guess."

Normal. Such a simple thing, such a simple request of humanity. Deaf people, mentally ill people, even gay people—just wanted to be treated like everyone else. Caleb looked over at his brother, guilt gnawing at him.

"I wasn't sure if they were still together. Matthew was with another guy last time I saw him," Sam added.

Caleb squirmed at the image of his boss out on a "date."

"So you're having one hell of a time, little brother. How are you holding up?"

Caleb stared into his own drink, measuring his words

carefully. "Okay. How are things going with your move?"

"I told you I don't know that I'm moving. I'm going to Atlanta next week. I want to stay a few days there, try to get a better feel for it. Tessa has a couple of gallery owners lined up to meet with me, and wants me to check out some studio space. But that doesn't mean I've made up my mind yet."

"Atlanta's a huge, busy place. Maybe twenty times the size of Westville."

"Yep. Tessa says there are two espresso bars for every resident."

"All that caffeine, you'll be working around the clock again. Churning out masterpiece after masterpiece. Making more money than Ted Turner," he signed.

"You really think so? Or do you think I'll fall on my butt? Give me your honest opinion."

Caleb started to pour out the usual platitudes: You'll do great Sam, We're all proud of you Sam, They'll be lucky to have you, Sam. But he thought better of it. "My honest opinion? Okay. But first, let me apologize in advance for pissing you off."

He noticed his brother stiffening.

Caleb went on, "I have no doubt that your career will continue to take off. That would happen here or in Atlanta or in Bora Bora, for that matter."

Sam looked perplexed so Caleb letter signed "Bora Bora" more slowly which made Sam look even more confused. Caleb studied his hands, wondering what to tell them to say next. Then suddenly, he signed, "Let me buy your bike."

"What?"

"Your bike. I'll buy it from you."

"You don't ride. You always tell me you're allergic to exercise."

"I'm gonna start. And it will be here when you're in town. Sell it to me."

"I ordered that bike from Italy. Get yourself a Schwinn. You'd probably need training wheels."

"I want yours."

Sam squinted at him. "You're not making any sense."

Caleb rubbed his hands together, then signed, "Here comes the part where I piss you off. I want you to leave your bike here because I don't want you to have it in Atlanta. I don't want you riding it there. Atlanta's a huge place with awful traffic. People drive like maniacs.

"You are an excellent cyclist but you are deaf. It scares the hell out of me to think of you in downtown Atlanta. After happy hour, some drunk weaving down the road, you can't hear him coming . . ." Caleb looked down at his hands, they were moving so fast and he didn't mean for them to. Something was leaking out, in his signing, on his face.

Sam noticed it, too. But he didn't understand it, Caleb could tell.

"Sorry," Caleb signed.

"I do realize that I'm deaf. I'm very careful."

"I'm not doubting you. But Atlanta. When you drive around in the van, at least you're protected. But on that bike, there's nothing between you and disaster." Caleb's hands trembled a little.

Sam held his gaze steady on Caleb for a long moment. Finally, he asked, "You're thinking about my accident, aren't you?"

Suddenly, memories flooded through Caleb's head: Sam laughing on the back of that Harley Davidson, without a helmet, Mom answering the phone, the unforgettable sound of her screaming. Then waiting, hour after interminable hour, for news. Dad calling to say Sam was bleeding in his head and unconscious and saying that they wouldn't know anything definite for a long time. And Caleb hearing the edge in his Dad's voice that said, *Why did it have to be Sam? Why couldn't it have been you?*

Sam studied him, seeing deeper than Caleb wanted him to. "You okay?"

"Not really."

"Would it help if I promise not to ride in the downtown area? I'm not suicidal, you know."

"Yes, it would help. I'd have less to worry about."

"And God knows, you do worry." Sam forced a weak smile and added, "So what else is going on? What aren't you telling me?"

Caleb shook his head. "I guess I'm just on overload. I shouldn't be trying to have a rational conversation with you right now. I should be locked in a cave somewhere."

"That's something we've all thought for years." Sam laid a hand on Caleb's shoulder and squeezed. "Talk to me."

Caleb ran both hands down his face, wishing he could erase the expression that was surely betraying him. "Shannon and I aren't going to make it. I guess that's no big surprise. She'll be moving out once everything's resolved with Maggie."

Sam glared at him, stunned. "You are such an idiot. Shannon is the best thing that ever happened to you. You guys are crazy about each other. So of course you're splitting up."

"It isn't exactly my idea, Shannon's the one who isn't happy. She wants something better. She wants a husband and a family and she deserves all that. I can't really blame her."

Sam made exasperated, growly noises at him. "You love her. She loves you desperately. Fix it."

"I can't give her what she wants, Sam."

"Seems to me, you're the only one who can. She wants to build a life with you, maybe have a kid. So do it."

"God, if it was only that easy."

"It is that easy. You're the one that's making it so damn complicated. I know you're still gun shy after the divorce from Mariel and I understand the idea of getting married again absolutely terrifies you. But Shannon is not Mariel. It won't be the same this time, Caleb."

Caleb couldn't find a reason to go on with this. Sam didn't understand. How could he, when Caleb didn't understand it himself? He thanked Sam for the soda and the advice, reached for his keys, and walked to his truck.

Caleb unlocked the kitchen door to find Chinese take-out containers lining the table. He opened the refrigerator, grabbed a beer, then looked around for Maggie and Shannon, who were nowhere to be found. Climbing the stairs, he heard music from the bedroom. "Shannon?"

"In here!" she called out from the bathroom.

"Can I come in?"

"Sure." He slipped open the door and a steamy fog rolled out. She lay in the tub surrounded by frothy bubbles, a half-filled glass of wine perched beside her. Her hair was gathered clumsily on the top of her head.

"You look like Pebbles. Julia would be very impressed."

"Uh huh," she said dreamily.

"Where's Maggie?"

"Off with Barry." She closed her eyes and slid down, letting the water close over her for a second before pulling herself back up and brushing the foam from her face.

"Getting relaxed?"

"Uh huh." She wiggled her arms to stir the water and more steam crawled up.

"Sorry I'm so late."

"It's okay. You said you had a million clients." She took a sip of wine. "I cooked dinner for us."

"I know. I saw the containers." Caleb closed the toilet seat and sat down. God, she was beautiful, he thought, his eyes sweeping across her. He could make out the muted contours of her breasts, the splash of pink just above the bubbles. A familiar stirring strained against his chinos.

"How's your chest?" she asked.

"Fine. I hardly feel it now."

"That's good," she said, all whispery. Her eyelids pulled down again so that she looked almost asleep, like she rested on the edge of a dreamy other-world.

He couldn't tear his eyes from her. At that moment, she was the most beautiful woman he'd ever seen. He ached for her. He wanted to pull off his clothes and join her in the tub, to wrap himself in her arms, to merge with her, as liquid as that warm, swirling water.

Maybe Sam was right. He should be able to give her what she wanted. She would be a wonderful wife, a terrific step-mom for Julia. It was Caleb who was the problem. He couldn't imagine becoming a husband again, giving all that trust to another person. Even if that person was this gorgeous creature in the tub.

"Caleb, are you looking at me?" she asked breathily, from behind her closed eyes.

"Yes, I am." He wondered if she heard his pulse thudding.

"And what are you thinking about?"

"How content you look. And beautiful."

She opened her eyes, gazing at him as though she could look through him. He sucked in a deep breath, his need for her terrifying him. He downed a swig of beer.

He heard her soft sigh, heard the edge of sadness in it. Here they were again. What was her word? Stalemate.

"Maybe you should go eat something. It's been a long day."

He nodded. He wanted to say more, but no words would come. The idiot white man strikes again.

Listening to the splash of water as she submerged herself again, he closed the door behind him.

The last of his beer accompanied cold fried rice, so he popped another. He knew he was drinking for the wrong reasons but he couldn't come up with any right ones. He took Cleo for a long walk to clear his marginally functional head, but it didn't work. He returned to the living room and dropped on the sofa, hoping the TV would chase away his dark thoughts.

He listened as Shannon stirred around upstairs, probably smoothing lotion on her body, slipping on her nightgown, brushing out her hair. He could feel his fingers in her hair, his lips on her flesh.

He reached for the remote control.

An hour later, he heard a car pull into the drive, probably Barry bringing Maggie home. They didn't come inside. He heard shuffling and whispers on the porch, Maggie's voice lifting and falling, a little laugh from Barry. He felt like a voyeur, but this was his home.

Something changed in Barry's tone, an insistence leaking out, as the key clicked in the door. When it opened and Caleb heard Maggie say, "Just leave now, Barry." The door slammed shut again.

Concerned, Caleb crossed into the hallway to listen. Barry's voice was so low it was barely discernible, but he could hear tension in it. Maggie said again, "Just leave," with an edge of desperation. Barry said, "No," loudly, then came shuffling sounds, then something banging against the door.

Caleb jerked the door open and hit the porch light. Barry glared at him and released his hold on Maggie's arm. Maggie stepped back, turning her head to hide her face from the light. "Maggie? You okay?" Caleb asked.

She nodded but she didn't look it.

Caleb stepped between them. "What's going on here, Barry?"

Barry's chin came out defiantly. "None of your damn business."

Caleb had three inches on him and used it, coming close, peering down. Barry's pupils—wide and black—meant Barry was high on something. Caleb said, "This is my home. What happens here is definitely my business. Maggie asked you to leave. You're still here, so we have a problem."

"It's okay, Caleb," Maggie said meekly.

"This is between us. It's none of your fucking concern," Barry spewed.

Caleb moved closer into his face. "You feeling a bit testy,

Barry? You between hits? What's your substance of choice these days?"

Barry came up on his toes, breathing hard into Caleb's face. Caleb laid a hand on Barry's shoulder, clinching, fighting a strong impulse to hurl him to the ground. But Maggie intervened, moving beside Barry and saying to him, "You need to leave. We're not accomplishing anything here. Just go, okay?"

Barry's furious glare fixed on her, but she met his stare with an uncertain smile that seemed to pacify him. He fished his keys from his pocket and said, "I'll call you tomorrow." He headed towards his car.

Caleb locked the door behind them and followed Maggie into the living room. She looked shaken. "Can I get you something?" he asked her.

"No. I'm sorry for all that."

"You have nothing to apologize for."

"It's embarrassing."

"Barry should feel embarrassed."

Maggie dropped into a chair and massaged her temples with trembling fingers. "I really believed he'd changed. He went through rehab, you know. He's been going to meetings. It seemed he was really trying this time."

"What's he using now?"

"Maybe crack. More likely heroin. That was always when he was the worst. And his favorite."

Caleb thought back to his conversation with Claudia Briscoe, when she had cautioned him about Barry Waters. The Narcotics Division had been investigating him. *Was Barry dealing?* Terrific, he thought. "Maggie, do you plan to keep seeing him?"

"No! I can't go through it again. That's what I told him tonight but he . . ." she hesitated, worried she'd disclosed too much.

"Did he hit you?" Caleb asked.

A shaky hand tugged nervously at her hair. "It wasn't bad.

When he gets all pumped up like that he . . ." her words trailed off, the excuse aborted.

Caleb reached for her hand. "You don't deserve to be hit, under any circumstances. He's out of control. You can't help him."

"I know, I know. I must look like one of those battered women you and Shannon counsel. I must look pathetic to you."

"Barry's the pathetic one. But I'll level with you. I don't feel comfortable having him around here. Julia will be here Thursday, then again this weekend. I don't think he's fit company for a four-year-old. Even if he is functioning at the same maturity level."

She tried a smile at that but it crumbled. She turned away. "I think I'll go to bed. It's been a long night."

chapter fifteen

Kevin Lumford wasn't happy about his therapy appointment. Caleb's keen therapeutic eye picked up on that right away.

"Fuck you," Kevin Lumford growled.

Caleb sipped his coffee and studied his new client, who had arrived twenty minutes late. Caleb had just about given up on him when Janice buzzed his extension. "I found him on the porch steps. He looks kind of shy," she had said.

Kevin was taller than his dad and thinner, if that was possible. He was a long, awkward kid who moved like he wasn't comfortable with his body yet. He had lost the battle against acne. Bumps and splotches crawled up his neck, his chin, and around his nose. His head was shaved like a rap-singer-wannabe, and his dark T-shirt read "Mean People Suck." A tarnished silver cross dangled from his left earlobe.

"Okay, Kevin. You haven't answered any of my questions. So maybe there's something that you want to talk about."

Kevin fidgeted in his chair. His gaze roamed all around the room before falling back on Caleb. "I hate you fuckin' shrinks."

"I'm not a shrink. I'm a social worker."

Kevin scowled Elvis-style, curling up one side of his lip. "Even worse."

Caleb smiled behind his coffee mug. "Sounds like you have some history with us helping professionals."

"What do you think?" he barked.

"I think you've probably seen a mess of counselors and therapists over the years. Your dad said it started before your mother died."

That got a rise out of him. "What the fuck do you know about my mother?"

"I know she had a drug problem," Caleb said, keeping his voice even.

"A drug problem? She was a fuckin' addict. She died a fuckin' hooker in a fuckin' ditch. Didn't live to see thirty." That seemed to have a special meaning to him. He leaned back, a spark of pride gleaming in his eye.

"You ever wonder what if? What if she'd straightened out? What if she hadn't died? What if she was still around?"

Kevin rolled his eyes in disgust and fixed them back on Caleb. "Why the fuck would I do that? She was a whore. She burned out like a short fuse—" He drew a line in the air with dirty fingers, then splayed them out in a mock explosion. "Boom. No more mother."

"How old were you?"

"Nine. Old enough to know what happened."

"But your dad had custody, right? Even before your mother died?"

"He took me when I was six. Then he dumped me on my grandmother."

"You see him much?"

Kevin grinned. It was wide and bitter, a flash of dirty teeth. "Not much lately. He's in jail, you know."

"Yes." Caleb let silence hang between them for a moment while Kevin squirmed and practiced new ways to register antipathy on his face. He smacked his lips. He narrowed his eyes into a steely squint. He crossed his arms against his chest and pulled back in his seat. "So what's that like for you, having your father in jail?" Caleb finally asked.

Kevin's fingers found his face and picked at a pimple. "My old man's fucked."

Kevin had quite a vocabulary, Caleb reflected. "What do you mean by that?"

"Fucked. Like in doomed. He'll get the chair for what he did."

"I hope not. I've talked with him a few times. I hope he'll get himself a good attorney to help."

Kevin laughed out loud, making a forced, artificial sound. "He's gonna be toast. They'll pull the switch, then poof!" Again, he mimed an explosion with his fingers.

"Sounds like you've given that some thought."

"Who hasn't? Every time you turn on the news, there's my old man. Everybody in Westville's heard of Murphy Lumford."

"And what's that like for you? As his son?"

His eyes betrayed him. He wanted to look surly, clicking his tongue and slouching in his chair, but the wound appeared somewhere behind his eyes. He quickly turned away.

"It's gotta be hard, Kevin."

He shrugged, his eyes averted. "Don't matter. It's what is."

"I think it matters. You've already lost your mother. I can't imagine how it all feels to you."

Kevin looked down at his hand. For the first time, Caleb noticed a tattoo on Kevin's knuckles, a cross with the initials "C.L." underneath. Kevin made a fist and stared at the tattoo.

"Is that from a religious affiliation?" Caleb asked.

Kevin smirked again. "I guess you could say that."

"What does 'C.L' stand for?"

"It stands for the 'City Lords.' You heard of them?"

Caleb grimaced, hoping Kevin didn't notice. "It's a gang. Are you a member?"

Kevin punched at the air with his fist. "Not yet. But my best friend is." Pride rang out in his voice.

"What's his name?"

"Leon. Been with the Lords since he was twelve."

"I don't know a whole lot about how gangs work. Why don't you tell me about the City Lords."

"Are you fucked? We don't talk it. It's sanc-ti-fied!" He exaggerated each syllable.

"I understand that a gang can become like your family."

"Close as brothers. We look out for each other."

"I guess that's especially important now. Since it must feel like your real family is falling apart."

Kevin made a fist again and studied it. "You fuckin' shrinks. Same fuckin' thing every time. A fuckin' game, isn't it?"

Caleb sat back, frustrated. He wasn't making headway in winning Kevin's trust. And Kevin had found his own solutions to his family crisis by connecting himself with a gang. It would offer him support, a feeling of belonging. Plus the added bonus of abundant drugs and the thrills of the violent gang lifestyle. The perfect vehicle of self-destruction. He was, after all, his parents' son.

Caleb pondered his next move. With rebellious adolescents, he usually took his time, sometimes weeks to build the relationship, longer to gain a real sense of trust. Kevin might not have that kind of time to play with. Caleb needed to get creative.

"Sorry, Kevin. I know you've been through counseling before. And it sounds like you've had some bad experiences with it." Caleb rocked back in his chair, hoping Kevin felt the pressure letting up. "I tell you what, maybe we can change our focus a bit. I'm working with your dad, and I'd like to understand him better. Would you mind helping me out?"

"What do you want to know?"

"Well, I know he has headaches. Pretty nasty ones. Has he always had them?"

"Long as I can remember. They been worse over the past couple of years. My grandma wants him to quit his job, start getting a government check. He ain't about to do that, though. Said it would make him look like a cripple."

"Did you notice any changes in him? When the headaches got worse?"

"That's when he dumped me with my grandmother. He said he couldn't take the noise any more. It made his head hurt worse." Kevin's voice softened.

"I remember my teenage years," Caleb said. "I kept the TV and stereo cranked up as high as I could get them. My brother, who's deaf, even complained. He said he could feel the floor vibrating. Said he was worried I'd start an earthquake."

Unexpectedly, Kevin smiled. "Yeah. That's how I like it, too. But I don't think the noise got to my old man, though. I think it was just having someone else around. He wanted to be by himself."

"Why?"

"His headaches made him do weird things. He'd stay for hours lying on the floor. Or he'd sit by the refrigerator, with the door open, and the side of his face pressed into a melon or even a hunk of cheese. Fuckin' weird, like I said. When I had my friends over, they always asked me about him." Kevin paused, then asked, "Your brother. He's deaf and dumb, huh?"

"He isn't dumb in any sense of the word. He's actually about the smartest person I know. And most deaf people can talk. It's just when they're born deaf, they sometimes can't pronounce words well because they can't hear how they sound." These were rote answers, Caleb always made it a point to educate people about hearing disabilities. Especially young, impressionable people. "My brother didn't lose his hearing until he was a little older than you, so his speech is easy to understand. And a speech therapist works with him to help with harder pronunciations."

Kevin rocked back in his chair like he was mulling that over. "Who takes care of him?"

"My brother? He takes care of himself. He's fiercely independent."

"And he can't hear nothin'?"

Caleb smiled. Strange, they were building a connection of

sorts, over this talk about Sam. "No, he can't hear anything. But he finished high school and college. He's a successful artist now."

Kevin rubbed his hand over his shiny head. "I used to want to be an artist."

"Really? Do you paint?"

"Yeah."

"Study art in school?"

He made a fist and punched the air again. "School's fucked. My art's more like the real world. It tells the story, you know?"

"Your story?" Caleb asked.

Kevin turned his head slightly and took in Caleb out of the corner of his eye. "My story ain't none of your fuckin' business. I know you fuckin' shrinks. Pardon me, you fuckin' social workers. I know your games."

"Okay. You've been clear you don't want to tell me about yourself. How about telling me about your art?" Caleb kept his voice even.

"I record the truth. During a war, somebody tells the story, right? Somebody takes pictures of the soldiers. They're the heroes. Well, we have our own heroes. I do the pictures."

"You do graffiti art, don't you?" Caleb had read about it. They were called "taggers," graffiti artists who recorded the gang's history on abandoned buildings, on bridges and overpasses, on the walls of schools and other scorned institutions. A gang death called for a memorial painting, a recounting of the violence in explosions of colors, done in spray paint. In New York City, these works were even recognized by the art world.

Kevin grinned with pride and stroked the fuzz on his lip that was a long way from becoming a mustache. "I'm the best."

"So if you did a painting of your life, what would it look like?"

He scowled again. "I wouldn't do my life. That work don't

get done until after I'm dead."

"I hope that doesn't happen for a lot of years."

"It don't matter. It'll happen or it won't." He ran his tongue across his teeth, again looking disgusted. "I'm done. I was suppose to come here, and I did. Now I'm fuckin' out of here." Kevin lifted himself out of the chair and strolled out. He didn't look back.

Caleb watched as Kevin's back disappeared down the hall, then spent a few minutes doing a therapist's version of Monday-morning quarter backing. He should have backed off, maybe walked the kid to McDonald's, bought him a Coke, discussed baseball or rock music. He should have stayed away from the family issues until Kevin could look at him without glowering.

The world was full of "should haves" Caleb reflected. And the reality was, Kevin would have bolted no matter what Caleb said. And he probably wouldn't be back.

He wished he had better news for Murphy Lumford about his son.

"Your eleven o'clock is here," Janice said sweetly through the phone.

"Thanks." Caleb glanced down at his schedule. Time for Emma. He found her in the waiting area sitting between Paul Callahan and her older brother. "Hello, Emma!"

"Hey, Caleb." As Paul Callahan stood to shake hands, Caleb noticed that he'd dropped more weight. His skin hung looser on his high cheekbones and his eyes looked more sunken.

"How you doing, Paul?"

"Hangin' in." His grin was forced, obviously for his children. "I understand you talked to Matthew. So everything's out in the open now, right?"

"Is it in the open with the police?"

"They know what they need to know. I'm doing my best to keep Matthew's name out of it."

Caleb stared at him. What would his boss have to do with this? Aside from being gay, from moving in the same social circles as Paul.

"You remember meeting Seth, don't you?" Paul asked.

"Sure." Caleb stooped down to reach for the boy's hand and was surprised by his strong grip. He had Emma's blond hair, but his eyes were darker and more wary. Caleb winked at the boy and crossed over to Emma, whose arms were clutching the bear.

"Can we go to the playroom?" She jumped out of the chair and reached for his hand. This unprompted gesture was so unexpected that both Caleb and Paul laughed.

"Well, I suppose so," Caleb replied. He turned to Paul. "You guys can wait here. There are some games in that basket in the corner if Seth gets bored."

Emma tugged his fingers, pulling him up the stairs, stopping at the door to the playroom. "Go right on in, Emma." She didn't need any more encouragement. She reached up for the knob, pushed open the door and headed straight for the crate of stuffed toys. Head first she tunneled into the crate, flinging bears and stuffed puppies and dinosaurs all over the room.

Caleb watched, fascinated.

She came up for air when she found the panda. Carefully, she positioned it in the center of the floor. She placed the smaller bear in front of it, tilting its head as though it was staring at the panda. Emma sat cross-legged beside them.

Caleb took his usual seat in the dwarf chair and said, "Those bears look like they're talking."

She looked over at him as if surprised he was there and returned her attention to the bears. Abruptly, she nudged the panda, toppling it on its side. She bent the smaller bear over it. "Mama! Get up!" she cried out. "Get up, Mama."

Caleb studied his young client, who seemed entranced by this play with bears. It was as if she didn't know where she was, or that he was there. The play was taking her somewhere else.

The smaller bear shook the panda with more vigor. "Get up, Mama!" Fear rang out in her voice now. Caleb leaned forward, ready to intervene.

Suddenly, Emma lifted the mother bear back into the sitting position. She squeezed the smaller bear onto its lap, wrapping the panda's paws around it. She moved closer and leaned the bears to one side, then the other, in a gentle rocking rhythm. Closing her eyes, she hummed to herself which soothed her. Soon, the fear melted from her small face.

"How does the little bear feel now?" Caleb asked.

Slowly, she opened her eyes to study it. "She's happy. She's with her mama."

"And before, the mama bear was lying down and wouldn't get up. Why?" He knew it was risky to ask this question, he was asking her for words she might not have yet. At age four, play was her most familiar language.

Emma didn't answer. She pulled the little bear away from the panda and held it close. After a moment, she knocked the panda over on its side again.

"What's wrong with the mama bear?" Caleb coaxed as he dropped out of the chair and stretched out on the floor. He wanted to be as close as she would allow, but noticed Emma's curious study of his moves. "I thought I'd get a better view if it's okay."

Her finger touched the panda's nose. The other hand released the small bear and gave it to him, which meant she was including him in the play. An important development. He held up the bear. "What do you want me to do with her?"

She pushed it into his chest and molded his fingers around it. "Okay. I'll hug her just like this," Caleb said, letting her know that he understood the weight of his responsibility.

Emma looked over at the crate where a dozen stuffed animals remained buried, then glanced around at the toys she'd scattered on the floor, like she was shopping for another figure to draw into her play. She scooted over to the crate and peered in, spotting a large stuffed "Barney." She pulled the purple dinosaur out by its tale and dragged it over to the panda.

What followed completely captivated Caleb. Emma positioned the mama panda so that it faced Caleb. Barney inched up behind, grabbed the panda, both arms encircling its stomach. Emma bent the mama bear so that it buckled over, head down, before collapsing on its side.

Suddenly Emma sucked in a deep breath, balled up her fist, and knocked Barney clear across the room. Her frantic eyes looked up at Caleb, who handed her the small bear. Emma pressed the bear against the panda's chest. "Get up, Mama! Get up!" She called out again in a pained, desperate cry. Too real. The play had ended.

Caleb looked in Emma's contorted face, tears trickling down. He reached over and gently laid a hand on her shoulder, summoning her back. "Emma? Look at me, sweetie."

Her tear-filled eyes sought him out. He leaned closer to her and slid his other arm around her. "It's okay. You're okay, Emma." She climbed up in his lap, tilting her head back against his chest.

Slowly, her body started to sway again and she closed her eyes, humming so softly he could barely hear it. Caleb rocked in her rhythm, his arms supporting her. It didn't take long. The fear evaporated from her, the tension fell from her face. She crawled out of his lap, putting the small bear there in her place.

She retrieved the conquered Barney and put it on the floor in front of her, scrutinizing it.

"Tell me about the dinosaur," Caleb said. "It hurt the mama?"

She nodded, her stare fixed on the dinosaur. Then suddenly, Emma repeated the attack. Barney grabbed the panda from behind, the panda toppled over, then laid very still.

Caleb closed his eyes as the terrible realization sank into his consciousness. Barney was her mother's murderer. Was Emma playing out something she'd seen? Had she witnessed Fran Callahan's death?

Emma grabbed the smaller bear from his hand. "Get up Mama!" she yelled, the bear nudging the unmoving panda. Then unexpectedly, she froze.

"Is the panda waking up?" he whispered.

She nodded. She laid down beside it and whispered, "Go hide, honey."

"Mama wants you to hide." Caleb said, just as softly.

"From the bad man." Emma and the small bear moved over behind a chair.

"You found a good hiding place," Caleb whispered. "You're safe there."

From behind the chair, Emma pointed at the panda.

"What should I do with it?"

"Mama chased the man. She yelled at him and chased him away."

Caleb nodded and did as instructed. He lifted the panda and pushed it toward Barney, his other hand helping Barney flee. As the panda closed in on the dinosaur, he hurled the purple beast across the room while Emma watched him, terrified. Maybe Emma had seen the man attack again, maybe she watched the man run out the front door, with a bleeding Fran struggling after him.

Caleb blinked back this realization. Healing would take time, he reminded himself. Memories would surface when Emma could cope with them. Not before. His job was to buttress her as they surfaced and, through play, help her work through them. But at least now, the process had begun.

Caleb retrieved the dinosaur. "How about we play something else?" He said, winking. They collected all the stuffed toys and returned them to the crate. He put the small tan bear on the table in case she needed to take it home again.

They spent the rest of the hour reading "Three Little Pigs"

and acting out the various characters. Emma knew the story and chimed in on her favorite parts. She was more alive now. A spark shone in her eyes, the flush of color returning to her face. When the session ended, he offered her the small bear. She took it without hesitation.

Caleb returned her to the waiting area. Paul Callahan noticed the change in her immediately. He lifted her on his lap and hugged her. "Thanks, Caleb."

"I'd like to see her again next Monday. Emma's doing better, as you can see. But I need to talk with you. Could you give me a call beforehand?"

Paul said he would and hugged his daughter again. Caleb stooped down and shook her hand, promising to see her again soon.

Back in his office, Caleb mulled over his session with Emma. She was such a brave kid. Losing her mother. Maybe even witnessing the murder.

He needed to tell Paul about it. Should he tell the police? But they would question her and that could be disastrous for Emma. He thought of the small, delicate girl sitting on his lap, struggling to untangle herself from the trauma of that night. She was so fragile now and needed to be treated with great care. Not a strong suit of the Westville Police Department.

Besides, they wouldn't give much credibility to a preschooler who played out the murder scene with a Barney doll. Maybe he could get more information from her in their next session. Maybe she could describe the attacker.

Whatever Caleb did, he knew he needed to be very careful.

chapter sixteen

Paul Callahan called that next morning. "I'm having a problem with Emma."

Caleb took his first sip of office coffee and said into the phone, "What's wrong?"

"She woke up in the middle of the night, screaming her head off. I tried everything I could think of to calm her down, rocking her, singing to her, giving her juice. Nothing worked. I guess she had a nightmare but she didn't remember it."

"Or it could have been a night terror, which can have the same effect. Were you able to settle her down?"

"After she sobbed uncontrollably for two hours. I thought she was doing better. I thought the therapy was helping." There was an accusatory edge in Paul's voice that Caleb chose to ignore.

"Did she say anything?"

Paul hesitated. "She asked for her mommy."

"That's to be expected. Look, Emma is just now beginning to deal with her loss. At her age, grief is raw and very primitive. It started yesterday in my session with her and we can expect more to churn up over the next several months. I know it's scary, but it really is a good sign."

"It's hard to see her like that."

"How is she now?"

"She's better. She and Seth are playing in the living

room."

"Good. Keep an eye on her. Call me this afternoon and give me an update."

Caleb glanced at his watch as he hung up the phone. He was ten minutes late for their usual weekly staff meeting. He fumbled through the mounds of papers on his desk, uncovered Emma's chart, and headed for Matthew's office.

As usual, Grey Lazarus had beaten him there. He leaned back on the sofa, draping his long, hairy, ape arm over the back, a large stack of files overflowing on his lap. "Nice of you to join us."

Matthew handed Caleb a chart. "Helen Fleck had a bad night. She got disoriented and wandered out of her room around two A.M. It took the nursing staff a half hour to find her."

"She okay?" Caleb asked.

"She's very agitated. They gave her a Vistaril injection, which means we can't do any tests on her today."

"That reminds me. I took a call for you, Caleb." Grey Lazarus groped in his pocket and pulled out a handful of wadded pink message slips. He sifted through them, handing one to Caleb. "It's from Helen's son."

"Jeffrey? When did he call?" Caleb asked.

"About an hour ago. I told him to call back at eleven. He didn't know Helen was in the hospital. Said he'd been trying to reach her."

"Well I've left messages for him."

"He sounded pretty upset," Grey added and Caleb wasn't sure what he was implying.

"Well, let's just say his wife, the Southern Ice Princess, may not have given him the messages. She's not exactly fond of Helen." He shook his head in disgust. "I'll try him again when we're done here."

Grey cleared his throat and opened one of his charts. "I'd like to go over this case. Caleb's been working with Murphy Lumford, our local gunman. I talked with his neurologist and got some information on him." He handed Matthew a report with lab slips attached.

"What did he say about Murphy's headaches?" Caleb asked.

"He said they were a severe form of cluster headaches, usually expressed on the right lobe. Lumford has not responded to treatment. He tried a daily regimen of Inderal, twenty milligrams, but that didn't help. They put him on Imitrex autoinjects, which have been very helpful in most migraine sufferers. But Lumford developed a cardiac arrhythmia, so they had to discontinue it."

"I don't know much about migraines but Lumford's are horrendous," Caleb commented. He relayed the incident when Lumford had pressed his eye into the rug.

"Dr. Foster said he was a very tough case. And the pain is most intense right behind that eye," Grey went on to explain. "That practice of grinding his head into the carpet caused a carpet burn. Infection's what caused the scar."

"Jesus," Caleb muttered, remembering how Kevin had described his father burying his face in a hunk of cheese. "Lumford's supposed suicide attempt, when he wrapped a sheet around his head. It was the same thing."

"Dr. Foster wanted to try Lumford on one of the newer medications, but Lumford had never followed up on appointments. Foster also referred him for counseling. He saw depression secondary to the pain and worried it might drive him to suicide."

Matthew flipped through the chart. "It may have driven him to homicide. Maybe the pain was so excruciating that he lost all self-control. He wanted to end the pain, maybe take his own life. But in desperation and confusion, he fired on those people around him."

Caleb took it in. While it seemed logical that the headaches played a part in Lumford's violence, the scenario Matthew described didn't fit. "The thing is, Lumford wasn't behaving irrationally. He was completely calm. The shooting was methodical."

Grey took off his bifocals and cleaned them with his necktie. "I'm afraid I agree. I believe Lumford knew exactly what he was doing when he shot those people."

"Are we still seeing him?" Matthew asked.

"I have another appointment with him on Friday," Caleb said. "Claudia Briscoe got him to sign a release. Wants to know his motive. Says he hasn't even hired an attorney. Claudia believes Lumford wants the death sentence."

"It sounds like he wants to be put out of his misery," Matthew said grimly. "Keep me posted on him. Since he's such a high-profile case, we can expect subpoenas. And maybe two or three wasted days in court. Who else do we have for staffing?"

Caleb waved his chart before Grey could speak. "I need advice on this one. Emma Callahan. I've got a new problem. I think she witnessed her mother's murder."

"God, I hope you're wrong." Matthew reached for the chart.

"I don't think I am. She enacted an attack with some stuffed toys. A stranger grabs her mother from behind, her mother collapses, then takes off after the attacker. What she described matches what I've heard about the crime. The police think Fran Callahan was stabbed inside, then went out the front door and died on the sidewalk."

Matthew took a long, hard look at Caleb before closing the file. He opened his desk drawer, retrieved his tobacco pouch, and unzipped it. He took his time packing the pipe and lighting it, which was what he usually did when he needed a moment to gather his thoughts. "So what do you do with this information?"

"You tell me. I suppose I have to tell the father, but what if he's a suspect himself? He might want us to talk with the police, especially since it could help clear him. But I'm not real excited about that prospect. They'll question Emma and that would be disastrous. Her verbal skills are limited and her memories are still sketchy. I'm afraid they'd push her into remembering more than she's ready to handle."

"Or maybe she'll remember things that didn't occur. You know children can be manipulated into believing things that didn't happen," Grey interjected.

Caleb glared at him, unsure what Grey meant with his comment. "And what possible motive would someone have to do that?"

Grey ran a nervous finger over one of his charts. "You would have no motive. But the father—who knows? Besides, I think we have to tell the police. There's a murder investigation going on. Don't we have to cooperate?"

Caleb found it interesting that Grey said "we" when it was Caleb who'd be dealing with the cops. Or worse, the solicitor.

"I think we need a legal consult." Matthew wrinkled his nose like he smelled something bad. "Caleb, give Phil Etheridge a call, do whatever he advises. You might also let him know about the Lumford case."

They spent the next hour reviewing a score of other cases, most of whom were new clients who never needed mental health care before Murphy Lumford. Caleb listened and took notes and quickly wearied. The sheer volume of new clients was overwhelming.

Janice paged Grey that he had two clients waiting, so he grumbled and excused himself from the meeting. Caleb started to leave, too, but hesitated at Matthew's door.

"Something else?" Matthew asked.

"I don't know." He eyed his boss uncomfortably. "This Callahan case. It's taking twists and turns I never expected. It's disconcerting."

Matthew placed the pipe stem against his lips and puffed. "That's what we have Phillip for."

"Paul Callahan said something weird the other day. He said he would tell the police what they need to know. And try to keep your name out of it. What do you think he meant?" Caleb studied his boss closely, measuring his response.

Matthew pulled the pipe from his mouth, studied the amber glow from the tobacco, then puffed again. "What are you asking me, Caleb?"

Caleb hesitated, surprised by the intensity of Matthew's gaze. "I guess I'm asking if you're involved with Paul Callahan. If you're more than just friends. Because if you are—"

"If I was, I would have never had him bring Emma here. I thought you knew me well enough to know that."

I used to think I knew you pretty well, Caleb started to say, but held back. He glanced down at Emma's chart in his hand. "I just didn't want anymore surprises."

Matthew dumped tobacco into his ashtray. "It's the nature of our work. We see deeper into other people than we even see into ourselves. But I can assure you that I had no romantic involvement with Paul Callahan. I've been his friend. I've gone to dinner with him and to movies with him, but nothing else. Are we clear on this?"

Caleb nodded, relieved. "Thanks, boss."

When he made it back to his office, Caleb left another message on Jeffrey Fleck's answering machine and hoped this one actually reached Helen's son. Call number two was to Phillip Etheridge, whose legal assistant said he was "in a deposition." Caleb had left his number and barely hung up when Janice buzzed his extension.

"Detective Briscoe's on line one for you."

He punched the line. "Hi, Claudia."

"My, my, my. You are a busy fellow, aren't you? I get this report about two gangs tangling over in the projects. And there's your name all over it. What the hell are you up to?" she snapped.

"Trying to stop bloodshed. I had no idea we had gangs like that in quiet little Westville."

"We stopped being quiet little Westville a decade ago. And I've got bad news about your on-the-streets social working.

The gang-bangers met up again around midnight, only this time there were more of them. We found two kids with knife wounds. One's critical."

"Jesus!"

"That's life in the gangs." Claudia didn't hide her disgust. "Average life expectancy's about twenty-one."

Caleb swallowed. "All that over drugs?"

"You better believe it. We found about five thousand dollars worth of cocaine in that abandoned house. And another three grand worth of smack."

"Smack? You mean heroin?"

"Yep. It's making another comeback, only they're mixing it with some crazy stuff. Shooting it up. Or smoking it. And kids are starting on it younger and younger. As if our kids need yet another way to fry their brains." He heard a dark edge in her voice.

"Anything new on Lumford? He hire an attorney yet?"

"No. In morning report today, jail staff said he wasn't eating. Keeps complaining of headaches. And our friend Solicitor Mayer stopped by. He isn't any too happy that Lumford's still seeing you. Guess you better get ready for a court appearance. Do you, like, own a tie?"

"Julia made me a bolo out of macaroni and glitter. Should look great in front of those court room cameras."

"It would guarantee to keep your testimony short."

Meredith Spencer was dressed all in black. Short black dress, black hose, shiny black high heels. Her wristwatch and purse were black. She looked like a grieving widow in a Hitchcock film.

Caleb pointed to a chair and she sat, crossing long, exposed, dark legs. Her hair hung loose around her shoulders, light brown with hints of gold. Her wide, beautiful eyes had flecks of gold, too. Counseling her would sure be easier if she wasn't so attractive. "How are you, Meredith?"

"Fine, thanks." She blinked the eyes at him, then said, "I

mean, that's the polite thing to say, right?"

"I suppose. But in therapy, that's not exactly what we're after."

"No. I guess you want the truth." She cocked her head, giving him a cool appraisal.

"That's right."

"Okay. The truth. I'm not doing very well at all. It takes hours to get to sleep, and when I finally do, I have nightmares. I wake up so exhausted that I feel I'd be better off if I stayed up all night. I can't eat. I find myself crying and can't think of a reason for it. I guess I'm a bit of a mess." She lowered her eyes as if ashamed. "You said you wanted the truth."

"I'm sorry you're having such a hard time. Have you had more panic attacks?"

She shook her head. "I haven't driven much. Only to the grocery store and back. And here."

"So you haven't gone back to work?"

"No. Alec thinks I should resign."

"And what do you think?" Caleb asked.

"I like my job. I miss the people there. I hope I'll get well and be able to go back."

"I think you will. Maybe sooner than you think."

She looked at him closely, as if she wanted to believe him. "My boss called yesterday and told me that Sally Weston's coming back to work next week. If she can get over this, I suppose I can, too."

"Do you know anything about the other guy who was shot?"

"Mike Beard? He's in the hospital but doing better. Seems things are sort of getting back to normal now."

"That's good. It will make it easier when you do go in." He paused, letting her take the lead.

Her long, dark fingernails played with a fat gold chain around her neck. "I remembered something. Late last night, when I couldn't sleep. I remembered our office picnic last month. We had it out at Douglas Park."

"Pretty cold season for a picnic, isn't it?"

"It wasn't that bad, actually. Cool, but pleasant. We'd had a tough month, most of our crews worked double shifts to put out a huge order. Since we met the deadline, the company president decided to throw us a party. That's one thing I like about Tindall. They treat us well."

"So what did you remember about the picnic?"

She softly drummed her long fingernails against her lips. "I remember seeing Mike Beard and Buck Swygert together. They were at a picnic table, drinking beer. Then later, I saw them behind the boathouse. They were talking to Murphy Lumford."

"Do you remember anything else?" Caleb asked.

"I think they were arguing. Murphy looked real mad. Buck Swygert wasn't taking him very seriously, though. He sort of laughed, which made Murphy even madder. Mike was trying to make peace between them."

"Any idea what they were arguing about?"

"I didn't want to intrude. After they settled down, I walked off." She ran her hand through her hair, then let it fly. "I was wondering if I should tell the police about that."

"It might be helpful. I know they're still investigating the shooting." Caleb hoped she would. Ethically, he couldn't tell Claudia something that had come up in a therapy session with Meredith, even though Claudia was looking for any possible link between Lumford and the shooting victims.

"Of course, the picnic was before Sally Weston was hired," she added.

He nodded. "Still, it could be useful information."

"I'll call them, then. If *you* think it would be of help." The way she emphasized the "you," he wondered if there was a hint of sarcasm.

He decided to change the subject. "Can you tell me more about your nightmares?"

"Yes." She closed her eyes and held her face up to the

light. "I remember one. It started out like the one we discussed last time. You know, the woman, lying in a bed, with the cuts on her wrists. The bed was drenched in her blood and there was more spilled onto the floor. And she held the knife in her hand—a long butcher knife."

"Like she'd cut her wrists?"

"Exactly. I went to the bed and shook it, thinking maybe she was asleep. She didn't move, of course. How could she? It's like I knew she was dead, but couldn't let myself believe it. So I kept shaking her, telling her to wake up."

"So you knew her."

"Yes," she whispered, her eyes remaining closed.

"What did you call her in your dream?"

She didn't answer him, and he noticed a change in her breathing. Her lips parted, air coming in and out at a fast, shallow pace. Perspiration seeped out on her forehead and neck. Her hand reached for her throat.

The sudden change concerned him. "Meredith?"

She was trying to catch her breath now, trying so hard that she wasn't giving oxygen a chance to enter her system. Her mouth sprung open, gasping, making guttural noises of sheer panic. She clawed at her chest like she was fighting an invisible monster there.

Caleb reached over and grabbed her trembling hand. "Look at me," he commanded. She obeyed, probably more out of desperation than trust. "This is just a panic attack. It might feel like a heart attack or something else, but it isn't. We can fix this if you do exactly as I say."

She nodded.

He reached in his desk and pulled out a small paper sack. He rolled the top edge of the bag down and handed it to her. "Put this over your nose and mouth. It will help keep you from hyperventilating. Now, I want you to listen to my voice and do exactly as I instruct you." He slowed and softened his speech as he took her through a progressive relaxation process, beginning with her hands and feet, moving inward,

to her breathing and her heart rate. It took a few moments for
her to settle down. When her respiration slowed to a
reasonable rate, he took the bag from her. "I know that scared
you."

She reached for a tissue and wiped the perspiration from
her face. "I couldn't breathe. I thought I was choking to
death."

"How do you feel now?"

"Tingly. Especially my hands and arms."

"That's called a parasthesia. It will go away soon."

She dabbed at her eyes and regarded him nervously. "I
hope this isn't going to keep happening. It's like I'm dying or
something."

"I know it's frightening. But no, you won't die. If it does
happen again, you can do what we just did. Keep a paper bag
with you, just in case." He leaned in, closing the distance
between them. "Do you know what brought it on?"

"We were talking about my dream. You asked me who the
woman was."

"Yes," he said.

"I remember who it was." Her eyes swept beyond him to
the window. In a childlike voice she added, "It was . . . it was
my mama."

"You dreamed your mother slit her wrists?"

She nodded. "I was a little girl. I went to the bed and there
she was. I remember the blood, the knife, the silence of the
room."

"From the dream?"

She shook her head. "No. God. It really happened. My
dream brought it back. I never remembered it until now. It
happened when I was eight years old."

Caleb sat back, confused. He remembered Meredith had
talked about her mother and described their relationship as
close. "I don't understand."

"When Teresa was killed by that car, my mother couldn't
handle it. She stayed in bed for days, crying all the time. She

couldn't stand to be around Sandra and me, I guess because we reminded her of Teresa."

"The death of a child—"

"I think she blamed me, because I was with Teresa when the car hit her." Meredith's hand went up to the window. Her finger trailed through the condensation on the glass. "That day—the day I dreamed about—was maybe a month after the accident. Mama was in her room. Sandra and I could hear her crying. I went in, trying to comfort her, I guess.

"She yelled at me to get out. She said to leave her alone, she couldn't stand to look at me. She said I would be the death of her one day." Her finger drew a slow spiral in the water droplets and her eyes followed it. "I went to my room. I remember crying and feeling horrible. I decided to tell mama how sorry I was. So I went back to her bedroom and found her. Just like in the dream."

"She tried to kill herself," Caleb whispered, understanding.

"Sandra got our neighbor, who bound her wrists and called an ambulance."

"Do you remember any other incidents like that one?"

"No. I remember she went away for a long time, but then she came back, and it was like nothing had happened. She was almost her old self. Except we, and I mean all of us, we never talked about Teresa's death. We just went back to our old life, but this time, pretending Teresa never existed."

Caleb reached for his coffee, now long chilled, and took a sip. He studied her from behind the cup. "Did you grieve for Teresa?"

"I suppose. I still miss her." Her finger blotted out the lines of the spiral, leaving a dark hole in the mist. "So why now? Why, after all these years, am I remembering what my mom did?"

He smiled reassuringly. "I suppose you're ready to deal with the memories. With what happened. As scary as it was, it means you are healing."

"Seeing Buck's body after he was shot . . . maybe that

stirred up my memories of the accident." A tremulous hand wiped her face. She was regaining control, but the devastation remained there, behind her eyes.

Caleb knew what lay ahead of her. For years, she had preserved a fantasy image of her childhood. The perfect, loving home. The healthy, Leave-it-to-Beaver parents. And now that fantasy lay in shards around her. More devastating memories might come, followed by raw grief, like Emma Callahan's. Meredith Spencer would need a great deal of support.

Caleb reached for the phone and buzzed Matthew, who said he could work her in. Caleb cradled the receiver. "I want you to see Dr. Rhyker now. He'll put you on a mild medication to help with the anxiety and maybe help you get some good, quality sleep."

She nodded. "Will I get to see you again?" The games had ended, she was desperate for help.

"Sure. How about day after tomorrow? And if you need to call in the meantime, you have the emergency number. Okay?"

She blew her nose boisterously, then stood, clutching her purse at her chest. "Thanks, Caleb."

chapter seventeen

Phillip Etheridge shook Caleb's hand with a solid, warm grip
before taking a seat in Caleb's office. Caleb pointed at the
attorney's hair, long over the collar, thinning on top. "They
let you in court like that?"

Phillip smiled. "When you're losing it on top, you tend to
overcompensate. Not that you'd know anything about that,
damn you." Phillip fumbled at the pocket of his tweed jacket,
pulled out a pack of Salem's and lit up. When Caleb pointed
at the "No Smoking" sign on his desk, Phillip flipped it over
so that the words were face down. Caleb growled as he
retrieved the ashtray he kept hidden in his desk. It was used
by only two people on the planet: a very anxious client who
averaged three packs a day, and Phillip Etheridge, attorney at
law.

"So I need your advice on a few of matters," Caleb said.

"So I hear. I just talked to Matthew. A couple of
interesting cases you got there, Sherlock."

Caleb nodded. "The Callahan kid. I guess I have to tell the
father that the girl witnessed her mother's murder. But I don't
want her questioned by the police because she's too young
and too fragile."

Phillip sucked on the cigarette as twirls of blue smoke
circled over him. "You have to tell the father, he's the legal

guardian and he signed the consent for treatment so he has a right to any information related to his kid. Your instincts are right on that one. The police are another matter. You can bet they'll want the kid questioned."

"So what can we do to protect her?"

"You, Caleb Knowles, esteemed counselor, are in a unique position here. You're on contract with the police department as a consultant. Which usually means you see suicidal or psychotic prisoners, right?"

"Yeah. Like Murphy Lumford."

Phillip balanced the cigarette on the edge of the ashtray and opened his embossed leather portfolio. "I was reviewing the contract with Matthew. It's pretty generic, which is in our favor here."

"How do you mean?"

"I mean, if the father consents and you don't have any objections, then you can interview Emma Callahan for the police. However you want to do it. Maybe the police can watch behind a two-way mirror, or maybe you videotape the session and give it over as evidence. She tells you she saw the murder, gives you a description of the assailant, you hand the tape to the police."

Caleb shook his head. "No way. I'm her therapist. It wouldn't be appropriate."

"Matthew told me you'd say that. But I asked him, and I'm asking you, would it be better if the police questioned her? Because that's going to be your only other option. No way they'll leave her alone. She's the only witness they have to the second most publicized murder this decade."

Caleb rubbed his eyes and wished he hadn't let Phillip Etheridge in his office.

"You know I'm right." Phillip tapped the cigarette on the ashtray in rhythm with his words.

"She's just a little girl. She's Julia's age. She has long blond hair and big, tragic blue eyes. She saw her mother get stabbed. She needs to heal from that and it's my job to help her heal. I want to keep it that way."

"It seems to me once the murderer's caught, the whole family can move on. That's helping her heal, isn't it?" Phillip's voice rose like he was arguing a point to a jury.

"What if Paul Callahan doesn't agree? What if he doesn't want me to question Emma?"

"He's a suspect. His daughter may help get him cleared. If it compromises your work with Emma, Matthew says he can have another therapist work with her."

"He does, does he?" Caleb's ire rose.

"Down boy," Phillip grinned. "Only as a last resort. Only if *you* decide your work with her is compromised. Matthew was insistent on that point." He drew on the cigarette again and breathed out a puff of smoke. "I promised my doctor I'd quit these before I turned forty. I got another month to go."

"So what do I do now?"

"Talk to the father. Then call me. I'll work out the details with the police when he gives us his consent. I know you don't like it, but it's the only way. And remember, you'll be helping them find a murderer. Your ethics can't oppose that, can they?"

It didn't feel right. It felt like betrayal. It would surely pollute the therapeutic relationship he had with his young client. But Caleb wasn't sure what choice he had.

"So. Can we move on to your other client? You certainly have some high profile cases."

Caleb reached for a file from his desk. "Murphy Lumford. I talked to Claudia Briscoe about him earlier. She said that the solicitor's coming after our records. Matthew's worried we'll all get subpoenas and spend weeks in court."

"Has the defense attorney requested your files?"

"Lumford hasn't retained counsel. Claudia thinks he wants the death penalty, sort of like he's letting the state carry out his suicide."

"And what do you think?"

"I'm inclined to agree. But I hope he'll change his mind. If he does, can you defend him?"

Phillip ground out the cigarette and ran his tongue over his lips. He wanted the case, Caleb could tell. Phillip loved a good courtroom battle as much as he loved a good game of poker. And he was the best lawyer in town. "You met our assistant solicitor, Powell Mayer?"

"Not yet. From what Claudia says, I'm not sure I want to."

"He's good. And he'll be hot on this one. Loves that media exposure." Phillip grinned, this seemed to make the case even more appealing.

"I know Lumford shot those people," Caleb said. "But I also know he's not a cold-blooded killer. He needs someone to defend him."

"If I take the case, you'll be on your own with Mayer," Phillip added.

"All he can do is go after my records, right? You've seen my handwriting."

Phillip laughed at him. "Yeah. For now, that's all he can do. When we get closer to trial, that's another story. I'll probably want you as a witness. He'll probably get competing testimony from another expert. It'll get ugly then."

Caleb had been down that road before. He'd testified in several trials where his competency and credentials were called into question. After all, what good's a social worker when you can hire a high-priced psychiatrist to say exactly what you pay him to say? "Look. I want Lumford to get a fair trial, which means you need to be his lawyer. The rest we'll deal with."

Phillip zipped his portfolio. "I'll wait to hear from him then. By the way, how's that brother of yours?"

"He's getting rich. He may be moving to Atlanta." It was the first time Caleb had said that without flinching.

"He did a piece for me, you know. I have it in my office. He's damn good."

"Yeah, he is." Caleb walked Phillip to the front door and watched him climb into his new Audi. It was black, with tinted windows and a sunroof. Caleb ruefully eyed his own '92 pick-up. But at least it was paid for, he thought.

* * *

Caleb wasn't due to pick up Julia until five, which left twenty minutes to visit Helen Fleck. After all, the hospital was practically on the way to his ex-wife's house. And since the morning conference with Matthew, he'd been worried about Helen's deteriorating state.

He sailed past the nurse's station and knocked on the door to her room.

"Come in," an unexpected male voice said.

Caleb re-checked the room number before opening the door. The voice belonged to a man sitting by Helen's bed. He was heavy-set, with thinning hair, a weary face, and brown eyes identical to the ones belonging to the patient in the bed. He had to be Helen's son.

"I'm Caleb Knowles." He extended a hand.

"Jeffrey Fleck. Mom's asleep, as you can see."

Caleb looked over at her. She was on her side, her head half on the pillow, her mouth opened wide. She had tucked her hand between her drawn up knees, the way a small child sleeps. "She looks down for the count."

Jeffrey nodded without smiling. "She's been out since her last medication. About two hours ago."

"When did you get in?" Caleb found a straight-backed chair and pulled it over beside him. His movements didn't disturb his sleeping client.

"Around eleven. I forget how long a drive it is from Richmond."

"I know she was glad to see you. She talks about you all the time."

Jeffrey let out a heavy sigh. "She didn't know who I was. When I came in, she was sleeping. I touched her to wake her up. She took one look at me and screamed like I'm attacking her."

Caleb glanced anxiously at Helen. "She's been pretty

confused over the past several months. Then the robbery and coming here made it even worse. But she's back on her medicine, so maybe she'll do better soon."

Jeffrey didn't say anything. His gaze roamed from Caleb, to his mother, then to the window, looking burdened.

"I've been trying to get in touch with you," Caleb said. "I'm glad you came down."

Jeffrey gave him a non-committal nod. "My wife didn't give me your messages at first. She doesn't take Mom's problem very seriously."

"And you?"

"Me? I hate seeing her like this. Not much I can do, though."

"Do your brothers know she's in the hospital?" Caleb asked.

"Yeah. I called them this morning."

"Are they coming down?"

"No. Mitchell works at a private school. It's impossible for him to take time off during the school year. Alford's another matter. He can't really deal with Mom's situation."

"It's gotta be hard on all of you."

"Yeah, well, when it comes to Mom, I guess we're used to it." An edge of anger leaked out in Jeffrey's voice.

"She's been sick a long time." Caleb didn't fight his impulse to defend Helen.

"You could say that. She's been a drunk since I was five. She left my Dad a dozen times. Once she left us while Dad was out of town and Alford had to take care of me and Mitchell for three days. He was only twelve years old. She was a lousy mother."

"Like you said, she was an alcoholic."

"And I suppose your point is that since she was sick, she's not accountable for her behavior?" His voice rose, shaking at the apex.

"No. My point is that she really did love you. And your brothers. But she made some bad mistakes." Caleb recognized himself in Jeffrey's eyes. He recognized the rage, the grief, the self-doubt that is the heritage in alcoholic families.

"My wife can't forgive Mom, either," Jeffrey said, quieter now. "We have two daughters. They mean everything to Gloria. She can't imagine leaving them alone for days without anyone taking care of them."

"I understand, real well, how your Mom's alcoholism has affected you and your brothers. But look at her. She's a victim, too. The alcoholism destroyed parts of her brain. And now the Alzheimer's." Caleb leaned in closer. "She can't live on her own any more. It's gotten bad enough that I'm not sure she remembers to eat."

"I know, I know. But what can I do? She can't live with us, we don't have room. Besides, we can't take care of her."

Caleb noted a flicker of guilt in Jeffrey's eyes and wanted to stifle it. "I understand. But maybe we could find a group home for her. Or a supervised retirement facility."

"What would that kind of place cost?"

"Most group homes will use her disability check. Retirement placements cost more, but we could find something manageable."

"Mom got a small inheritance from Dad that I manage for her. It's a couple of hundred a month. With her disability check, she gets close to a thousand. Do you think that's enough?"

"I could give you the names of a few programs, if you want. You could call around, maybe visit one or two. How long will you be in town?"

"A day or two." Jeffrey looked back at his mother. She stirred a little, as if an unwelcome dream had infiltrated her sleep. "She's never going to get better, is she?"

"I wish I could tell you she was."

"She'll get worse and worse. Until she forgets to breathe or something."

"We can't really predict what course her illness will take,

but we're doing what we can for her."

Jeffrey nodded soberly. Helen stirred again and her head teetered off the pillow. Jeffrey stood to lean over her. "She doesn't look very comfortable. I keep worrying that she'll roll over on her broken arm."

Caleb walked over to the other side of the bed and gently lifted her shoulders so that she was back on the pillow. She made a little groaning noise, then a slow sigh heaved out of her. He gave Jeffrey his card with the center's phone number and Jeffrey said he'd call tomorrow.

Quietly, Caleb slipped out of the room.

chapter eighteen

Caleb eased his pick-up behind his ex-wife's Volvo. He took his time about opening the door, climbing out, and sauntering up the walkway. He hoped Julia would emerge before he had to ring the bell and confront Mariel's terminally disapproving face. Their divorce two and a half years ago had been ugly. Now, they could be civil to one another, they could bear each other's company when it was in Julia's best interest, but the overall climate between them hovered at arctic chill.

The door knob turned, the heavy oak door inched open, and a red headed child peeked out.

"Hey, monkey-face!" Caleb said, grinning.

"Hi, Daddy," she said, with less enthusiasm than usual. She stepped onto the porch, reaching up for him to lift her in his arms. She was warm and wiggly against his chest.

"You've grown another three inches. Soon I won't be able to lift you. Does your mom know you're leaving with me?"

She squirmed her way back down, stuck her head back through the door and bellowed, "Mama!! I'm going!!"

He heard some sort of muffled response as Julia slammed the door shut. Good. Another avoided Mariel encounter.

His daughter trotted over to the truck and opened the door without his help. She had buckled herself in the seat by the time he made it around to the driver's side. Growing up so fast, he thought.

"How was your day?" he asked, wheeling out of the drive.

"I don't like Billy Stoddard," she answered.

"And what did Billy Stoddard do that upset you?" Feeling her gaze on him, he turned to read her expression. She looked very serious, her mouth bent in a solemn frown, her wide amber eyes like looking in a miniature mirror.

"Billy Stoddard said there's a killer and he comes to your house at night and kills your mama," she blurted out.

"What?" he turned again, sensing she was checking out his response. "Billy Stoddard makes up stories," he said.

"He said he saw it on the TV. He said the killer might come after his mama next."

Caleb turned on his turn signal and pulled off the road. Swiveling to face her, he said, "Billy is talking about a woman who was killed in town. Her name was Frances Callahan and she was Maggie's friend."

Julia narrowed her eyes at him, the way she did when she was concentrating very hard. "Who killed her?"

"A very bad man, sweetie. And the police are going to find him and put him in prison."

"Did the lady have a little child?"

He nodded, curiously touched by her wording. Again, the faces of Emma and Seth Callahan flashed on the mental screen of his mind. How senseless, how unfair it was. Once Emma must have been like his Julia, with the same wondering mind, the same excitement over things like eating peanut butter off the spoon or finding a lost Matchbox car.

But now, in an instant, Emma's world had transformed into a dark place of shadows and fear. She needed to heal. And it was Caleb's job to make that happen.

He reached over to squeeze Julia's hand. "The woman who died had two children and they miss her very much. But their Daddy loves them and will take very good care of them."

"Where is the bad man?" she asked. "Does he know where I live?"

Caleb unbuckled his seatbelt and shifted closer to her,

slipping his arm around her. "No, the bad man doesn't know where you live. He won't come near you, sweetheart. I promise."

"He won't hurt Mama?"

"No," he said definitively. "He cannot hurt your mom. She is safe. She'll be waiting for you tomorrow after kindergarten. But if you want, we'll call her tonight and check on her." After a long moment, she nodded, and it looked like some of the fear had lifted. Caleb slid back over to the steering wheel and drove them home.

Cleo met the truck as it pulled up in the drive. As soon as Julia opened the door, the sheepdog bounced up and plopped onto the girl's lap. "Looks like somebody's missed you," Caleb said.

He watched as Julia bounded after Cleo, climbed on to the swing, and did her best to dodge sheepdog kisses. He motioned that he'd be inside and opened the door to the kitchen, where he found Shannon at the table surrounded by stacks of files and insurance forms. "Welcome to paperwork hell," she commented.

"I just left that at the office."

She tilted her head up like she wanted him to kiss her. He obliged, grinning. These little familiar movements had new meaning to him—bridges that spanned the distance, if only for a second. "The girls are in the back."

"Good. Cleo's been waiting. I thought we'd do burgers on the grill."

"Sounds good." Caleb opened the fridge to find patties already formed on a plate.

"We're out of buns but I needed to go to the store anyway." Shannon tapped the end of her pen on the table and grimaced at the paper around her.

Caleb lifted one of the sheets to study it. "What is this?"

"It's a justification for continued stay. If a client's in the hospital for more than three days, the physician has to submit it to us. Then we decide if the stay is justified and if we're going to pay for it."

"I've heard of these. So, say I'm bipolar and get suicidal. I go to the hospital, and I only have three days to get well?" he asked incredulously.

"Three days to get you stabilized, then off you go to out-patient treatment." She shook her head. "I really hate this part of my job. The main office says I'm too lenient, that I'm costing them money. They say we have to take risks to assure cost-effectiveness. I say the risks are with people's lives, and it's not worth it. Welcome to the age of Managed Care."

Caleb glanced out the window. Julia sat cross-legged on the ground and Cleo had wedged as much of her body as she could on Julia's lap. Caleb looked back at Shannon, noticing the lines of tension around her eyes. "I wish you were happier with your work."

"I'm happy about the money. When do social workers get to say that?" She let out an ironic laugh. "But the work isn't satisfying. I'm a salmon swimming upstream in that place."

Caleb nodded. He met Shannon back when they both worked for Matthew at the counseling center. When she moved in with him, they decided it was best to separate home life from work, so Shannon had taken the job at the First Care Company. It seemed things had been going steadily down hill since then.

He sat across from her. "Your clients miss you. You're a great therapist, Shannon. Maybe you need to get back to it."

"I know I do. But I've only been in this job a year."

"And we both know why you took it. Maybe I should have been the one to find something else. You'd still be working with Matthew doing what you love." He couldn't keep the guilt out of his voice.

She leaned forward. "When I feel sorry for myself about this job, one thing always helps. I imagine you in it. I imagine you in a tie, sitting in those corporate meetings, playing with a slinky under the table. I imagine the main office calling you about the expense of a patient's treatment, and you call them

Fascists and hang up on them." She laughed out loud. "You'd make it about fifteen minutes in my world, Caleb Knowles. And Managed Care might never be the same."

She collected all her papers in one tidy pile that she dropped in her briefcase. "Maggie went to happy hour with friends from work, so it's just us for dinner. I'll take the girls with me to the store." She grabbed her car keys and headed out the back door.

With all the females gone, Caleb went out to the garage to rummage for charcoal and lighter fluid. He rolled the grill onto the patio, poured out the briquettes and stacked them in a pyramid. He was generous with the lighter fluid, then tossed on a match. Flames erupted into dancing fingers of yellow and blue. It was gratifying, this making of fire, like it touched a primal memory in his Cro-Magnon DNA.

He sat in a lawn chair beside his masterpiece and watched dusk descend on his world. The air was crisp and dry, with the kind of cold that sneaks up on you. He watched as his breath emitted a white fog that quickly dissipated, pondering how anyone could stand to live up north where winter temperatures rarely climbed above fifty. South Carolina might have summers that might serve as dress rehearsal for hell, but at least a guy could sit outside in March without his eyeballs freezing over.

"Caleb! I knew someone had to be home."

Caleb closed his eyes, praying that voice would go away. He heard the clinking of the gate latch, the groan as the gate swung open, his own groan as Barry Waters let himself into the yard.

"Is Maggie around?" Barry asked as he helped himself to the other lawn chair.

"No. It's always a good idea to call before you drop by. That way you'll know if she's here."

"Yeah, well, I wasn't sure she'd take my call."

"That might be a hint, Barry."

Barry grinned, his deep dimples cockeyed on his face. He

needed a haircut, his mop of curls laying in peculiar alignment on the crown of his head. His collarless linen shirt looked like it had been slept in. "I know she was pissed at me. But she's had a few days to cool off."

"It may take more than that. And honestly, I'd rather you didn't show up here."

Barry smiled again like he didn't take Caleb seriously. "I should think that you, of all people, would understand where I'm coming from. I love Maggie and I want to work it out with her."

"Why should I, 'of all people', have any inkling of what goes on in that head of yours? You hit her. You were strung out and you smacked her. So you need to leave her alone. And you certainly don't need to show up here."

Barry turned his head, his face shedding its cocky arrogance. His eyes swept past Caleb to the cool, dusky sky. After a long moment, he said, "I guess I really blew it this time."

"Yeah, you did."

"I didn't mean to hurt her." He balled his hands into fists, then relaxed them. "I was doing good for a while there. I was straight for three months. Did she tell you that?" He sounded like it was an unexpected good report card.

"Three months isn't long when it comes to recovery. It may feel like an eternity, but it's really just the start. Way too soon to get into a relationship."

"That's what they said at the meetings. NA. I was going for a while. Dropped out when Maggie came back. I thought she was all I needed."

"That kind of thinking proves how far you had to go," Caleb commented. "So how much are you using now?"

He heaved his shoulders up. "Anything is too much, right?"

Caleb looked at him for a long moment. It was like he was back at the office, confronting a regressed, demanding client. He didn't want to be at the office. He wanted to be home, enjoying this quiet time alone.

But there was something pathetic about Barry. And there was Maggie to consider, too. "Maybe you should go back to rehab."

Barry's fist rubbed his nose and lingered in front of his mouth. "I think it may be too late for that."

"Come off it, Barry. You're what, thirty-five? You can't undo what you've done, but you can change where you go from here."

"You don't get it. It's more than detox and twelve-step meetings. It's a world that sucks you in and holds you by the balls."

"So what are we talking here? The drug culture? You dealing?"

"Everybody's a player in that world. It's not like you have a choice."

"That sounds like addicted thinking to me," Caleb said.

Barry shook his head. "You don't have a clue. You have this sweet little perfect life. Your kid. Shannon. God, I wish I was you." He looked like he meant it.

"You keep acting like it's too late for you. Get yourself some help."

Barry looked over at him without saying anything. After a long moment, he stood up and shoved his hands deep in his pockets. "Tell Maggie— I don't know. Maybe you shouldn't tell her anything. Maybe it's time to cut her loose."

Caleb watched as Barry let himself out the gate and climbed into the BMW. Barry Waters was a tragic man, he reflected. Only the tragedy was his own creation, with consequences he couldn't escape. There would be fall-out, there would be other victims of his addiction, which was why Caleb didn't want Barry Waters anywhere near his family.

When Shannon, Julia, and Cleo returned, the burgers were done. As they ate, Julia regaled them with tales of daycare and her career plans, which currently included flying the space shuttle to Mars. While Caleb and Shannon cleaned up, she called her mother and seemed assured that she was safe and sound. She conned Caleb and Shannon into ice cream for dessert, then came a dozen card games, and then the usual battle over bath time. She lingered in the tub with her plastic horse collection and gradually wore herself down. Caleb held the towel as she climbed out and leaned into it, a warm little fish nestled against him. He slipped a gown over her tired shoulders and carried her into bed. He was three pages into "Curious George" when her eyelids lost the battle and closed themselves.

He kissed Julia's cheek, turned out the light, and shut her door.

Shannon was sipping wine in the living room. He poured himself half a glass of merlot and joined her. "She's out cold."

"She's an amazing kid." Her voice was soft, reflective.

"She is. She's the best of all of us, all three of her parents. Thanks for tonight. For not letting our problems affect her."

Shannon took a sip and held the claret-colored liquid to the light, studying it. Her long, graceful fingers twirled the stem of the glass, making the wine gently roll like a tiny captive sea. "I love her, Caleb. No matter what happens, that won't change." She looked away from him, the corners of her eyes weighted down. "If you and I split, my love for her won't mean a thing. I have no rights to her. I'm not her mother. I'm no relation at all. Not even a distant aunt, a cousin by marriage. I love that kid, but I have no family or legal connection to her."

This talk of separation chilled him. He took a gulp of the wine, wishing it could warm the icy places. "Julia needs you in her life. No matter what, I want you to have a relationship with her."

She leaned over to him, her pale eyes direct beams on his. "I wish you understood. But you just don't get it."

He squirmed, struggling to find the right words. "I'm trying . . ."

Her eyes softened. "I know you are." She sipped the wine and set it down. Her hand reached over for his. "I know you're doing your best, Caleb."

"But it isn't enough, is it?"

She laced her fingers in his and squeezed. "I don't understand why you expect perfection from yourself. You can't marry me unless you can be the perfect husband. Which means I'm destined to be single forever."

"And you? What do you expect from me?" He asked it without thinking, scaring himself.

"Me? I want you just the way you are right now. I want to have kids with you and retire with you and spend the last days of my life rocking on a porch beside you. I want you to give yourself permission to have all that." She stretched out her fingers between his and slid her hand free. "But thinking you won't let it happen makes this hole in my gut. It scares me."

He wanted her to feel better. He wanted to take her in his arms and promise her anything. He wanted to take their clothes off and lie naked together, to make love to her in a way that was all her, every place on her touched, kissed, loved, so that she would know how much she meant to him. If he could just reach for her . . .

Her moist eyes looked through him again. He tried to smile, but it fell apart. Suddenly the atmosphere around them was heavier than lead. He couldn't move under the weight of it.

"Maybe I'll get some more work done before bed," she said quietly. She lifted her wine glass and took it with her to the kitchen. His eyes followed her and watched the door close softly behind her.

chapter nineteen

Paul Callahan sat motionless and silent as Caleb finished relaying his suspicions about Emma. Paul had arrived unexpectedly at eight-thirty, anxious to confer about his daughter's worsening nightmares. He had no idea Emma had witnessed Fran's murder.

"It's not definite. But what she acted out in play sure looked like it. She described a stranger coming up behind her mother. His arms came around her, then she buckled over," Caleb told him.

"Did she understand that Fran was stabbed?" Paul asked.

"No. I suppose Fran was unconscious for a few minutes, then came to again and told Emma to hide."

Paul's eyes moved, ghost-like, around the room. "Dear God. She saw it. My poor baby saw the whole thing."

"I'm afraid so. And she's starting to remember. As she feels safer, more memories will emerge. She'll probably play them out. With the memories come the feelings. The terror, the grief. They'll leak out in lots of ways. Nightmares are especially common. Do what you normally do. Comfort her, rock her, stay with her until she gets to sleep. She'll have a rough few months, but she will get better."

"How can she? How can this not affect her the rest of her life?" Paul squeezed his hands together so tight the knuckles whitened. "I can't believe this!"

"Are you going to mention this to the police?"

Paul's eyes widened. "I want Fran's murderer caught. It's all I think about. If the person is arrested and tried, then maybe I can go on. Everything is on hold now. I live—" he paused, sucking in a deep breath.

Caleb nodded, he'd heard it all before. Crime victims often fixated on the perpetrator, on the court system carrying out some semblance of revenge. But even when the system works, there is never any real satisfaction. After the victims see the perpetrators punished, they're left alone, face-to-face, with their loss and grief.

"So one option is to tell all this to the police. It would help their investigation," Caleb tried to keep the skeptical tone out of his voice.

"But you don't like the idea, I can tell."

"I'm nervous about it. They'll question Emma, and it could hurt her. If they coax her into remembering more than she's ready to, she may regress."

"I can't let that happen. She's finally talking and eating. Even sleeping some. I can't let her go backwards." Paul's voice was a mixture of resolve and confusion. "Do you have any suggestions?"

"I discussed this with our attorney. This is what he says." Caleb filled him in on Phillip's idea: Caleb would work with Emma in the playroom and the police could watch behind the two-way mirror. If the police had a specific question, they could phone Caleb in the playroom and if Caleb thought Emma could provide an answer, he'd ask the question. But he'd claim the right to refuse any line of inquiry that was counter-therapeutic. "I'm not wild about the idea, I have to admit. But it does seem the least dangerous for Emma. What do you think?"

Paul looked out the window. His angular shoulders pulled down, under an invisible load. "I want to do the right thing. For Emma. And for Fran."

"You can take some time and think about it, if you want."

"No. I really can't. I have to get this over with." He heaved himself out of the chair and looked down at his counselor.

"Do it. I'll tell the police how they have to work it. If they refuse, then we'll see. Maybe we could set it up this week."

"If that's what you want."

"I'll call after I've talked to them."

"You've had several calls," Janice stopped Caleb in front of the stairs. "Alec Spencer wants you to phone him regarding his wife. Here's the number." She sifted through a stack of message slips and handed him one. "You also got three calls from a young man who wouldn't identify himself. He sounded distressed. I offered to put the call through to Grey but he said he'd only talk to you. I told him you'd have a break at noon."

"Was the voice familiar?"

She shook her head. "Not really."

"Whoever he is, put him through if he calls back," Caleb said. Weary legs hauled the rest of him up stairs that seemed to have multiplied in recent days. He wasn't sure of the exact source of his fatigue. Maybe it was the erratic sleep, after his talk with Shannon. Maybe it was due to the slow recovery from having his ribs pounded by the thugs in Maggie's house.

Or maybe he was just pathetically out of shape. Sam had tried to drag him to the gym a number of times, but he always resisted. Here he was, age thirty-six, winded after one flight of stairs.

He sat at his desk, held up the message slips, and dialed the number to Alec Spencer's office. He was concerned after his last session with Meredith when she had left in a precarious state. Caleb hoped there was no emergency.

The Center for Human Studies at the university put him on hold. Caleb was about to hang up when Alec Spencer's distinctive British voice said, "Mr. Knowles? Thanks so much for ringing back."

"I just have a moment, Dr. Spencer. Is Meredith okay?"

"Call me Alec, please. Meredith is quite distraught, as you might imagine after your last session. These new memories are devastating to her. She can only sleep if medicated, and she resists that."

"I'm due to see her Friday, but if she needs to come in today . . ."

"No, she says she can wait. Meredith wanted me to tell you that she contacted the police. She was directed to a Detective Briscoe, who's handling the murder at the mill. Apparently this detective knows you. Anyway, Meredith related what she told you about the office picnic, about the scuffle between Mr. Lumford and those other men. The detective was very appreciative of the information. I must say, though, that I have concerns about this. If Meredith becomes some sort of witness, if she's required to testify . . . I'm not sure she could handle it. Not in her present condition."

"We don't need to cross that bridge right now, Alec."

"I suppose not. Anyway, Lumford's confessed to the shootings. I don't imagine there will be a real trial. You know this detective. What do you think?" Alec had taken on a probing tone that Caleb found confusing.

"I think we need to help Meredith get better. Tell her I'll see her Friday."

After Caleb hung up, he plodded through another day of session after session. When he finally had a break to finish up some paper work, he stopped by Janice's area to pick up a few charts.

Janice motioned him over to her desk. She was nodding into a phone and scribbling down on a note, *This is your mystery client.*

"I'll take it in my office." He took the stairs two at a time and closed the office door behind him. "This is Caleb Knowles," he panted into the phone.

"I couldn't think of who else to call." The voice sounded panicked and oddly familiar.

"Is this Kevin?" Caleb asked.

"Yeah. It's me."

"What's wrong?" Caleb heard frantic, sucking breaths and the click of Kevin's tongue as he started to say something but held back. "It's okay, Kevin. Just tell me what's wrong."

"He's dead."

"What? Who's dead?"

"They shacked him. There was nothing I could do so I ran." Kevin choked on his words.

"Slow down. Now tell me what happened."

"Leon. They got Leon. We were taking a shortcut through a parking lot behind an old warehouse. They came out of nowhere, maybe a dozen of them. They swarmed us. They pulled us apart and they shacked him in the throat!" He paused and Caleb again heard his shallow, anxious breaths.

Caleb closed his eyes, immediately picturing the faces of the gang members he had seen. "Easy, Kevin. Where are you?"

"I got away. I'm at a pay phone," he whispered. "I didn't know what to do. It was the Blades!"

"How do you know it was them?"

"Their jackets, stupid! They killed him!"

"Who?"

"Leon. They're gonna pay, I swear it. Those fuckers didn't give us a chance!" Anger and terror competed in Kevin's voice.

"Listen, you need to get somewhere safe. Tell me exactly where you are."

"I didn't know what to do, I—"

"I'll come for you, then we'll take it from there."

He didn't answer.

"Kevin?"

"Why the fuck should I trust you?"

"Because I'm the one you called. I'll help if you let me."

Kevin gave him an address outside a bar in the Briarwood area, near the projects. Caleb told him to hold tight, he'd be there soon. He punched another line and called Claudia. "Murphy Lumford's kid just called. He's in a mess. Said he witnessed a murder. I told him I'd pick him up. Can you come?"

"A murder? Where?"

"Somewhere in Briarwood."

"We didn't get a report. You sure it's legit?"

"You didn't hear the kid. He's a wreck. Apparently he just saw the whole thing. Come in your car. If he sees a police cruiser, he'll take off."

Caleb told Janice he had to leave and she pointed at the large gathering in the waiting room. "Reschedule my appointments. I'll get back as soon as I can." He zipped his jacket and headed out the door.

Dark clouds filtered the sun, casting a cold shadow over the day. On the porch of the clinic, pansies in clay planters shivered against the chilly breeze. Caleb had to keep moving to stay warm. He was pacing back and forth when Claudia's CRV squealed to a stop.

"Where to?" she asked as he climbed in.

He directed her to the bar in an old strip mall where Kevin was hiding. She jerked the steering wheel so that the car careened into heavy traffic. "So what can you tell me about this kid?"

"Not much that I haven't already told you."

"It would help if I knew what I was walking into here." Her tone was cool.

"I can tell you what he said to me." Caleb repeated, verbatim, the call from Kevin. He knew the dead body was a police matter and he needed Claudia's help to protect his client. "He used the term 'shacked.'"

"Means stabbed. Sounds like a gang hit." Her eyes fixed on him from the corners, gauging his reaction.

"That's what I was afraid of."

"What you described—the swarming behavior, the victim singled out and then the slashed throat—that's a gang-style execution. It's meant to send a message to a rival group."

"Jesus," Caleb muttered.

"Your client's bought himself some serious trouble. He may be more his father's son than you realized." Claudia pulled into the asphalt lot and parked under the billboard that read "Lucky Day Saloon."

Caleb glanced around the lot but didn't spot his client. He looked over at the bar. Metal strips welded to the windows and door made it look like a prison. An orange neon sign above flashed "OPE." "I'll check in there. You wait until I call you over, okay?" Caleb didn't give her a chance to argue before climbing out of her car.

The place smelled like beer. Old beer. Beer that had probably been spilled in a Viking revelry and never cleaned up. The woman at the bar had bleached out hair that stood tall over her forehead as if she'd just been hit by a typhoon. At least five different shades had been drawn on her eyelids, like an elementary school display of the primary colors. She wore a T-shirt with large red letters over her chest: "It ain't PMS. I'm just a BITCH." She smiled at him, remarkably unself-conscious about all her missing teeth, and asked, "You want anything? Beer? Something stronger?"

"I'm looking for a friend."

She arched an eyebrow that must have been drawn on by a felt tip pen. "I could be your friend."

Caleb grinned. "I bet you could. But I need to get this kid. He called me and told me I'd find him here." He squinted as he looked around. The place was lit like a cave. "But I don't see him."

"What does he look like?"

"He's fourteen. Shaved head. Frowns a lot."

Her gapped-tooth smile returned. "Check the men's room. He's been in there a long time. Tell him if he's been sick, he's gotta clean up."

Caleb headed down the dark hall off to the left, found the men's room, and rapped lightly on the door. "Kevin?" He didn't get an answer right away, so he opened the door and stepped inside.

Kevin sat on the closed lid of a toilet, his head buried in his trembling hands. A stub of cigarette dangled precariously from his lips. His left eye was red and swollen, and traces of dried blood streaked his nose and cheeks. Caleb stooped down in front of him. "You okay?"

"Those fuckers are gonna pay," he mumbled.

"Listen, we have some important things to do. I need you to tell me where Leon's body is, then we need to get you somewhere safe."

"Where the hell is that? Ain't nowhere safe." Kevin's voice tried on a macho edge, but his eyes betrayed him. The boy looked scared to death.

"Kevin, I brought a friend with me. She's a detective. She—"

"You brought the fuckin' police? I trusted you!"

"I know. And you need to trust me now. The police have to know about Leon so they can find his murderer. Isn't that what you want?"

"We got our own way of doing things."

"Look, we can debate that later. But right now, Leon's body is lying all alone in some parking lot. Do you want that for him? Would his family want that? We need to take care of him. And Detective Briscoe will know what to do." Caleb coaxed him with a hand and Kevin relented. Despite all his bravado, the kid needed to be led. Caleb took him out of the men's room, past the bar, and out into the parking lot.

Claudia's car idled out front and Caleb urged Kevin inside. He introduced Claudia, telling him, "Tell her where to take us." Reluctantly, he directed her behind the strip mall to a long dirt road. Passing a line of rental storage buildings and a small herd of rusted out cars, the road ended at an ominous looking deserted warehouse. Every window had been shattered, rust had chewed away at the tin siding. Neon graffiti glowed on every wall of the sagging structure. Graffiti art, like Kevin did.

"Pull around the back." Kevin's eyes shifted warily from the car's side window to the rear as Claudia wheeled the CRV onto a paved drive that paralleled the warehouse. Carefully maneuvering between the rusty paint cans and broken bottles scattered everywhere, she turned into a parking lot behind the building.

"There." Kevin pointed across the expanse of asphalt to a small, dark heap. Claudia parked the car, reached for her radio, and told the police dispatcher to send the forensic team and the coroner.

Caleb opened his door and climbed out, followed by his hesitant client. The place seemed as isolated as the surface of the moon. It was eerily quiet, except for the sound of glass fragments crunching beneath their feet as they inched towards the corpse.

"Not too close. Don't touch anything," Claudia cautioned, passing them. She knelt down to examine the body.

Caleb didn't want to get close. He didn't want to see the face of this kid who would never have the rest of his life. But somehow, he couldn't tear himself away.

The boy was young, maybe Kevin's age, with skin the color of an old penny. His empty eyes stared blankly at the overcast day. The flaps of his black leather jacket opened out beside him. The boy's head was tilted back, a long crimson gash opened the throat like a bloody mouth. "Jesus," Caleb gasped.

"Gruesome, huh?" Claudia moved her pen down to the hand on the body. "See that? The cross tattoo? He's a member of the City Lords. It's definitely a gang hit." She looked up at Kevin. "You mentioned the Blades. It would help if we knew what this gang war was about. Before more bodies start piling up."

Kevin looked away.

"Okay. You said the kid's name is Leon. I need a last name and a home address."

Kevin looked back at the body and clutched at his stomach. He looked shaky. "Leon Spears. His mom lives over on Dover Street. But Leon didn't stay there much."

"How old was he?"

"Fifteen."

Claudia pointed at Leon's feet. "Look at those basketball shoes. They run about three hundred bucks and they look brand new. How do you suppose Leon got that kind of money?"

Kevin leveled a glare at her and looked like he was about to take off, so Caleb stepped between them. "Anything you tell Detective Briscoe will help us find Leon's killer. I know that's what you want."

Wiping his nose with the back of his hand, Kevin glanced down at the body. "I don't know where he got his money."

Claudia's attention drifted from the corpse to a trail of brown spatters on the asphalt. Carefully, she followed it for about four feet, then stooped down to study a larger rust-colored shape.

"What is it?" Caleb asked.

"A foot print. Stay back, so we don't mess it up for forensics."

Caleb glanced at Kevin, who seemed unable to look away from his fallen comrade. "Do you have any idea why they killed him?" Caleb asked.

Kevin didn't answer.

Claudia scribbled down a few notes and said, "Let me call for back-up. I don't like the set-up here, we're too isolated." She looked back at the corpse. "I guess we'll get in touch with Leon's mother to let her know."

Caleb watched as she returned to the car, imagining what it would be like when Mrs. Spears got the call. How would she feel? Would she think of the child she had carried in her womb, the infant she had cradled in her arms and nursed at her breast? Or had she already grieved the loss, when Leon turned his life over to the streets?

Caleb's gaze shifted back to Kevin, who was staring at the warehouse. Caleb followed his gaze and noticed a car winding its way down the clay road. The car's tires kicked up a cloud of orange dust and Caleb hoped it was an unmarked police car responding to Claudia's summons. It turned off the dirt road onto the paved driveway, picking up speed and grinding the broken glass under its wheels.

Caleb stepped closer to Kevin as he eyed the car. As it passed the warehouse, he could tell it was not a police vehicle. It was an old monster of a car, with dented fenders and a patchwork paint job. Its tires squealed in protest as it swerved into the parking lot.

"It's them!" Kevin screamed.

Before Caleb could speak the car accelerated, lunging towards them. Caleb grabbed Kevin's arm and spun around, unsure which way to run. He caught a flash of metal in the back window of the car before he heard the unmistakable explosion of gunfire.

"Down! Get down!" He hurled Kevin on the ground, dropping on top of him. Bullets sprayed around them, coming so fast, so loud. The car swerved in a full arc as more gunfire blasted. Shaking, Caleb held onto the kid and tried to make himself as flat as he could. Soon more shots rang out. The slower, baritone report from Claudia's gun.

Caleb turned enough to catch a glimpse of Claudia Briscoe standing in the road and firing. Her last shot took out its left tail light before the car sped away.

"Caleb! You guys hit?" she yelled.

"I don't know." Caleb stared down at his own body, which seemed intact. He lifted himself off Kevin and asked, "You okay?"

Kevin nodded, fear twitching him like electricity. "You sure?" Caleb asked. "Let me take a good look at you." He helped the kid stand up and noticed a spot on Kevin's pants where he'd wet himself. Kevin quickly pulled away.

"I think we're okay," Caleb yelled at Claudia.

Claudia ran to her car and radioed the dispatcher what had happened and soon a parade of police cars swarmed onto the property. She barked out orders and pointed in the direction that the car had taken. Four cruisers sped off after their attackers.

Claudia motioned Caleb over and introduced him to a uniformed officer. For the next twenty minutes, he answered questions as best he could, but there was little that he remembered about the vehicle. He recalled the collage of colors and the busted tail light, but mostly he remembered the gun, which seemed to have been twelve-feet long and pointed straight at him. That image wouldn't leave his mind.

"Maybe Kevin remembers more," he told the officer. He looked around at the hordes of police personnel, but didn't see his young client. "Claudia! Where's Kevin?"

She glanced across the chaos and questioned a few officers beside her. Caleb walked over and heard a policewoman say, "Sorry, Detective. He disappeared."

"Damn it!" Claudia muttered.

"So we have no idea where he is?" Caleb didn't hide his concern. "Those gang members were gunning for him! They find him, they'll kill him."

"You don't have to remind me," she barked. She turned to the officer and instructed her to issue an all-points bulletin. She gave a thorough description of Kevin Lumford, including his earring, his tattoo, his faded black jeans, and his scuffed army boots. Claudia had a keen eye for detail. Then she asked Caleb, "Anything you want to add?"

"He hangs out in the Briarwood area. And yes, he's involved in a gang called the City Lords."

"No kidding."

"I think he's more of a gang wanna-be than a full-fledged member. He's a lost kid, Claudia. He just wants to belong somewhere."

She chewed on the end of her pen. "The bad news is, he'd be safer if he was a member. It looks like we got the beginnings of an all-out gang war. If he belonged to a gang, he'd have protection. Living on the streets like he is, he needs it."

Caleb leaned back on Claudia's car. Suddenly, he felt very weak. He squeezed his eyes shut and watched a movie play on the back of his eyelids. Flickering in stylized slow motion, the car comes towards them, then the gun emerges, then bullets spray the air. Bullets seeking him. He popped his eyes open to stop the film.

"You okay?" Claudia asked.

"I've never been shot at before. Guess I'm kind of shaky."

"Me, too. We were lucky."

"You were quick, Claudia. I blinked, and then there you were with your gun, like Clint Eastwood or something."

"I should have seen it coming. I saw the car. I know all about drive-bys. I should have been more cautious."

"Can I go now?"

"I'll have someone drive you home."

chapter twenty

It was after eleven when Caleb piled into bed. He kept thinking about Leon Spears, about how his short life had been jerked out from under him. And Caleb was still shaky, not wanting to think what might have happened when that car screeched into the abandoned lot. When he closed his eyes, he could hear the gunshots all over again. A close call. Too damn close.

He heard Shannon climb the stairs and open the door. She'd just returned from an evening of shopping and dinner with Maggie. He watched as she took off her suit, clipped her hair on top of her head, and slipped into one of his old T-shirts. She disappeared into the bathroom for a moment and returned, crawling into her side of the bed. Propping her head on her hand, she faced him. "Okay. Something's on your mind. What is it?"

Caleb didn't want to tell her about the afternoon's events, it would just terrify her and he didn't trust himself to tell it without trembling, so he opted for safer subjects. A distraction. That was what he needed. "Let's see. On the home front, Barry stopped by yesterday, but I ran him off. And did I mention that Matthew's gay?"

She smiled. "Like you haven't known for years."

"No, no. Didn't need to know. I'd have been fine if he never said that word out loud."

"Feeling a bit homophobic, are we?"

"Don't ask, don't tell. The only thing about the military I agree with." He shook his head, embarrassed by the truth in those words. Matthew was his friend. A close friend. Caleb needed to get over what ever hang-ups he still had. "He didn't hide it from you, did he?"

"I figured it out a long time ago. I think it was easier to talk to me because I'm a woman."

"It's easier to talk to you because you're you. It's those eyes of yours. They look into your soul. It's impossible to hide from them, you know."

"You seem to manage." Her voice sounded more resigned than angry.

"No I don't. But I get scared, I guess. If I start to count on you, you may disappear."

She rolled over, resting her chin on her arms crossed on the pillow. "I thought you'd figure out that I'm not Mariel. I won't get bored with you or have an affair. If I leave, it will be because you left me first. You may physically be here, but emotionally, you've left the building. It makes me crazy."

The truth in her words chilled him. He studied her profile, softened in the haze of light from a small lamp. She looked so far away.

She turned her head toward him, her long fingers slowly raking the tresses from her face, her eyes probing the miles between them. "What are you so afraid of?"

"Losing you," was all he could say.

"I don't want to go anywhere. But I want us to get to the next step. That's all I'm asking." Her hand reached over and touched his face—an unexpected, gentle brush of flesh. He tilted his head so that his lips found her fingers and held them. He closed his eyes, savoring the taste of her. Without thought, his arms sought her out and pulled her to him. Her lips kissed him lightly, as timid as a young girl.

"Shannon," he whispered, aching for her. Suddenly her arms were around him, strong and eager, and their mouths melted together. She moved into him, her breasts warm against his chest. She reached down and touched him as he trembled. He groaned with need for her. He arched up, high above her, then gently lowered himself to merge with her, her legs cupping around him, moving with his rhythm. He kissed her again and again, wanting to love every inch of her. Their lovemaking was wild, breathless desperation, it was two people holding each other like they could transcend the bounds of flesh.

And when they finished, Caleb collapsed beside her. He slipped an arm around her and she fell across him, her moist flesh heating his flushed skin. "Wow," he panted.

"No kidding. We keep making love like that, I'm gonna have to go back to aerobics. Build up some endurance."

He turned to kiss her forehead. "I sure like it when you talk about us in the present tense," he whispered.

She turned her glassy eyes on him, assessing. "You know that's what I want, don't you? I want the present. And a future with you."

"You said I'm not ready for you. But I want to be. Please don't give up on us." He was surprised, and embarrassed, by the fear leaking out in his voice.

She heard it, too. She clutched him tighter, as if trying to reassure him. He closed his eyes, overwhelmed by the comfort in that bed. "I love you, Shannon."

He had wanted a distraction, he thought, and smiled.

"Good morning," Claudia's voice sounded unusually chirpy for the early hour.

"Did you catch the people who tried to kill us?" Caleb balanced the receiver between his chin and shoulder, freeing his hands to load the coffee maker.

"I'm fine. How are you?" Claudia said.

"Sorry. Almost getting killed makes me lose my Southern manners."

"I'll bet. The answer is no, we haven't arrested anyone yet.

Have you heard from Kevin Lumford?"

"No. I'm worried about that kid."

"You should be. That other gang, the Blades, they're after him and they'll find him. I don't think he has the street smarts to stay alive."

"Does his father know what happened?"

"Yeah, and he's taking it hard," Claudia said. "He wants to see you as soon as he can."

Caleb tried to remember his schedule at the office. Lumford had an appointment some time, maybe Friday. It would be impossible to work him in any earlier, not with the schedule as tight as it had been.

"Another thing," Claudia added. "Yesterday, we found a bloody footprint near the body, remember? Well forensics got a match on it. It's identical to a shoe print we found at the Callahan scene."

"For real?"

"Yep. Guess that clears Paul Callahan. His wife was probably murdered by someone in the Blades, just like the kid yesterday. We still have no idea about motive. So it's doubly important that we talk to Kevin Lumford soon. And of course, we need to question our other witness. Emma Callahan."

"I think we're making other arrangements," Caleb said evasively.

"Yeah, yeah. We heard all that from your lawyer. Etheridge dropped in on the solicitor yesterday. Powell Mayer got so mad they heard him screaming on three floors. Then Etheridge left his office with this shit-eating grin on his face."

"So round one goes to Phillip," Caleb smiled.

"I guess. But I'm not so sure about round two. Mayer's called your office and had all your afternoon appointments canceled. He's bringing his legions in, and Paul Callahan's been ordered to bring Emma. Mayer plans on using the two-way mirror in your interview room."

"Play room. It's not an interview room," Caleb wanted to

be clear on that point.

"Whatever. It looks like you get to interrogate the kid."

"Anyway I can put a stop on this?"

"I doubt it. Make sure Phillip's there to keep an eye on Mayer. I'll do my best to get there."

"Great," Caleb muttered to no one after he hung up. This was not how he wanted to start his day. He glanced up at the clock, which read seven. He'd promised to stop in at the hospital and check on Helen. Maybe he could catch Matthew later for sage advice on how to handle the solicitor.

Maggie stumbled into the kitchen wearing a white terry robe gathered tight, warming her against the morning chill. She reached for the cup of coffee he offered. "You're up mighty early."

"My job sucks." He sipped the coffee, glad he had made it strong.

"So I hear. Look, I want to thank you again for putting up with me."

"What's to put up with? We hardly even see you."

She removed the towel that was draped over her shoulders and used it on her wet hair. Her olive face was pretty, even without makeup. "I want to move back home as soon as the police say it's okay. I'm underfoot here. And I really miss my things, you know?"

"Have you heard anything from Barry?"

She carefully replaced the towel around her neck, her hair cascading down in moist tendrils. "No. I keep expecting him to call, but so far, nothing." She used the edge of the towel to dab around her eyes and nose. "I had a weak moment yesterday and dialed his number. But I hung up before he could answer. It was stupid, I know. But sometimes I really miss him. I know he's bad for me, I know nothing would be any different. But that doesn't stop me from feeling it."

He studied her over his cup. "Maybe it would help if you started seeing other people."

Her eyes rolled up at that. "Like who? You men don't

really have a clue. It's not like I have a lot of options."

He nodded, accepting the chastisement as he had when he'd given the same advice to Sam. "Well, it shouldn't take long. You're a beautiful woman, Maggie. You're funny and intelligent. Your culinary handicaps can be easily overlooked. Just make sure you hold out for a man worthy of you this time."

She hid behind the towel like she was embarrassed. He downed the rest of his coffee and placed the cup in the sink. "When sleeping beauty wakes up, tell her I'll be home around six."

"So tell me," Meredith Spencer said between sips of black coffee. "What do you do after you find out your whole life has been a lie?"

Caleb shrugged back at her, realizing she probably didn't expect a response.

"Not my whole life, exactly. Just the first twenty years or so." She set the cup down, spilling a brown pool on the edge of his desk. He handed her a tissue.

"Can you tell me about the lie?"

Her unpolished fingernails rested against her lips as if holding back a flood of words that might betray her.

"Silence only gives it more power."

She nodded, almost imperceptibly, but said nothing.

Caleb sipped at his own coffee, watching his client. She was so different today. Not a trace of make-up. A dark, unflattering sweatsuit. Hair pulled back in a severe knot. Though still a striking woman, she looked like she was ready to join a convent.

"My mother is the kindest person I know," she started. "You remember those old Kool-Aid commercials? The house where all the children were welcomed? Where the mother served snacks and invented little games to entertain all the neighborhood kids? That was Mom." She rolled the tissue into a tight ball. "And Dad. Totally devoted to her. And he made each of us kids feel special. He had little nicknames for us. I was Birdy because I learned to whistle when I was ten months old. Sandra was Slugger. She was the tomboy." Meredith made another attempt at the coffee, but her shaking hands barely got the cup to her lips.

"And Theresa?"

"Dimples. Theresa was always smiling. I remember her big, goofy grin, with a missing front tooth. And big dimples like holes poked in dough." The memory brought a mournful smile. "Teresa's with me more now. Images flash through my mind. Playing dolls with her. Sitting beside her, watching the 'Wizard of Oz.' She was terrified of the flying monkeys. She'd hide behind Dad's chair so they couldn't fly out of the TV and swoop her up."

"How do these memories make you feel?"

"Sad. Happy. Mad as hell. Sometimes all at once." She paused, fixing her eyes on his. "It's your fault, you know."

"My fault?" Caleb studied her expression, looking for a sign of accusation that wasn't there.

"My session with you last time. We talked about her, remember? We conjured her up. I keep thinking about what she was like, about her death. About Mom's suicide attempt.

"After Teresa died, Mom went crazy. I think grief made her psychotic, if that's possible. She wouldn't dress, eat, or talk to us. I kept trying to get through to her, but she'd just stare out like I wasn't there."

"You were just a kid. That must have really hurt you."

"Yes." Her voice faltered. She cleared her throat and continued, "I didn't understand it. We were a happy family, but this darkness took over. I had counted on Mom for everything, but suddenly, she wouldn't get out of bed. Sandra did her best to get our breakfast. Dad brought home dinner. Mom stayed in bed, staring out at nothing. I kept going to her, trying to reach her somehow, but she couldn't hear me."

"Then she tried to kill herself," Caleb said.

She nodded. "Yes. She wanted to be with her baby, with

Teresa. It's like Sandra and I didn't mean anything to her. I was so terrified when we found her after she'd cut her wrists. I remember thinking that if Mom died, we'd die, too. I was afraid of dying."

"That's a lot for a kid to handle." Caleb shook his head.

"So after Mom got back from the hospital and started acting sort of normal again, I was so relieved. She cooked our meals and played with us. We were the Cleavers all over again. Except there was this powerful unvoiced rule—Don't ever mention Teresa. Her pictures, her clothes, her bed, all disappeared. It was like she never existed."

"So your family never had a chance to grieve."

She reached for another tissue and wiped the tears cascading down her face. "I do this so much now," she whispered, gesturing at her eyes. "I seem to have an endless supply."

"Not endless. Just twenty years' worth."

Her eyes slowly drifted around the room, at last coming to rest on the window. "I never forgot Teresa. I couldn't talk about her to anyone. The subject was taboo. But I never forgot I had a little sister. And she came to me in my dreams. Especially if I had a scary or sad dream, she'd appear. This tiny silhouette, watching me and telling me I wasn't alone, comforting me in my sleep. But I'd wake up missing her so much."

"You kept her alive in the most private place you had. Your dreams."

"I suppose." She blew her nose and tossed the tissue in the trash. "So tell me, how long am I going to feel like this? I'm tired of being a basket case. I'm starting to wonder if I'll turn into Mom and end up catatonic."

He gave her a sad smile. "You're letting yourself feel what your mother was afraid of. She probably did the best she could, but you're stronger and braver than she was."

"Oh, I'm *feeling*, that's for sure. I'm feeling all the time. It's damn exhausting." She stretched her back, massaging her neck.

He eyed her carefully. "I know one thing that might help you work through this."

"I'll try anything."

"You're honoring Teresa with your tears and your grief. Maybe there's another way to honor her. Maybe you can do something symbolic to say goodbye."

She drew a long breath and let it out slowly. A deep, purging breath. Unexpectedly, her face broke into a smile. "Funny, I've been thinking about that. I've never been to her grave. I was thinking I could get some daisies and take them to her. They were always her favorite."

"I think that's a great place to start."

chapter twenty-one

Caleb wasn't at all happy with the set up. The playroom looked the same, except the curtain that they usually kept drawn over the two-way mirror had been opened. Beyond it, the small supervision room had been transformed into what looked like a television studio. A video camera and sound system had been installed to face the window. Two uniformed officers barely fit in the tiny room, and three chairs behind them meant other occupants were expected.

"Who's idea was this?" Caleb asked one of the officers.

"Solicitor Mayer's. He has a court order." The officer looked barely old enough to shave.

"Hope you all took showers. Ya'll will be wedged in here like sardines. Where is the solicitor?"

The young officer didn't need to respond. A voice boomed out behind Caleb, "Where is that goddamn microphone? The omni-directional. The round, flat one, not this!" A standard mike was tossed on the table with enough force that the officer cringed. He muttered something about it being in the squad car, squeezed past Caleb and headed down the stairs.

"You Powell Mayer?" Caleb said.

"And you must be Knowles." He didn't try to shake hands. His deep, rumbling voice conflicted with his thin, lanky body. He had bristly pewter hair that didn't match his jet black brows. He wore a trim three-piece suit with a pocket-watch chain dangling from a vest pocket, like the rabbit in Alice in Wonderland. "Maybe you can help us with the lighting. We need fluorescents or something else that will brighten things up in there." His thumb gestured toward the playroom.

"We prefer natural lighting. It's more conducive to therapy. Which is what we do here, by the way."

"So I hear. But today you're interviewing a witness. A witness to a murder. You have any confusion about that, you can call Judge Garvin. Do I make myself clear?" He was a fidgety man. His hands moved from his briefcase, to his watch, to a notepad he took from his pocket. His steel-gray eyes fidgeted, too, darting about the tiny room until fixing on Caleb. He opened the notepad and handed Caleb a sheet. "Here are the questions that you need to cover. I don't really care what order you take them. Just get the kid to give you as much detail as you can."

Caleb stared down at the paper and thought about where he'd like to tell the solicitor to put it. "I don't think I'll be needing this."

"I can question her, if you like."

"Maybe you should hook her up to a lie detector. Administer a little shock if she doesn't answer the way you like. Or maybe try sodium Pentothal?" Caleb shook his head in disgust. "Emma is a four-year-old kid. A fragile four-year-old kid. And if you ask for details, well, she won't be able to give them to you. She won't remember his height, all adults look huge to her. She won't remember his eye color or weight. She might remember something strange, like if there was hair on his hands or if he was missing teeth. Or if he talked like Big Bird on Sesame Street. Other than that, don't expect much."

Mayer lifted a hand, toying with the large class ring on his fourth finger. A Citadel graduate, Caleb realized. That fit, he had all the makings of a military guy. Marines, if Caleb had to make a bet.

"I have kids myself, Knowles. So I know what to expect

from preschoolers. What I don't know is what to expect from you."

The young officer returned with a disk-shaped object attached to a long, black cord. He handed it to Mayer. "This should do it. Tape it down on that table in there, then secure the cord so nobody trips over it."

Caleb glanced around the small room. He'd lost the battle with Mayer and he wasn't sure how. And if he had, the real loser would be Emma Callahan.

"This looks like quite a set-up, Powell." The voice behind Caleb was a welcome sound.

"I wasn't expecting you, counselor," Mayer mumbled.

"Now, Powell," Phillip Etheridge peered at him over his bifocals. "You know I represent this agency. I have to make sure your actions don't compromise the therapeutic relationship between Mr. Knowles and his client. I thought we all understood that." He didn't wait for a response before turning back to Caleb. "Your young client is here. She brought a teddy bear."

Caleb motioned Phillip out the door. "I've never been so glad to see your face."

"Mayer is a barracuda. I wouldn't let you swim in the same tank with him alone. I also asked Detective Briscoe to attend. Hope she makes it." Phillip pulled out a notepad and returned to the small viewing room. He made himself as comfortable as he could in one of the folding chairs before reaching in his pocket for a cigarette. He grinned at Caleb as he lit it. When the camera operator took his place, the room was crowded and miserable and the smoke from Phillip's cigarette sure wasn't helping. Powell Mayer coughed and glared at Phillip, who winked at Caleb as he started to close the door.

"Wait for me!" Claudia Briscoe hurried to the door and let herself in, waving away the cloud of smoke billowing out.

Caleb found Paul and Emma in the waiting room and escorted them to the door of the playroom. "I hope this isn't a big mistake," Paul said.

"Look, I intend to treat this like a regular session. The solicitor may or may not get what he wants."

A small hand tugged on Caleb's pants. He grinned down at Emma, whose arm was wrapped tightly around the bear. "I see you brought your friend."

Paul lifted her. "Are you kidding? She hardly ever puts that thing down. I barely saved it from the bathtub last night."

Caleb reached over and touched Emma's small hand. Unexpectedly, she reached out for him.

Caleb took her in his arms, her tiny hands coming around his neck. "Are you ready to go to the playroom?"

She nodded eagerly. Caleb turned to Paul, took in a deep breath, and said, "I guess we'll see you later."

The playroom looked the same, which meant Powell Mayer must have conceded the battle over lighting. The small, round mike was barely noticeable on the small art table. The stuffed animals rested in their usual bin. The doll house, with its minuscule furniture and tiny family, lay on its stand, undisturbed. Above it, open curtains framed the two-way mirror.

Caleb took Emma's hand and walked her over to it. "Can you see yourself, Emma?"

She nodded.

"This is a special mirror. Behind it, there are some people. They can see us, but we can't see them. They'll be watching us today."

She looked up at him, puzzled. "You don't have to worry, though. They won't bother us." He imagined Powell Mayer frowning beyond the glass.

Emma went straight to the doll house. She positioned her bear on the floor and reached for the infant doll that was nestled in its cradle. As she held it up, to inspect it, Caleb lowered himself on the floor beside her.

"Don't cry," she whispered to the baby. Gently, lovingly, she cupped the doll in her hands and rocked it.

"You're taking good care of that baby," Caleb commented.

She swayed it back and forth with her eyes closed. She looked relaxed, like she was absorbing the comfort she offered the doll. Caleb enjoyed watching Emma's little self-healing ritual almost as much as he enjoyed the mental image of Powell Mayer gawking at the two of them. Maybe the solicitor would get bored and leave, Caleb hoped.

Emma's eyes sprung open and she dropped the doll. Her hands froze in mid-air as she stared into the doll house, her eyes wide with terror. Caleb moved closer. "It's okay, Emma."

She blinked at him, as if she'd been called back from a far away internal place. She scooped up the doll, threw it aside, and made her way over to the crate of stuffed animals. With her thumb wedged in her mouth, she peered down at the protruding Barney dinosaur.

"You can play with anything in here, Emma. Do you see something?"

She nodded, pulling Barney from his box and laying him on the floor. Next, she dug out the panda bear. Caleb mentally braced himself, glancing up at the mirror.

Emma placed the panda in the center of the floor and retrieved the smaller bear that she had brought. The two animals faced each other, Emma's hands holding each of them up. "You go to bed now," Emma said.

"Is the mama bear talking?"

She nodded. "It's late. You go to bed now." She slid the younger bear behind the panda and braced it against the leg of the art table. She bent over and whispered to it, "Shhhh!"

"Is that bear hiding from the mama?"

She nodded again before turning to Barney. Her thumb found its way back into her mouth as she stared at the dinosaur. Caleb wondered if the men behind the glass had any idea about the relevance of this play.

Finally, she moved. She jerked her thumb out of her mouth and clutched Barney. She scrunched up her face and dragged the dinosaur over to the panda. Positioning it over the bear, she tilted its head down so that its face was very close to the panda's. Emma scowled at it.

"I want water," She said in a forced, low voice.

Surprised, Caleb asked, "Are you thirsty, honey?"

She shook her head vehemently. "I want water!" She shook the dinosaur in rhythm with her words.

Suddenly, Caleb remembered an earlier session with Emma. Like now, she'd asked for water, but when he'd brought some to her, she'd ignored him.

"I want water!" she exclaimed again. It was the dinosaur, Caleb noted. The murderer must have spoken to her mother before the attack. And he wanted water?

"I want water! Where is he?" The dinosaur shouted in Emma's gruff voice.

Confused, Caleb asked, "Where is who, Emma?"

But she didn't answer. What followed was exactly what had played out before. The dinosaur moved behind the panda, its arms embracing it. The panda collapsed and the smaller bear came out from its hiding place. It shook the panda, saying "Mama, wake up!" Emma's screams sounded so desperate that Caleb almost intervened when she suddenly pulled back, returning the small bear to its hiding place.

She stood the panda and said, "Get out of here!"

Barney backed away.

She made the panda scream, "Get out of here!" and shoved it toward the dinosaur, which retreated over beside the animal bin. The panda bear joined it. Emma returned to the middle of the room, resting on her knees and sucking her thumb.

After a moment, Caleb reached for the smaller bear. "Do you think this bear is scared, Emma?"

She nodded without speaking.

"It must have seen something scary. The mama bear yelled at the dinosaur. Was she scared, too?"

Emma nodded again, her eyes fixed on the animal in Caleb's hand. Caleb glanced up at the mirror.

"Do you know why she was scared of it?"

"He was a bad man."

Caleb handed her the small bear, which she squeezed against her chest. Caleb then grabbed the dinosaur. "I'll hold onto this guy so he doesn't hurt your bear. You just hug your bear and tell her she is safe, okay?"

She nodded, maintaining her vigilant watch of the Barney doll.

"What can you tell me about this bad man, Emma?"

She pointed at him accusingly with her forefinger. "He had on a jacket like Daddy's. 'Cept it was red."

"What kind of jacket, sweetie? Did it have a zipper?"

She nodded. "The bad man drew a knife on his."

Caleb swallowed. He remembered the jacketed men in front of Helen Fleck's house. He remembered the "Blades" wearing their red jackets with the bloodied knife emblazoned on the back. He remembered the body of Kevin's friend in the parking lot after he'd been killed by that gang. And the matching footprint found at Fran Callahan's house.

Frances Callahan had been killed by a gang member. But why? And why had the gang member wanted water?

Not water, he suddenly realized. Waters. The man must have been looking for Barry Waters. Barry had lived with Maggie Wells up until last month. The man had come looking for Barry, but arrived at the wrong house and killed the wrong person. Fran Callahan's death had been a tragic mistake.

He glanced up at the mirror, wondering if they had made the same connection.

But then he turned back to his young client whose eyes remained fixed on the purple dinosaur. "So what are we going to do with you?" Caleb asked Barney. "Emma, what do you want to do?"

"He's bad!" she cried out.

"You are bad," Caleb repeated to Barney, before positioning him on the floor. He turned to his young client. "I'll bet your little bear would like to talk to him."

Emma peeled the bear from her chest and held it in front of the dinosaur for a second. Suddenly, she grabbed the smaller animal and swung it into Barney, hurling him across the room. Immediately, she ran to where it landed and pounded it with the small bear. "Bad, bad, bad!" she screamed.

"It's very bad." Caleb fueled her play and her aggression. She needed to overpower the enemy that had taken her mother; she needed to have that control.

Soon, the bear lay on the floor and Emma's fists pounded Barney. Her inflamed face dripped sweat, her hair swung wildly in the air. Caleb stayed beside her, amazed by the fury pouring out of her frenetic, flailing arms. It was as if the rage flooding out of her could actually fill the room.

Gradually, her arms slowed and pounded the dinosaur with less vigor. Her face calmed, her fists relaxed. With a final punch, she knocked the dinosaur away.

"Emma?"

When she looked up at him, her eyes were half-closed by exhaustion. She pulled herself up on all fours and crawled to him, dropping down in his lap. Caleb wrapped his arms around her, feeling the heat radiating from her small body.

"You've worked hard today," he whispered. "And now I'll bet you're tired."

She didn't answer. Her heavy eyes closed and her thumb returned to her mouth. She leaned back against his chest, nearly melting into sleep. He jostled her and said, "Okay, Sleepyhead! Let's put the animals back in their crate, okay?"

Her sluggish hands reached for Barney. She straightened the bend she'd pounded into his tail and dropped him in the bin. Caleb handed her the panda, which she placed beside Barney. Then she lifted the smaller bear.

"You can take it home again if you want," Caleb said, watching to see what she would do.

She stared down at it, as her mouth continued to work on the thumb. Then carefully, she placed it in the lap of the panda. Caleb smiled. It looked like Emma no longer needed the bear. "I guess it will stay here then. With its mother."

Emma nodded and reached to touch the panda. "You go to sleep now," she told it.

"So what do you think?" Caleb asked Phillip and Claudia, who'd followed him into his office. Phillip dropped in a chair, immediately reaching for a cigarette and lighting up.

"Don't give me that shit about your no smoking policy. After being locked in a closet with Powell Mayer, I deserve this and maybe a drink."

Caleb pulled the secret ash tray from his desk. "I'm just glad he didn't burst into the session."

"He wanted to," Claudia said. "When Emma talked about the jacket that the assailant wore, Mayer wanted her to draw it. And when she re-enacted the attack with the bears, he wanted to move the TV camera inside the room."

"I acted like I was a bouncer, not letting him out," Phillip added. "Matthew's gonna owe me big. I figure a dinner at McVie's, with an expensive wine." The cigarette dangled from Phillip's lip as he sifted through his notes. "You got some good stuff out of the kid. The gang logo on the jacket, that should be a help."

"I have a question," Claudia said. "Early on, when the kid talked about the assailant, she imitated him and said 'I want water'. Not 'I want *some* water', which would make more sense. And she asked, 'Where is he?'"

"I know." Caleb looked at Claudia, aware she had reached the same conclusion he had.

"She meant Barry Waters. The gang member may have come looking for him, probably scoring drugs. Waters lived with your friend, right?" she asked.

"Yeah. He stayed there . . . I don't know. Six months or so. He moved out last month."

"So the punk goes looking for Barry Waters, gets the houses mixed up. They're right across the street from each other."

"Yes," Caleb said.

"Then the night of the break-in at Ms. Wells' house, Waters showed up. I thought that was weird. I bet he knew then that they were after him. And they finally got to the right house."

"They were searching for something."

"Drugs, I'd say," Claudia answered. "Our pal Barry's a dealer."

Caleb wondered what kind of trouble Barry Waters had bought for himself this time. "So, what now?"

"I've got an all-points out on Waters. He's slippery, though. He hasn't showed up at his apartment in a week. His work hasn't seen hide nor hair of him. You had any contact?"

Caleb thought back to his back yard conversation with Barry Waters. "Two days ago. He came by the house, looking for Maggie. He was pretty messed up. Now I guess I understand why."

Phillip had watched their interchange with obvious interest. "So Detective, you got what you needed. You shouldn't need to question the girl anymore, right?"

"That's up to your friend Mr. Mayer, counselor." She stood and approached the door. "Caleb, you hear from Waters, you let me know. You have my home number."

Phillip ground the stub of cigarette and stood up. "I guess I'd better get back to my office. I've got a new client that's taking up all my time."

"This someone I know?" Caleb asked.

He grinned, his blue eyes crinkling up behind the bifocals. "You'll be my star witness. I'm defending Murphy Lumford."

chapter twenty-two

As soon as Caleb let himself in the front door, Cleo found him. She used her massive head to nudge him to her food dish which, to her obvious horror, was empty. As soon as he filled the bowl her face was buried in it, devouring the food in noisy gulps. Caleb patted her and whispered, "Easy girl. You'll get indigestion."

He grabbed himself a beer and twisted off the top. The first ice cold swallow jolted his innards, but the second went down easier. He hardly even felt the third. Satisfied, he opened the refrigerator again and was trying to imagine what he could assemble for supper when the doorbell rang.

"I thought you'd be on your way to Atlanta." Caleb's hands grumbled at his brother, who frowned back at him.

"I postponed it till tomorrow. And right now, I need a place to light because Vanessa's showing my house." Sam followed him into the kitchen and took the soda Caleb offered.

"So you may have a buyer?" Caleb asked.

"Maybe, maybe not. I hate being there. It's weird having strangers stare at your things."

"I'll bet."

"So. Things settling down with you?" Sam asked.

"Not hardly. I had a pretty interesting afternoon yesterday." Caleb set down his drink so he could sign what had happened without mentioning Kevin's name.

Sam's eyes never flinched, absorbing the terrifying meaning of every word. When Caleb finished, Sam reached for his soda and downed a good bit of it. He replaced the can on the table and stared at Caleb for a long moment. "I don't relish the idea of one day being called to identify your body."

"You said you wanted to be kept informed."

"Are you okay?"

"Yeah, but the kid—my client—I don't know where he is. And that gang is gunning for him."

"But you don't need to get pulled into it. You're his therapist, not his guardian."

"His mom's dead. His dad's in jail. I'm all he's got."

Sam shook his head. "I have a feeling you're going to do something stupid. Can't you let the police—let Claudia handle it?"

"I wish I could. But he doesn't trust the police. And I doubt he trusts me either since I pulled Claudia into this."

"Look, if you hear from this kid, don't do anything on your own. You call the police or you get me. Promise me that."

Caleb grinned at his older brother, remembering back when he was ten years old and Sam had defended him against neighborhood bullies on the basketball court. Then and now, Sam had a three inch and twenty pound advantage over Caleb.

"Have you eaten yet?" Sam asked.

Caleb explained how he had just started figuring out supper so Sam, as usual, took over. He found chicken, peppers, and onions in the fridge and conjured up a stir fry. Caleb helped with the rice pilaf and put frozen broccoli in the microwave. Soon, the unfamiliar scent of food being cooked wafted through the kitchen. Caleb's gaze drifted up to the clock. Almost seven. Shannon should be home any minute.

When the wall phone rang Caleb signed to Sam and answered it.

"Is Maggie there?" The voice sounded low and strained.

Caleb grimaced. "Barry?"

"When will she be in?"

"Barry, listen. I need to talk to you."

The phone clicked dead. Caleb replaced the receiver and felt eyes burning into his back.

"Everything okay?" Sam asked.

"That was Maggie's ex-boyfriend. I think he's in trouble."

"What did he want?"

"Maggie. He needs to stay out of her life."

Sam looked at him for a long moment, then handed Caleb a wooden spoon and said, "Check your rice. You're about to burn it."

Just as Sam dumped the stir fry on a platter, Shannon unlocked the back door. She wore a new suit, a teal blue number with a paisley scarf swaying loose around her neck. Her hair had freed itself from the barrette to hang in wild curls around her face. She gave Caleb a soft kiss and glanced at the food on the stove. "Heaven. I'm famished. Thank God you're here, Sam. I could almost resort to cannibalism."

"You hear from our houseguest?" Caleb asked as Sam divvied up the food.

"Not since this morning. She said she'd come home after work."

"Barry Waters just called."

"Great." She scowled. "Just when I think he's out of the picture. What did he want?"

"I'm not sure. But I doubt it's good news." Caleb looked over at Sam. They weren't signing because of the cutlery in their hands, and Caleb wanted to be sure Sam could follow the conversation.

The back door creaked open and Maggie appeared. She set her briefcase on the counter and stared at the gathering in the kitchen as if they were the posse she needed to evade.

"Hey, Maggie. The men cooked for us. Come eat," Shannon coaxed her.

"That's all right. I'm not hungry."

"You're barely skin and bones. And this is real, home-cooked food. Better not turn it down." Shannon loaded a plate for her friend and placed it in front of an empty chair. Maggie dropped in the seat and looked down at the food like it was something foreign to her. Shannon's assessment had been right, Caleb realized, Maggie had lost too much weight. She wore a black cotton sweater gathered bulkily at the waist by a belt that had new holes punched in it. Her eyes moved quickly from the food to the faces watching her.

Shannon coaxed, "Sam is the best cook I know. You have to try this."

Maggie lifted a fork and picked at it. "It does look good."

The phone rang again, Caleb eying Shannon as he reached for the receiver. "Hello."

"Let me talk to Maggie. I know she's there, I saw her car in the drive," Barry Waters said.

"Hold on a second," Caleb muttered. He covered the mouthpiece and turned to Maggie. "It's Barry, but you don't have to take it. I'd love to tell him to go to hell. Just give me the word."

He watched her eyes widen into saucers. Shannon said, "Let Caleb handle it."

Maggie shook her head. "I'll take it in the living room," she whispered, rising and hurrying out the door. A second later, she said into the phone, "Hang up, Caleb."

He obeyed. Shannon followed Maggie, leaving Caleb and Sam alone in a tense silence. Suddenly, the food lost all appeal.

Caleb became aware of a strange uneasiness. He didn't want Barry Waters in his house, not even his voice. Barry Waters was dangerous and would no doubt embroil Maggie in his problems. She didn't have the strength to turn him away.

When Maggie and Shannon returned to the kitchen, Maggie was crying.

"Tell him," Shannon whispered.

"Barry's in trouble," Maggie said. "It's never been this bad. I'm really scared for him."

"What did he want?"

Maggie wiped her nose and looked over at Shannon, who said, "Tell him everything He can help."

"I have to go get him. Before it's too late." Maggie reached for her keys.

Caleb moved closer to her. "I think I know what's going on with Barry."

Maggie glared at him. "What do you know?"

"I know that someone wants to kill him. He's the reason Fran's dead. They came looking for Barry, went to the wrong house, and killed her. Barry's dealing drugs. Now he's got a street gang gunning for him. So there's no way we're letting you go after him."

Tears glistened on her cheeks. She wiped them defiantly. "You don't know what you're talking about."

"Yes I do. I can't tell you how I know this, but you can believe it's true. Where is he?"

Angry eyes surveyed the faces around her. "Why the hell should I tell you! You'll just go to the police."

"He needs the police. Maybe they can protect him."

Shannon crossed over to her. "Maggie, we love you. We don't want you to get hurt. Please, let us help."

"Don't you get it? There's nothing you can do."

He watched the two women staring at each other in a weird stalemate. Finally, he whispered, "I'll go. I won't call the police. But I'll try to convince him to. If he refuses, I'll take him wherever he wants. I promise. As long as you stay here with Shannon."

She searched Caleb's face, then Shannon's. "I don't know."

Sam, who'd been watching the exchange in some confusion, said to Caleb, "You aren't going anywhere without me."

"Okay. We'll both go. Where is he, Maggie?"

She sighed in resignation. "There's a bar in the Riverwalk area called Abe's. He's there."

Caleb nodded and signed the name for Sam, who pulled out his van keys. Shannon approached Caleb and slid her arms around him. "You'll be careful?"

"Absolutely."

She squeezed tighter. "No heroics, okay?"

"Don't have a heroic bone in my body." He gave her a gentle kiss and headed after Sam out the door.

Sam unlocked the passenger door to his van and Caleb climbed in. Behind him, assorted tools rattled on special racks suspended above a large pile of lumber. The familiar smell of sawdust filled Caleb's nostrils.

Sam backed the van out of the drive and headed downtown where traffic was surprisingly sparse. In the moonless sky, a spray of stars dotted the black night. Caleb cracked open his window to let in the cool air. The swirling breeze took hold of Sam's tool belt and sent it swaying noisily on its hook. Caleb reached behind him to secure it.

They drove in silence for a while, each absorbed in thoughts about what lay ahead of them. A knot of anxiety tightened in Caleb's chest. He glanced over at Sam, whose somber eyes were fixed on the road. Suddenly, Sam pulled into the lot of a convenience store and switched off the ignition.

"We better talk," he said.

After reaching to turn on the van's dome light, Caleb turned in his seat and signed, "You really didn't need to get pulled into this."

"I sure as hell did. No way you're going after Waters on your own." He shook his head. "I want to be sure I know everything."

"Okay."

"What I got was that Barry's into drugs pretty bad. You think someone's after him because of a conversation you had with Claudia. And all this has something to do with Fran

Callahan's death."

Caleb filled him in on missing details, Sam's face tensing as he watched Caleb's signs. When Caleb finished, Sam said, "Tell me how you know all this."

"I know all this because I helped the police question a witness. This person was with Fran when she was killed and heard Fran's murderer ask for Waters."

Sam narrowed his eyes at Caleb. After a moment, he said, "I'm not liking this."

"And you don't have to go along with it." Caleb felt a pang of guilt for involving Sam in the mess. "Just take me back to my truck—"

"No!" Sam's voice was sharp. "What I don't like is how tangled up you are in all this violence. First, the break-in at Maggie's. A guy attacks you, nearly kills you. Then you go after a client who takes you to a dead body, and a minute later you're in a gun battle with gang members. Now, here we are going to help a man that we know people are trying to kill. A man you don't even like.

"When did you fall into this world? Why are you putting yourself and the rest of us in this kind of danger?" Sam balled his massive hand into a fist and thumped it against the seat, punctuating his words.

Caleb stared at his brother, surprised by the uncharacteristic anger in his eyes. "I have no interest in getting myself or anyone else hurt."

"Good. Julia's too young to lose her father."

"Maybe your coming along isn't such a good idea," Caleb signed crisply.

"I'm here because I have to be here because I'm your brother. Your safety is important to me." He paused, as if measuring his words. "So what do you plan to do with Waters?"

"Talk to him. Convince him to go to the police. It's the only way he'll stay alive. You saw Maggie. She would have come after him. And what would have happened to her?

Maggie is Shannon's best friend, I feel like I have to do what I can." Caleb tried to read Sam's face. The anger had evaporated, but he looked far away. Caleb reached over and tapped his shoulder. "Do you understand?"

"Yeah. I guess we'd better get going," he said.

"You sure?"

"I'm sure." Sam started the van and pulled onto Main Street.

The Riverwalk never slept. At nine that evening, it was bustling with the first shift of the city's night life. Like a changing of the guard, another crowd would soon descend, and the bars and clubs would stay alive until the sun woke up and sent the young folk home.

The long strip of restaurants, cafes, shops, and bars that looked out on the Cherokee River had long been the center of nightlife for Westville. It had a unique Bohemian flavor and Caleb had spent many hours of his youth as one of the long-haired, tie-dyed patrons on "The Walk." Now, he made it down there maybe three or four times a year. After a play or movie, he and Shannon would stop in for coffee and people-watching. It was funny how the kids looked the same. Long pony tails, Birkenstocks, folk guitars. Déjà vu, twenty years later. It made Caleb feel old.

Sam parked in the crowded lot behind the largest night club and they climbed out of the van. Caleb waited as Sam locked his door and joined him. Together, they headed towards the boardwalk that fronted the river.

They say olfactory memories are the strongest, Caleb reflected, as he lifted his nose in the air and caught the sweet, very memorable scent of marijuana. Sam noticed it, too, and cocked his head in the direction of five kids huddled under a tree. Caleb grinned, remembering his own "tree" days during college and graduate school. Of course, that was light years ago, back when the world was young and safe.

Despite the cold, the boardwalk held a dozen or so coffee

bar patrons sipping cappuccino. A young woman on roller blades zoomed past them, singing loudly with her iPod. "This place is getting dangerous," Caleb signed. Sam pointed up at a canopied door. A brass plaque under the porthole window spelled out "Abe's" in swirling, over-done letters. Glancing once again at his brother, Caleb pulled the door open and went inside.

Strains of jazz piano chords drifted out from speakers on the wall. Clusters of people lined the bar, an elaborate wooden monstrosity far too large for the narrow room. Above it, mirrors and neon beer signs hung on a coral-colored wall. The bartender, a tall, rail-thin blond, had her eyes on a young Hispanic man with a toothy smile and a wad of cash in his hand. Leaning over the bar, he whispered something in her ear that made her grin.

Caleb glanced around the smoky room, and when he didn't see anyone familiar, he motioned at Sam to follow him to the rear of the bar. In the last booth, he spotted a mop of dark hair over the seat back. "That's him," he signed to Sam.

They made it over to Barry's table. He looked rough. A black shadow of beard covered his chin. His eyes looked sleep deprived and twitchy. His Brooks Brothers shirt now resembled a Salvation Army reject. With a trembling hand, Barry brought a bottle of Rolling Rock to his lips and gulped down about a third of it.

"What are you doing here?" he blurted out.

Caleb signed the question for Sam and then answered, "Maggie sent us. For some damn reason, she's worried about you."

Caleb dropped into the seat beside Barry and Sam sat across from him, positioning himself so he could read the conversation.

"Shit," Barry grumbled, raking his hands through his uncombed hair. "I wanted her. Not you."

"Well, you get me. You know why, Barry? Because I know there are people trying to kill you. I thought it was too dangerous for Maggie. If you loved her like you claim you do, you'd agree."

He glowered at Caleb for a long moment, then said, "You know, you really don't have a clue, do you?"

Caleb looked over at his brother who seemed to be ignoring them. Sam's eyes were fixed on the people at the bar. Caleb shrugged and continued signing as he spoke. "Fran Callahan was killed because of you, did you know that? The murderer went to the wrong house. They thought you still lived with Maggie and they came looking for you. What I want to know is, why? Why are gang members gunning for you? Is it drugs? Money? What?"

Barry started to speak but his mouth weakened. "Shit," was all he said.

"Yes, I suppose it's deep shit. How long has it been going on?"

Barry tightened his grip on the beer bottle. "A few weeks, I guess. I mean, I knew they were after me. They showed up at my apartment, tore the place up. Then I got a few threatening calls. But I had no idea that they killed Fran. I mean it, Caleb. I didn't know."

Caleb leaned into him and said, "What about the break-in at Maggie's? You remember, the one where I was assaulted? You showed up that night. You knew then, didn't you? You knew they were looking for you."

For the first time, Barry looked up at Caleb. There was real fear gleaming in his eyes. "Yes. I just didn't know what to do. I was so glad Maggie was with you guys, where she'd be safe."

"Why? What are they after?"

He peered at Caleb, as if trying to see through a veil of smoke. After a long moment, he said quietly, "I told you before. I'm in this other world, and it won't let go. I try to quit, I try to get away, it doesn't matter. Nothing matters.

"I used to deal a lot. When I was using heavy, it was the only way to make it. Lately, I've been trying to stop, but that isn't easy." He took another swallow. "I have this sort of colleague over in the projects. We used to deal back and forth. If he had a shipment, I bought from him. If I had one, he bought from me. He was low and couldn't meet the demands of his buyers. I needed cash bad, so I agreed to help him out. He fronted me twenty thousand and I arranged a buy. My supplier had some new stuff, a stronger kind of heroin. Stuff he called Spider Blue."

That sounded familiar. Caleb thought back to the break in at Maggie's, to the thug who mentioned something about a spider. They must have come to Maggie's looking for Barry's stash.

"He gave me a good price on the stuff," Barry continued. "I pocketed five grand as the go-between. Problem was, the stuff was bad. My guy deals to his usual crowd but they wind up getting sick. One kid even died. I swear, I had no idea the stuff was tainted.

"I went looking for my supplier. Only I can't find him because it turns out he's dead. He worked for that mill where one of the employees went berserk and gunned down a bunch of people. Buck Swygert, my connection, was one of them." Barry shook his head in apparent disgust. "Such a goddamn waste."

Caleb sat back, sucking in air. Earth was suddenly a damn small planet. He thought about Murphy Lumford and his hatred of drugs. Maybe the shooting at Tindall was not so random after all. A hundred questions reeled through Caleb's head and he started to fire them at Barry. But Sam reached over and tapped his hand.

"We have to get out of here," Sam signed.

"What?"

Sam leaned in close and whispered, "The Hispanic guy at the end of the bar. He's been on his cell phone. He mentioned Barry's name. Told someone to meet him here. He mentioned a gun. I don't know if he has it, or if he asked them to bring it."

Caleb tried to look casual as he turned to glance behind him. The man was talking to the bartender again, but his eyes were fixed on their booth. "Good thing you read lips so well. What should we do?"

"We're getting the hell out of here." Sam turned to Barry. "Is there another door?"

"In the back. Beyond the restrooms."

"Good. Caleb, you go first. Act like you're going to the men's room, then go outside and wait."

Caleb didn't like it. "Maybe we should go together."

"Oh yeah. That would be subtle. Just once, do what I ask." Sam gave him a stern look and Caleb nodded. Caleb stood up, stretched, and slipped his hands in his pockets. He smiled down at them as though they had shared a very funny joke and gestured that he needed to take a whiz. Eyeing Sam, he headed to the back. He swung open the door to the men's room then maneuvered around it. He slipped out the exit before the restroom door closed.

He found himself in a secluded alleyway that looked like it ran the length of the Riverwalk strip. Arching overhead lamps topped each doorway and spilled circles of light onto the grimy asphalt. Along the back wall, several over-flowing dumpsters reeked of rotting seafood and old beer. Two drunks meandered down the narrow lane, dressed in old torn jackets that probably did little to combat the cold. Perhaps the liquor bottle they passed between them accomplished that job.

Caleb stared at the door, wanting it to open, wanting Barry and Sam to come out. It seemed like he waited for hours. Finally, the door creaked open and Barry rushed into the alley.

"Where's Sam?"

"He's still in there," Barry said, gesturing with his thumb. "He had me scoot down in the booth so that guy couldn't see my head, and he nodded and talked to me so the guy would know I was still there. Then the guy gets another call on his cell phone, and Sam tells me to run out. He said he'd come as soon as he could."

Caleb glared at him and then back at the bar. "I don't like this," he whispered. He focused all his energy on the door, as if he could will it open and will his brother out here where it was safe. But the door didn't move. Scarcely breathing, he tried to listen beyond the door, to hear sound of movement, but all was silent. He stood there, frozen. Waiting.

And then he heard the gunshot.

"Jesus!" Barry yelled.

"Sam . . . Sam!" Caleb grabbed the door handle and tugged with all his might.

"That won't work. It's a fire exit. We have to go around," Barry grabbed his arm and guided him down the alley. Caleb passed him, his feet flying, his arms pumping, doing all that he could to get to the front door. Rounding the corner, he nearly crashed into a young couple. He offered no apologies and kept on running.

At the front entrance to Abe's, a crowd had gathered. Caleb pushed through them and grabbed the door knob. As soon as he opened it, a large black man clutched his arm, herding him back outside. "Stay out of there. We got trouble."

Caleb pulled himself free and went for the door again, but the man blocked him. "You didn't hear me. There's a guy with a gun. You don't want to go in."

Caleb looked at the man's concerned face and pleaded, "My brother's in there."

The man stepped aside.

The music had stopped. A heavy pall had fallen on the small tavern as the patrons gathered by the door stared at the back of the room. Caleb wove through the crowd, searched the stunned faces for his brother. He wasn't there. Neither was the Hispanic man. Confused, Caleb moved to the back booth where they had sat. Empty. He glanced around and found the bartender. "Where is he? The man that was in this booth?"

Tears brimmed in her eyes and spilled out, leaving black

streaks down her cheek.

"Where is he?" Caleb shouted, grabbing her arm.

She pointed to the back. "He had a gun. He pulled it on the big guy. He fired a shot into the floor, then pressed the gun against the big guy's head—" a shiver ran through her.

"Where did they go?"

"Out back," she whispered. "We called the police!"

He rushed past her, shaking when he reached the door. It was like a strange dream, like he was watching himself from somewhere far away. He watched his hand press the bar handle on the fire exit. He watched the door open, letting him out. He didn't feel the cold, damp air as he scanned up and down the alley. His eyes strained to adapt to the darkness, to see movement in the scattered pools of light.

The wrought-iron steps clanged as he ran down them. As if in response, a rustling noise erupted at the end of the alley. A man screamed out.

"Sam!" Caleb yelled.

More scuffling sounds. "Sam!" He knew it was irrational, knew Sam couldn't hear him. He bolted towards the sound.

There. Two figures struggled beside a dumpster, arms locked. Bodies careening against each other. Sam's profile darting in and out of the lamp light. Caleb kept moving. Closing in.

The assailant screamed out. The two of them buckled over and crashed onto the asphalt. They twisted and turned and Caleb couldn't tell which was Sam. Then their bodies froze, locked together. Caleb came to a dead stop, unsure what to do. No one moved.

A shot rang out.

"Sam!" Caleb cried, but little sound came out. He couldn't move fast now, his legs were like lead. He could barely breath as he approached the tangle of bodies.

The stranger's body straddled Sam, his head resting on Sam's chest. Sam's eyes were open, unblinking. Caleb collapsed to his knees, trying to fathom it. Not wanting to. He reached for Sam's arm under the man and felt for a pulse.

The hand grabbed his, squeezing tight.

Caleb stared at it and then at Sam's face as he moved to look up at him. "Sam?"

Sam slowly turned toward the lifeless man on top of him. Jumping up on his haunches, Caleb grabbed the man's shoulder and hoisted him off his brother. The body was heavier than he expected and his head rolled awkwardly as Caleb heaved him against the dumpster. A large gun clattered from the man's fingers to the ground.

Caleb knelt beside Sam again, spotting a dark wet spot on Sam's stomach. "Christ," he whispered, lifting Sam's jacket to see the wound.

"I'm okay. It's his blood." Sam pushed his palms against the asphalt and lifted himself up. He bent over the other man and asked, "Is he alive?"

Caleb checked the man's carotid. Nothing. He groped along his chest, his hand finding too much blood, no heart beat. He extended both hands out, one palm up, the other palm down, and rolled them over. "Dead," he signed.

Sam shook his head in disbelief and peered into the man's lifeless face. "We need an ambulance."

Caleb read confusion on Sam's face. Behind him, a crowd had gathered. He could hear a crescendo wail of sirens coming in their direction. When Sam looked at him again, Caleb signed gently, "Help is on the way."

Sam asked, "Where is Barry?"

Caleb glanced around and realized that he hadn't seen Barry since they ran down the alley. "I guess he took off," Caleb signed with disgust.

The Emergency Medical Technicians gave Sam a clean bill of health. They made no efforts to save the other man, there was no point. The bullet had apparently hit his heart. He was identified as Rafael Hernando, an eighteen-year-old kid with a police record that spanned volumes and a known leader of the "Blades" street gang.

Yellow police tape was strewn across the alley in fluorescent zig-zags, marking off the crime scene perimeter. After questioning Caleb, the bartender, and a dozen witnesses in the bar, the police turned their attention to Sam. Caleb interpreted their questions and Sam detailed what happened.

When Rafael Hernando had taken the call on his cell phone, Sam had seen it as Barry's opportunity to get away. Sam continued to nod at the empty booth, as though Waters never left. The man finished his call, put the phone in his pocket, and strolled back to the booth before Sam could leave.

Finding Waters gone enraged Hernando. He pulled out the gun and started screaming at Sam. Sam had a hard time reading his lips and suspected he might have a heavy accent. When Sam didn't answer him, Hernando fired his gun. He guessed the guy thought that should get Sam's attention, so Sam tried to explain that he was deaf. But that just fueled Hernando's fury.

As the crowd scrambled to get away from the gun, Hernando grew more agitated. He pressed the gun behind Sam's ear and guided him out of the bar. As soon as they entered the abandoned alleyway, Sam knew he had to get away or Hernando would kill him. They were moving fast across the asphalt when something startled Hernando, probably Caleb clanging down the iron steps. Realizing it was his only chance, Sam lunged at Hernando, who grabbed on to him for balance. They fell to the asphalt and Sam tore at the man's fingers, trying to dislodge the gun. Sam felt the kick as the gun discharged and wasn't sure who had been hit. That was when Caleb found them.

The young officer taking Sam's statement asked a few questions, then carried his notepad to his squad car and spoke into the radio. Caleb followed him over and asked, "Could you get in touch with Detective Briscoe? Tell her this is about Barry Waters, the guy Hernando was after. She'll want to know."

Caleb returned to his brother and checked him over carefully. "How you doing?"

He shook his head.

Caleb tapped his wrist to get his attention then said, "Maybe they'll let us go soon." He wanted to get away from this place and its grim reminders. He wanted to get his brother home.

Damn, it had been a close call. Caleb remembered hearing the shot from inside the bar. It was like the bullet went through his own heart. His mind filled with the image of Sam lying so still on the asphalt. So damn close. And it was all Caleb's fault.

Sam didn't want to be a part of this. He was nervous about it, too. He'd come tonight out of concern for Caleb and it almost got him killed. Caleb glanced over at his silent sibling. Thank God he was alive. Somehow, Caleb would make this up to him.

The young officer came back over. He handed Sam a business card and said, "If you remember anything else, give us a call."

Caleb signed the instructions then asked, "Can we go now?"

"Yeah. Detective Briscoe's tied up in interrogation, but she said she'd talk to you tomorrow. If we need to question him again, we'll let you know."

Caleb nodded and signed, "Let's get out of here."

Sam relinquished his van keys to Caleb who drove them directly to Sam's house. When they unlocked the kitchen door, they found a sheet of paper on the table.

The note was from his realtor. *They want to make an offer. Looks good. I'll stop by tomorrow. Vanessa.* Her signature swirled elaborately down two-thirds of the page.

"That's good news, huh?" Caleb asked.

Sam stared at it and didn't respond. His eyes had the same vacant look as before.

"I wish you'd say something," Caleb signed.

Sam looked at him, blinked, and said, "You can take my van home. I'll ride my bike over and get it in the morning."

"No. I think I'll hang around here tonight. Shannon can get me tomorrow."

"Okay," Sam said. He touched the blood that covered his chest. "I need to wash up."

Caleb watched as his brother climbed the stairs. He should call home, he decided. In the living room, he disconnected the TDD, a telecommunication device that enabled Sam to make calls. Caleb dialed the number and Shannon picked up before the second ring.

"Caleb?"

"Yeah." Just hearing her voice stirred up something inside him. He told her what had happened and that he needed to stay with Sam.

"God, Caleb. What can I do?" Her voice quaked.

"Pick me up in the morning. Bring clothes." He paused, then said, "I guess you better tell Maggie."

"I will. She already knows most of it. Barry called about an hour ago. He was sobbing, begging her forgiveness. He said he wouldn't be calling again because he wanted her to be safe. He says it's too late for him."

"He's probably right. Look, I need to go."

"Okay. I love you, Caleb." The words felt like balm and he closed his eyes, savoring them.

"I love you, too."

A while later, Sam came back downstairs and poured himself a glass of juice. He sat down at the table and downed it in long gulps.

"So, I should have listened to you," Caleb signed. "I should have left Barry to deal with his own problems."

Sam didn't answer. He stared into his empty glass.

Caleb reached over and tapped his hand. "You need anything?"

Sam shook his head, letting the silence hang between

them. Caleb waited.

"How old was he?" Sam asked suddenly.

"Who?"

"The boy I killed. Raphael Hernando." He pronounced the name slowly.

"What the hell are you talking about? You didn't kill anyone," Caleb signed.

Sam shook his head. "He was just a teenager."

Caleb signed, "Hernando was a hood before he reached puberty. He was a gang member involved in drug trafficking. He came at you with the gun. And when I pulled him off you, the gun fell out of Hernando's hand. He tried to shoot you, but in the struggle, the position of the gun changed. Thank God it did, Sam." Caleb sank back in his chair. "Thank God it did."

Sam didn't seem to be listening. His gaze drifted from Caleb, to the forest green walls, to the polished slat-board ceiling. It looked like he was searching the room for answers that weren't there. Finally, his eyes rested back on his younger brother. "I think I'll go on to bed." Sam rose from the table, placed his glass on the counter, and climbed up the stairs.

Soon after, Caleb made his way up to the small guest room. He crawled into the bed, wrapping the covers tightly around him. He didn't close his eyes. Sleep was not something he expected soon.

chapter twenty-three

The next morning, Caleb didn't hear movement in Sam's room as he stumbled into the bathroom. He took a quick shower that didn't refresh him, toweled off, and put on last night's jeans. Still no sound from Sam, so he headed downstairs.

The fragrance of brewed caffeine greeted him in the kitchen where he found a note from Sam, *I couldn't get to sleep. Went on to Atlanta. Will see you later. S.*

Caleb couldn't really blame him. After last night, Sam had every right to get as far away from Westville as possible. The move to Atlanta probably looked very attractive now. And with the potential sale of his home, nothing stood in his way. Atlanta could mean a fresh start for his brother. Sam certainly deserved it.

Caleb took a sip of strong coffee and noticed the flashing door signal. Before he could answer, the door opened and Shannon let herself in with Sam's hidden key. She threw her arms around him and he buried his face in her hair.

"I couldn't sleep," she said. "I just wanted to be here. I wanted to hold you and know you were all right. Are you?"

"Getting there." He played with a curl that wound its way around his finger. "God, you feel good."

She handed him a large bag containing his clothes and a smaller one that held donuts. "Where's Sam?"

"He went on to Atlanta. He had a bad night. It was so close, Shannon. I really thought Sam was dead."

"But he's okay."

"Yeah. Physically, he is." He swallowed hard.

She squeezed his hand. "This is not your fault, you know. It's Barry's fault. It's that gang member's fault. Hell, it's partially my fault, for not stopping you last night. But don't you blame yourself. Just don't go there."

He stared into her serious eyes that read him so well. "Okay. I'll try not to go there. I need to be grateful I'm alive and Sam's okay. And that you're still in my life."

She slid her arms around him and held him close. "And I don't plan on going anywhere."

As soon as Caleb unlocked his office, he checked his appointment book. Good, Murphy Lumford was due in at 9:30. He switched on his lamps, swept the papers scattered all over his desk into one pile, and placed the steamy coffee mug beside the phone. He had barely touched the receiver when he heard a rap on his door.

"Come on in," he beckoned.

The door inched open and Claudia Briscoe appeared. "Got a second?" As usual, she didn't wait for an answer before making herself comfortable in a chair and pulling out her notepad. "I really don't know what I'm going to do with you," she berated. "I'm not sure you want to live to see forty."

"My brother made the same point last night. Of course, he was the one that almost got cheated out of a few birthdays."

She nodded soberly. "How's he doing?"

"He's in bad shape. Having someone try to shoot you, then watching them die from the bullet meant for you, well that can be sort of upsetting. I swear, this town is like a war zone or something."

"Parts of it are. You've been spending some quality time in the dark underbelly, I guess."

Caleb sipped his coffee and wished the caffeine would kick in. "So, you have any news for me?"

She nodded, pulling out a file. "Rafael Hernando. Street punk. Heroin addict. First arrest at age twelve for arson. Three years in Juvenile Justice, where he stabbed another inmate in a fight. Two months after his release, arrested on a B and E charge and for resisting arrest. Jumped bail. Picked up later for dealing cocaine and possession of an illegal weapon. Served three more years. Been out since last year. Suspect in a couple of gang-related crimes, including a gang rape of a fifteen-year-old girl. Charming, huh?"

"I'll say."

"And all this before he reached nineteen."

"How long was he in the Blades?"

"Since birth," she said sarcastically. "I don't know. His younger brother, Luis, was a gang leader for years. Luis's doing life at Manning Correctional. We caught him on a drive-by, where he gunned down three City Lord gang members. One died. Rafael was in the car with him, but he didn't get charged. Some family heritage, huh?"

"You got any news on my pal Barry Waters?"

"He hasn't turned up. We're looking, but he's slippery. I read your statement to the officers from last night. Waters admitted to dealing. Admitted to owing twenty thousand dollars to a street gang. I suspect they'll be dragging his body out of the Cherokee River soon." She closed the cover of her file and put it back in the portfolio. "We also haven't seen Kevin Lumford. You heard from him?"

Caleb shook his head. "I'm worried about that kid. After last night, I hate to think of what's going to happen to him. His dad's due to see me this morning. Maybe he knows where Kevin is."

"I hope he tells you more than he did me. I read your statement about the drug connection between Buck Swygert and Waters, so I questioned Lumford about it. But he didn't budge. Said he wasn't saying one word without his lawyer being there. I think you created a monster." She smirked at him, but at least Lumford was defending himself. "So, you got anything else for me? Anything else from last night?"

He shook his head. "I'd actually like very much to forget last night. And forget the drive-by shooting three days ago. And forget the attack at Maggie's house. That answer your question?"

"I suppose it does. But promise me this. You hear from Waters, or from Kevin Lumford, let me handle it. You got my cell number. Use it. Don't go involving yourself in anything else, okay?"

Caleb rubbed his fatigued eyes. "Believe me, I have no intention of involving myself in anything except my work and my family. You have my word on it."

The police officers removed Murphy Lumford's handcuffs before Caleb even asked. They left him in Caleb's office, saying they'd be right behind the door if Caleb needed them. Caleb thanked them and turned to his client.

Murphy looked ill. The scar around his eye looked more inflamed, bright red against his chalky skin. He'd always been a slight man, but now he looked nearly skeletal. He didn't smell too good, either. He stank of sweat and neglect, an odor like the jail that was now his home.

"How's it going, Murphy?" Caleb asked.

Murphy shook his head stiffly and scanned the room as if looking for an exit.

Caleb leaned forward. "I think it's time we talked about what happened at Tindall."

Murphy's head swung around. "Why? What the hell good would it do?"

Surprised, Caleb moved back, giving his client space. He didn't answer.

"You heard anything from my son?" Murphy asked.

"No. Not since the other day. You?"

Murphy shook his head, looking deeply troubled. "He's

just a kid. He doesn't need to be out on the street."

"He's living in a very dangerous world. There are people trying to kill him. I saw what they did to his friend. The kid died a gruesome death."

"Don't you think I know all that?" Murphy snapped.

"I guess I wanted to make sure you understood how serious this is. Because if you have any idea about where Kevin is, you need to tell the police."

Lumford glowered at Caleb. "I don't know where he is. God, I wish I did know. But he hasn't called me, or my mom. I just pray he's alive. I pray it isn't too late."

"Like it is for you? That's what you mean, isn't it?" Caleb said.

"Yeah. I guess it is. And like I told you before, it doesn't matter."

Caleb reached for his mug and took a sip of the lukewarm coffee. He wanted to let the silence do its work. Finally, he said, "I've figured out a few things about you. About why you shot those people."

His eyes widened behind the Coke-bottle lenses. "What are you talking about?"

"I'm talking about drugs. I know how you feel about them. I know that you lost your wife to a heroin addiction. I heard that you got into a big argument with Buck Swygert at the company picnic. Now I think I know why."

Lumford's hands moved up to his head and started massaging his temples. A flush spread around his nose, inflaming the scar again. "Buck Swygert was a pig. That's no secret."

"Yeah. And he was a drug dealer. You knew that, didn't you? How? Did he approach you?"

He shook his head. His eyes squeezed shut, tiny web-like wrinkles stretching out from the corners. "Swygert had more sense than that. He knew how I felt about his little side business."

"How did he know?"

"We had a little talk about it a couple of months ago. We were both on second shift. Took our break close to midnight. My head was hurting, so I went out back to get some air. Sometimes, when it's cold, the fresh air helps. Buck and his pal, Mike Beard, were standing behind Buck's truck. They had a soda can with a hole drilled in it. I saw the flash of a lighter. Then I caught the smell. You can't ever forget that smell, once you know it. Crack.

"My head was really killing me and the odor made it worse. Swygert sees me and invites me over. So damn cocky, like he thinks everybody does that stuff." Lumford paused, flinching like he'd tasted something sour.

"What did you do?"

"I walked over to them. Mike held the can, Buck held the lighter like they were gonna fix me up good. I knocked the can clean across the parking lot. Bright orange ashes sprayed everywhere. Some even landed on Mike. Man, he was pissed. He swatted the sparks off his pants, then came after me. Buck held him back, said he'd take care of me later."

"So he threatened you."

"He was all talk, he and I both knew it. Anyway, I went back on in and finished my shift. But I kept my eye on the two of them. Swygert spent the rest of his shift hitting on a new girl. Mike Beard's the systems electrician, so he was crawling all over this pretty dangerous equipment, even though he was high as a kite. It's a wonder he didn't kill himself."

"I'm beginning to see you weren't exactly a fan of Swygert and Beard."

"I didn't have much use for them."

Caleb studied Lumford for a long moment. He expected to find a flicker of antipathy, a glint in his eye that would betray him, that would explain why he had shot those men. But none was there. Murphy looked detached, as if his thoughts were turned inward. "So What happened at the company picnic?"

Suddenly, Lumford jerked back as if he'd been struck.

"That's none of your fuckin' business," he yelled, words spewing from behind clenched teeth.

"You're wrong there. I'm your therapist. So it is very much my business." He kept his eyes on Lumford, hoping his unease wasn't evident on his face.

Lumford narrowed his eyes at Caleb, trying to appear threatening, but it didn't last long. He twitched in his chair like he was in an examining room with ominous dental tools poised above him. The change was dramatic. The first time Caleb had seen Lumford so rattled. Caleb glanced at the door, hoping the police officers had kept their promise to stick close by. Of course, Caleb had about five inches and forty pounds on Lumford, but Lumford had killed someone. This was something Caleb couldn't afford to forget.

I don't understand what upsets you about that subject," Caleb said, watching closely. "About the picnic."

Lumford sank in his chair, deflated. He mumbled, "I should never have gone. I thought it was a good idea. Me and Kevin could spend time together, maybe play some ball, maybe joke around together like a normal family. But it was a big mistake.

"Kevin's always been real shy, so he wouldn't talk to the other kids. He wouldn't play in the softball game, which was okay by me because this killer headache came on me. Sort of like now." Murphy pinched the bridge of his nose with dirty fingers.

"It's pretty bad again?"

"They come five, six times a day now. Nothing makes them go away. I suspect that one day, I'll just have the headache without it ever stopping. Hell, that may even be better. There's nothin' worse than feeling it coming on, knowing how bad it will be, and there's nothing I can do about it."

Caleb tried to imagine what it was like being Murphy, battling against the excruciating waves of mind-numbing pain. There was never a reprieve, never a truce. "You want some water or something?"

"No." Murphy rubbed his brow bone, where the scar was. "We were talking about the picnic. I told you about how my head was hurting so I walked down to the pond, where it was quiet. Kevin went off by himself, like he usually does. Anyway, after a half hour or so, I start feeling better. So I go looking for him, but I can't find him anywhere. I start to get worried, so I ask around about him. One of the men that works my shift says he'd seen him heading off in the woods with two other guys, so I go after them. It takes about twenty minutes, but I find the three of them in the woods. Smoking crack." Murphy paused and squeezed his eyes shut tight. It looked as though the pain had intensified.

"Who was he with?"

"Come on, Knowles. You can figure that one out. Buck Swygert. Mike Beard. Those gutless assholes."

"But why Kevin?"

"Because Swygert's a predator. He notices that tattoo on Kev's hand, the 'C.L.' written across his knuckles. Swygert knows right away what it means. He's already dealing to one of the other gangs, and he decides Kevin can be his connection to the City Lords. He gives Kevin a couple of rocks, says there's more where that came from. Then when I show up, he tells Kevin he'll be in touch."

"What did you do?"

"I was so mad, I wanted to kill them. I take Kevin by the shoulder and tell him we're going. He didn't put up a fight, he knew he was in trouble."

"And you ran into Swygert and Beard later."

"Yeah. I didn't mean to make a scene. But when I found that crack on Kevin, I blew a gasket. I told Swygert that if he ever got near my boy again I would kill him. And I meant it."

"I suppose you did," Caleb said, letting the information sink in. "What happened then?"

Murphy took off his thick glasses and rubbed his eyes. Tiny droplets of sweat beaded on his face, even though the room was cool. "I kept my eyes on Swygert and Beard," Lumford said. "Over the next two weeks, I watched them close and learned a lot about them. Swygert has a country band, he plays on Wednesdays and weekend nights that he doesn't work second shift at the mill. Beard plays with him, on keyboard. I went to a place called Mac's Tavern to hear them. They were okay, but nothing to write home about. When they take breaks, they have a whole other business going on in the parking lot. Just like at the plant. Swygert had balls, I'll tell you. No getting around that.

"Mike sees me at the tavern. He gets all flustered, runs and tells Buck. Buck comes over to me, winks, says he hopes I enjoyed the show. Balls, like I said. That next day, I pull in the parking lot, right behind Buck's truck. A big ugly sedan pulls up in front of Buck. Buck gets out, goes over, and soon there's a deal going down. A couple of kids get out of the car, and I recognize one of them. Kevin's friend."

"Leon Spears?" Caleb asked.

He nodded. "Leon sees me sitting in my car and gets real nervous. He points me out to Buck, but Buck doesn't care. Anyway, the kids get back in the car and drive away. Buck comes over to me and he's got this shit-eating grin on his face. 'How's that boy of yours?' he says, looking after the car that was driving off.

"I realized then what he was doing. He was dealing to that gang, through Leon. That was how he would get to Kevin. I thought about all the kids he was hurting, all the families he would destroy with drugs. And he really didn't give a shit about any of that. As long as he made his money, as long as he could get high." Murphy paused and turned toward the window. The day was gray and dismal, with leafless trees waving spindly arms in the chilling breeze. Dark swollen clouds hung over buildings like they were ready to burst, ready to wash the dirty day with rain. Murphy stared out, lost somewhere in those clouds.

Caleb coaxed, "So then you went into the mill?"

He nodded. The gesture was so slight it was almost imperceptible.

"And you worked a few hours, right?" Caleb asked.

Murphy's eyes took a long, slow journey around the walls of the office until they found Caleb's again. "Yes. I was working on a threader, and it was real loud and hot in there. I started getting a headache. It was a bad one, like an awful giant had my head in some tweezers and was squeezing real tight. I could barely think, it hurt so bad. I wished it would end. I wished I could just die, right then, if it would make my headache end. I wound up in the bathroom, hugging the toilet, vomiting my guts out.

"When we took break, I went outside for some air. I sat in my car for a long time, staring at Buck's truck. Then I reached in my glove box and pulled out my gun. I stuck it in my pants and when the break was over I went back inside.

"I remember everything I did that day. Every detail. I remember going back over to the threader and working for a while, keeping one eye on Buck. After a bit, Mike Beard goes over to him. They whisper to each other, then Mike starts walking off. I knew it was time. I walked over to the center of the floor, pulled out my gun, and shot them." He paused, took in a deep breath, and closed his eyes. Caleb watched him closely, watched his eyeballs shimmy behind the eyelids, like they were studying something on a secret screen in his mind.

Caleb asked, "What about Sally Weston? Why did you shoot her?"

Murphy's eyes sprung open again in a look of surprise. "That was an accident. She stepped in the way when I was aiming for Mike. I didn't mean to hurt her. I feel bad about that. But not bad about Buck. He was a predator. He destroyed everyone that he touched. I couldn't let him destroy my boy."

"So you feel no guilt."

"I feel guilty. About Kevin. About what I'm puttin' my mom through. But no, I feel no guilt about Buck Swygert or

Mike Beard. I gave them what they deserved."

Caleb fingered the rim of his coffee cup and wondered how far he should push Lumford. He decided to take a gamble. "So you're sort of a self-appointed executioner."

Unexpectedly, Murphy laughed. It was a strange sound, low and boisterous, from deep in his belly.

"You find that funny?" Caleb asked.

"Well, yeah. It makes me sound noble or something. I wanted to kill Buck. And I hoped the police would come and kill me. If I had just held on to the gun, you know, acted like I was taking hostages. Then the police would storm in and take me out, maybe shoot me in the temple, maybe shoot that fuckin' headache right out of me . . ." He shook his head. "That would have been so easy, so quick."

"Suicide by cop," Caleb muttered. "But that's not what happened. You laid the gun down."

"After I shot Mike, I looked around. All those people were staring at me, terrified. They thought I was gonna shoot them, too. I saw all those horrified faces. People I worked with. People I liked.

"I looked down at the gun. I wanted to point it at my own head and blow myself away. But I couldn't. I got scared and I couldn't do it. So I laid down the gun and waited for security to come."

"Do you regret that decision?"

"No. I didn't want to hurt anyone else. And I'm glad I'm not dead, not with Kevin in all the trouble he's in. I need to stick around for him."

"Yes. He needs you. How do you think you can help him?"

"That, I don't know. But there has to be something."

There was a gentle rap on the door. Janice stuck her head in and said, "Dr. Lazarus is ready for Mr. Lumford."

Caleb glanced at his watch. The session with Murphy had gone over by ten minutes, and Grey was on a tight schedule. "I guess we need to wrap up."

Murphy looked exhausted. "I got nothing else to say."

"Well, you've told me a lot today. I appreciate your being honest with me."

Murphy stood up, wincing as his stiff legs straightened underneath him. "You've been good to me, Knowles. And what I just told you, that Solicitor Mayer's gonna love. I just confessed that my killing of Buck Swygert was premeditated. I want you to write that down in your notes. I want him to know.

"They sentence me to death, I got at least five years on appeals. Kevin will be twenty. He should be all right by then." Murphy reached over and shook Caleb's hand. He thanked him for his help, then opened the office door.

chapter twenty-four

The ringing phone sent a shock wave through Caleb's sleep. He jerked up, eyes wide open, and stared at the clock. 3:21 A.M. The phone rang again and he grabbed it before it could wake Shannon.

"Hello?" After recent events, this could only be bad news.

"Caleb? Sorry to wake you." Claudia Briscoe sounded rushed.

"What's wrong?"

"It's bad. A security guard at Tri-Star Quarry found Barry Waters."

"Dead?" Caleb swallowed.

"Very. Probably happened yesterday, from the looks of him."

"Jesus." Caleb glanced over at Shannon, who stirred a little then settled down under the comforter. "Murdered?"

"Yes, though we don't know the exact cause of death. Could have been a number of things. They tortured him. Burned him. His throat is slit, ear to ear, just like that Spears kid we found. Definitely a gang hit. Probably drug related." Her dry tone made the words even more chilling. Caleb wondered if she had become too hardened by her work, by these repeated ventures to gruesome murder scenes. "I'm on my way to the site," she went on. "Thought you'd want to know."

"Yeah, thanks." Caleb hung up the phone and leaned back against the headboard. His stomach was doing some interesting gymnastics, and it didn't feel like it planned to calm down any time soon. Bad news always hit him in the gut.

Carefully, he slid his legs onto the floor and stood, doing his best not to jar the bed. Shannon rolled over and burrowed deeper in the covers as Caleb eased out of the bedroom.

The hall light clicked on. "I heard the phone," Maggie said. She was leaning against the wall by her door, looking lost.

"Yeah," Caleb muttered.

"Something's happened." Maggie searched Caleb's face. "Tell me."

He turned his head, not wanting to.

"It's Barry."

"Yes."

Her hands came out, fingers splaying against the wall. Bracing herself. "I have to go to him."

"No. It's too late. He's dead." He wished he could take back the words even as he spoke them. He watched as she fell back against the wall and slid down, her bones losing their hold, and he grabbed her, holding tight. "I'm so sorry," he whispered.

She made a keening sound, raw and wounded, as though the pain couldn't be formed into words.

"I know you loved him. I know." He kept holding on, feeling her quake with sobs she couldn't let out.

"I have to see him," she whispered, pulling away.

"No. Look, there's nothing you can do for him now." He wasn't getting through. She pushed by him and disappeared into her room. A moment later, she came out, dressed in jeans and holding a pair of boots.

"Come downstairs and I'll tell you what I know," Caleb said.

Maggie followed him into the kitchen and sat, looking at

him with wide, empty eyes. He pulled a chair close and said, "They found Barry's body at the Tri-star Quarry. He died sometime yesterday. It was a terrible death. You don't want to see him like that."

She blinked. "I know where the quarry is." She slipped on a boot and laced it with quick, nimble fingers.

"Think about it!" he pleaded. "Do you want that to be your last memory of him?"

She finished with the other shoe and stood. "Tell Shannon," she paused, taking in a hitched breath. "Tell Shannon I'll call later."

"No." Caleb shook his head, knowing this was a bad idea but not seeing any alternative. "If you're going there, you're not going alone. But first, let's tell Shannon what's happened. I don't want her waking up to find us both gone. Okay?"

Twenty minutes later, they climbed into Caleb's truck. It was a crisp, black night. A half-coin moon had perched itself low on the horizon. There were no cars on Maple Street and the stop lights and neon signs flashed like eerie beacons in the pre-dawn stillness. Maggie was quiet, her hands wrapped around the door handle as if she wanted to escape.

Caleb wished he could turn the truck around. From Claudia's description of Barry, he knew it was more than Maggie could handle. Hell, more than he could handle. He slowed the truck, praying the coroner would remove Barry's corpse before they arrived. "You sure you want to do this?"

"You don't have to take me."

"Right. Shannon would hang me by my ears if I didn't. Or she'd have brought you herself. I wasn't too wild about that idea."

Maggie didn't respond. She leaned forward on the edge of the seat, her body rigid as Caleb turned on to the gravel road leading to the quarry. In the distance, portable lights had been mounted around the crater where sandstone was blasted out and cut down to marketable chunks. Beside the huge pit, strobing blue lights on the police cars made the scene almost surreal, like a space ship had landed to make contact with earth.

Caleb parked his truck a good distance away. He glanced over at Maggie, who stared out at the quarry, a look of strange bewilderment on her face. Caleb reached over and laid a hand on her shoulder.

They watched two men lift the black body bag and secure it to a narrow gurney. That done, they shoved it into a waiting ambulance. "That's his body they're taking away. You see? There's nothing we can do for him now."

She didn't look at Caleb as she opened the door and climbed out of the truck. Caleb grabbed his gloves from under the seat and followed her toward the police officers. He scanned the faces under the lights, hoping to spot Claudia.

An older officer noticed Maggie and pointed her out to his colleagues. He walked over to her, raising his hand to prevent her approach. "Can I help you, Ma'am?" A fog of breath puffed out of his mouth.

Maggie was about to answer when she heard the ambulance door slam shut. She jerked back, shuddering.

"Mind telling me what you folks are doing here?" The officer said.

"This is Maggie Wells, she was a friend of Mr. Waters. I'm Caleb Knowles. Where's Detective Briscoe?"

The officer cocked his thumb toward the pit, and Caleb noticed Claudia down in the rubble, a small team of men working around her. The men wore gray jumpsuits that Caleb recognized from his visits to Claudia's office. The Forensic Team from the State Law Enforcement Division. Wearing latex gloves, they collected clumps of debris and dirt and placed them in plastic bags.

The officer beside Caleb removed the radio from his belt. The loud, crackling static startled Maggie, who jumped as though given an electric shock.

"I got a Mr. Knowles and Miss Wells up here, Detective. They asked for you," the officer said into the radio.

"What are they doing here? I'll be right up." He heard the radio click off and watched as Claudia brushed dirt from her jeans and began the difficult assent from the quarry pit. When she reached the crest, she directed the officer to assist the men below. He didn't look too pleased with the suggestion, but something in her expression gave him the good sense to comply.

"Ms. Wells, I'm sorry for your loss," Claudia said soberly as she approached them. Maggie stared down at the blood traces on Claudia's jeans.

"When I told Maggie about Barry, she wanted to see him. I don't think it's a good idea."

"Your coming at all wasn't too bright." Claudia eyed him sharply.

"I see SLED's here. They find anything?"

"Like I'd tell you if they did. Look, Barry Waters was brutally murdered, probably by one of the gangs. If either of you can tell us anything helpful, I'd appreciate it."

Maggie stepped forward and asked, "What do you want to know?"

Claudia pulled a notepad out of her jacket pocket. "We know he was trafficking drugs. You got any names for us?"

"He never told me specifics," she said quietly. "There was a country music band called Buck and the Silver Spurs, or something like that. Barry hated country music, but he always went to this little dive where they played. So I put two and two together."

"Did he admit he got drugs there?"

"I asked him about it once. We were going to a play and he insisted on stopping by the club first. He told me to wait in the car. The band had just gotten there and was unloading equipment. He motioned one of the guys inside and came back out twenty minutes later. He was wired, so I knew he'd done a hit. I asked him if that was his supplier and all he said was, 'You don't really want me to answer that, do you?' I got mad as hell and made him take me home. We broke up that next day."

"When was this?"

"Last October. Then, around Christmas, he calls me again. Says he's been in recovery for four weeks and plans to stick with it. He was lonely, and I was lonely, and it was Christmas, so we sort of fell together again. We had a nice couple of weeks, then New Year's came, and Barry showed up high as a kite. We had one of our worst battles ever." She wiped tears from her cheek with the palm of her hand.

Caleb asked, "Is that the first time he hit you?"

"No, it wasn't the first. But it was the most out of control I ever saw him. At one point, he had me on the floor with his hands around my throat. I thought I was going to die, that he was going to kill me. I got dizzy and almost passed out before he let me go."

"What happened then?" Caleb asked.

"He sat on the floor beside me, crying, begging me to forgive him. He said he loved me and I was all he had left. I was terrified and ran out of my house. I drove over to your house, Caleb, and Shannon gave me some cash for a hotel room."

"I remember. She was upset when you left, but wouldn't tell me why."

"I made her promise. I was so ashamed, and a part of me still wanted to protect Barry. I know it's sick, but that's how I felt. Anyway, I came back two days later, packed up all Barry's stuff and put it in my garage. Changed my locks. He didn't fight it. He took his things and told me again how sorry he was. I didn't hear from him again until he showed up at my house the night of the break-in."

Claudia jotted down a few notes then looked up at her. "Besides the country music band, do you know of any other possible drug connections?"

"Barry was on the road all the time with his work. It suited him, because he was hyperactive by nature. Even off the drugs, he was never still. He didn't talk much about where he was going, or why. And I didn't ask, I guess because I really didn't want to know. Denial is a handy thing."

"Do you use?" Claudia asked abruptly. Caleb stared at her, perturbed.

"I tried coke once. It felt pretty damn good. For about ten minutes. I wanted more and I knew that was a bad sign. So I never went near it again. I'm glad I tried it because it helped me understand Barry better. It helped me understand how bad the cravings can be." She looked embarrassed by the admission.

Caleb turned to Claudia. "You need anything else from us?"

She shook her head. "I think Ms. Wells can use some sleep. You can help her notify the family, I guess. It'll take a day or two for the coroner to release the body."

Swirling red lights and a quick siren blast signaled the departure of the ambulance. They heard the crunch of gravel and the steady rumble of the engine as it passed, ghost-like, away from them.

It was just a few minutes after Caleb went back to bed, it seemed, when the alarm sounded. He woke to the clatter of dishes and the smell of coffee. He drifted down the stairs and into the kitchen, where he found Shannon hovering over Maggie, coaxing her to eat a piece of partially burned toast.

"How we doing?" Caleb asked.

Shannon came over to him and gave him a quick hug. "She hasn't slept. She won't eat a thing."

Caleb bent over to study the black-edged toast. "I'm not sure I blame her. Should I make pancakes?"

Shannon swatted him, which prompted a hint of a smile from Maggie. "No thanks. I don't think I can digest quite yet."

Caleb took his usual chair and studied their houseguest. A pink flush had spread around Maggie's eyelids and nose, but there was something new in her eyes. They didn't waver.

Didn't hesitate to make direct contact.

They had lost their fear.

"So what are your plans for today, Maggie?" he asked.

"I called Barry's parents and told them what happened. His mother's devastated. But she wasn't surprised, really. She said she knew one day she'd get a call like this. But she always prayed Barry'd turn around, get his life together before it was too late. I only met her once because Barry stayed away from his family when he was using. But talking to her last night, I realized how much she loved him. How much he missed out on because of the stupid decisions he made."

"His parents coming to town?"

"No. His younger brother lives in Carrolton. I said I'd meet him at my house later this morning." Maggie stretched, her long, thin arms steepling over her head. "I know you guys are worried about me, but I promise I'll be all right. I'm sad, yes. I'll miss Barry, yes. But I have my life and I plan to get back to it. And that means moving back to my home and going back to my job and getting on with things."

Shannon reached over and squeezed her hand. "I'm glad you're doing better. But you aren't moving back home until Claudia says it's safe. If you try, I'll move right in with you. And I'll bring Caleb and Cleo. You think you're miserable now . . ."

Maggie laughed. It was a light, musical sound that trickled through the air and made them all smile. They hadn't heard it in weeks. "Okay, Mom," Maggie said.

Caleb plowed through a long morning of intake appointments, phone calls, and neglected paperwork. Lack of sleep left his mind marginal at best; fortunately, no crisis arose to test his faculties. He was about to sign out for lunch when Janice buzzed him.

"Dr. Wheeler's on line one."

Caleb dropped back down in his seat and punched the

extension.

"Hey, Caleb. We have a problem. Your client, Helen Fleck, took off this morning, AMA. Her confusion's been worse, so there's a risk of self-endangerment. Any ideas where she could be?"

"She may have gone home. I'll stop by her place and check. Her son in town?"

"I think he left yesterday. He agreed to an assisted living placement, and our social worker was lucky enough to find a vacancy at The Meadows."

"Does Helen know?"

"He told her before he left. But I don't know if she processed it. Like I said, she's deteriorated."

Caleb promised he'd spend his lunch hour looking for their escapee and told Bryant he'd call back with a report. He buzzed Janice to say he'd be taking a long lunch.

Rain thrummed against the windshield. A wet breath of wind nudged against the truck and swayed the traffic lights above him. The air had a piercing chill to it. This was no weather for Helen to be out in. He needed to find her.

Caleb pulled into the front entrance of the hospital, then out Wheat Drive. If Helen knew where she was, which was a big if, this was the logical road to take back to her house. Caleb decided he'd try this route first, then maybe the streets to the clinic. If he didn't spot her in an hour or so, he'd call the police and report her as a missing person.

The rain picked up, sheets pummeling the truck and obscuring his search. He kept his speed at twenty and stayed in the right lane, his eyes fixed on the narrow sidewalk that paralleled the pavement. Pedestrian traffic was sporadic, a few raincoat-clad women struggling to hold umbrellas being snatched by the wind. Two black youths in dark jackets sauntered slowly in the downpour, as if they needed no rain gear, as if the water couldn't touch them.

Caleb studied them closely. They looked to be about

sixteen, school-aged kids taking their education from the streets. He wondered if they belonged to a gang, if they knew Leon or Kevin. Or Rafael Hernando. He wondered if they carried automatic weapons or drugs. The youths stopped at an intersection, waited for the traffic light to turn red, then crossed in front of Caleb's truck. Caleb watched as they trotted up the sidewalk, then mounted the steps to the Midlands Vocational School.

So much for assumptions, Caleb muttered to himself.

It was when Caleb turned onto Sunset that he spotted the other youth standing in a bus stop shelter. His hands were buried deep in the pockets of a red jacket, his shaved head shielded by a black baseball cap. He leaned against the graffiti-covered wall of the shelter, his bowed face obscured by shadows and rain. But the sunken posture of the kid was immediately recognizable. Kevin Lumford.

Caleb wheeled the truck into a Seven-Eleven parking lot behind the bus stop and climbed out. Kevin didn't notice his approach. He kept his head down, studying the holes in his soaked, tattered jeans. Caleb eased over beside him. "How ya doing, Kev?"

The kid turned toward Caleb and glared.

Caleb smiled back. "I've been kind of worried about you."

Kevin did his best to screw his face up into a sneer. "I'll bet."

"Your dad is, too. He doesn't like you staying on the streets."

"My old man's fucked," Kevin growled.

"Your old man's scared. He doesn't want anything to happen to you. Says you're all he has left."

Kevin craned his neck back and started banging his head against the wall. It looked painful, but Kevin was too angry to notice. "Just leave me the fuck alone."

Caleb took a good look at his client. He was filthy, new pimples had erupted on his forehead, across his nose, down to the bottom of his neck. He smelled like old sweat and stale cigarette smoke. "Where you staying?"

"Here and there."

"You got some place dry to go tonight?"

He shrugged. The wind picked up, carrying sheets of rain that sought them out through the open wall of the shelter.

"You still have a place at your grandmother's house. You could go home, have a hot shower, a meal, sleep in a nice warm bed."

"They'd find me there. They might hurt her. Or worse."

"You mean Leon's killers? They're after you?"

He didn't answer. He shivered as the chilling wind blew against them once more.

"Tell you what. It's miserable out here. How about you come with me? I'll buy you a bowl of hot soup and help you find a place to stay."

"I already trusted you once. You called the cops. Almost got me killed."

"Come on, it was Detective Briscoe who saved your butt when those gang members drove up. She's the best friend you could have right now. Your best chance is for her to arrest Leon's killers and get them off the street." Caleb heard a rumble of thunder. He looked up at dark, threatening clouds blowing in. He glanced back at the road, noticing a junker of a car inching by, its occupants checking out who was in the bus shelter. "Let's get out of this mess and go somewhere we can talk."

Kevin nodded, more out of resignation than agreement. He followed Caleb to the truck and crawled in. Caleb turned the heat on high, directing the vents at his drenched client. "There's a restaurant a few blocks from here. They have good soup." Without waiting for his companion to respond, Caleb wheeled out of the parking lot.

Rain thudding the windshield blurred his view and made travel so difficult that he didn't get the truck out of second gear before turning into the restaurant's lot. Once inside, they made their way to a table in the back where Caleb ordered coffee for both of them. "When was the last time you had a hot meal?"

Kevin was still shivering. He took the coffee and hugged it with his hands. "Couple of days ago." His gaze trailed up to the window. Rivulets of rain played tricks on the glass, distorting the gray view of the asphalt lot. "Leon was a good guy," he said softly. "He never hurt no one. What they did to him—" He paused, shaking his head.

"What who did? Tell me."

"Leon's my age, you know. His mama's raising six kids by herself, and now she's burying one of them. For no fuckin' reason."

"Claudia said it was a gang hit. Over drugs."

"Leon wasn't into that shit."

"You don't have to use to deal."

Kevin rolled his eyes like he was talking to an imbecile. "Leon didn't deal. The Blades killed him because he was the Lords' youngest, the newest member. It was what they call a message hit."

"And what was the message?"

Kevin shrunk down in his chair as the waitress brought the soup. When she left, he grabbed his spoon and dove in, slurping like he was half-starved.

"What was the message?" Caleb repeated.

"The message is, 'you fucked with us, so we're fuckin' with you.'" He put down the spoon and wiped his mouth with the back of his hand. "Why do you want to know all this?"

"Because I want to understand why a fourteen-year-old kid is dead. And why Rafael Hernando is dead. I'm getting sick of all the bodies."

Kevin jerked back with such force that he knocked the table, sloshing soup onto the table. "Rafael's dead?"

"Yep. So tell me, what is this war between the Blades and the City Lords all about?"

Kevin looked out the window for a long moment. "You ever heard of Spider Blue?"

"That's the new drug on the streets."

"Yeah. It's a new drug. It's also a fuckin' nightmare. A white guy sold a mess of it to the Lords. It turned out to be really bad shit. Heroin, cut with some nightmare shit.

"A few weeks ago Miguel Hernando, that's Rafael's brother, just got out of the joint and was looking to celebrate. The Blades connection was dry, so they came to Tito."

"Who's Tito?"

"He's sort of the leader of the Lords. They were hard up, coming to Tito like that. Anyway, Tito sold him some of the Spider Blue, before he knew how bad it was. Miguel shot up two hits and got real sick. They got him to the emergency room, but his heart stopped and he died. Rafael's been on a tear ever since."

Caleb thought back to his visit to the emergency room, to the young man who'd gone berserk on heroin mixed with Scopolamine. Bryant Wheeler had mentioned another patient, a young man who'd died from the drug. "So Rafael was after Tito, because he sold Miguel the bad stuff—this Spider Blue?"

Kevin slurped at the soup again. "Yeah. And they were after this white guy they knew sold the shit to Tito. Tito was hiding out, they couldn't get their hands on him. So Rafael did Leon, to make his point."

"They ever find the white guy?"

"One of the Blades finally did. I think they iced him."

An unwelcome image of Barry Waters' corpse flashed in Caleb's mind and churned up something in his stomach. He stared down at his uneaten soup. "So this war goes on and on, until everybody's dead. Is that how it works?"

Kevin blinked at him. "I don't know how it works. I don't know when it all stops."

"And in the meantime, you just keep running, keep hiding. Who is it that's after you?" Caleb asked.

"Tito."

"Why? I thought you were tight with the City Lords."

"Because of you," Kevin barked. "Tito saw me bring you and that detective to Leon's body. He thinks I'm narcing him out."

Caleb leaned forward and said, "Have you tried talking to him, telling him the truth?"

Kevin stared at him incredulously, as if Caleb had just reported a Santa Claus sighting. "Yeah, right. I'll just sit Tito down and tell him it was all a coincidence that me and you and the police were together at that abandoned building. Beside Leon's body."

"Okay, okay. I see your point. So what are your options?"

Kevin shook his head resignedly. "I don't know. I'm doing my best just to stay alive. Like you pointed out, the bodies are piling up."

Caleb watched him for a moment, watched the tough guy veneer dissolve as the face of a terrified kid emerged. Caleb leaned closer in. "Try this on, Kev. We take you to Claudia. You tell her what you know. Then maybe the police can help you get out of town. You got relatives you can stay with?"

He scowled, but muttered, "Got an aunt. Up in Richmond."

"You go there, maybe finish school. Maybe go to college, or an art institute. You live long enough to see thirty. Or maybe even sixty."

Kevin gave him that Santa Claus look again.

"Okay, you got any better ideas? You want to keep living on the street, hiding from a gang that wants to kill you?"

Kevin stared out the rain streaked window, his eyes wide and fearful. "Why do you care what happens to me?"

"Because you're just a kid and you deserve to have a chance at life. And because of your father."

His eyes shot back at Caleb. "What's he got to do with this?"

"I saw him yesterday. He doesn't look too good. He's worried to death about you. I promised I'd do what I could."

Kevin's stare returned to the window. "I don't know what

to do," he said, sounding more like a scared kid again.

"Come on. Let's go see Claudia."

Caleb dropped a ten on the table and stood to leave. Kevin said he needed to visit the men's room, so Caleb used his cell to check in with the office. "Any word on Helen?" he asked Janice.

"Yes, thank goodness. They found her behind one of the medical office buildings. A janitor brought her back to the hospital. They gave her a tranquilizer to settle her down."

Caleb sighed with relief. "Good. Now I need you to do me a favor. Call Claudia Briscoe and tell her to meet me at the clinic. Tell her I'm bringing Kevin Lumford." He hung up and Kevin appeared behind him. He had scrubbed the grime from his face and his hands. Beads of water dripped from his chin. "You ready to go?" Caleb asked.

Kevin didn't answer, but let Caleb lead him outside.

The rain had let up a little, but a brisk breeze swirled wet, cold air around them as they headed to the truck. Kevin climbed into the passenger seat and Caleb started the ignition. The truck bounced over a pothole, splashing an arc of water, then turned into the street.

Traffic was steady and unforgiving. Caleb nudged his way into the left lane, ignoring irate horn blares from a black Cadillac. He kept the speedometer at forty, aware that the wet road could be treacherous at higher speeds. The Cadillac didn't seem to agree. It wheeled around Caleb and sped off, water spraying the truck in its wake. Caleb cursed under his breath as he switched the wipers to the high setting, clearing off the sheets of rain. Kevin continued his vigil, staring out the passenger window.

"Shit!" Kevin suddenly yelled, his body tensing as if hit with an electrical current.

"What?"

"Tito!" Kevin pointed out the side window as he sank down in the seat.

Caleb immediately recognized the car in the right lane.

The patchwork paint job, the rusted, dented front fenders. The same car from the abandoned warehouse. The gunmen's car.

"They see you?" Caleb slammed his foot on the accelerator.

He caught a glimpse of Kevin's panicked nod as he wheeled around a beige Camry. The patchwork car mimicked his moves, dangerously close to his back bumper.

Caleb glanced at the mirror. The driver was big, dark, maybe a bandana tied around his head. The passenger sat lower, an arm draped across the seat. Caleb heard the throbbing, bass pulse from the car's stereo. His own heart pounded in the same rhythm.

He looked over the two congested lanes, unsure what to do. If he pulled into a side street, he could maneuver better, but he'd be more vulnerable. He could speed ahead, like they do in movies, but he'd likely lose control on the slick asphalt.

His mind flashed back to the abandoned warehouse. The car had spun around, the passenger leaning out the window, two hands on a gun splaying bullets. He didn't need a repeat performance. He had to put some distance between them and the patchwork car.

He wove his truck back in to the right lane, tapped the brake, slowing to forty. The car did the same. Caleb kept an eye fixed on his side mirror as an eighteen-wheeler sped past. Behind it, another truck was fast approaching. Caleb held his breath, stomped the accelerator, and careened into the small space between the two large trucks. A horn blared and the rear truck slid, just managing to miss Caleb's left bumper. The patchwork car tried to change lanes but couldn't squeeze in.

The traffic light at First and Loring turned red. "Hold on!" Caleb yelled, swerving into oncoming traffic to make the left turn. A cacophony of horns blasted and he prayed a police car had spotted him. He sped into the line of cars, braking to get control of the truck, then pressed the accelerator again.

"Jesus!" Kevin yelled.

"You buckled in?" Caleb checked the mirror again to see the patchwork car squeal onto Loring. "Keep your head down!"

"Where are we going?"

"I don't know," Caleb stammered. Loring Road led into the industrial park. No help there. Police coverage of that area was probably minimal. If he could turn around, make it back downtown, get on Third Avenue to the police station . . .

He pulled into the left lane, scanning the grass-covered ditch that formed the median. No getting over that. The patchwork car crept up on the right. Caleb crossed lanes again, hoping to remain a moving target. The car surged forward, now only inches from his tailgate. "Damn!"

In the mirror he caught a flash of movement. The car's passenger window opened. "Damn!" Caleb screamed again.

He saw a steel-gray blur. A gun. A head appeared, then hands stabilizing the pistol. "Get down!" he yelled at Kevin.

Caleb sank down in his seat, trying to eye the road through the steering wheel. He could almost feel the patchwork car breathing on them.

A short burst of shots rang out. He flinched, pressing harder on the accelerator. "Come on," he muttered, begging the old truck to have just a little more to give. Another shot and the truck jerked to the left. Caleb tugged on the steering wheel and hit the brakes, desperately trying to avoid the steep ditch that would surely flip the truck. Another blast of bullets shattered the cab's rear window, spraying them with small gems of glass.

"Hold on!" he screamed, lifting up so that his weight hung on the steering wheel. Finally, the truck responded. He swerved to the right lane, into the path of the patchwork car.

Caleb heard the grating gnaw of metal against metal. Saw the spider web shatter of his windshield as the car hit, bounced off the truckbed and careened off the road. Felt the pain lance through him as his forehead hit the wheel.

In slow motion, the truck continued its pirouette. Caleb

made a last, weak attempt to steer, but it continued its macabre dance, gliding to the left, and off the road.

Caleb grabbed Kevin, clutching his jacket as the truck tumbled, flipping once, then twice.

Then down, down . . .

Caleb mentally commanded his eyes to open, but they didn't comply. His body seemed to be submerged in some black current. No air there. It was a silent, cold place, this current. He wanted to leave it, but couldn't. He drifted at its mercy, desperate for breath as it carried him farther and farther away.

A hot knife of pain sliced through his consciousness. He felt himself being lifted, heard the screech of metal tearing metal. He blinked his eyes open, tried to focus. A fireman in a yellow coat leaned through the shattered windshield and tugged at the seatbelt that suspended Caleb upside down in the overturned truck. As it clicked open, the fireman braced his shoulder against Caleb's stomach, cushioning his fall. Pain screamed in Caleb's chest. He closed his eyes again, letting the darkness carry him away.

"Caleb? Caleb!" the voice insisted.

He tried to focus on the face. He knew it, knew the voice, and summoned all his mental resources to respond. "Claudia," he whispered into the oxygen mask that covered his face.

"Hey, you," she said softly. Her eyes were wet, even though the rain had stopped. "They're taking you to the hospital."

Caleb turned his head to look at the mangled mass of steel that was once his truck. "Kevin?" he gasped.

An EMT held him still. "Easy, sir. You have a punctured lung. You need to lay still."

Caleb's gaze sought out Claudia, who squeezed his hand. "The kid's okay. Just a few cuts is all. He crawled out of the truck, ran a half mile up the road to get help. Your friends in the other car wrapped themselves around an oak tree. One's dead, the other's close to it. How you doing?"

It was a good question. There was that inconvenient block of lead on his chest. His right knee was on fire and a strange cloudiness filled his head. "Had better years," he mumbled, as they lifted his gurney into the ambulance.

chapter twenty-five

The next few days were a blur. A collage of faces, some familiar, some unknown. Tubes going into his arm, another on his leg. *Ugh.* An annoying plastic mask pinching his mouth and nose. A haziness filling his brain, obscuring memories, filtering thoughts so that one couldn't connect with another. Strange sleep, invaded by surreal images of guns and twisted metal.

He blinked away the nightmare and looked around the room. He looked at the same sterile white walls, the machine beeping beside him. In the corner, there was a chair with a large man in it. "Hey," he tried to say, his throat like sandpaper.

The large man didn't respond. Of course, he couldn't, Caleb realized. He fixed a stare, hoping to get his attention through telepathy, but after a few seconds, he felt himself being pulled back to the cloud.

"Caleb?" Sam hauled himself off the chair and came over to the bed. He took Caleb's hand and gave it a squeeze. "Can you stay awake a minute?"

Caleb nodded, looking up at the beleaguered face of his older brother. A few days' growth of beard had darkened his chin and upper lip. Skin under his eyes sagged like he had a bad hangover.

"You're doing pretty good," Sam said. "You had a

punctured lung, so they kept you on oxygen for a few days. But that's better now. They operated on your knee because you shattered it when you flipped the truck, but it's looking good, too. You had a concussion, but that thick skull of yours kept most of your brains intact. They've had you on lots of drugs, that's why you're so out of it. Do you understand me?"

He nodded again, and lifted his sluggish hands to sign. "How long?" he managed, without tangling the tubes.

"Three days. Shannon just left an hour ago to get a shower. She's been here round the clock. She'll hate it that she missed seeing you awake."

Caleb had a dozen questions but couldn't get his hands to communicate them. He shrugged, frustrated.

"How about I fill you in," Sam said. "Kevin Lumford's fine. Claudia's hiding him out somewhere, until they finish their investigation. The car that hit you had two gang members in it. One's name was Tito Ramirez, he's dead. The other was a newcomer to the City Lords named Billy Weldon, he was driving. He's got a broken back, but he's been talking to Claudia. He told her that Tito killed Barry because of a bad drug deal. Barry dealt Tito heroin laced with a nasty drug that killed a few people."

"Spider Blue," Caleb said aloud, hoping Sam could read his lips.

"Yeah," Sam said, surprised. "The guy at the bar was with another gang, called the Blades, who were after Barry for the same reason. His brother took the tainted heroin and died. So Rafael went looking for Barry, ended up in the Callahan's house. He thought Fran was Barry's live-in girl friend. He meant to kill Maggie as a message to Barry."

"Jesus."

"Claudia says the case is pretty well wrapped up. When she finishes with some of the details, she'll send Kevin to live with relatives up north." Sam passed a hand over his face and rested it against his chin.

Caleb just blinked at him. So. It was all over. Emma

Callahan wouldn't have to testify. Paul could get on with his life. Murphy Lumford had accomplished his only goal, getting his kid somewhere safe.

Caleb 's eyes drifted to a window. A few fat clouds lazed along a bright blue sky; it was the first clear day he'd seen in weeks. Sam's hand squeezed again.

"You still with me?" Sam asked.

"Yeah." He stared into his brother's tired eyes. "You sell your place?"

"I accepted a contract this morning. An offer I couldn't refuse, as they say."

Caleb swallowed. "That's great, Sam. Maybe in a few weeks, I'll be up to helping you move. Find a place in Atlanta yet?"

"You will be no help at all. Your truck, which I was counting on by the way, is totaled. And you'll be tied up in physical therapy for a month or so."

An image of the loyal old Toyota, an upside down mass of mangled metal, filled Caleb's mind and made him shudder.

"So anyway," Sam went on. "I'll hire a few high school kids to help with the move. You can supervise from your wheelchair, or you can stretch out on my deck until it's all done."

Caleb squinted at Sam, feeling like the fog machine had turned back on in his brain.

"I bought a house on the lake," Sam said. "Ten minutes from you and Shannon."

"So you're not moving to Atlanta."

"I'm not moving to Atlanta," Sam repeated.

"But you sold your house so you could move there. You had gallery deals and—"

"Then I leave for just a few days, you almost get yourself killed. Again." He shook his head. "I decided I'd better stick close enough to keep an eye on you."

Caleb blinked, trying to understand it all, but then remembered and turned back to Sam. "How you doing? I mean, the boy. Rafael." He knew he wasn't making much sense, but the change in Sam's expression told him his brother understood.

"It's hard. Not something I can really talk about." He took Caleb's hand again. "But it's not as hard as seeing you in the E.R. after your wreck. You're my family, you know. You and Shannon and Julia. Besides, Shannon says she can't raise you all by herself."

Caleb wanted to tell him how sorry he was for dragging him into this mess and for making him worry and for a number of other sins, but instead closed his eyes and drifted off again. When he awakened later, Shannon was there, leaning over him. She kissed the tips of his fingers, the palm of his hand, and then his lips, her wet hair brushing against his cheek.

Printed in the United States
42976LVS00005B/1-27

9 780974 768564